BETHESDA

A NOVEL

Paul A. Nigro

RIVER
OAK
PUBLISHING

Bethesda
ISBN 1-58919-006-8
Copyright © 2003 by Paul A. Nigro
Published by RiverOak Publishing,
An Imprint of Cook Communications Ministries
4050 Lee Vance View
Colorado Springs, CO 80918

O human race, born to fly upward,
wherefore at a little wind dost thou so fall?

—Dante

I AM SEATED IN my place on the platform looking down the aisle as the mourners file in. I should be among them, but the circumstances dictate otherwise.

The pallbearers are fine men, carefully selected. They stand in the vestibule at attention while the ushers show the relatively few mourners to their pews with practiced compassion. The organ draws out the final notes of the hymn; the melody offers comfort, if one knows the words.

I look down at the sleek silver casket that cradles the body of my friend. It is a terrible and mystifying grace that God provides, which must wait until we have come to the end of ourselves before it begins to do its work. I see in the faces of the congregation the impact of the one life that was lost. God has used this one life to try to teach us many things. One life lost; how many will be found?

The family is small in number, bewildered, unsure of what to do. They come from far away. I watch them intently. The director is pulling them along, turning back often to make sure they are still there. They look like they are being pushed by an unseen hand. They are distant relatives, here out of necessity alone. If I didn't know better I would assume their relationships are fragmented and strained. I do know better. They are.

We stand in honor of them as they enter. They are visibly uncomfortable in such a place, which they have long associated with death and have avoided most of their lives.

I wince at my own observation. In a sense, this is indeed a place of death. It doesn't take long to die here. I know this only too well. I could write a book about it.

PART 1:

THE STIRRING OF THE WATERS

CHAPTER ONE

THE AFTERNOON GREW CLOUDY and suited my cold mood. The days were becoming increasingly unproductive as the season of Lent dragged on mournfully toward Good Friday, a day which marked a tragedy so great it took forty days to observe it properly, yet in pathetically inadequate ways. As a little girl growing up Catholic, I once struggled mightily to give up thumb sucking during Lent and reveled in my victory until the absurdity of the observance struck me: What's so great about giving up something I shouldn't be doing anyway? Suddenly my eight-year-old eyes were opened to a host of similar inconsistencies in my faith, and I concluded that this practice and others like it did not make much sense. So even back in 1975, I knew I was a Protestant at heart, and in that year I gave up Catholicism along with my thumb for Lent. These days I sometimes wonder if I entered the ministry purely out of some deeply hidden inner desire to prove that I was right.

The small square envelope sat above the stack of sermon notes, photocopied articles, and open commentaries on my cluttered desk, demanding immediate attention. I had shuffled it around for the past several hours, but it somehow seemed to float back to the top of the pile. Its bright linen sheen radiated under the soft light of the desk lamp, as if my little sister had packaged every ounce of her sweetness inside, and it glowed through the paper. The envelope was addressed to "Aunt Carla" and could therefore only mean one thing. I would have to open it eventually.

Out of my window, I could see Isabella Ruiz coming up the walk dragging her three-year-old daughter Miranda. I closed my eyes before punching the intercom.

"Mrs. Dickson?" I spoke into the phone. "Any benevolence kits left?"

"No, Reverend. You haven't put any together yet this week." Her voice was tired and irritated. I probably interrupted her in the homestretch of a soap opera crossword puzzle.

"Could you make one up for me, please?"

"Of course, Reverend. Now, how many bars of soap go in one of these?"

"Well, that would depend on what we've got in the benevolence closet, wouldn't it?"

There was a short pause.

"Fine. We have lots of beets in there. Should we double up on beets then?"

I sighed. "It might be better if I just did it myself. Sorry to trouble you." I let go of the button sharply, breaking my nail. Mrs. Dickson often abused me mercilessly in ways like this. She evidently resented having a woman boss. I was used to her behavior, but it was frustrating nevertheless.

She was not the only one of the members who wasn't yet sold on the idea of having a female minister, to be sure. It was clear I was the best they could get since the church had declined so dramatically over the past few decades, along with the neighborhood. I was not complaining, though, because I had spent years toiling as an assistant in various places, St. Fred's gave me my first shot at the pulpit. I presided over a lovely stone building, which had been modeled in miniature after some European cathedral no one could remember. The place was crumbling around me, and its two hundred aging members— the vast majority of them inactive but presumably entitled to my pastoral services—were surrounded by a community of needy people who saw the church primarily as a dispensary for food and clothing.

I pushed the envelope aside once more and began the frantic search for the emery board I knew was buried somewhere under the mess. I'm disorganized by nature, and the office was a disaster area. I rarely met with people there but used a sitting room down the hall for counseling, for if they could see the environment in which I was most comfortable, they might be hesitant to take my advice. Not that they took it anyway—most people already had their minds made up and came to me to justify their twisted views of life, which I hardly ever did. Except for people like Isabella Ruiz, of course, for whom life was a much simpler matter.

I buzzed the intercom again. "Mrs. Dickson, has Mrs. Ruiz come in by chance?"

"Yes, but she's left already."

I was puzzled. "What did she want?"

"She wanted a handout, Reverend." Her voice hinted at the indignation that she harbored toward every needy person who entered the building. "I told her we had no benevolence kits to give her and to come back another time."

"Did it occur to you to let me know she was here?"

"I'm sorry, Reverend, but she didn't ask for you, and the child was whining."

Not sure what this had to do with the Ruiz family's needs, I ended the conversation with a lecture on how to handle these situations, realizing it made no difference to this master of passive aggression who happened to be the church secretary.

It was nearing four o'clock, and I was no closer to meeting my day's objectives than I had been when I wrote them down at nine. I had figured the whole day for study, but everything changed when I arrived at the church to discover a major plumbing problem, which dominated the morning, followed by a call to the hospital to visit a member admitted with chest pains. Upon my return, the newsletter required serious editorial work before it could be printed, a skill which Mrs. Dickson clearly lacked, and a handful of phone messages awaited, including one from Al Lintz, concerned about my use of the word *darn* in a recent sermon. Good old Al. Where would I be without his constructive criticism? Just as things settled down, there now seemed to be a pressing need to make up benevolence kits. Then, of course, my emotions had been unexpectedly derailed by the little square envelope in the mail. Such was a day in the life of Carla Donovan, Senior Pastor.

I found the emery board stuck in one of the Bible translations on my desk, perhaps put there to mark a particular passage, but I yanked it out before checking to see which one. I filed away with one eye on the broken nail and the other on the glowing square below. Impatiently I grabbed the envelope and slipped the emery board under the flap. The paper was of a high quality, naturally, and would not easily submit, so I sawed at it in frustration, breaking both the flimsy board and another nail in the process. But finally, I was in.

Ryan Castleton Cavanaugh III weighed 7 pounds, 6 ounces at birth and measured nineteen inches from head to sole. My sister, being perfect in every respect, had spared no expense in the preparation of her son's first appearance in print, and the birth announcement was classic Margaret—right down to the blue satin bow stitched into the card and what appeared to be a hand-colored border of baby toys. I wondered if she colored this one herself, just for me, or if she delegated this important task to one of her ladies-in-waiting. As the wife of one of the youngest law partners in Boston, she could certainly afford it.

I put down the card and gazed out the window at the dreary day. The town always appeared dreary to me for some reason, but maybe it was because I had only been here for five months and, though the winter thaw had begun, I had yet to see the signs of spring. I had always wanted to live in upstate New York, attracted by the lure of colorful autumns and Christmases in the mountains, but the snow around here soon turned a dirty brown, and the falling leaves had been a nasty wet nuisance in my little yard since the day I moved in. The real color of this town, I soon discovered, came alive in the faces of its people—Italian, Polish, Slavic, and increasingly Hispanic and African-American, each one strong and vibrant in its own way. These did not represent my congregation, however, a strange mix of WASPs who had managed to band together out of mutual distaste for their own churches and purchase St. Fred's from the Catholic diocese more than thirty years ago.

I leaned back in my chair, reflecting. It wasn't all that bad being here. I loved the old building, though we could not afford to see to the ongoing repairs and do effective ministry at the same time. But then, the members were content with having worship one day a week, and they seemed to ignore the dilapidation around them. In its day the church must have been gorgeous, with its shiny marble floors in the vestibule and its stained glass in the windows, most of which could only be imagined, having been replaced by a cheaper kind, the kind of stuff one would see in a colored beer bottle. There was even a small swimming pool in the basement, though it had long been out of service and was marred by deep fissures in the shell. Plumbing and electrical problems were constant, and there was a slight odor in the front hall, from a source as yet undetermined. But I cherished the place, even so.

There were other advantages. For one, I was my own boss, but in a sense I had two hundred bosses, each of them assuming authority at various times for various reasons. And there was Michael Montefiore, the cute—though somewhat quirky—pastor of a small church on the other side of town who was head of the local ministers' alliance. I was hopeful that he might take an interest in me, assuming he felt it was providentially ordained. We would make an interesting couple—me in my clerical garb and wire-rimmed glasses, and him with his snazzy neckties and emotional exuberance. I wondered why he was still single, but as long as he stayed that way, I could hope.

I stuffed the card back into the envelope and slumped in my squeaky chair. My sister Margaret was living the life of her dreams, but where was I? When I went to seminary, full of ideals and vigor, I had no idea what life as a minister would actually be like. I fancied a blissful existence in which I floated along in a spiritually charged mist all the time, with my devoted parishioners smiling adoringly up at me as I walked gracefully among them, dispensing wisdom and tenderness as I went. My days would be rich with deep, fruitful study and personal growth, sharpened through application to a number of vital ministries. Lives would be changed daily due to my skillful practice of the pastoral art, and my words would spark a revolution of meaning that would shape the culture around me. Long nights absorbed in prayer and scholarship would empower me to make critical leadership decisions that would have implications lasting beyond my lifetime. And now, nearly ten years later, the toughest decision facing me was what to do with all those cans of beets.

Perhaps it wouldn't have been so frustrating if I hadn't been constantly reminded of the charmed life my little sis was living. When I phoned home to tell my parents I had been called to my first assistant pastorate, all they wanted to talk about was Margaret's acceptance to Radcliffe. When I asked them to come hear my first sermon, they had to stay home because Margaret was inviting her boyfriend (Ryan II, of course) home that weekend. Then it was "Margaret and Ryan are engaged!" Soon after, "Margaret got a job as a staff writer for *Boomers* magazine!" (although she wasn't even old enough to be a Boomer). And now my beautiful baby sister—who appeared to have gained maybe a whopping fifteen ounces during her pregnancy—had been "blessed with a beautiful baby boy, and heavens-to-Betsy, Carla, what are you doing that's so important that you can't come to the baptism?"

I knew I couldn't compete with Margaret, but at least I could excel in my own endeavors, right? I could win my parents' approval by streaking to the top in my own chosen field, right? Well, reality has a way of killing off our dreams over time. When it became clear that I wasn't exactly flying up the rungs on the clerical ladder, and that my parents weren't exactly thrilled about my career path anyway, I quit worrying about their approval and adjusted my expectations. I wanted to help people know God the way I knew him; I wanted them to know the peace that I had found in faith. It was such a simple goal, but so much got in the way of it that I sacrificed it just to stay afloat in my profession. As a pastor I had to keep the church going, tend to the members' endless complaints, play the mascot at all times, and generally be available to be whatever anyone wanted me to be. When all this was done, there would be time for long nights of prayer and study, time to help the spiritually ignorant, the poor, and the hopeless. But there was never any energy. All that had been used up.

I suppose my dreams started to fade when I realized that, being female, there was an immediate conflict between what I believed God had said to me and what many in the Christian community believed about women in ministry. Some of these leaders had publicly stated that it was inconsistent with his Word for God to call a woman into pastoral service. I was branded as a liberal before I arrived at my post, a charge that still followed me after several months. A letter to the editor of the local paper suggested we amend the church's name to Our Lady of St. Fred's. Even many in the congregation seemed to resent my presence, as if I had no right to be there. Only Michael had been encouraging, bringing up the delicate matter indirectly himself, saying to the ministers gathered for a recent meeting, "You alone can know what God is leading you to do. No one else can. That's why leadership is lonely." He glanced in my direction as he said it, and I could not help but feel his words were mainly for my benefit.

I certainly knew about loneliness, but it had less to do with the burden of leadership than it did being without any close friends, colleagues, or romantic interest to spice up the days. I loved my sister, but we had nothing in common, and I embarrassed my parents, who had become even less religious since their children moved out than they had been while we were there; they struggled with how to tell their Catholic friends back in Boston what their oldest child was doing. I did have a cat, Motorhead, whose loud, obnoxious purring filled every cranny of my small house on Congress Street, but even he disappeared for long stretches on occasion. And there was Pete, the eight-year-old latchkey kid who lived next door.

By four-thirty I had given up on shaping my nails properly, having resorted to chewing nervously on them all the while I had been reflecting. Mrs. Dickson would already have gone home—the only act she performed promptly—so I could wander down the hall to the benevolence closet without fear of a confrontation. A sudden loud pounding quickened my steps as I set out.

I rushed to the front entrance to find the plumbers standing outside, their dirty white jumpsuits blending in with the snow piled high and crusted over the curb.

"Hey there, Miz Donovan. You'll never guess why we came back," said Joe with a grin. If I didn't know better, I would have thought Joe was flirting with me. The scary part was, I really didn't know better. The least I could do was play along.

"Let's see, you've come to fix the sink?"

Joe's grin melted into confusion. "No . . . is it broke?"

Trying hard not to laugh, I simply shook my head and tried again. "Nope. You got me. Why'd you guys come back?"

"You won't believe it," said Joe, grinning again. I was praying it wasn't to ask me out for a beer after work or to go to the plumbers' black jumpsuit dinner on Saturday night.

"I give up," I cried. "I'm really stumped, Joe."

"We left a pipe wrench down in the basement." The other guy smirked and looked embarrassed. Somehow I didn't have any trouble believing these two clowns had worked half the day without their pipe wrench.

Relieved, I swung wide the door as they tramped in. Isabella Ruiz was just coming up the walk with Miranda in tow. "Mrs. Dickson gone?" she queried from the sidewalk.

I was glad to see them. "Yep. Come on in, and we'll fix you right up." She smiled broadly and tugged on Miranda's coat sleeve.

The first time I met Isabella was while shopping for groceries. I was in line ahead of her wearing my clerical collar, having run in to stock up on our depleted supply of grape juice on a Saturday night, since our communion committee had simply let the inventory expire. We had communion only twice a year, they insisted, not four times, as I had scheduled, and they threatened to boycott the next observance if I didn't change it back. When I checked the cabinet that morning, I realized that they were serious, and I had no choice but to stock up myself. So there I was in line, attracting a lot of attention, no doubt due to the bottles of sparkling grape juice in my cart, which I found out later was the seed for a rumor that the new local lady minister might also be something of a dipsomaniac. Behind me was Isabella; glancing in her direction I noticed a large bruise on her face, and she saw that I noticed. Instinctively I tried to lighten the tense moment by engaging in kid talk with Miranda, who was clutching a candy bar and staring hopefully at her mother.

"And what's your name, little girl?" I chirped.

"She no hear you," said her mother, making swirling gestures around her ear.

I nodded, kneeling down to Miranda's level. "Can I buy this for you?" I asked, pointing to the candy. Her face glowed in a smile of understanding.

"She's very lovely," I said to Isabella as I stood. "I hope you don't mind." The smile she returned reflected her daughter's and nearly erased the dark bruise.

We talked for some time outside the market, where I learned that Isabella's husband had been unemployed for an extended period, that they had lost their home as a result, and that she and Miranda were now living with her mother in a cramped apartment. She had managed to find work at a local bar, but hoped to get a better job soon. Her meager groceries verified the needs she described. I explained that the church was restocking the benevolence closet and that she could come to get a few things if she wanted. Since that day she had visited weekly and was always grateful for the few items we offered. I was glad she hadn't let Mrs. Dickson scare her off today; I needed a good dose of her optimism. Despite her circumstances, she always had something positive to say.

"You're in luck. We're running a special on beets this week," I said, inviting them in. Miranda ran inside and jumped up in the chair in front of Mrs. Dickson's desk like it was her own living room.

"She run wild all day," quipped Isabella.

"I heard she was whining earlier."

"Oh, that." Isabella was shaking her long black locks. "That because she no like Mrs. Dickson today."

I took Miranda by the hand and walked her behind the desk where I boosted her up on a telephone directory in Mrs. Dickson's chair. She laughed as I spun her around. I found a few sheets of paper and crayons from the supply cabinet for her to use while her mother and I shopped down the hall in the benevolence closet. She was visibly delighted.

"You so nice to us, Carla," said Isabella warmly, patting my arm as we went. Looking into the room and seeing the stacked cans of beets, she laughed. "I take five cans."

The benevolence kits were small boxes designed to hold a few packaged food and sanitary items. My intention was to develop the ministry further, but I had not had time or support from the congregation as yet. I envisioned a visitation program to go along with the food and clothing closet, with a system for paying bills, making home repairs, running errands for those without transportation, providing counseling and medical care, but I seemed to have lost interest myself. As with so many other things, I had learned to settle for what was easy and convenient; in that regard, I had become very much like the people I served, members and nonmembers alike. All except Isabella Ruiz. She never complained, always worked hard, and consistently showed compassion for others. I doubted that she was a Christian, but she was certainly an inspiration.

I stopped packing a large box and looked her squarely in the eye. "Isabella," I said cautiously, "do you believe in Jesus?"

"Yes," she replied, not surprised at all. "Do you?"

The question stunned me. "Uh, of course. He's been my Lord and Savior since I was very young."

She nodded agreement. "He make sun rise every day"—she said this with a sweeping gesture—"and shine his love on all of us."

"Are you . . ." I wasn't sure how to ask the next question. "Do you . . ."

"Catholic," she said. "No go to church since I work at the bar. I think priest no like I serve whiskey, though he drink plenty wine." We laughed, recalling the circumstances when we met.

"Isabella, I hope you know you're welcome here."

She did not respond for a moment, then said, "I know you welcome me."

We finished packing the box and walked back out toward the front desk. Turning the corner, we stopped abruptly. Isabella raised her hand to her mouth, and I dropped the box in a heap. Crayons were scattered on the floor beside the desk.

Miranda was gone.

I quickly scanned the office. The door at the end of the hall that led to the basement was left open, apparently by the plumbers on their way to fix the pipes. Normally this door was locked, because the downstairs classrooms were used only for storage, and the old, crumbling pool had been drained long ago—presenting a hazard to anyone who might wander in. Worse, there were no working light fixtures in the pool area, since they were high above the empty shell and impossible to reach without rented equipment. The only illumination was afforded by equally inaccessible, small rectangular windows located at ground level outside the building. They had become streaked and clouded by the passing of many winters, and the shaded light they allowed seemed to collect like an eerie fog in the cavernous hollow space. For this reason, I avoided the pool room myself. It gave me the creeps.

"You try outside," I said to Isabella. No sense her risking getting hurt down there too. "I'll check the basement."

Isabella obeyed immediately, and I walked toward the darkened gateway. *Stay calm, Carla,* I told myself. *She'll be fine.*

The mysterious portal reflected a soft orange glow from the hall below, just enough to attract an adventurous child. Concern gave way to fear. The horrific vision of an unsuspecting little girl falling into the dark pool forced its way into my mind, and I nearly tripped on the stairs at the thought, descending so fast that I bounced off the wall near the landing. Luckily, Joe had his back turned as I ungracefully entered the hall, barely keeping my balance. The plumbers were working in a small room across the way, hunched over like surgeons preparing to make an incision.

"Joe," I said, momentarily catching my breath, "I've got an emergency." He studied the panic on my face for a moment, then grinned.

The big fellow laughed loudly. "Sorry. We got down here and saw the pipe was still leaking, so we're gonna bypass the line. Had to turn the water off again. We'll have it fixed in about twenty minutes. Can you hold it that long?"

"No, no, no." This was no time for bathroom humor. "Listen, a little girl may have wandered down here. She's deaf. Have you seen her?" I spoke as calmly as the situation would allow. Isabella came hurriedly down the stairs as the plumbers shook their heads.

"She no outside," Isabella said, her voice cracking with anxious fatigue.

My brain tingled with the possibilities. Could Miranda have run away from the church so fast? And *why?* Isabella's eyes communicated that this would have been impossible. Could she have been snatched? No—that was too terrifying to consider. There was only one thing to do.

We should press on.

Joe and his helper put down their tools and joined the search. We proceeded in silence, like archaeologists exploring an uncharted passageway deep beneath the earth.

The basement hall had several classrooms along one side. Finding these empty except for the assorted junk the members had stockpiled over the years, we headed toward the one remaining door on the opposite side at the far end. There was no way out other than the way we had come. I held my breath, hoping, *praying* that we would find her.

I became aware of a dank smell as we came to the end of the hall. It was moist, almost salty—I didn't recognize it. It swirled around me, strangely triggering my resolve. Miranda *had* to be down here somewhere, and there was only one place she could be.

We approached the last door, the one that led to the pool.

The air seemed barely breathable now. Or was it just my frazzled nerves tightening around my windpipe?

The door swung open easily. Light filtered in from the basement windows at the top of the wall, snow resting against the glass like frozen waves. We stared in disbelief, more puzzled than alarmed at what we saw.

There was Miranda sitting in the deep end of the pool, water bubbling up around her, splashing around with delight.

"Where'd all that water come from, Joe?"

The big man could not answer his assistant. "Don't know," was all he said.

The relief of finding her daughter forced an overflow of emotion from Isabella. "Miranda!" she shouted, her cry echoing off the block tile walls and reverberating in the large open room.

We watched in stone-cold silence as the child abruptly turned to face us, responding for the first time in her life to the sound of her mother's voice.

CHAPTER TWO

"IT's A MIRACLE!" ISABELLA Ruiz kept insisting as we mounted the stairs back to the first floor. Dripping wet and extraordinarily happy, Miranda shrieked and swayed in her mother's arms.

The whole scene made me uncomfortable, though Joe initially had no trouble believing. He came deliberately up the stairs behind us, talking as much to himself as to anyone else. "I know that water line was shut off. I did it myself, didn't I, Fred?" His partner agreed.

"Look, I don't think we should jump to conclusions," I said. "We ought to have Miranda examined by a doctor."

Isabella shook her head violently. She set Miranda down in the chair opposite the secretary's desk and spoke to her directly. "Miranda. Do you hear?" The little girl squealed at the sounds and attempted to mimic them.

The woman spun around to face me. "You see? Why you no believe?" She spoke accusingly but concerned.

I did not know what to say, so I said nothing and uttered a silent prayer. *I do believe; Lord, help my unbelief.* I smiled at her and nodded approval. She threw her arms around me and sobbed.

I picked up the box of food, but thought it might be wise to replace Miranda's wet clothing before we walked out into the damp, cold air. The most suitable item in the closet turned out to be an adult-sized gray sweatshirt with SIENA emblazoned across the front in faded block letters. It swallowed her, but she was delighted nevertheless, swinging her empty sleeves about like a shrunken majorette and filling the room with unintelligible chatter.

In the excitement Joe forgot his pipe wrench again and went to retrieve it as I bid the Ruizs goodbye. Still too overwhelmed to speak, Isabella hugged me again and walked briskly toward home with her box under one arm and

Miranda's armless sleeve in her hand. The child skipped ahead like a dog that had been shut up in the house all day and yearned for a good romp outdoors.

Joe returned a moment later with the wrench slung over his shoulder. "I checked it again, Miz Donovan. That valve was closed." His voice was emphatic. "When I opened it up again, I went to check the pool to see if it had drained out, but that little bit of water was still bubblin' up in the deep end. There must have been some back pressure in the system somewhere, but there's no tellin' where or how it got there."

"It's an old church, and I'm sure there are lots of funny quirks in the mechanical system we don't know about," I said.

He nodded and looked down before speaking again, quietly. "I never seen nothin' like that before, Miz Donovan. Was that kid really deaf before she went down in that pool?" He seemed overly humble, so different from the way he had acted earlier.

"That's what her mother always said. I just assumed it was true, though I admit I never watched her carefully. She couldn't make many words, but she was always responsive when I talked to her."

The big guy shrugged. "Well, I don't mean no disrespect or nothin', but, um, do you think she might want somethin'?"

"What do you mean?" I asked.

"Oh, just that, well, I don't know. You can't be too careful nowadays."

I paused, trying to get the drift of his intent. "Are you suggesting Mrs. Ruiz has been *faking* this deaf daughter thing all along just for charity? I can't imagine why she would, I mean, we've never judged her or failed to offer help when we could." My expression changed from confusion to certainty. "No. Isabella wouldn't do that."

"Don't get the wrong idea, now, please, Miz Donovan." He seemed to be regretful of the insinuation. "It looked like a miracle to me; at least I can't explain it, plumbin' -wise anyway. I got no reason to doubt her, 'cept—"

"Except what?"

He looked away again as if ashamed. "'Cept you didn't seem too excited over it, and I thought, with you bein' a reverend and all, well, that you woulda been. So I just figured maybe—"

"Listen, Joe," I said firmly, cutting him off. "We both saw the same thing down there. You can draw your own conclusions about it."

Throughout this exchange Joe's buddy had been waiting patiently in the truck. He finally honked the horn as lightly as he could, but the sound was still harsh enough to feel like a judgment on my words. It was, however, excellent timing. As the two men drove away, I went back inside to lock up, eager to get home.

My legs felt like stone as I flicked off the lights and checked all the doors. There was an intense pain in my spirit like a pinprick or a toothache, sharp and yet dull at the same time. Why had I been so short with Joe? He had given me a perfect opportunity to share my faith. There, just there, as the words echoed in my mind, the guilt intensified. I blew it, and I knew it. Just minutes earlier, I had attempted to evangelize Isabella Ruiz, and then somehow, she ended up testifying to me. What went wrong?

Maybe I was just tired. Could be the seasonal blahs, though it was March, and most people gained a lift by the melting snow and the coming warmth of spring. Maybe it was just the stress of a new job, a new place, all catching up with me at once. Maybe it was a new round of depression sparked by this latest milestone in my sister's life, reminding me of all that I didn't have, though I was ten years older. Perhaps I had given up on myself, but had I given up on God too? A few years ago, I would not have hesitated for a moment in declaring that child healed of her deafness. But today I stood there like a doubting Thomas, surrounded by a simple faith that, despite all my learning, I couldn't muster. Worse, my cynicism seemed to have rubbed off on Joe.

I pulled the front door closed and sloshed down Congress Street in the melting snow to my duplex apartment. I could see the green awning over the door from here, and Pete fidgeting on the concrete steps below. His mother was not yet home. He saw me coming and waved, as if he had been looking out for me for some time. I returned the greeting.

"Carla!" he yelled, jumping up and nearly tripping in his oversized rubber boots as I approached. "Can I have some hot chocolate? Puhleeeez?" His begging seemed to anticipate rejection.

"Yeah," I said, not really feeling like company but not wanting to be alone either. "Your mom will be home pretty soon, so no hanging around all night watching TV." His expression indicated disappointment, though I could tell he hadn't expected a long visit.

"Okay. Do you have the spray kind?" I said yes, evoking a shriek of joy. To Pete, the whipped cream was the whole point of having hot chocolate, and he much preferred the nozzle to the spoon. He was a chubby boy for his age, and sometimes I felt guilty about stuffing him with junk all the time, but he craved attention, and I couldn't stand to see him pout.

Motorhead was purring loudly as we practically crashed through the front door, Pete collapsing onto the kitchen floor, tugging at his boots in the posture of a contortionist, spinning on his rear as he yanked. The cat looked up from his perch in the kitchen windowsill, leaped down with a thud onto the linoleum, and waltzed over to Pete, the purring now intensified. He sniffed at the boy's damp clothes, and his nostrils flared at the whiff of the chill outside.

"Hey, Head!" shouted Pete, using the shortened version of my pet's name which he alone preferred. The beast blinked a few times and rolled on one side, stretching.

I stepped over the two of them and opened the pantry in search of the familiar brown powder. There was just enough for one Pete-sized mug, which would be half a cup for most people. Pete filled the top half of his with whipped cream.

In five minutes, Pete was seated at the table shooting cream out of the nozzle until it sputtered. Motorhead stretched out on the plastic place mat to Pete's right, and I sat directly across from him eating a rock-like thing Mrs. Grasso had described as a pepper cookie when she delivered a half-dozen a few days ago. Mrs. Grasso was always getting packages of food from the old country and often distributed its contents up and down the street like Santa Claus on Christmas morning. Motorhead's purring, my crunching, and Pete's slurping conjoined in a bizarre harmony that filled the little kitchen.

"You like wearing that?" Pete asked, referring to my clerical collar.

"Not particularly."

"Then how come you wear it?"

"I don't know."

"Do they make you wear it?"

"Well . . ." I paused. Did they make me wear it? "No, they don't *make* me, but it *is* sort of expected."

"Why?"

"So people can tell I'm a minister."

"Why?"

I squirmed a bit and brushed pepper cookie crumbs from my plain gray shirt, suddenly self-conscious. "Well . . . in case they might need something."

Pete seemed confused. "Like what?" he wondered innocently.

Good question. I had often wondered about it myself. Did I expect people to stop me in the street to ask for help? If so, they never did, not like they did Jesus. He gave them answers. He solved their problems. He got plenty of attention, and he didn't even wear the flowing robes of the scribes and Pharisees.

"I don't know . . . something, that's all. You want some more whipped cream? There's another can in the fridge." The boy's gooey smile indicated that I had successfully maneuvered out from under his interrogation. What a chicken.

It was after sundown when Pete's mother phoned and asked him to come home. We had met only once, and it wasn't a pleasant encounter, at least not from my perspective. Sheila was young but looked older than her years, a receptionist/billing clerk for a local garage who never seemed to make it home before seven. Pete was usually at my place or down at St. Fred's after school, but he visited the church only if he was especially lonely.

Out of character for her, Mrs. Dickson had taken a liking to him and kept him occupied with some silly thing or another. His vocabulary was exceptional, she said, and she rather enjoyed working with him on his letters. They were engaged in this very exercise when Sheila burst in late one afternoon, angry that Pete had not answered the phone at home, causing her to leave work early. She had seen his bike out front, and her parental concern had changed quickly to wrath by the time she came inside. I introduced myself and assumed my best pastoral character, though she was agitated the whole time we spoke. Perhaps she felt shame over the obvious truth that her child shouldn't have been in the care of total strangers, compounded by guilt in that these caregivers were associated with organized religion. Still, despite our lack of personal contact thereafter, she permitted Pete to hang around with me whenever he wanted.

Motorhead licked up the spilled hot chocolate and cream where Pete's mug had been as I washed it in the sink. The darkness outside turned the window into a mirror of sorts, and I beheld my reflection with disconsolation. I had to do something about this lifeless hair. Maybe I could trade in these old granny spectacles for some iceberg-blue contacts. I took off the glasses and squinted at myself, imagining the possibility that Margaret's cherubic face could somehow be reproduced in mine. I had been considered pretty once, before the ordination had plunged my dating life into oblivion, and I had quit caring about my appearance. One thing was for certain—I *would* dump the stupid collar. In a flash, my wet hands were at the back of my neck, pulling the white band out and dropping it on the steel counter. I was tempted to cast off the goofy shirt too, but not in front of the window.

A half-hour later I was settled into a warm bath. The bathroom was my favorite room, with its freestanding sink, claw-foot tub, and white tile, all original to the house. I sunk deeper into the water as Motorhead announced his coming with a deep purr seconds before he nudged the door open and hopped up on the commode to keep me company. I closed my eyes and heard nothing beyond the purr. My mind quickly recalled the events of the afternoon. *What happened down in that basement pool?* Water trickled into my ears and plugged them—I sat up with a start, then settled back again. I was thinking of Miranda, of the rush of new sound into her brain, like being born into a whole new world. What a magical moment that must have been—if, in fact, something miraculous had really occurred. But if it had, why? There had to be some plausible explanation.

I tried to relax, forcing myself to unwind. I thought of the park in the Boston suburb where I played as a child, the heat of the bath substituting for the summer sun. There were flowers everywhere—tulips and roses—and a gazebo where a young girl could play house and dream of her future. There were new homes placed charmingly together nearby, and one of them was mine, the one with the tan siding and bay window in the front. The village was quaint and existed strangely unto itself in the heart of the big city—a fairy-tale place, a picture of the life I could have, **should** have had.

The water was cooling, but I tried to ignore it and make the daydream last. I thought of Michael, so interesting and thoughtful, not what one would call handsome, but so full of confidence. His clothes didn't match—those colors!—but smart people are like that, I think. Maybe he's looking for his intellectual equal. All those years in the library might pay off after all; I mean, who else is there in Schenectady for him to discuss the synoptic problem with on a cold winter's night? Just me, little ol' bespectacled me. No, I mustn't get discouraged. There's something there, even if I might be a few years older. I'll get the contact lenses, that's for sure. The hair is no big deal either. Shoot, it will take only a little effort; I mean, it's in the genes. After all, wasn't my kid sister the homecoming queen? The water is almost cold now, but I'm really enjoying this. Who knows, maybe Michael will call. Why wouldn't he call? Yeah, why wouldn't he!

The phone rings, and I gasp, swallowing soapy water.

"Oh my God!" I fly out of the tub, dousing Motorhead's motor and head, sending him leaping toward the door. I almost slip on the tile as I reach for my robe. It is the one I preach in, of course, hanging up on the back of the door where it doubles as evening wear, but I am usually dry and at least semi-clothed when I put it on. Dripping, I head for the kitchen and grab the phone on the fifth ring.

"Miss Carla, this Isabella."

Words could scarcely describe my disappointment. Clutching at my robe as if someone were in the room with me, I cruised into reality nicely with a proper ministerial greeting. "Isabella. How are you this evening?"

A brief silence on the other end suggested caution. She could tell it was a bad time, or possibly that I just wasn't in much of a mood to talk.

"So sorry to bother you at home." *Right, as if I had a social life.* "I want you to talk to Miranda."

"Oh. Okay," I said quietly.

The little girl came to the phone. "Hah," she said. "Manda. Manda." This was followed by a squeal, and then some Spanish gibberish as her mother snatched the phone. "She say her name," Isabella said excitedly.

"That's wonderful. I'm so happy for you." And I really was.

"You open pool tomorrow?"

The words stunned me. "What?"

"The pool. The healing pool. Where Jesus heal my daughter today."

This is the kind of thing ministers are trained to handle yet all of us fail miserably at handling—how to tell a person of simple faith that miracles just do not fall from the sky like raindrops. They are special interventions of God that serve his purposes, not ours. "I'll certainly give it some thought," I said, a tad too clinical in my tone.

"You no believe?"

"No, no, it's not that," I lied. "It's just that, well, the pool isn't really safe. We can't have people down there until—"

"You no believe," she interrupted in a flat tone.

"No, Isabella, really, please try to understand. I just want to check things out, you know? I mean, we can't advertise for miracles and then have the health department shut us down." It was a poor attempt at levity, as if a little humor might get her to drop the subject.

She laughed, but not at my joke. "Okay, Carla. You very smart woman with a very good heart. You think too much though. I wait 'til you believe." Her voice was not condemning, and I was relieved. I thanked her for calling.

"Oh, Carla? We all enjoy the beets." Now it was my turn to laugh.

There was water all over the kitchen floor, beginning where Pete had taken off his boots earlier and continuing all the way to the bathroom along the path of my flight from the tub. I tore off a paper towel and sopped up some of it with my foot. Motorhead watched me from his place mat, sitting in what humans call the "cat position." The robe was clinging to my skin, and my hair was drying in clumps. I dropped more paper towels and slid them along until I reached the refrigerator. Realizing how hungry I was, I opened the door to a blast of arctic air, which left me shivering. The box from Ann's Pizzeria seemed to call my name. I snatched it up and, backtracking toward the microwave, caught my reflection again in the window. I stopped for a moment as if I meant to talk to this person looking back at me, but I had nothing of import to say. I was numb.

Motorhead followed me into the den, hoping to snag a bit of mozzarella. I stared at the TV, but could not find escape in the drivel it pandered. I was in a serious rut. What kind of woman of God am I? I'm supposed to be in the faith business, but a miracle happens right in front of me, and I deny it. What am I afraid of? Why can't I just go with it? Maybe I'm just too educated for my own good, because if faith is so simple, if the issues are so black and white, then who needs a pastor with a seminary degree? I wanted to be needed, to be essential, but blast the sermon—let's just run down to the pool and soak up what God's dishing out.

I reflected on this last thought for a while, realizing this is exactly what happened to the teachers of the Law when Jesus appeared on the scene. They rejected him because the people's acceptance of Jesus' simple truths and miracles meant rejection of them and their big fancy religion. Had they been schooled in modern science, they would have put forth rational explanations for what they saw—the same way some contemporary scholars view Moses' burning bush as a vivid sunset embellished for effect in the Holy Writings. But, not being thus enlightened, they murdered the Troublemaker instead. Anything to stop the threat to their domain.

Had I become one of them? No way, not me. I was no arrogant Pharisee. What then? My head was telling me that a miracle just can't happen in an abandoned swimming pool in Schenectady, but my heart was grieving over what my head insisted had to be true. I believed that such a thing *could* happen, but I struggled with the idea that it *did* happen. I suppose I should admit that these years of fighting the establishment had made me cynical. If God wouldn't bless me, how dare he bless anyone else?

Once, while in seminary, a group of my fellow students were discussing an article that had appeared in a gossip newspaper. It disclosed a secret venture to dig down to the center of the earth, an effort that was abandoned when, according to an inside source close to the operation, the screams of tortured souls became audible as the expedition drew near. Most of the students were laughing about it, but one fellow adamantly argued that this surely proved the existence of hell. I can still feel the stitch in my side as I sought to repress the laughter. I often told the story, even from the pulpit, as an example of ignorance in action, and how religious people are the most gullible of all. Ignorance, I said, is the enemy. But I don't tell the story anymore, since I read in the alumni magazine a few months back that this same student had been called to a huge church in Ohio as senior pastor. Call it ignorance or simple faith—he had it in abundant supply, along with a prominent pulpit. And I was jealous.

Okay. So I have more talent in my pinkie than nine out of ten male ministers have in their heads, and they always get the nod over me. So what? So I have to defend myself constantly to those who don't take me seriously because I'm not a man. Who cares? So all the notoriety I get is negative. Big deal. So First Mega Church is never going to call. Okay, I can live with that. So Michael Montefiore might never call either. And I can live with that too.

Motorhead was standing in the greasy box, tearing cheese from my pizza with his incisors, oblivious to my pain. My cheeks were suddenly wet with tears. *Oh, God, what happened in that pool?*

The cat, now satisfied, plopped into my lap, licking his face as far as his tongue could reach. I sighed, and he purred. It's the simple things, I reasoned, that make life worthwhile. *Look for meaning in the simple things,* I mused in a kind of mantra; then, exhausted, I nodded off to sleep.

C H A P T E R   T H R E E

THE NEXT MORNING BEGAN with a fresh enthusiasm, initially inspired by the first sunny day in more than a week. I was determined to get at the root of what had happened on the previous afternoon, if only to avert an impending crisis of faith. I hoped it would be easily explained, and the theological problem of healing waters bubbling up in the church basement conveniently set aside. The first issue to be resolved was the source of the water, which, the more I thought about it, possibly indicated some serious structural fault in the building. I summoned Mr. Delvecchio, the part-time custodian, to investigate the matter.

He shuffled in with the look of a tired hound, his Italian features drooping with age. He was in his mid-fifties, with wispy white hair and a pleasant smile, which hinted strangely of a sad resignation. I really liked Mr. Delvecchio because he was sincere, a true servant whose capabilities were limited, but not for lack of effort. He split his time between St. Fred's and a nearby Catholic church, earning just enough to care for his elderly father, a victim of Alzheimer's who rarely left their home.

I nearly blushed when he greeted me. "Miss Donovan, you look wonderful today," he said in his rocky voice, which was tender at the same time. "I don't think I've ever seen you without the collar before. Any special occasion?"

No, I thought, *except that I want to look like a real person for a change.* "Actually, I was discussing it with a friend, and he thought it was a bit conspicuous."

"Oh, I see," he said with a wink. I decided not to inform him that my gentleman friend was only eight and slurping up whipped cream while we were discussing the matter.

I motioned for him to sit down, at which time I noticed a small white box in his hand. "Canoli," he whispered. "Fresh from the bakery on Crane Street." He handed the box to me gently. "All for you this time." The reference to Mrs. Dickson's recent surreptitious purloin of his last pastry delivery, of which I enjoyed exactly none, was perfectly understood.

"Mr. Delvecchio," I began in a solemn tone, "a little girl got lost in the church yesterday."

His expression showed concern, awaiting the rest.

"She found her way to the basement, into the swimming pool."

"Was she hurt?" he asked, his expression unchanging.

I laughed. "No, actually she's fine. Better than ever, in fact." He looked puzzled.

"She was playing in the deep end of the pool when we found her," I continued. "There was water bubbling up from the drain, and I was wondering if you might know how it got there. The plumbers were here at the time, and supposedly they had turned the water off to make repairs. Any ideas?"

He thought for a moment before he spoke. "What you say happened is impossible."

I was a bit startled by this response. After all, I had seen the water myself, and there was no reason for me to be making it up. "Are you suggesting I was seeing things?" I asked.

"Yes, I think so," he answered. He regarded me the way my mother did when I told her I had seen reindeer on the roof one Christmas Eve.

"Look," I said firmly, "just because the plumbers said the water was off doesn't mean it actually *was* off. These guys aren't exactly rocket scientists. What I want to know is, assuming they were mistaken, how could water back up into the drain at all?"

"It can't." His voice was as firm as mine.

"Well, I just don't understand that, Mr. Delvecchio." Now *I* sounded like my mother. "Couldn't something have broken down there?"

"Wouldn't have made any difference."

I stood up. "Okay, fine. Why don't you come with me, and I'll show you why you're all wet." I hoped my pun would offset the intense frustration I was feeling.

"Miss Donovan, please listen. There cannot be any water in that pool." He looked up at me with that sad, peaceful face of his and saw I wasn't buying it. "All right," he sighed, getting up slowly. "Let's go have a look-see."

As we headed down the hall, I secretly worried that the water might have receded during the night, and our custodian's suspicions about my emotional state might be confirmed. It would only be a matter of time before the congregation knew. Oh well, there went my career, right down the drain. And then I thought, *What career?* The irony of it made me chuckle out loud, arousing the curiosity of Mrs. Dickson as we walked by.

We descended the steps slowly, at my companion's pace. The door at the bottom was old and opened with a loud creak. A musty smell surrounded us as we walked through the lower hall toward the room where the pool was located.

I paused before entering. "Now, no matter who's right, no rubbing it in, okay?" He grinned, and I opened the door.

The room was brighter than it had been on the previous day, due to the sunshine flooding in from the windows at the top of the wall. It glimmered on the water, which rested in the bowl of the deep end, no more than a few feet in depth.

Mr. Delvecchio stepped quickly along the deck and peered down at the water. "This is impossible," he exclaimed.

"That's what the plumbers said," I quipped, thankful that I was vindicated. "Now you're the guy who has to figure out the mystery."

"Well," he said, his hands in his pockets, that look of resignation returning, "unless something has changed . . ." He looked at me. "C'mon. Let's check it out."

I obeyed his command and followed him toward the far end of the pool. Suddenly he stopped and pointed at the deck area above the deep end. There was a rusty curved pipe sticking out of the deck and hanging over the pool edge.

"See that? That's the fill spout. It's connected to the fresh water line. That's how they used to fill the pool."

"So the water doesn't bubble up from the drain?" I asked, ashamed of my ignorance.

"Well, it could, I suppose, but only if water was trapped in the line. If that were the case, it would've happened twenty years ago when they shut down the pool, not yesterday. Normally, water leaves the pool through the main drain. After it goes through the filter, it comes back in through those inlets you see in the floor. So, if water came in last night, it would have had to come in through the fill spout. And that just can't be."

I was stumped. "Why not?"

"Go on over to the spout and stick your finger in it."

I did as I was told, kneeling down to feel inside the opening. It was bone dry, and pieces of rusty metal flicked off in my hand.

"Think any water came through there lately?" he asked. I nodded negatively. "Now I'll show you why it couldn't have."

I followed him to the corner of the room where a large steel plate with a handle lay on the floor. Mr. Delvecchio knelt on the tile floor and opened the hatch with great effort. He peered down into the dark hole and then got up. "Wait here," he said. "We'll need a flashlight."

I waited by myself in the still room. I had the ominous feeling that I wasn't alone. Were angels all around me? I looked down into the pool at the opaque, glassy water. I felt like Zacharias, alone in the Holy of Holies, a priest elected to burn incense on the biggest day of his life. Nothing was supposed to happen. Or was it? He would go into the temple, do his thing, and go home, just as it had been done by priests for hundreds of years without incident. A simple religious ritual. Nothing more. But on that particular day, an angel showed up in there with him with a major announcement. God was about to do something awesome, and Zacharias had a role to play in it. Unfortunately, he couldn't believe the news and was struck dumb for his lack of faith. He was old, tired, cynical. A good man—in fact, that's why he had been chosen—but too beaten down by the world. Had Miranda seen an angel? I looked all over the room, not knowing what I expected to see, grateful that there was nothing.

The abrupt return of Mr. Delvecchio snapped me back into reality. As we prepared to descend, he stopped to lecture me like a camp counselor before the big kayak race. "Now, Miss Donovan, be careful on these rungs." He seemed to possess a new assurance. "If we are to solve the mystery today, we'll find the answer down here."

He lowered himself down, and I followed. I'm not particularly agile, and the effort required all my concentration and skill. At one point, I stepped on Mr. Delvecchio's hand, but he managed to yank it out from under my loafer before I could raise my foot again. In seconds, we were standing together in a small windowless room.

He shined the light on the concrete wall. "That wall is shared by this room and the pool. Where you're standing is actually below the pool bottom." He swung his light around to the opposite side, where a huge rusted tank filled the space from floor to ceiling. "That's the filter, and down there next to it on the wall is the fresh water line." I was looking at a large spigot.

"It's not connected to anything," I observed.

"That's right," he said. "That's a gear-operated valve. You turn that wheel, and water comes out, just like on the side of your house. There used to be a pipe hooked up to it that ran to the fill spout . . . see it there?" He aimed the light at a section of pipe lying on the ground that had been removed from below the spigot. "Took it out myself years back, to make sure none of the kids got down here and filled the pool."

"But they could've flooded the room, couldn't they?" I wondered.

"Nope. There are drains in the floor running to the sewer." He used his light to point out the drains, then slowly moved it along the floor, saying nothing for what seemed like minutes.

"Mr. Delvecchio?"

We were standing in relative darkness, gazing at the circle of light. It revealed cobwebs and dirt, an occasional empty soda can, and some trash.

"Let's go," he said. "There'll be no solution to the mystery today."

When we emerged, he went back to the pool and shook his head at the water below. "It's a strange thing, Miss Donovan. I would have thought that the floor down there would be damp from rainwater seeping under the building. Or even from a leak in our water lines somewhere else, but you would have noticed your bills going way up, 'cause that's a lot of water. Maybe if the main drain line was cracked, some water could come back up into the pool. That's happened before, but never this much water; it's at least a foot deep in the bowl down there. But you saw the floor—no cracks from settlement. And dry as dust. I'm sorry, but I just can't figure this thing out."

We said nothing for a few moments, both of us looking down into the pool.

"There's something I haven't told you," I said quietly.

He stared into my eyes as if he knew this whole affair was about something much bigger than a water leak.

"The little girl who wandered down here, she was deaf. At least, she was before she played around in that water." I pointed.

He hesitated, "And now?"

"And now she can hear," I said, exhaling. "I know it's crazy, but she can. Or I think she can. Her mother hasn't taken her to a doctor yet, but I told her she should. I don't know. It's weird."

He looked to be trembling slightly, saying nothing, still fixing his eyes on the water below. At last he spoke. "This is a healing pool," he said matter-of-factly, "like in the Bible."

"A healing pool?" I asked.

"Like in the Bible," he repeated.

Mr. Delvecchio said no more as we made our way back upstairs. His mind was preoccupied, that was obvious. I assumed he would leave me and go about his duties, but as we walked by a perplexed Doris Dickson, he indicated that he intended to follow me back to my office. As we entered, he closed the door behind him.

"You need to go see Cornelia Shepherd. As soon as you can."

I knew I was remiss about visiting in the nursing homes, but I was confused as to the reason he would bring up the subject now. "I was meaning to, really, it's just that—"

"No, no, Carla." Strange, that he would call me by my first name. I guess he felt the shared revelation had brought us closer somehow. "You need to go see her and ask her about the pool." He turned to go.

I wasn't following the logic. "What do you . . . I don't . . ."

"Just go," he said quietly and in a grandfatherly way, like he did when he handed over the pastry, "and ask her about the pool."

He left me bewildered, not only by his words but also by his strange manner. A tightness visited my stomach. The anxiety of the previous evening was nothing compared to this sensation. It felt something like those dreams of free falling we all have as kids. I did not want to face it, whatever it was.

The intercom buzzed. "You had a call from Mrs. Ruiz while you were in the basement." Mrs. Dickson spoke with her typical sarcasm. "I knew it must be important, so I said you would call her right back."

Great.

I sat back in my executive's chair and pondered my situation. I couldn't avoid Isabella forever, and eventually I would have to either acknowledge that her daughter had been healed—or deny it. The repercussions from one choice were no better or worse than the other, and even if I did accept Miranda's miracle, that didn't mean I had to open the pool for miracles on demand.

I punched out the numbers, and Mrs. Ruiz answered on the first ring.

"You think about opening pool?" Her voice was cheerful, as always.

"I have thought about it," I answered, "but I'm not sure we should do that right now."

"You still no believe." Her tone was discouraged, but not angry.

"On the contrary, Isabella—there's something extraordinary going on, and I don't doubt for one minute that your daughter can hear—"

With that, she interrupted, sounding excited again. "She hear everything and talking good."

"I am so pleased for her. Thank God," I said.

"Oh, yes, praise to God," she exclaimed, her voice breaking.

"But think with me for a minute. What if God intended to heal Miranda—and *only* Miranda? What if her healing had nothing to do with the pool at all? What would happen if we let others in and nothing happened?"

There was a pause on the other end. "They no believe," she answered.

"Right. Now, I know you're thrilled over this—and you should be—but please, let's not tell anyone how this happened or, well, we might have some publicity we don't need. We don't want to be forced into anything that might not be in the best interests of the community."

"I understand. You seem very wise about this." She sounded satisfied.

I hung up the phone with the guilty feeling that I had said the right thing for the wrong reason. Would she have been so understanding had she seen what I had seen this morning? Probably not; in fact, she would likely have been more demanding than before that the good news be spread. Okay. So I don't know how that water got into the pool. Fine. And I don't know how that kid started hearing again either. What I do know is that, miracle or not, the church board was not going to sanction a "Swim for Miracles" crusade.

It was nearing eleven o'clock and, as usual, my To Do list was untouched. The big item, Sunday's sermon, screamed at me from the notepad. I still had no text, much less an outline. However, I was far too preoccupied to think about it right now. More than likely I'd be serving up another Saturday night special. I would be useless until I dealt with this pool thing, and that was no easy trick. First I had to satisfy myself that angels were indeed in the building, and then— assuming I took the side of faith—I would have to act on it somehow.

There wasn't much I could do about the mystery of the pool water other than jackhammer the shell until I got some answers, but neither I nor the church building could endure the stress of such a task without collapsing. Still, I had to do something. I couldn't very well go to the church board with a wild story like this one without some hard evidence. That was it exactly—I needed an objective, certifiable, expert opinion before I could do anything else.

The situation was obvious. The old pool suddenly started filling up with water. I figured something was wrong, so I would have someone come out to look at it. It was logical. Any pastor would do the same.

Looking under Swimming Pools in the Yellow Pages, I found a company called Trident Pools that specialized in commercial work. The ad listed renovations among the firm's services. I dialed the toll-free number, and a young woman with a Southern accent greeted me.

"Trident Pools," she said with a happy drawl.

"Uh, yes, I've got a pool problem," I said stupidly. I was holding the receiver in a death grip.

"Just one minute, and I'll transfer you to someone who can help."

Wow. That was quick.

I was rather enjoying Tom Jones's earthy vocals while on hold when another chirpy girl came on the line. The contrast was startling. She asked me lots of questions about the pool's size, age, and location. She seemed especially interested in the fact that it was situated in the basement. I could hear her tapping on the keyboard as I gave the answers.

"Now, exactly what did you say the problem was?" she asked.

"Well . . ." *How should I say this?* "It's got water in it."

"I see." She paused. "And how is that a problem?"

Perceiving that she thought me an idiot, I summarized the issue succinctly. "The pool is supposed to be empty—it's been closed for years—and when the water appeared, I thought there might be a leak or something."

"And you would like it fixed?" She had resumed tapping.

"Yes, of course." I cringed as I said the words. It's terrible when ministers lie.

"So you're planning to open the pool?"

The irony of her question summed up the problem perfectly. "Possibly," I said.

"Wonderful!" she squealed. The woman clearly loved her job. "We have a representative just down the road from you in Albany who would be glad to come by and make a proposal. We can assist you with complete drawings for your renovation and all the equipment you need. We custom make recirculating systems and filters, deck equipment—anything required to make the pool just like new. And our local franchised builder can do the work."

Whoa. "How much is all this going to cost?"

"Well, our representative will give you an estimate when he comes by, but his consultation is free."

That was a relief. She went on to say that Trident Pools was the oldest and largest organization in the commercial pool industry, and that she would like to send me some literature and photos of a similar renovation. I gave her my name and address, and she indicated that she would have the representative call before the day's end to schedule an appointment. It was a little over the top, but I felt relieved that these people knew what they were doing and were apparently the best in the field. If they couldn't get to the bottom of this, no one could, I figured. At least, no one on earth.

Determined to solve the mystery, and encouraged by the promise of progress, I advised Mrs. Dickson that I was expecting the call. I left her awaiting an explanation as I strolled out the door to grab an early lunch before dropping in on Cornelia Shepherd.

CHAPTER FOUR

THE MORNING AIR HAD the brisk quality of autumn, and sunshine struck places in the cracked street where the snow had melted away to expose its aged condition. It was football weather, even for spring, and the dampness of the passing season seemed to be retreating before the coming one. Though I had been warned against walking in the neighborhood alone at any time of day, I walked to my house where my Cavalier awaited obediently. I often left the car at home, thinking it a waste to drive it three blocks to work. I loved the little car more since it turned 100,000 miles, a milestone all of my previous vehicles had reached before the eventual trade on a newer, but still used, model. Each new car was older and less valuable when I bought it, and I doubted I would get much in trade for the little red Chevy, so I had decided it would be mine until the day of its demise. I find that personal commitment breeds endearment—to cars and people alike.

My fast-food choices were limited. I am not overweight and never paid attention to those who argued that burgers were time bombs for heart disease until one day, after consuming a particularly delicious one, I noticed the wrapper all sopped with grease, and I was suddenly repulsed at what I had done. Now I go for the salads, none of which are fresh; but since I can't feel my arteries hardening as I chew up the lettuce, I figure I'm ahead in the game. Unfortunately, I can't eat a salad and drive, which on this day I had in mind to do. Then an idea hit me. I backed out to the road, pulled up in front of St. Fred's, and scampered back to my office.

Mrs. Dickson, looking up from her mayonnaise-lathered turkey and mushroom pita, was not able to swallow fast enough to interrogate me as I ran by. White goo was dribbling down her chin, and she was scrubbing herself clean when I came zipping back. If she spoke, I was already gone, the box of canolis tucked under my arm like a football. I jumped into the cockpit and drove off, lunch in hand.

Had I been acting according to any rational code of behavior whatsoever, I would have checked the hospital list before I headed out to the nursing home, since the former lay along the route to the latter. But I had only one thing on my mind: Mr. Delvecchio's bizarre comment about the pool and Cornelia Shepherd, a balding, ice-blue-eyed lady, date of birth unknown, who, to my knowledge, had never been what you might call active in church, even when she was well. I chomped on the last bite of canoli number one as I approached downtown.

The city was unusually alive, though it was hard to determine where the people were going to or coming from. There was not much down there to attract anyone, and there hadn't been since the malls lured the shoppers and merchants away twenty years ago. I liked the city anyway. It had character. And plenty of parking.

By the time I reached the nursing home, three consumed canolis were making their presence known. They were small to look at and sweet to taste, but they were also heavy suckers that sat like unexploded grenades in my stomach. It must have been nervous energy that provoked my binge—a terrible, lifelong habit—and soon, I knew, I would be paying for it.

Nursing homes are not my favorite settings for ministry. I find it amusing that so many people assume that all ministers—especially me, who by all accounts am considered tenderhearted and sympathetic to those in need—are naturally imbued with a gift for comforting the infirmed and dying,. Extending sympathy is one thing, but providing personal care is quite another; a few minutes around suffering, and I'm usually headed for the nurses' station myself, ordering up something to untie the knot in my stomach. For the same reason, I always flick the channel whenever one of those commercials comes on about starving children. It's not that I don't care. I do—and I send money when I can. It's just that seeing all those emaciated people makes me horribly uncomfortable. Same thing in the nursing home. I especially dread passing the wheelchair-bound residents who have been indiscriminately parked in the corridor, left to linger there in some ratty nightdress for all the passersby to see, while the attendant takes a smoke break. I want to speak to them, but I know that the sounds that emerge in response will be unintelligible, and I will eventually have to say something pathetic like, "Yes, yes, I know." But really, I don't know. Who can really know what it's like to be in such a condition? It leaves me feeling ill and, instead of feeling grateful, strangely guilty for being relatively young and healthy.

The receptionist was not particularly responsive today. I stood there for several minutes while she shuffled papers. I was ashamed to ask for assistance. I should have known the system, but this was only my second visit, and the first had been with a parishioner who had escorted me to the proper room. In the lobby behind me, several wheelchair-bound ladies fixed their eyes on me, hoping, I figured, that I may have come to see them. They loved to touch their visitors, to cling to them in some kind of desperation, as if they were starved for affection. Anyone would do—relative, friend, or local minister. The last canoli seemed to lurch upward in my stomach at the thought of it, like a frightened hamster who suddenly realized there was no way out of the cage but up. Had I been wearing my collar, the residents may have falsely assumed that I exuded warmth and compassion and rolled themselves toward me with reckless abandon to get some.

"Excuse me, but I need a little help here," I said, the irritation in my voice springing directly from the little hamster down below. The receptionist looked up, surprised. She was particularly unattractive and apparently not used to interruptions. "I'm Reverend Donovan of St. Fred's." She looked me over, her expression unchanged. "I'm here to see one of our members, Ms. Shepherd?"

"One oh eight," she said flatly.

"Thank you," I said with a return shot of Bostonian arrogance. I hoped she was offended.

Remarkably, the corridor was clear all the way to the room as I sprinted forth. The door was closed, and I hesitated before knocking, afraid that I might interrupt a sponge bath or some heinous medical experiment that outsiders must not be permitted to see. Instead, I just peeked my head in and entered quietly.

Cornelia Shepherd sat in a vinyl chair, gazing out the window. She was draped in a multicolored afghan. I could tell she had no idea that someone was in the room with her. I stood there for an awkward moment before speaking.

"Mrs. Shepherd?"

She didn't seem to hear me. I stepped closer and called out again, somewhat louder.

"I heard you the first time," she said with a sigh, still looking out the window. She turned to face me. "I'm only ten feet away, you know."

Her demeanor was so dramatically different from the ladies in the lobby that I questioned whether she even belonged in the home. She appeared to be close to ninety, but her eyes still sparkled and, apparently, her hearing was quite normal. Her sprigs of white hair were long and in disarray; her mouth sagged at the corners as she spoke.

"I'm not sure we've met before. How do you know me?" She looked sad but slightly interested.

I revealed my identity and awaited her response. At length she smiled crookedly.

"You were here once before. And I've heard about you. Sit." She pointed at the bed.

I started in with the ministerial routine. "So, how have you been?" I said in my best happy voice.

"What do you want?" She quipped, not irritated, but clearly not charmed either. This lady was all business.

"Well, there is something," I started. "I wanted to talk with you about something that happened at the church yesterday."

"Haven't been to church in thirty years." She turned to gaze out the window.

"Yes, I know. I guess you're out of the loop. I've been meaning to visit more often, of course, it's just that—"

She sighed, loudly. "So what did you want to tell me?" If she was at all interested, she had me fooled.

"Look, maybe I should go," I said, standing up.

"Don't think so," she said quickly. "Be a year before you come back. Sit."

I took a deep breath and sat down again. "Okay. I need your help," I confessed.

The old white head turned back to face me. The crooked smile was back. "Thought so," she said. "But I don't have any money."

"Oh, no, Mrs. Shepherd, I wouldn't come here to—"

"Give you anything you needed if I had some."

I just stared at her. *Did I hear correctly?*

"I know, they all think I'm nuts down there, if they're even still alive. Stupid old cows, all of 'em. They can all take a long walk off a short pier, for all I care." For the first time, she began to show emotion. Her face flushed. "But I love that church." She stared wistfully out the window again.

"Mrs. Shepherd, please don't be upset. I really do need your help."

She sat motionless and silent, looking off into the distance, as she had been when I entered.

"It's about the pool."

The old woman's body tensed at the words. "The pool?" she asked. Her voice was suddenly childlike.

I had obviously struck a nerve. "That's right. The pool. It's been abandoned for decades—"

"Since 1971, last day of August." She turned toward me, her eyes brimming with a youthful intensity. "That's when they shut it down."

"You remember that, all those years ago?" I was intrigued.

"Oh, certainly, dear. It's my fault, you know. He told me not to tell."

Something about these words and the tone in which she spoke them made me question Cornelia Shepherd's mental health, as if the mood swings at the slightest provocation I had already witnessed were not evidence enough of some deficiency. *"He?"* I asked.

"He told me they wouldn't believe and not to tell." She seemed to be talking to herself now.

"Mrs. Shepherd, you're going to have to be more specific. I'm not following you. *Who* said not to tell?" I was leaning in toward her so far I almost slid off the bed.

"You don't know him?" She queried, quite surprised.

I took a shot in the dark. "Is it Mr. Delvecchio?"

She stared blankly for a moment. Then her eyes flashed. "Of course not!" Her body trembled slightly, and she turned away again.

"Mrs. Shepherd? Look, I don't have a clue as to what you're talking about." My frustration was showing.

There was no response.

"Mr. Delvecchio told me to come here. He told me to ask you about the pool. It's filling up with water, and he can't explain it."

She seemed to be listening.

"He calls it a healing pool, like in the Bible. He told me to ask you." She was hearing me, but did not seem to want to discuss the matter.

"Mrs. Shepherd?"

My pleading got me nowhere. I stood up to go.

I was almost to the door when she spoke. "They all said I was crazy," she said softly.

I paused. *Crazy at worst, eccentric at best,* I reasoned to myself. "I'm very sorry," I said. "Church people can be cruel."

I waited to see if she might continue.

"You say the pool is filling up?" she asked.

"Yes."

"Why?"

"I don't know. I thought you could tell me."

"And you say you haven't seen him?"

"No, I guess I haven't. *Who?*"

She swiveled her head around and stared me down. "Sit," she said. I obeyed.

"There was a time, many years ago, when St. Winnie's was full of life, when the neighborhood was full of young people," she said. "It could have been a *Jesus* church." My face must have given away my confusion. "You know, like in the sixties?" I nodded, still unsure.

"We were a church of old ladies, all bent over and miserable, wearing black all the time . . . you know. The priest got into trouble with the bishop over something. So they decided to sell the building. There were these Protestants who wanted to buy it, so they sold it. Now, I was just in my sixties then. My husband was dead, and I wanted to live a little bit. So I stayed with the Protestants."

"So you were part of the old Catholic church, and you converted?" I asked, impressed.

"Yes, that's right; that's exactly right," she answered emphatically. "But you know what? The new people were serious Bible-thumpers, all buttoned up and everything. They were constantly fighting about music and hair and bell-bottoms, things like that. Uptight all the time. Made me mad. Let the kids live a little, right? That's what I said. They let you have your say in church, you know, at these meetings they had. Well, you know. Of course you know." She looked somewhat embarrassed once she realized I was one of them.

"Why are you smiling?" she asked.

"I am? Oh, well, I'm just really enjoying this. I mean, you were something of a rebel. I can relate, being a female minister."

"I don't really believe in those," she said flatly.

"Oh."

"So anyway," she continued, "it was a few years after they bought the church that things started to happen. We were having these Bible studies, and new people were coming. I used to wear a lot of fringe in those days."

Now why would anyone think this woman is crazy? I mused.

"The only thing I did with the old people was swim. They didn't use the pool much but opened it for the seniors, and I went with them because it helped my arthritis. Laps in the morning, back and forth, back and forth, every day. They kept the water very warm. Good for the old bones.

"I was swimming at the far end of the pool one day, approaching the wall, when I saw these great boots. I looked up and saw this man. Hip huggers, fringe jacket, long hair. He said, 'Shhh.' Had his finger over his lips like this." She made the librarian's favorite gesture.

"I hung on to the wall, and he said again, 'Shhh. Don't tell anybody.' I didn't know what he was talking about, and I was about to ask, and he was gone. I blinked, and he was gone."

I was engrossed, I'm ashamed to admit.

"So I just pushed off and headed back, then I knew right away." She sat back in her chair, looking pleased.

"Yes . . . ?" I started, hoping she would finish.

"Well, I was healed. No arthritis." She sat back again, beaming.

"And the man . . . ?"

"Jesus," she said, as if it were the most natural thing in the world.

I sat there and nodded, taking this in. "So . . . how does Mr. Delvecchio figure in?"

"Frankie? He was just out of high school then. Working for GE during the day, custodian at St. Winnie's at night. He was a good boy, and the Protestants liked him, so he stayed on. He just knew."

"He knew you were healed?" I wondered.

"Yes, he did. He believed me. He heard it through the grapevine, and he asked. I told him, and he believed. That's what he said. He's a good boy."

I recalled Mr. Delvecchio's expression when I told him about Miranda, and how he tried to convince me—and himself—that it couldn't be so. Perhaps he did believe . . . thirty years after the fact.

"You have a wonderful testimony," I said, trying not to sound condescending. "But why did they shut the pool down?"

"Right after I was healed, they did that. They said I was stirring up trouble. Nobody believed me. He said they wouldn't. He said not to tell."

"Jesus?" I confirmed.

"Jesus," she agreed.

We talked for a while about other matters, girl stuff mainly. I went through the long story of why I entered the ministry, which by now I had almost memorized. The words were carefully selected to minimize potential objections. She found the saga interesting, but she didn't seem particularly empathetic. Not too many people did.

I promised to return, which she appreciated. As I was rising to go, she reached out and clutched my arm.

"It will happen again," she whispered.

I couldn't bring myself to tell her that some people thought it already had.

The interview with Mrs. Shepherd had exhausted and energized me at the same time. I wanted to believe her, if for no other reason than to inject some excitement into my otherwise mundane existence. What if she had recalled an actual experience? Of course, the hippie-Jesus vision must have been at least a little embellished. It could have been the sugar from all that Italian crème stimulating my mind to new dimensions in spirituality, but I kept feeling this urgent desire to *do* something, to act swiftly and demonstratively in defense of my fragile faith, which, sugar or not, seemed to be unusually vigorous. Just a pinch of doubt, though, and it would shrivel into the old familiar cynicism. I had to do something to keep it alive—something *drastic*.

I gripped the wheel with both hands and veered across the traffic into a hardware store parking lot, where I quickly made a sharp three-point turnabout into the street, heading back the way I had come. I sneaked under two yellow lights and careened past the college's athletic fields, zipped through the old neighborhoods, one after the other, and finally sailed across the river where a winding rural route took me to the gravel drive leading to Shekinah Community Church.

I hopped out, slammed the door, and examined my reflection in the dirty window. A sudden wave of air lifted the back of my hair into a wing, and I cocked my head against the flow until it fell back. I was pumped.

The door to the church was locked. It was a ranch-style building with wood siding and a little porch in front; if not for the sign, no one would recognize it as a house of worship. In fact, I don't think I could be comfortable worshipping in such a casual setting, but I would never tell Michael that. He had deliberately revitalized the dying congregation, changed its name, and moved it to this contemporary setting so that he could effectively reach a new generation of unchurched people. I stood there for a minute as my confidence ebbed away. My intentions were to discuss the miracle pool with Michael, maybe over coffee—or even dinner. Flying over there in my little car, I had envisioned this quasi-romantic encounter in some bookish joint down near the college, leaning across the table, postulating theories in the style of some intellectual flirt, while Michael listened intently, enraptured. But when that doorknob wouldn't turn, I woke up. He was probably out visiting and could come back at any minute. What was I doing? Had my bathtub revelations seeped into my skin with the suds, merging fantasy into reality? I had to get out of there. I felt so naked without my collar.

The wind wafted my hair once again as I sprung from the porch. I nervously flung myself into the car and drove deliberately toward the highway. I made a right just ahead of a silver Honda coming slowly from the left. I glanced in the mirror. It was Michael.

As I sped away, I could not find one shred of my earlier enthusiasm, which I should have realized was not sustainable. I felt like slouching down under the wheel, ashamed at what I had almost done. *Michael! Glad to catch you in. So . . . let's you and me head down to the bistro for a latte–I have important news.* Oh, yeah, like what? Like I've got Jesus in fringe wandering around in the church basement, offering unction to old ladies' joints? My own stupidity was startling. Human beings are such emotionally fragile creatures.

It started to rain. My wipers were old—original to the car, as I liked to say—and they made a violent rubbery scraping sound as they obediently applied themselves to the task, up and down, up and down—just like my mental state—worn out and struggling, barely getting the job done.

The peculiar thing about my momentary transfiguration was that it suggested there might be a part of me that still cared way down deep, that all I needed was a little *oomph* to get the old juices flowing. That thought was encouraging.

I arrived at the church with the determination not to let this thing drop. Isabella was overly excitable, simplistic, and maybe even opportunistic. Cornelia was loopy at best and possibly unstable. The two supposed miracles could not be easily substantiated. Even so, I liked the way it felt to believe that such things might be so. If not, why bother to serve? Why preach? I could not let it go. It gave me purpose.

Mrs. Dickson was sitting at her little desk doing a crossword. In a short forty-five minutes she would be going home, and I hesitated asking her for anything. Not that it wasn't within my rights, of course. I just didn't want to deal with the attitude.

"I need something."

She looked up, empty-faced.

"I'll need the minutes of those early business meetings, back in the seventies. The first five years."

We looked at each other for a few seconds. At last, she scribbled a note on her pad.

"Mrs. Dickson, I would really like to have them to read over tonight."

She was miffed. "I'll have to go down to the basement to get them," she retorted. The basement room where the records were kept was poorly organized, and this statement suggested she might not have enough time to perform this difficult task and still leave on schedule. It ticked me off.

I looked over her shoulder at the crossword. "What's a four-letter word beginning with *L* and rhyming with *crazy?*" I snapped.

Her eyes got big at that remark. Pushing her chair back from the little desk, she lifted herself with a snooty air and marched off to the basement.

CHAPTER FIVE

THE SERMON I HAD chosen to bring on the upcoming Sunday was a real clunker. In seminary I had a professor who often said there is a big difference between having a sermon to preach and having to preach a sermon, and lately the gap was widening. I stared at the notepad, swirling cyclones of blue ink on the paper, my mind in limbo. I was in the middle of a series from the parables, the wise and foolish virgins presenting themselves as my subject for this week. The converted bedroom office in my house was lit only by my desk lamp, which cast an embarrassing brightness on the empty page. My eyes kept glancing nervously to a spot on the side table just beyond the ring of light, where the ledgers containing the old church minutes were stacked.

It was already dark outside and all throughout the house, except for the desk in my home office. I had dropped the ledgers in my frantic effort to get at the sermon, suddenly possessed with a mixture of worry and fear that always accompanied the realization of the relentless, looming return of the Sabbath for which I was unprepared. My place had two bedrooms and, though I called one an office, it was really just a room with a desk and piles of books, papers, files, unpacked boxes from the move, and assorted clutter. I had set myself directly to the task of writing the sermon upon arriving at home, and I must have sat for more than an hour, giving only token attention to the virgins and producing exactly nothing of value. With a sigh I put down my pen, closed the Bible, and reached for the ledgers.

One thing I had gleaned from my haphazard study of the text before me was that the foolish virgins were shortsighted and unprepared for the abrupt return of the Master. With this thought tickling my mind, I began to leaf through the old minutes. What was I expecting? A firsthand account of the sudden appearance of Jesus in the church basement?

The church did appear to be making great strides in those days. Names I failed to recognize were cited for various contributions to a number of ministries, many of them experimental and quite successful, if only briefly. The Performing Arts Center in Saratoga was the scene of an evangelistic rally at a Steppenwolf concert, which produced several converts. One group in the church had organized to help find work for veterans returning from Vietnam. Cornelia's memory of home Bible studies was accurate; they had been springing up everywhere in the records.

And then came the stunning account of a special meeting called to discuss one member's activity, that being one Mrs. Shepherd, whose "vision" had become known in the community and was drawing unwelcome attention to the church as—if I interpreted the subtle report correctly—something of a hippie hangout.

Certain names were familiar—Egan, Hamber, Kerry, and Lutz—all still very active in church affairs. Hamber was the clerk then, and author of the minutes, and chairman of the board now. Lutz and Egan were also now on the church board, and Kerry was currently serving as treasurer. These men had been key leaders in their young adult years, the driving force to acquire the property from the Catholic church, and had apparently led the charge to close the pool.

The darkness was somewhat distracting now, and Motorhead's heavy presence against my leg suggested even he was ready for me to get up and do something about it. I reached down to scratch his neck; the throaty purr resonated in the room, soft and warm, like a quilt on a chilly night. I was comfortable in the security of that lighted space, as if somewhere beyond it lay a threat to things as they were. Maybe in my mind I was on the brink of discovering some dread secret that was better kept hidden, especially for me. I could stop at any time, and I knew it. Perhaps I should have.

The telephone interrupted my contemplation, as only the phone can do with its harsh, intrusive clamor. My back hurt as I stood. My legs were stiff as I walked to the kitchen, flicking light switches as I went.

"Did we miss each other earlier?" the voice said pleasantly.

"*Michael?*" I felt the throb of my pulse as I squeezed the receiver.

"Yeah . . . that was you, wasn't it?" He sounded less confident, but still sure of himself. "I only had time to check my messages before running down to the soup kitchen. Just got back, or I would have called sooner."

I searched feverishly for words. "That's . . . okay," I said. "No problem."
What was I going to say next?

"So. Did you want something?" He seemed especially curious.

The ball was definitely in my court. "Well, there *was* something I wanted
to talk to you about. It's no big deal." I closed my eyes and held my breath.

"Gosh, I'm sorry I missed you. You sure it isn't urgent?"

"No, nothing really important." I hoped he couldn't hear me swallow.

"Tell you what," he said with that chummy boldness so frequently found
in ministers. "I'm free tomorrow if you want to get together—day or night—
your call."

If I want to get together? "Sure," I said. "How about dinner . . . Erie Diner
. . . around seven?"

"Great," he said. I was sure I could hear a little laugh as he said it. "See
you then."

I stood there for a moment, hanging onto the phone. Suddenly I realized I
was talking to the cat, saying something like, "Erie Diner? I invited him to
Erie Diner?" Motorhead did not condemn me, which is the great thing about
cats. They just rub your leg and hop onto your lap no matter how stupid you
are. Not that there's anything wrong with this particular eating establishment—open twenty-four hours a day, great steak sandwich—it's just not the
most romantic place in the world, a far cry from my fantasy earlier in the day.
But it was the first place that came to mind, and it would have to do.

Now that the date was set, what was I going to talk about? Maybe the
sermon for Sunday—no, not the foolish virgins. Maybe small talk and where-
ya-from, who're-your-folks kinda stuff—no, why would I drive down to his
office just for that?

With a sigh I went back to my study and plopped down at the desk. Wait
a minute. Who said this was a date anyway? He didn't exactly ask me out or
anything. He's not even picking me up. This is just business. Two colleagues
talking shop. No big deal. Why worry?

I plunked my head down on the open ledger book, devastated.

Perhaps if I tried hard enough, I might be able to recover my earlier
mood. What was it Lutz had said?

I flipped a page and found it.

Mrs. Shepherd made a long speech insisting again that she had
seen this man, but that only later did she recognize him as Jesus. She

continued by calling the church leaders Pharisees and cited Scripture from Matthew 23. There was a disruption at the back of the auditorium, several people rose to speak, and Mr. Belcher called for order. Mrs. Shepherd was asked to finish, and she began to cry softly before speaking. She said that she had such high hopes for the church. At that point, Mr. Lutz was recognized, and he apologized for his earlier hostility. He made his case plainly, asking who would believe such a story, and saying that if the pool was kept open, it would attract all kinds of unruly people, as it has nowadays, and so it should be closed. Without further discussion, the matter was put to a vote, and Mr. Lutz's proposal carried.

"Who would believe such a story?" Lutz had said. If the church didn't believe it then, how could I expect Michael to believe it now? I wasn't sure I believed it myself. Maybe that's how I should approach it—just tell him the facts and let him reach his own conclusions. After all, any person with a mustard seed of faith would naturally be at least a little open-minded about such things. Who could fault a woman of the cloth for that?

Saturday morning rocked its way into my head with the coming of the sunshine through my bedroom window, even though it was nearly nine before it forced my eyelids open. Suddenly awake, I was struck with the panic of having no sermon ready for the next day and the stress of a first quasi date with Prince Charming-iore that night, which, based on the agenda for the evening, might well be the last. Motorhead seemed to sense my nerves and rolled off the bed like a fat slinky, padding his way toward the empty dish in the kitchen. Cats have no long-term memory, and I knew he would return to that empty dish every two minutes, whining between visits, until I filled it.

I sat for a moment on the edge of the bed, pondering my options: shower, dress, fix breakfast, read the paper, call Mother, maybe catch a bit of Wide World Wrestling, head to the office, crack some books, get the sermon on paper, come home to a leftover canoli for lunch, do some housework, put in a load of laundry, devote myself to major grooming. No way was this going to work, with me being so uptight. My revised schedule went like this: dress, take a canoli to the office for breakfast, get the sermon done, play the rest by ear.

I pulled on my jeans and stuffed my feet into my Adidas, no socks. I decided to stay with the blue long-sleeved T-shirt I had slept in, waiting to shower until just before I would head to the diner to insure maximum freshness for the meeting with Michael. I didn't plan on seeing anyone until then anyway. I did brush my teeth, for my own benefit, and snatched my Red Sox cap to cover my matted hair, just in case I might be seen from afar. Dropping some Friskies into Motorhead's dish, I picked up my keys and was headed out the front door, when the telephone rang. It was Mother.

"I'm calling from Margaret's. Your nephew is sitting right here in my arms." The speakerphone made her shrill voice sound like it was coming from the bottom of a barrel, and the urgent gurgling in the background suggested Ryan III wasn't exactly comfortable with the arrangement. "He was wondering when you were coming to see him."

"He was wondering?"

"Well, we all are, actually. He's a month old, Carla." The familiar nasal tone was snappy, and I could feel the old wounded child in me rising to meet it. "You missed the birth, you missed the baptism—are you the least bit interested in this major event in your sister's life? Or are you too busy caring for others to remember your own family?" I resented the condescending tone.

"It's not intentional, Mother. Tell Margaret I'll be there next weekend, okay?" I was barely containing my resentment.

"We were thinking about this afternoon."

"What, *today?* But I can't—"

"It's a Saturday, dear. Do they make you work on Saturday? It's only 166 miles, for heaven's sake. And it's a gorgeous day for a drive."

"But I still have work to do on my sermon, and I've got things planned."

"You mean you still haven't done your sermon? Shame on you, Carla." I closed my eyes, preparing for the put-down. "How hard can it be anyway? You people don't have any rituals to remember; you just give a little talk, right? Your sister can help—she's written some wonderful pieces on the family for *Boomer* magazine."

"Mother, please listen. I can't come, and that's it. I've . . ." My pulse was rapid now, my breathing shallow. "I've got a date tonight."

There was a heavy silence. Even Ryan III paused his grunting, presumably alarmed at the shock that had momentarily paralyzed his grandmother. I heard whispering. It was Margaret in the background, repeating my statement in interrogatory form.

"That's right, I have a date. So I can't come."

There was a sharp noise; Margaret had snatched up the receiver. Her cutesy voice rang clear in my ears. "Carla. This is awesome. You've *got* to come today. Right now, jump in the car—you'll be here by lunch. We'll spend the afternoon getting you ready."

I hesitated. That might not be a bad idea after all. I wouldn't have to stay long, and if anybody could prep me for a quasi-romantic encounter, it was Margaret. "Well, I don't know—"

"We'll look for you by one at the latest. I've got a closet full of stuff I can't wear yet—this will be great." She paused. "We're still the same size, right?"

"Well, I . . . I guess so."

"She's been on a binge again," I heard my mother say in the background. "I can tell by the sound of her voice, such a nervous Nellie. Just like in high school when she got asked out by that trombone player, and she ate an entire box of chocolates and couldn't go."

"As a matter of fact, I'm *not* overeating, and I *am* still the same size as Margaret!" I shouted to Margaret by mistake. Guilt and panic broke out on my skin in tiny droplets. "And I'll be there at one o'clock to prove it!"

My mother said nothing further, and I let Margaret rattle on about the superhuman exploits of Ryan III, who seemed destined to follow his parents' pattern of excellence in everything. By the time I hung up, I was literally trembling with anxiety over the suddenly full day ahead and the encounters that awaited me.

◆ ◆ ◆

It was indeed a glorious day. Driving past St. Fred's, I saw a white, very dirty Oldsmobile parked out front. From it emerged a stocky gray-haired man carrying a briefcase and dressed in a houndstooth jacket, white shirt, and black pants.

"Reverend Donovan?" he asked as I rolled down the window. He seemed as surprised to see me as I was to see him. "Did you get my message?"

I shrunk down in my seat, looking for a way to escape without running this fool over. I was trapped. Thank God, I had at least grabbed the baseball cap. "And you are . . .?" I said with hesitation.

"I guess not," he said, answering his own question first. "I'm Phil Garrison. Trident Pools. I spoke to your secretary yesterday, a Missus—"

"Dickson," I blurted out, realizing at last what was going on.

He was holding his briefcase in front of him with both hands on the handle. Seeing me up close seemed to make him suddenly uncomfortable.

"That's right. I explained that you had called our corporate headquarters, and that I would be out of town all next week, but I could drop by this morning if it was okay with you, and she suggested around nine."

I folded my arms across my chest and said stiffly, "Well, I didn't get the message. I was out all afternoon." There was an awkward pause, as neither of us knew quite what to do.

"Look," he said. "I'd be glad to come back another time."

I did not immediately respond, and he turned back toward his car. "Wait, it's fine, really." I didn't think I could live with the mystery for another week. "You'll have to excuse my appearance, though. I didn't—"

"Shoot, don't worry about that," he said happily, bounding over to the car. He appeared relieved that I had implied that I didn't look like this all the time. "I usually don't shave on Saturdays myself."

How nice.

We stumbled inside, me pasted against the door as I opened it, body language screaming discomfort at being seen in such shabby condition. I jammed my chin down and sniffed, sure that I must stink at least a little, though not a trace of odor could be detected. Phil was talking the whole time as he followed me in, yapping about old churches, and how interesting to find a pool in one, and God knows what else. Typical salesman banter.

I stopped at Mrs. Dickson's desk and whirled around. "I guess you're wondering why I asked for you," I muttered, still extremely self-conscious. "The pool has been out of service for years, and, well, there's water coming in from somewhere, and I'd like to know from where." I was nervously waving my hands in the air as I spoke, perhaps in a subconscious attempt to draw his attention away from my person.

"Have you called a plumber?" he asked. He looked serious, but I could tell he already thought me something of a nut.

"Yeah," I sighed. "He was no help."

He laughed. "Okay. How about your water bill? Has it been higher than usual?"

Now that was an excellent question. "You know," I said thoughtfully, relaxing a bit, "I haven't even looked at it."

"Might be a good idea. You could be losing water somewhere, and it's coming up under the pool. Is the shell cracked?" He was getting a little smug.

"Looks like it. It's an old pool. But our custodian insists that's not the problem."

"Oh, well, have you checked the piping?"

"Bone dry."

"Bone dry?"

"Yep, and the water was off when the water came up. In fact, the fresh water line isn't even connected anymore." *How's that, Smarty Pants?*

Phil Garrison seemed momentarily bewildered. "Well, I guess you better let me have a look at the pool, huh?" Suddenly he smiled broadly, and I got the impression that he really didn't care all that much about my water problem.

"Sure. Listen," I said, "we really don't want it fixed. I mean, I haven't even told the board about this whole thing yet. I just thought there might be a simple explanation, that's all."

He nodded, as if he was used to this kind of speech. "I understand. So let's have a look anyway. I'm here, and I love pools. What can I say?" He was cute in a teddy bear kind of way, and I happily led him to the basement.

Phil Garrison gushed upon first sight of the pool, like a collector of fine porcelain might swoon over some obscure vase discovered in a cluttered antiques warehouse that only the serious collector would recognize as having value. He knelt on the tile deck and ran his hands over the lip of the concrete trough. "Has anyone checked these drains?" he asked, swiveling his jar-like head in my general direction.

"What drains?" I asked back. "There are drains in there?"

He stood up and swatted his knees, though there was no dust on the trousers. "Oh yes, spaced about twenty feet apart, all along there, see?" He pointed, and I leaned over, peering down the side of the pool. "From the feel of the plaster I would say the pool has moved," he said confidently.

"Moved?"

He nodded.

"That's bad?"

He nodded again.

The stupidity of this whole situation was beginning to make something twitch in my neck. "Where did it go?"

He laughed uproariously. "No, no, Reverend . . ."

"Call me Carla."

He paused. "Okay . . . Carla." He was swallowing a chuckle, realizing I didn't think my ignorance was anything to laugh about. "Look down into the trough. See that black line going all the way down? That's a crack. Now, pick up your eyes and look at the deck across the pool. What do you see there?"

I opened my mouth, fully expecting to see something, but nothing materialized when I needed the words.

"There's a bump," he said. "See it?"

With some effort, I did see it. "Oh, yeah . . . a bump."

"Do you know what that is?"

I looked at him strangely. "Is this a trick question?"

He threw his head back to laugh but nothing came out. "This pool was constructed with poured concrete. Forms were built and the walls were made when the concrete was poured down into them. Over time, the ground will settle, and the structure may crack or shift. When that happens, pipes break, and—"

"The pool leaks," I said confidently.

"Right. Hey, you're catching on." His big smile almost made me blush. "These drains in the gutter are connected by piping, and I'll bet it's cracked, especially at that bump over there."

"So?"

"So, your custodian's wrong. If those drain lines are cracked, it's likely the piping underneath the shell is too, and water is coming in underneath it. This is an old building. You've got plumbing problems, Carla."

"But the plumbers checked that out already, and they—"

"But you said you haven't checked your water bill."

"Uh, no—"

"So you could be losing water somewhere, and it's coming up under the pool."

I shook my head vehemently. "You don't understand—"

"*I* don't understand?" He was smiling.

"Okay, I realize you're the expert, but I'm sure it isn't a leak."

"One way to find out," he said smugly. He pulled a small jar out of his briefcase. "We'll just take a sample of the water to see exactly where it's coming from." With that, he was climbing down a wobbly ladder into the pool and creeping toward the deep end.

"I think you ought to talk to Mr. Delvecchio," I called out. I shuddered as he reached out toward the lifeless water, expecting something, not knowing what.

"The water sample is free," he said as he clambered up the slope. "But I can tell you right now, this is gonna be an expensive fix." He was puffing as he hoisted himself back onto the deck from the ladder.

"Look, we've been over this before—"

"Hey, I'm not selling anything, just trying to help. But you've got either bad pipes, or a structural problem that will only get worse. Shoot, this whole building could fall in maybe."

I could only stare blankly.

"Well, probably not. Let's test the water first. I'll call when the results come in. Deal?"

Of course it was a deal. Still, I felt obligated to listen to his claptrap about installing some kind of steel system on the pool, and then I let him wander around down near the filter. I could hear him talking to himself down there as I waited alone above. The disembodied voice was eerie, even though I knew where it was coming from.

He climbed up from the hole in the floor slowly, as if the morning's sales work had been as grueling as a five-mile run. "Something odd about it all," he said. "A church this old with a pool. When was it built?"

"The church? Almost a hundred years ago," I answered.

"Well, tell you one thing, this pool isn't half that old. I wonder what made the church decide to put it in?"

"Couldn't say." Honestly, I had never given it much thought.

"A new pool like this would cost at least a quarter million. If I were you, I'd have this baby renovated one day. It's the kind of thing that brings in the young families, you know."

I didn't appreciate the pool guy telling me my business, but he was correct in his assessment. Perhaps I should bring the idea to the board after all. But bringing in new people wasn't exactly high on the board's list of priorities. Neither was spending money. And surely they wouldn't want the ladies of the church flopping around down here in bathing suits. I just smiled and listened as Phil Garrison dreamed out loud of St. Fred's Indoor Water Park, complete with garish water features spritzing gushers from the mouths of the saints, an ark for the kids to climb on, and a fiberglass whale in whose gullet disobedient toddlers could be sent for time-out. We made our way out of the darkened belly of the basement, he ebullient with vision, me hunched over and hiding from the glare of the morning, feeling a bit like the petulant Jonah spit out on a land I had never wished to see.

CHAPTER SIX

STILL SMARTING FROM MY mother's quip, I resisted the urge to swing by a drive-through eatery as I whizzed along the Mass Pike toward the historic and refined suburb of Newton, the quaint composite of a dozen or so quaint villages west of Boston where nearly all of my family still resided. The road was practically deserted, and my thoughts drifted back in time to childhood Sundays, where I once sat, similarly catatonic, in the pew at the stately Mary Immaculate of Lourdes Church, and where my parents would likely be sitting the next morning. I noticed that snow was still collected, crusted with brown stains at the curbside, and dotted with footprints on the wide lawns of Upper Falls. A blackbird fluttered down and perched atop the mailbox of my sister's home, a grim omen, which quickened my pulse as I rolled along the drive and parked behind my mother's Volvo. The presence of Mother's car suggested that my father wasn't there—another bad sign, for if I had a defender in the family, it was Dad, despite my choice of vocation that had caused him so much grief.

I tramped my wet shoes on the front porch, and the door opened before I rang the bell. "Carla!" squealed Margaret as she extended an arm outward while cradling the baby in the other. I prepared for a hug, but her hand just grazed my shoulder lightly and she drew back quickly, rocking the infant in both arms. I stood there on the stoop, watching her nuzzle the tiny pink face swathed in blue blankets, realizing that this was my cue to say something. Mother's squinting eyes appeared behind Margaret; her snippy voice broke the silence first. "Are you coming in, or do you want the baby to freeze to death?" Margaret chided her halfheartedly, and I followed them as they backed inside.

Margaret bent over to lay Ryan III in a Moses basket embroidered in yellow, and Mom swooped down to tuck the blanket around him. Standing stiffly with her hand on her lower back, Margaret smiled and opened her arms wide to me once more. This time I embraced my baby sister gladly. Despite the roiling of my insides at being there, it was good to see her.

She was, of course, as perfect as she had been three months ago when last I had been home. The statement about not fitting into her old clothes was clearly made to make me feel better, since it was obvious that she had recovered her naturally curvaceous form, which had been toned on treadmills and rowing machines since high school. "He's beautiful," I said with true sincerity. We stepped back and beheld each other awkwardly. "I'm an aunt!" I said, and we laughed.

Margaret—now called Meg, Megs, Mags, or Maggie by outsiders—never seemed to show anything but affection toward me. We were nearly ten years apart, and therefore noncompetitive, except, from my perspective, for my parents' admiration. I was the child who had rejected my family's affluence and superficiality, along with their ambitions for my life that went with it. My sister, however, had managed to please them and yet remain her own person; everything came easy to her, and she never seemed to have any lost opportunities or bad luck. I often wondered if her positive attitude created her good fortune, or vice versa. If she had any inkling of my resentment, she never brought it up, and after a few moments with her, it seemed not to exist at all.

It was agreed that Ryan III, who had been fed only moments before my arrival, was suffering from some sort of intestinal problem that required his grandmother's full attention. Margaret and I retreated to the guest room, where she had laid out a half-dozen dresses on the bed, and the adjoining bathroom had been converted into a salon, with all the pertinent tools for my transformation displayed. Ryan's warbling had now become a full-scale cry, and Margaret closed the door on him and our mother's desperate words of consolation. "You can play with him in a few hours, when he's in a better mood," she said. "Now, tell me about your date." She seemed more excited than I was.

During the next few minutes, I realized that, as important as this was to me, it was also important to her, yet in a much different aspect. We had very little in common, and, until now, I had not understood that my little sister wanted to relate to me in some way, to forge a bond in adulthood that, because of distance and circumstances, had never really existed beyond our shared childhood, most of which she didn't even remember. I had come to pay homage to the prince, but she was making me feel like royalty instead.

I held up the clothes against my body in front of the mirror, listening to Margaret's suggestions. Seeing her beside me, I realized the differences between us were amazingly small. She was slightly fuller or narrower in a few key places, but the effect of her careful attention to the details—hair, skin, makeup, nails—was overwhelming, dramatically illustrating my shameful neglect of such basics. Was it possible that which I had considered narcissism these last ten years was merely good grooming?

She chose for me a forest-green pleated wool skirt (which I later vetoed and replaced with black slacks), a white long-sleeved blouse, and a tan suede vest that cinched snugly around my waist. Then we considered jewelry, nail polish, eye shadow, and hair coloring—which she selected from a vast array of products I had never even heard of. The hairstyle would be important, she said, to complement the shape of my face and my wire-rimmed glasses to give me what she called "a classy, intelligent look." But the real magic would be contained in a cleansing, lotion-laden bath, a series of skin treatments, and her expertise in applying the makeup, which Margaret insisted would take years off my age. I had heard such banter from women all my life; why had I decided that none of it applied to me?

As it turned out, the prince exhausted himself in Mother's care and fell into a deep slumber from which he did not awaken until Margaret nudged him with motherly impatience after I emerged from "the spa," as she called it. Though groggy, Ryan III was surprisingly compliant (and no doubt enchanted by the exotic scent of this stranger) as I held him and stroked his chin. He wrapped his fingers around my pinkie and once more drifted off to sleep. Mother took advantage of the chance to observe how good I was with children, and I bristled under the obvious implication.

Forty-five minutes later, when I marched forth from the bedroom in full dating regalia, my mother was speechless. When she finally did speak, she was complimentary and supportive, as if the daughter she had always wanted had finally appeared. I would have resented her for it, if it weren't so nice to hear.

I kissed Ryan III on the nose and said my farewells. There was no time to stop by and see Dad, who was at home watching the NCAA basketball tournament with Ryan II, and this was unfortunate, because he would have been so pleased. It's funny how the outward appearance can be so important to some people who never take the time to look deeper. And yet, perhaps I was no prettier on the inside than I had been on the outside over these many years, and it was better for that secret side of me to remain undisclosed.

I drove past the road I often traveled so many years ago when a student at Andover Newton, where the fragmentation of Carla Donovan had begun. How strange that in the seminary—the "seedbed" of learning—my belief in God was strengthened and shaped at the expense of my belief in myself. The long days in class, long nights of study, and the demands of my pastoral internship, all under the disapproving glare of my parents and friends who pursued more traditional paths, soon began to crush my spirit even as God attempted to lift it. But rather than suffocate in the isolation, I continued to feed it, pouring myself into the needs of others, forgetting my own. The pattern had continued in each congregation I served, until now, at thirty-five, the years of personal neglect had come home to roost. Perhaps I could yet overcome the underconfidence and disillusionment that plagued my days, if God would grant me the faith to do it. As I accelerated onto the wide expanse of the turnpike, I looked back at myself in the rearview mirror and decided I liked what I saw. I settled in for the ride home, thinking about how far I had to go.

◆　◆　◆

When I strolled into the fabled Erie Diner I realized why my subconscious mind had found it the perfect locale for a rendezvous with Michael and dispatched the information to my blabbering mouth before either my heart or logical mind could offer their suggestions. The heart would have chosen a more romantic place, for the diner's torn vinyl booths and clientele of truckers and factory workers failed to attract many lovebirds. Logic would have dictated a trendier, or at least more tasteful, place where one could impress another with one's sophistication. No danger of that here, where the food was cheap but good, and the menu was stained with the excesses of previous oversized portions delivered by waitresses in three-sizes-too-big uniforms, which bore stains that matched the menus. This was a very safe place.

Michael slid out to greet me from his seat in a booth near the door. He was dressed in clashing colors, as usual, and seemed to be smirking. His Italian features were a little too extreme for him to be considered really good-looking, but the strong impression he made was undeniable. He was the type that commanded everyone's attention when he walked into a room, and he was doing it now.

"I hear the steak sandwich here is excellent," he said, inviting me to slide in opposite him. I got hung up momentarily on some thick fuzzy substance protruding from a crack in the stuffed seat, but then settled in nicely with a low squeak. "Not for me, I'm dieting," I said foolishly, my subconscious mind once again flinging out a traditionally feminine response under pressure, as if to ward off the overwhelmingly brutish atmosphere. The reality was, I was ravenous, having had almost nothing to eat all day. He decided not to pursue this line of conversation further, and I was grateful.

"You look terrific," he said. "You know, I've never seen you without your collar."

I stared. "Oh yes, *that.*" I reached for my naked throat. Should I tell the truth? *Well, it's like this, Michael, I just can't envision getting cozy with a man while wearing clerical vestments.* I decided to skirt the whole issue of my new and improved appearance. "Didn't want to get any tomato sauce on it before tomorrow," I said.

He laughed. *He laughed!* A husky waitress with dark hair on her forearms arrived with the laminated menus and two glasses of water. Michael ordered two coffees, and she left abruptly. He folded his arms on top of the menu and leaned in. "Now, what did you want to talk to me about?"

The question startled me back into reality. I looked furtively around in the deluded fear that someone nearby might actually be eavesdropping. "Well, I'm struggling with a spiritual problem," I said. "I thought you might help me with it."

He looked concerned. "Have you prayed about it?"

The waitress returned to take the order, and Michael waved her away. "No, I mean yes, but look, it's not that serious," I whispered. "There are some weird things happening at St. Fred's, and I'm having difficulty accepting that God may be doing something . . . out of the ordinary."

"I'm not following you."

"Miracles, Michael. In the church basement."

The waitress returned with refills on the coffee and a notepad. She set down the carafe and waited, pen poised above the paper, indicating there would be no further delays. Michael ordered two steak sandwiches for us to hasten her exit, apparently not buying my statement about dieting. I thought him a bit presumptuous. Did he always choose what his friends ate for dinner?

"The basement? Isn't your church the one with the . . ."

"Pool," I finished for him.

He nodded his head thoughtfully, eyeing me warily. "So, are people walking on water down there, or what?"

"I can see that you're already skeptical. I'm the same way. I guess I'm just looking for someone to tell me I'm not nuts."

His features relaxed into sympathy, sensing my anxiety. "Okay, tell me what happened."

I sighed and related the story in summary fashion: Cornelia Shepherd's claims and the subsequent closing of the pool, the recent spring bubbling up in the deep end, the inability to find a rational explanation for the water, the apparent healing of Miranda's deafness, and the pressure I felt to believe.

"Your problem is that it seems so easy for this Isabella person to embrace the miraculous," he said. "It's very common in her culture, uncommon in ours. Her simple faith threw you a curve. You reacted defensively, and now you're beating yourself up over it. You need to see the bigger picture."

I waited for him to elaborate on whatever he was obviously thinking. Was that it? I didn't much like his tone, which seemed a little . . . arrogant. I was looking for his interpretation of the events, not psychoanalysis. "I guess I'm missing your point," I said at last.

"Well, the way I see it, this woman Cornelia might be a bit daffy, so you can't really base your conclusions on her testimony. As for this mother, she is focusing everything on her daughter. You, on the other hand, are worrying about your job."

Big oval plates with huge open-faced sandwiches were suddenly dropped on the table. The waitress tore the ticket off her pad and left it face down under Michael's saucer, where it soaked up the liquid from her last careless overfilling.

"What?"

"Your job, Carla. It's obvious," he insisted, steam rising in front of his face. "She's pressuring you to open the pool because she thinks God is suddenly dispensing miracles like food stamps. You won't do it because you feel that God doesn't act that way. So do a lot of other people, and you're afraid if you open the pool they'll think—"

"That I'm nuts."

"Yeah."

The steak sandwiches were deeply layered and required more heavy machinery than a cheap knife and fork to adequately disassemble them for consumption. He continued philosophizing as we toiled with the inadequate tools.

"If I were in your shoes, I'd probably do the same thing. Check out all the angles on how the water got there. If you can't find a simple answer, start asking other questions, like 'what is God trying to show us here?' Miracles always happen for a reason. They're not intended for their own sake. They point to something. God may be trying to get your attention in some way."

"The bigger picture."

"Exactly."

He went on to recall an experience he had with a member of his church whose cancer disappeared without explanation. The man took it as a sign that God wanted him to be more dependent on him, so he sold his business and used part of the money to go on a short-term mission trip to Africa, which changed his life dramatically and led to a second career in vocational ministry. "Maybe God has something to teach this Ruiz lady, and you're the one he wants to help her figure it out."

"She'd probably make a great preacher," I said, "but I don't think this town's big enough for two of us."

This evoked a chuckle from Michael, and I was relieved that my soul-baring did not seem to diminish his view of me too much.

"That's actually part of your problem too, I think, the woman preacher thing. Could it be that you have an inferiority complex?"

This guy thinks he has all the answers I thought to myself. *Could this be why he's unattached?* "I wouldn't go *that* far, Michael." I squirmed a little and looked away, because of course he was right.

"All I meant was that you seem to be awfully tough on yourself for questioning the supernatural." He was backpedaling; I sensed from his tone that he regretted the last remark, and I let down my defenses in response.

"I know. It's just that the supernatural is supposed to be our business, right?"

"Yes, but most churches don't promote bathing for blessings either."

We shoveled around in our sandwiches and babbled on about ourselves, but I offered only a minimum of basic information. I learned that he was a Schenectady native, raised Catholic like me, but went with a girl in high school who was Dutch Reformed, and thus his conversion, which he related in a long, complicated story. He was two years younger than me, dated often, but said the demands of the ministry made relationships difficult. Though I was attracted by his boldness, he struck me as quite high on himself and something of a control freak in the way he talked about other women's short-comings, speaking as if he felt he had to make excuses for his singleness. I guess at our age this was natural, and I was glad he did most of the talking.

In the midst of this rambling, Michael made the tactical error of trying to actually pick up his food and eat it, a move that proved disastrous for his sweater and stopped the flow of his monologue. I could tell he wanted to say something that came to mind as he was chewing, and he accelerated the process, mumbling his intent.

"Tell me," he said, forcing the last of the mouthful down. "Why does a church build a pool in the basement anyway?"

I shook my head, daintily dabbing the corners of my mouth with a paper napkin. "It's funny you should ask. The pool expert I had come in this morning said that the pool was only about fifty years old. The church is twice that, of course."

He seemed intrigued. "So somebody had the bright idea to put it in after-wards, in the fifties or sixties," he observed. "Can you find out about that?"

"I guess so. I have the records and minute books at home. I don't think I have anything from before the former Catholic congregation dissolved though. Why?"

He shrugged. "I don't know. It's a bit unusual, don't you think, especially for those days?" I nodded. "There might be a history we don't know that could shed some light on the situation. If it's documented, it might help us figure this out."

"How so?"

"I don't know." He seemed flustered that I questioned him. "Maybe somebody saw the Virgin Mary on that spot, like over in Europe, or some-thing spooky like that." He was referring to Lourdes, a subject with which I had some familiarity. Now it was my turn to make his ideas sound goofy.

"And she said to build a swimming pool?"

"Okay, well, maybe not. But there's a reason that pool was built, and if miracles really are occurring down there, I would guess your Mrs. Shepherd wasn't the first."

This sounded reasonable, so I let him off the hook. "How do you plan to get the information if I don't have it in the records?"

"There's a way, but you check the books first, and we'll go from there." He smiled. "We're in this together."

His words were almost tenderhearted, but I wouldn't let myself get carried away. I looked down at my plate and noticed I had nervously devoured nearly all of my sandwich, while Michael had given up halfway through his, though the spillage had probably ruined his appetite. There was limited seating, and several people were waiting. Michael grabbed the check and slid out of the booth to pay at the register. I followed, and, while standing in line to pay, he suggested we stop by a coffeehouse he knew. I wasn't prepared for this invitation and declined awkwardly, mumbling something about finishing up tomorrow's sermon, and he looked surprised but not disappointed. We didn't speak again until we approached my car parallel parked in the street out front.

"Let's touch base tomorrow afternoon to see what you find out," he suggested. "I might like to swing by and get a look at this pool of wonders, if it's convenient."

"Sure," I said coolly. "I'll give you a call. Thanks for dinner."

He laughed and nodded in acknowledgment, then walked off to his car, hands thrust in pockets.

I was two miles down the road before a steady drizzle on the windshield awakened me from the daze into which I had slipped when Michael mentioned the coffee shop. I switched on the worn wipers, which gave out a horrendous scraping sound against the glass. I was driving too fast, berating myself for missing the opportunity to extend the evening. It was the subconscious mind again, my deepest fears rising to the occasion to protect me, as always. If I were an objective observer, I might assume that Michael actually liked me, but then, that couldn't be possible . . . could it?

The drizzle grew into a heavy rain. I slowed the car, squinting into the blurry glare of oncoming headlights. For a moment I thought I had lost my way, that mental meandering had affected my steering. But the torrent subsided, allowing me to confirm my position, before slapping the little car hard with a sudden wave of water, then another. The weather forced me to concentrate on my driving, which was good. God was getting my attention.

I crept along, occasionally dropping a tire into one of the many potholes along the route, now made invisible by the deluge. Each time I hit one, I recovered quickly from the jolt and continued on my way. What was I afraid of? Why didn't I just say, "Yeah, Michael, let's make this a real date, sneak off to a nice dimly lit joint, with cloth napkins sculpted into old-style nuns' habits and waiters with cummerbunds, and discuss the finer points of antinomianism over cups of cappuccino." Why not just come right out and say it, and let the chips fall where they may? Why not test the waters and see what was there? If it turned out that we weren't a good match, life would go on, wouldn't it? Sure, just a little bump in the road. A jilt or a jolt. No big deal.

But it *was* a big deal it seemed, since I had developed a disconcerting fear of failure, and I avoided tough decisions. My attitude was defensive about almost everything in those days. Afraid to take risks, I almost always settled for whatever lot fell to me. As I drove through the steady rain, I pondered again how I had come to be so wishy-washy, a weak-in-the-knees little girl who was abused by her own secretary. It was as if I had built an emotional cocoon around my life and was satisfied to remain inside it forever, content to ride out any and every storm. But the sunshine never seemed to come anymore. I was safe. And sorry.

After the nice afternoon I had spent with Margaret, it seemed silly now to blame my problems on my family. Perhaps it wasn't fair to hang so much of it on the demands of my calling either, but I had to find a scapegoat for my shame. No matter how good I might be as a preacher, or counselor, or administrator, I would never be a man, and therefore I couldn't be good enough. Years of being reminded of this fact had undoubtedly had an adverse effect on my already wounded confidence, reducing me to little more than a yes-girl, intimidated by everyone from the church board to a Hispanic bartender living off of dry goods and canned beets. Somewhere along the line, it had become easier to surrender than fight and repeatedly lose. The thought that my own sense of inadequacy had turned me into a failed leader deeply troubled me. It occurred to me that it might have been this very aspect of my personality that had been attractive to the people at St. Fred's in the first place—I was someone who wouldn't challenge the power core, who would be happy just to have the job, who wouldn't meddle with the way they'd always done things. Sadness washed over me like the sheets of rain. I felt ashamed.

I noticed something unusual in my peripheral vision as I rumbled down my narrow driveway behind my house—a moving shadow under the porch lamp, concealed by the wetness on the window. Naturally I had no umbrella, so I raced to the front of the house, galumphing across newly formed puddles in the gravel, only to stop dead at the sight of my drenched cat, shrieking pathetically on the stoop.

"Motorhead! How did you . . . ?"

This was most unusual. Motorhead was an indoor cat who only made tentative forays outside when I was in the yard, and then only in balmy weather. He leaned hard into the door, his eyes fixed on the handle above, howling in some primeval growl I had never heard before. I slung open the storm door and fumbled with my keys; he slipped inside and bounded across the porch and into the kitchen, vanishing in the darkness, probably to our bedspread, which he would leave wet with matted fur.

I flipped on the light and headed for the back of the house, where I thought I might find the back door left ajar, and perhaps a tear in the screen that enclosed the porch. Motorhead might have hopped on the porch furniture and scrambled out, not realizing that the hole in the screen was too high to access from the ground outside. I expected to feel a chill from the open door as I approached, but the house was warm as I exited the kitchen and dining area. I was startled to see that the table lamps were already lit in the den—they were the kind that detected motion and came on—and from where I stood, I could see that the back door was closed. There could only be one explanation. I squinted to see if the dead bolt was turned in the locked position.

There was a clamor of hissing and spitting. Then, a wild feline wail. Motorhead sprang from the back bedroom where I kept my study, his eyes fully dilated and his ears pinned back in terror. I jumped aside as he sped past, turning my head just in time to see a figure dressed in black with a red knitted ski mask hurtling toward me. The sudden shock at the sight of him caused me to lose my balance, and a gloved hand sent me sprawling, crashing into one of the lamps, extinguishing the light. I swung my foot out to trip the intruder, but he was already gone; I heard the heavy thud of the front door as I painfully pulled myself to a sitting position.

Breathless—more from fear than exhaustion—I rose to my feet and rushed to the kitchen window. I peered through the rain-streaked glass out into the dim light of the street. The dark figure was nowhere in sight. Half relieved, I leaned back against the counter and tried to concentrate, my brain slowly catching up with the frightening sequence of events. Images photographed and stored in my short-term memory flashed into focus behind my eyelids: a terrified cat, a bright red blur, the toppling lampshade, and the paralyzing fear that gripped me in that split second when my assailant stared directly at me. I was still breathing hard, shaking all over, trying to calm myself. Moments passed. Motorhead appeared from his hiding place, crying in self-pity. Now more rational, I began to come to terms with the fact that I had been robbed. There had been a rash of break-ins in the neighborhood, and my number had come up. I was sure the thief had met with profound disappointment at the paucity of valuables in my possession, and the thought of it nearly made me laugh out loud. There was my grandmother's jewelry, none of it particularly expensive, since Margaret got all the good stuff, but it was old and might be attractive to a hurried burglar who didn't know better. There was an antique clock, but it was still on the wall. There was the silver (which Mother periodically hinted that I might want to surrender to Margaret since I never had occasion to use it), but it was stored in a wooden case and kept under the sink, of all places. I bent down and opened the cabinet to find it right where it should be. I headed to the bedroom.

My jewelry box was emptied and turned over on the dresser. It was clear that the intruder had just entered from the back porch and must have darted into the room when he heard me coming in. I went to the back door and found it closed, but unlocked, and there were scratches, which indicated the lock might have been picked.

I walked out onto the unheated porch. The storm door was banging lightly against the jamb in the wind. It had been pried open with a crowbar or some similar tool. I tried to close it, but the latch was bent and wouldn't work. Eager to leave the exposure of the porch, I left it alone and went back into the house, bolting the door behind me.

I slipped back into the bedroom-turned-study and turned on the light. My desk, normally covered with stacks of books, was clean. My computer monitor had been knocked to the floor. I knelt down and lifted it, feeling an intense pain in my right wrist, no doubt from my earlier attempt to soften my landing as I fell across the lamp. Setting the monitor on the desk, I noticed the church ledgers strewn about. I took a deep breath and began to stack them. As I did so, I checked the contents of each book, since only a few of the covers were inscribed. Everything was there.

I walked to the phone.

"Carla?" I had spoken his name first and knew instantly that I had to slow down or this was going to come out all wrong.

"Somebody broke in. I—" I jumped at an imagined sound and lost my train of thought.

"What?" Michael sounded too stunned to process the information. "When did this happen?"

"A few minutes ago. I came in and surprised him. He knocked me down and ran out. I hurt my wrist."

"Have you called the police?"

"Not yet."

"Carla . . . you need to call—"

"The back storm door was jimmied open," I continued. Suddenly I began to panic. "I'm scared, Michael. I . . . I can't stay here."

"Look, I'll call the police right now. Then I'll be right over to pick you up—you can stay at my mother's house tonight." It was more of a command than an invitation, and he said it with such a paternal, protective tone that I consented. "Just hold tight," he said. "It'll be okay."

CHAPTER SEVEN

It Was Still Dark when Michael's mother knocked on the door, summoning me to a breakfast of Pop Tarts and juice, apologizing for it without knowing it was better than I would have had at home. She was an absolute gem of a lady, and I got the impression hospitality was her primary concern in life. The only problem—she was allergic to cats. Michael had to keep Motorhead at his house overnight, which worried me, because my cat didn't respond well to strange places or the strangers who inhabited them. The plan was that Michael would pick me up early and deliver us back to my place before church. I expected Motorhead to still be showing signs of emotional trauma from the rainstorm, the intruder, the car ride, the separation anxiety, and the exile to the strange apartment, but I was sure he would recover once deposited safely at home.

Michael had an early worship service, and I knew he would be coming by early to get me. I had been sleeping in his old bedroom, which made me more than a little uncomfortable, but his mother's personality was stronger than his, and I didn't feel it my place to raise an objection. I had stayed awake for at least an hour the night before, lying stiffly in Michael's old bed, afraid to move. Once the lights were out, and I was cocooned in Michael's most private adolescent domain, I retreated to prayer in order to keep my mind from entertaining other less noble notions. The experience of invading Michael's homestead had a paralyzing effect, causing me to periodically forget about the pool, or the theft, or the sermon I had to preach in just a few hours.

The bedroom had been intimate enough, but the single bathroom shared by the family was far worse. Just before turning on the shower, I heard Michael's voice and knew he had already arrived. I froze, like a deer caught in the headlights, overcome by the anxiety of being where I was, doing what I was doing. I was standing naked in the shower, rehearsing the finer points of my imminent message concerning wise and foolish virgins, separated only by a hollow door, from an eligible man whom I hardly knew, yet upon whom I had romantic designs.

When I strolled forth in my clerical garb and collar, Michael smiled, comparing the shower to Superman's phone booth, which transformed an ordinary woman into "super-sermon-woman" or something like that, though I was so self-conscious that the words didn't register at the time. I laughed nervously in response while scanning the room for my cat, which was probably crouching behind a door somewhere. I called and he appeared, head thrumming loudly, miraculously cured.

Michael and I talked of ministerial things while Mrs. Montefiore scurried about. He was preaching from Deuteronomy and was engrossed in the life of Moses. His whole emphasis was on leadership in this series of sermons, trying to define it biblically and apply the principles to his church. I never did tell him the truth—that I was preaching from the parables for exactly the opposite reason. They allowed me to make strong points of a theological nature without confronting the church directly about its shortcomings, which would undoubtedly expose my own. Instead, I dispensed platitudes with only a minimum of application. But I was running out of parables, and the opportunity to effect any significant change in congregational life was almost up as well; the pulpit established my leadership style, and once the people grew accustomed to my weak preaching, they would likely never accept me any other way.

Michael and I agreed to meet later on to begin our investigation into the history of the pool. As he dropped me off at home, we wished each other luck and went our separate ways.

◊ ◊ ◊

"The party doesn't start until the Lord shows up," I was saying, probably too often, emphasizing the importance of readiness as a divine principle. To illustrate, I recalled my fifteenth-year high school reunion, which was awkward and boring for nearly two hours until the more fashionable class members arrived and brought with them an almost instant excitement. "No matter that they had grown up to be mechanics, sanitation engineers, and postal workers—they were once cool, and for the rest of the evening we reveled in their presence." It was an unfortunate choice of a story, for such occupations were honorable and duly represented in the congregation, and puzzled looks greeted my words as I strained to make the point. "Had we given up on the reunion too early, we would have missed the great event it became. In the same way, if we are preoccupied with our own affairs like the foolish virgins, we'll miss the Lord's blessings when he returns. Everything we do now is but preparation for that day. He is the life of the party, and the light of our lives."

The sermon was a stinker, and I was grasping for words to justify my claim on what appeared to be a wasted twenty minutes of my hearers' time on this earth. Desperate, I released myself from my incomplete notes and quit thinking, surrendering instead to my ever ready subconscious mind, which I knew wouldn't produce anything risky. What did I think the parable really meant? "You know," I said like a wise grandma, "I sometimes think the Lord has already come and gone, and we're so oblivious to spiritual things that we never knew it."

Derrold Hamber, recently elected chairman of the church board, was one of the first to greet me at the door. I noticed he wasn't sitting in his usual spot up front, and I speculated that his place at the end of the pew in the back had been chosen for a quick exit for some reason. Taking my hand, he said softly into my ear, "The board would like to meet with you for a few minutes before you close up shop this morning." He smiled as he said it, but I knew this couldn't be good, despite his light demeanor. I prepared for the worst, swallowing my fear as I greeted my flock one by one, nodding in appreciation for their empty compliments. As the board members went by, they waited on the front steps like a jury, until the last member departed. Then Hamber led them back into the sanctuary, with me following behind like an obedient puppy.

Hamber directed the board members to be seated in the back pew, and I sat a few rows in front of them, leaning over the smooth wood, almost hiding. Hamber stood in the aisle; the informality of the arrangement suggested it would be short and sweet.

"We all want to have some lunch, so I'll be brief," he began. "I received a call from Mrs. Dickson, and—"

"Okay, Derrold, I have to apologize for that," I interrupted. "I know I shouldn't have spoken to her that way. But we do have something of a problem working together. It's not that she's lazy, actually, and I regret the remark. It's just that she can be resistant at times. That's all. And I'm sure in time we can work this out. It's really not . . ."

"Carla."

". . . that big of a deal." I paused, seeing his stern look. "Yes?"

"It's about the pool."

"The pool?"

"Yes. I understand that you have made inquiries about having it renovated. I don't recall the board giving you the authority to do that."

I was stunned. "I'm sorry. The pool has water in it. A little girl wandered down there and caused quite a scare. I was just—"

"We've already instructed Mr. Delvecchio to have dead bolts installed in the doors to the basement, and if you had asked, you would have known that this is not a new problem. Water has come up through the drains on occasion before; we know the building has settled, and there's likely a crack somewhere in the piping. When we have heavy rains, it sometimes makes its way up into the pool shell."

"But there hasn't been much rain, and there's a lot of water. I did ask Mr. —"

"It's rained enough. We've also had a lot of snow, Reverend, and if you haven't noticed, it's melting." This quip came from Corning Lutz, my least favorite of the bunch. "But we don't really have to explain this to you. The point is that you serve this church under the authority of the board, and we expect you to respect that authority. You are not to concern yourself with the swimming pool in any way."

"Fine. Is that all?" My voice trembled; I was having difficulty masking my anger.

"Actually, no," said Hamber. "There is the matter of your personal life."

I blinked. "I'm afraid I don't understand," I said honestly.

Hamber cleared his throat as if to imply discomfort at what he was about to say, but I could tell he couldn't wait to get the words out. "It has come to our attention that you've been dating a young minister, and—"

"Excuse me," I interrupted, now becoming rattled, "but I don't think that's any of the board's business."

"Good. You admit it. And you're correct, it is none of our business. But I think you would agree that it is a matter of grave concern when a minister of the gospel of our Lord and Savior Jesus Christ spends the night with her boyfriend, who is also a pastor, then comes to church and delivers a sermon." He was strident, his face red with emotion.

My anger and embarrassment must have been obvious. Rage turned to shame, and I felt tears collecting in my eyes. "For your information, sir, I have no boyfriend, and I have done nothing inappropriate."

"You expect us to believe you two were translating Greek all night then?" Lutz chuckled, eyes darting to the others for support. "Be careful what you say, Miss Donovan. You were seen early this morning when he dropped you off at home, already dressed for the service. I would have thought that you would've been more discreet."

I was steaming. "For your information, the parsonage was robbed last night, and I stayed with Michael's mother at her house. I admit that what happened this morning looks bad and, in hindsight, I should have realized it. However, I was very upset last night and didn't think the situation through. It won't happen again. I can show you the police report if you don't believe me."

"Are you all right? Is the house unsafe?" It was Jameson Kerry. Amazingly, he sounded sympathetic.

"I'm fine. But I suggest you ask Mr. Delvecchio to change the locks there too."

Kerry nodded, but no one else said a word. Hamber dismissed the meeting, and I walked away from them toward my office, furious and scared at the same time, now unable to hold back the tears, which I refused to let them see. I vanished through the door adjacent to the chancel, sat down in my office, and had a good cry. I sat there for quite a long time, my thoughts drifting across time back to when I first began to sense a call to this miserable vocation. Why had God sent me to a place I would never have chosen, to a people who wanted to control my every action? Either I had made a terrible mistake about even being in the ministry at all, or I had taken a wrong turn somewhere and ended up far from where God intended to send me. One or the other of these errors in judgment had to be true, since the alternative was unfathomable: that I was exactly where God wanted me, doing a work that I was at best unsuited for and at worst unwilling to attempt.

It was clear to me that these people had a paranoia about my deciding anything on my own. The pool issue was merely peripheral to their desire for total control. I doubted they suspected that something had happened beyond what I had told them; if they knew what we really might be dealing with, they would be loath to embrace it. If this was, indeed, the beginning of a spiritual battle, it could only lead to further conflict. And I was stuck smack in the middle.

I decided at length to go home and tend to Motorhead, call my sister as promised to tell her about the date with Michael, whip up some lunch, and kick back a while. I could use the break, maybe even a nap. It was warming up outside, and I might even go for a bike ride. I would try to forget about my troubles for at least a few hours, recharge my batteries, and prepare to dive in again when Michael showed up later that afternoon.

As it turned out, I never got the nap or the bike ride. Pete was waiting on my stoop, chattering about the Yankees down in Florida, saying he had a great-uncle down there who wanted him to come down and watch the spring training games. We both knew it would never happen, but he had two gloves with him and a rubber ball, so we played catch in the yard. He followed me inside, and I offered him lunch, which consisted of cereal and dry toast, after which some inner alarm told him he had to go home. With the afternoon half gone, I decided to act on the gnawing urge to drop by to see Cornelia Shepherd and ask her a question.

◆　◆　◆

Cornelia was glad to see me, but it struck me that I could have been anybody—she was just glad to have company. It was hard to follow her conversation, so I cut to the chase.

"Do you remember why the pool was built down at the church?"

"What church?"

I sighed. "St. Fred's. Your church, Mrs. Shepherd."

"I didn't go to any St. Fred's," she said. "I went to St. Winnie's."

I bit my lip in wonder. "Okay, whatever. The church with the pool."

"The healing pool!" she shouted excitedly.

"That's the one."

She frowned, looked out the window for a moment, and then turned back to me. "He told me not to tell," she said softly.

Not wanting to revisit the story again, I tried to direct her thoughts. "I know. I'm trying to find out how the pool came to be built. Do you know?"

Her eyes suddenly became clear. "There was never any good explanation, but Catholics don't exactly ask the laypeople for their approval before doing something, you know. There was talk that the priest was doing something in secret down in that basement, before they built the pool. I remember my husband had been on the priest's side, but he never talked much about it." She smiled pleasantly, and her eyes glazed a bit. "Those were interesting times, dear, not like now." She was zoning out again, and I thanked God silently for the few moments of coherence, which I concluded were divinely provided.

I didn't know what Michael had up his sleeve aside from digging around in the records, but this information was enough to indicate that there were indeed secrets surrounding the pool. It encouraged me that whatever persecution I was about to face might have some value after all.

As I drove home, I considered the passion of our Lord, who took upon himself the sin and shame belonging to each of us, simply because he loved us. In the Lenten season, when ironically so much is made of our trivial sacrifices that bring more glory to ourselves than to God, we tend to forget that all of our secret sins are known, paid for, and forgotten. They could not be held against us if we would only confess them. And yet, with every tiny act of resistance to grace, we store up consequences as in a great thunderhead such as was gathering above the city once again, ominously foretelling a mighty rain, the first drops of which were just beginning to fall.

♦ ♦ ♦

It was well past nightfall when Michael finally called to say he was on the way. He had also called hours earlier to say he wouldn't make it until after his evening service because of a series of odd occurrences that, frankly, I had difficulty following. He asked if I had found anything in the church records yet, which I hadn't because I hadn't looked, and he seemed a bit impatient when I explained I assumed we would do that together. He was obviously stressed out, and I suggested he take his time getting to St. Fred's, and we could have a cup of hot coffee and sift through the paperwork then. He calmed a bit at that, and when the second call came, he sounded like a different person. I smiled as I hung up; Sundays tend to make even the most well-adjusted ministers a little uptight, and there's no better feeling than getting all the responsibilities out of the way at day's end. I was grateful that, like all the churches I had served, St. Fred's closed up at noon on Sunday.

I piled the old books into the car and drove over to the church to put the coffee on. It was a nasty night, and I became drenched in the process. My fear was under control by then, but just in case, I left every light in the house on, and the television as well—turned up extra loud.

I arrived to find Mr. Delvecchio's truck parked out front, and the door to the office part of the building unlocked. *It's an odd time to be working on securing the building,* I thought. I stepped inside to see my custodian friend in the middle of the office, supporting a much older man who was leaning on him. My entrance surprised them both, and they nearly fell.

"Carla . . . this . . . is my father . . . Paul. I told you about him before, I think." I looked into the older man's eyes and saw a clear resemblance. Paul Delvecchio was agitated and mumbling something incomprehensible while his son patted his shoulder repeatedly in an attempt to calm him down.

"Derrold Hamber called today," he said, "telling me to change the locks on all the entrances. It's urgent, he said, and he's coming by tomorrow morning to make sure I got it done. I didn't have anyone to watch Pops, so . . ." I walked alongside them and rubbed the elder Delvecchio's arm. He was wet and fidgety, obviously disoriented. He looked to be nearing eighty-five and, though in apparently good physical condition for a man his age, the Alzheimer's had clearly ravaged his mind, and I wondered if he even recognized his own son.

"He also said he wanted to have me pump out the water in the pool, so I . . . I . . ." Mr. Delvecchio was distracted now himself, unsure of how to tell me what he had planned to do, although from his demeanor I already knew. He searched for the right words. "I thought . . . maybe I could—"

Michael unexpectedly burst in from the torrent and stopped cold, dripping, trying to make sense of the scene. I turned to face him and attempted to explain.

"This is Frankie Delvecchio, our church custodian," I announced. "Mr. Delvecchio, this is Michael Montefiore." They nodded reservedly to each other like men sometimes do. "And his father, Paul. Remember what I told you about Cornelia Shepherd—what Mr. Delvecchio said about the pool?" Michael narrowed his eyes at me, then looked intently at the two men, and slowly, a look of understanding crossed his face.

Minutes later, I was following behind Michael and Mr. Delvecchio as they carefully helped his father down the back stairs.

"Frankie?" the elderly gentleman croaked in fear, trembling now from the chill in his wet clothes. I felt so sorry for him. He didn't understand what was going on.

"That's good, Pops. Just come along with me now, and we'll be going back home soon."

They led him carefully to the basement. The old man gripped his son's arm tightly as he was led out on the pool deck. "It's okay, Pops," Mr. Delvecchio said. "Trust me."

Michael went down the ladder in the shallow end, then assisted Mr. Delvecchio as he helped his father into the pool. The old man's steps were tentative, and his breathing uneven. His son steadied him as the three walked across the cracked plaster to where the floor transitioned to the deep end. Michael backed away, and his eyes met mine. This was a personal moment for this father and son. Perhaps, even a sacred one.

Mr. Delvecchio sat his bewildered father down gently on the slope. With one hand, he helped him inch his way toward the water's edge. With the other, he made the sign of the cross.

PART TWO:

WAITING FOR THE ANGEL

CHAPTER EIGHT

THE MAN LOOKING BACK at me was a completely different person.

He was still confused, but now cogent; still unsure of himself and his surroundings, but now capable of forming the appropriate questions. He looked at his hands the way a baby does upon their discovery. He held his son close and wept at the news that his wife was gone. She had been dead for five years.

I knew the story in Mark's gospel of how Jesus had expelled the "legion" of demons from the wild man of Gadara, and the passage presented the first biblical image that came to mind when I gazed into the eyes of Paul Delvecchio. The demon-possessed man in the biblical story was violent, prone to breaking chains and howling in the night. Paul Delvecchio in his illness was not. And yet, they shared a certain kind of lonely suffering, an isolation so complete that it sealed them off, not only from others, but from part of themselves as well. The man in the story was transformed; whereas before he had torn at his clothes and no man could subdue him, once Jesus confronted the legion and sent them away, the man became the picture of civility—quiet, subservient, dressed, and in control of all his faculties. The metamorphosis of Paul Delvecchio was not as dramatic, but certainly as evident to the three of us.

The two men with me experienced a catharsis of their own. Frankie Delvecchio, the gruff custodian, had grown considerably more contemplative since first hearing of Miranda's "miracle," and now he was almost childlike in his humility. I don't know what it is like to care for an aged parent, much less one who has the mind of a small child, but the burden must have been heavy, for now that it was lifted my friend could do little but mutter his thanks to God between intermittent tears. As for Michael, he was clearly shaken by the holy power of what he had seen, and a moment later nearly fell back into the pool when Paul Delvecchio turned to him and said, with a voice as clear as a brass bell: "Are you my grandson?"

The fact that Frankie Jr. was alive and well and managing a supermarket on Long Island seemed to calm the elder Delvecchio, but that was all the good news we could find to give him. Amazingly, we were so awed by the miracle that we failed to share excitement about his healing, and could only answer his questions. His companion of sixty years had died of cancer; Paul had been too sick to care for her. In the time that his mind had been clouded, he had lost many friends. Mr. Delvecchio soon turned to me to rectify the situation, as he feared his father, despite the miracle, would soon fall into despair. We were to blame for this situation. We had handled it poorly. Although, who could have experience in knowing exactly what to do and say in such a situation? I know now why, when angels confront men in the Bible, the element of fear and the acknowledgment of sin is always present. When one comes this close to the touch of God, it takes time to recover.

This I attempted to do, being trained in such matters. Michael, for all his leadership skills, was ill-equipped for dispensing mercy. I laughed inside my head at this fact, remembering his blunt assessment of my "inferiority complex," and it eased my anxieties. Here was a hurting person I could help—no blood, or cries of agony, or tubing hanging out to frighten me—just a man in need. I could do what came naturally.

"Mr. Delvecchio," I said, grasping the old gentleman's hand, "I can't imagine what you may be feeling, perhaps something like waking up from a long sleep and finding things have changed, hmm?" I smiled at him, rubbing his hand. "I guess right now you think it might be better to just go back to sleep, right?"

"Yes." His voice was firmer than I would have liked.

"I understand." I waited for a moment. "But you know something, sir? God has done something incredible here before our eyes. He healed you—he brought you back into the world, to your son. Do you know what that means, Mr. Delvecchio?"

He opened his mouth to speak, but thought better to listen. A deep furrow of concern appeared in his wrinkled brow.

"It means that God—who knows all things—has known your suffering. Yet, he didn't want you to die alone, trapped in the prison of your mind. He loved you enough to do something he doesn't do every day for just anyone. He who healed your mind will share the burden of whatever it is you must face now. He knows you intimately well, Paul Delvecchio. And he has decided that you shall *live*."

The old man whimpered and nodded heavily. Father and son embraced. Michael paced, visibly moved. We helped the two men back to the truck, and Mr. Delvecchio hugged me robustly, the way Italians do, unconcerned about the torrent swirling around us. My shoes filled with icy water and my feet went numb, and for the first time, I felt safe enough to cry.

Meanwhile, Michael lugged the box of record books from my car back to the office. I found him inside, laying each one out on the floor. He was taking great care with them, like someone unpacking antique china.

"That was impressive," he said, not looking up.

I walked to the coffee cart. Predictably, all we had was instant. "Makes me feel like an idiot for ever doubting in the first place," I said, wiping the water from my face and hair with a paper towel. I sensed we both felt a pleasant relief from the intense emotion of the past hour.

"I wasn't referring to the pool, Carla." I turned back to see he was looking over his shoulder at me. "I was talking about *you*, how you handled the situation. You're gifted."

I wanted to cry again, so deeply pleased was I to be at the receiving end of the compliment, but instead I just said, "Thanks."

He went back to the ledgers while I went to fill the pot with water. Michael jokingly suggested I might dip the pot in the pool to create what he called "Jehovah's Java"—some kind of heavenly hazelnut blend that would give us wisdom for every situation.

"Including this one?" I shouted back from the bathroom. When I returned with the full pot, he was off the floor with about a half-dozen books under his arm. "We might actually find the answers in here," he said, now suddenly serious. "What we saw tonight was incredible, Carla, but what I don't get is why the board is so uptight about the pool? My guess is that they're scared of something. If you're going to deal with them in this, you need to find out what it is."

"If *I'm* going to deal with them? I thought we were in this thing together?" I was only kidding, naturally, and he laughed. I didn't quite agree with his assessment of the board's suspicions. To me, they were just plain mean.

"Well, let's put it this way. You have my unwavering moral support."

I narrowed my eyes at him playfully.

"And, if things don't go well with the board, I'm sure I can get you on the staff at Shekinah—then we'll *still* be together. How's that?"

The coffeemaker had a bad case of gastritis, and I could not ignore the racket any longer. I stuck a cup filled with coffee powder under the drip and waited for it to fill up, then deftly handed it to Michael while I stuck a second one under. He was already poring over the first ledger when I met up with him in the conference room.

Two hours and six cups of horribly bitter coffee later, we closed the last book. Not only were there no records from the Catholic era to be found, but neither were there any references to it later. Not a word about the construction or use of the pool was given—except for the controversy I had already found involving Cornelia Shepherd.

"We'll have to dig back further," Michael said at last. "I'm off tomorrow, so if you want, we can do some investigative research. I'm from around here— I know the right folks to ask. Can you meet me at Shekinah around nine?"

I could do nothing but agree and, after a time of concerted prayer for guidance, we slipped out into the storm, our minds and hearts full of the awe and mystery of our God, who we knew—now perhaps more than ever before—would never fail us, or leave us alone.

◆　◆　◆

Shekinah Church rested peacefully beside the road. I drove up into the gravel lot and parked in front of the office entrance, then thought better of leaving my car in plain view of the highway. One never knew when the "hounds of heaven" might be watching.

I pulled around to the back, carefully checking my makeup in the rearview mirror before heading inside. I had tried to learn from Margaret, but the hairstyling hadn't quite worked—though I had been up past midnight fussing with it—and the lipstick was entirely too bold. I rubbed some of the gloss away. The mascara was too heavy also. And the rouge. The contrast to my normal appearance was alarming, and I feared I had gone too far. Too late now to do much about it.

The forest-green wool skirt was a snug fit and actually quite flattering, despite the slight stretching across the hips. I wore an embroidered, form-fitting sleeveless blouse with a scoop neck, and the only drawback might have been the overexposure of my upper arms, which were not toned and thus betrayed my sedentary lifestyle.

The diminutive part-time secretary was expecting me. She looked dramatically Italian, like Michael, but old enough to be his mother. Her pleasant demeanor was incredibly refreshing, given what I had to deal with at St. Fred's.

"Did you bring the collar?" asked Michael as he emerged from his office. He stopped abruptly. "Wow," he said.

It was an awkward moment. I blushed and imagined my face soon exploding as the heat prickled in my cheeks. I couldn't tell if the "wow" meant I looked great or "Gosh, Carla, what did you do to yourself?" I assumed the former and tried to hide my obvious satisfaction. "I have no idea where we're going, and my mother always said it was better to be overdressed," I said meekly.

Michael just smiled, and I had no idea what he was thinking. I handed him the collar. "Uh, can you help me put it on?" he said. "I've never worn one of these things." I noticed he was wearing solid black slacks and a black short-sleeved polo shirt. I laughed. "Seriously? What, are you masquerading as a priest or something?"

"That's against the law, I think," the secretary chirped, concerned. She was cute.

"Listen, you guys," he insisted. "We've got to get the information from the diocese. They won't give it to us if we don't look official."

"Whatever," I said. "But this shirt doesn't exactly go with the collar."

"That's okay," he said. "I'll start a new trend."

I stood behind him and buttoned the clerical collar at the back of his neck, then folded the knit shirt collar over it. I grasped both shoulders and turned him around to face me. "Tight," I observed. He nodded stiffly, as if unable to speak.

Michael's Honda wasn't new and made a mechanical grinding sound as he accelerated onto the paved road, but the ride was smooth. He was fiddling with the collar as he explained his plan. There had to be an official record of how the pool came to be constructed, he reasoned, the theory being some miraculous event had precipitated it. "Catholics keep up with things like that," he said.

I squinted in the sunlight, listening. He was a born preacher, persuasive in even the weakest of arguments. He had no doubts now that there were spiritual forces at work in the pool, and this assurance made him all the more convincing. "The scary part of the whole thing is that there are people trying to keep this a secret. They want to keep God in a box, to coin a phrase. This could get ugly real fast."

His excitement was at least a little irritating. "Let's not forget in all this prophetic zeal that someone's job may be hanging in the balance," I reminded him. "It's tough enough for a girl to get a decent pulpit these days, much less one who got fired in her first year."

"Sure, I understand your point; don't fret about that," he said, almost apologetically. "But hey, the way I see it, you've got to answer to God, not just the board. Let's find out what he's up to here. Stick with him. He'll see you through it."

That was easy for him to say, of course. He couldn't possibly relate to my position. Theoretically speaking, however, he was right. I needed to borrow a little of his confidence.

The diocesan offices were located in an old brick building with a wooden sign out front. I didn't know what to expect and was pleased when Michael suggested he do all the talking. We entered a musty waiting area where thin floorboards, painted a dull white, creaked beneath our feet. Michael approached an older woman whose great height was evident even as she sat behind a green metal desk. She eyed Michael curiously, no doubt assessing the interesting manner in which he wore his collar.

"I'm Michael Montefiore, and I'm interested in finding some historical documents related to a local parish, St. Frederick's church, which dissolved more than thirty years ago. Could you help me?"

She studied him. "And what is the nature of your inquiry?" she asked in a manly voice. It was clear she wasn't going to just open up the files to us.

"Well, I'm trying to settle a dispute actually," he answered smoothly. I could see he was struggling to come up with something that wasn't a lie. "There's this friend of mine who claims . . . well, this might sound silly, but . . . he claims that he was healed there, saw a vision or something. He's quite old now and doing some nutty things, and I've been asked by one of his grand-children to help sort it out. Nobody in his family believes him, of course." He leaned in and whispered with a hand covering his mouth, "They're all Episcopalians now."

The tall lady suppressed a smile. "I'm afraid I don't believe him either," she said.

Michael looked at me, somewhat worriedly. He had no response to her declaration other than, "Why is that?"

"Because there is no church in the diocese named St. Frederick's. Never has been."

Michael pulled at his collar. "Well, actually, there is. Surely you've heard of it; the building's still there. It has a woman pastor."

A spark of recognition came to the woman's face. "Ah, yes. That would have been St. Winefrid's."

At this, Cornelia Shepherd's words rang in my ears. "St. Winnie's!" I blurted out. "Now called St. Fred's."

The lady nodded. "Okay, then. I see at least one of you is familiar with it," she said to me. "Are you a family member to the gentleman?"

"Uh, no, I'm just a friend of Fath . . . of Reverend Montefiore's."

"Is that so?" She scrutinized my figure in the tight wool dress and shot a quick reproving glance at Michael. "Well," she said, looking now exclusively at me, "if you want information on St. Winefrid's, you'll need to speak with Sister Louise. She was a contemporary of Father Calabrese. Just one moment, please." She arose, towering over us, and walked, giraffe-like, down the corridor and disappeared into a side door.

"St. Winnie's?" Michael asked quietly.

"Hey, look, I don't know," I said in a hushed tone. "That's what Cornelia called it. Naturally I thought she was a bit loopy at the time, but . . ." I stopped and we both stood at attention. The giant was escorting an ancient woman wearing a navy blazer and skirt with a nun's habit. "This is Sister Louise," announced the giant. "Please come with me," the little nun beckoned.

Her office was tiny and loaded with books and papers. I felt an immediate affinity for her. She was energetic and intense, despite her age, and I pictured her as a young woman, full of spunk and devotion. "St. Winefrid's is an interesting place," she said. "Have they changed it at all?"

"Very little," I said. "At least, not lately."

She nodded. "Are you reporters?" The voice was not vindictive. "You, sir, are definitely not a priest."

Michael turned red, but I could only laugh. "Truthfully, we're both non-denominational pastors," I said, still laughing as Michael reached back to undo the collar. When he removed it and unbuttoned the top two buttons of his shirt, the imprint of the band could be seen on his neck.

"We thought you would think we were crazy if we told you why we really came here, but I guess you think we're crazy already," I confessed.

"Go on," said the nun, amused.

"Well, I'm the pastor at St. Fred's. We have a pool in the basement that hasn't been used in years. I had a pool company come out to look it over, and the board just got all upset. I wondered why we even have a pool if nobody wants to use it. I thought there might be some kind of story behind it."

"You are right about that, dear. And this board—have they been members a long time?"

"Yes, in fact they were active in the transition, when the building was sold."

The nun looked off somewhere wistfully. "They don't want the story to come out again. That's what killed St. Winefrid's."

"So there is some secret behind the pool?" Michael asked.

"Oh, yes, and I see no harm in telling it now."

We sat quietly, listening intently.

"Bruno Calabrese was a good man, an older priest, and St. Winefrid's was a good appointment back then. Schenectady was booming, and many families were moving to the area. Father Calabrese had a heart for the poor, but he had difficulty motivating his more prosperous parishioners to give of themselves. He prayed about this constantly, and I with him. Then, he had a vision."

My eyes bulged. "Really?"

She laughed. "Well, supposedly. There was a story circulating afterward that he claimed to have seen Winefrid herself, in several places throughout the unfinished basement, kneeling and weeping—where the pool is now."

"Did you believe it?" I asked.

She closed her eyes. "I like to think he would have told me, if it were true. Nevertheless, most of us did wonder if he had truly lost his mind. Bruno was somewhat odd, a deeply meditative man, much less worldly than I was in those days."

Michael inched forward on the wooden folding chair. "What was the nature of this vision?" he asked, intrigued, his embarrassment forgotten.

"Do you know the story of St. Winefrid?" she asked. We shook our heads. "She was a princess, in Wales, and deeply devoted to Christ. She lived in the seventh century. Her death came when she resisted the advances of a local prince. She fled for safety to a nearby church, but he caught up to her and cut off her head in anger. The legend holds that in the place where her blood spilled, a spring rose from the ground, and for centuries, pilgrims have attested to the power of its healing waters. There is a crypt there today called the Holy Well, and it is widely known. I'm surprised you've never heard of it."

"That's incredible!" exclaimed Michael, sounding a bit like a little boy. "I see now why you had trouble believing. So he started digging for a holy well under the church?"

"Yes, that's what they said he did, without permission, of course."

"And?" I said anxiously.

She fidgeted a little. "Well, Bruno's version of the story was quite different. He was convinced that there were graves under there. That much, he did tell me, and honestly, this sounded as bizarre as the official story of the vision the Church put out later. He managed to find some very old unofficial records, he said, evidence that pointed to a so-called potter's field being located somewhere in the area. He speculated that the diocese purchased the land rather cheaply and eventually built St. Winefrid's on that spot, long after the cemetery had been forgotten. He was ashamed by what the church had done and believed God had directed him to raise the bodies and give them a proper burial. Word got out about the digging, of course, and there was a superstitious fear of a curse being cast on the church for disturbing the graves. Others objected to offering Christian burial for the heathen, as they were called. People stopped attending mass. So, embarrassed by the whole affair, the Church transferred Father Calabrese to the Southwest to be treated for his mental illness, and the official story was that St. Winnie's would construct a pool out of the gaping hole in the basement to meet the recreational needs of the young families. Of course, the idea never caught on, and I'm sorry to say that Bruno has never returned to contest the Church's position. The last I heard, he had left the priesthood and was living in New Mexico."

"And the church kind of went down after that, I guess," said Michael.

"Yes, indeed it did. Though in truth, I think it was more due to the loss of Father Calabrese than the other issues," the nun said.

"There was a stigma though," I surmised. "There must have been. That's why the new group altered the name to St. Fred's."

The nun nodded in agreement. We all sat quietly for a moment, reflecting. I stood up. "Thank you, Sister. You've been most helpful."

Her eyes sparkled, and she looked at me warmly. "He was the most compassionate and just man I've ever known. I've always believed in his vision. To help the poor, I mean," she said. "To bring healing to the poor."

The words haunted us as we made our way back to the car. Michael held the door for me and then went around to his side. Upon shutting the door he turned to me with a serious look and said, "You do agree with me that this thing is just a bit too eerie to be coincidental, I hope."

I fought off the urge to give in. "You thought that before we went in there," I said smartly.

Michael clenched his jaw. "Don't be so cynical, Carla. Look at the facts. There are probably elements of truth in both versions of the story. Think about it. A Catholic church builds on a graveyard. Its namesake appears to a priest half a century later and exposes the truth. A good priest wants to make peace with the past, but his intentions only create controversy. Don't you think the decline of the church was a divine judgment against their unwilling-ness to respond to God?"

"So this Winefrid thing . . . you actually believe that?"

He shrugged. "I don't really have an opinion. God speaks to people in ways they understand. You and I might check ourselves in at the psych ward if we saw something like that, but consider what we *have* seen. This priest was deeply affected by whatever he believed, he was sensitive to issues of oppression and discrimination, and he had concerns for the poor. He was the right man at that time to deal with the injustice of the past, and perhaps to spark something good in his own time."

"Okay, so God basically led him to the slaughter. His vision didn't amount to much, did it?" I was stiffening with defensiveness and didn't know why.

"What's wrong with you?" Michael's eyes blazed. "Don't you see what's going on here? The healings in that pool were—and are—God's way of bringing the message to a new group of people. The old priest's vision—as Sister Louise referred to it—is still alive. That church is supposed to be a house of mercy."

"But again, the leadership stopped it. They drained the pool. They couldn't handle it. It wasn't what they wanted." I felt like I was making my point, but it was getting me nowhere.

"Right. Now, empty pool or not, stubborn board or not, God is speaking again. Only this time, he's not asking for cooperation. He's demanding it."

I looked away, wishing he would start the car and forget the whole thing.

"He has been waiting for the right leader to make this vision a reality, Carla. That's you, I'm convinced of it. I think you should open the pool."

I fumed. "There is no way, Michael. Maybe the Holy Rollers down at your place go for that sort of thing, but I'm not particularly keen on handing out miracles on demand. So what's next—shall we bottle the water and sell it to the needy? Or maybe I'll cut up strips of my vestments and hand them out as prayer cloths this Sunday. Or maybe distribute postcards of St. Winnie sitting with her head on her lap."

He cranked the engine and gunned it. "I can't figure you out." His voice carried a lilt of contempt. "One minute you're convinced of the supernatural, the next you're convinced such things can't be so. Why am I wasting my time on this anyway?"

"You volunteered," I seethed.

He glared at me. "I . . ." He wanted to say something important, but stopped himself. He yanked the wheel and accelerated onto the street.

"You don't have to be so hard on me," I said after a moment. "I'm the one who'll have to pay for all these miracles. You'd be afraid, too, if you were in my position."

"Faith," he said firmly, "trumps fear."

We rode in silence for quite a while. He suggested we pick up some lunch, but I declined, perceiving that he had asked only out of obligation. We didn't speak again until I was walking to my car. I had difficulty looking at him as I smiled weakly and said goodbye, wishing that, by turning away, I could simply banish him from my thoughts. Upon turning back and finding him gone, I regretted making the wish.

CHAPTER NINE

THE LOUD THRUMMING OF Motorhead's purr roused me from an unusually deep sleep. Despite the strained discussion with Michael, I felt a strange sense of resolution about the pool, as if I had convinced myself that the heavy cloud of speculation had finally drifted away.

The cat was standing on my chest, thrusting his head under my chin. I chunked him to the floor and sat up, light-headed. In seconds, I was following my furry friend toward the kitchen, when I heard a scraping sound from the back porch. I froze; grabbing a pewter candlestick out of a dusty china cabinet, I backed against the wall in fear. Sunlight was streaming in through the windows, but someone was definitely fiddling with my back door.

I crept lightly into the bathroom and threw on my robe, pulling the sleeves down to hide my makeshift weapon. I tiptoed out the front door into the bright, crisp morning, and peered around the side of the house. There, in the street, was the back end of a truck I recognized.

Relieved, I walked barefooted around the house and came up behind Mr. Delvecchio, who was busy repairing the damage to the storm door caused by the intruder. He saw my reflection in the glass and spoke first.

"I woulda had this done yesterday, but I had to drive across town to get a new latch for this thing." He chatted on for a few minutes before I could say a word, and I got the impression he kept talking to steer the conversation to some inevitable but dreadful topic.

I finally interrupted him. "How's your father today?" I asked brightly, hoping there had not been a relapse.

He turned around. He seemed embarrassed in a way, like he'd heard something I wished he hadn't. "Oh, Pops is fine," he answered. "A little upset, but fine."

I smiled, hiding the worry. "It'll take time, but he'll be okay. Just let me know if you need me to talk to him. Anytime." It puzzled me that this didn't seem to satisfy him.

He stared down sheepishly. "Actually, that's not exactly the problem."

The doorbell rang from inside the house. Somebody was apparently at the front door. I trotted around to find Isabella Ruiz waiting for me.

"Carla! You *do* believe! You open the pool now!"

I hesitated. "No . . . in fact, I've been told just the opposite by the board. Before we do anything, we need to discuss it with them first."

"But Mr. Delvekki . . . he said you were there when God healed his crazy head."

I stammered out an unintelligible answer just as Mr. Delvecchio appeared behind me. "That's what I wanted to tell you, Carla," he began. "I had to pump the water out yesterday—Hamber was right there watching. Pops was a little upset about it. I think he went down to the bar last night."

"Yes, yes. He tell all of us how God heal him in the pool," Isabella repeated. "But you no open it? It not okay with you?"

"No, Isabella. Like I said, we can't—"

"Okay, then let's go tell them you not coming."

I looked at Mr. Delvecchio, who sighed and looked away, then back at Isabella. "There are people at the church—right now?" I gasped.

"I told him not to discuss it, Carla."

I whirled to face the custodian. "No, this is my fault—I should have cautioned him." I thought about all the people Jesus had told not to blab about their healing, who went right ahead and did it anyway—including Cornelia Shepherd.

Mr. Delvecchio looked me in the eye for the first time. "It might be good if you got over there before you-know-who."

"Mrs. Dickson?" Isabella wondered, catching the drift of the problem.

"Yeah."

With that, I was already running into the house, leaping over the famished, caterwauling Motorhead, throwing on a pair of jeans, and hopping into my Cavalier.

Minutes later, I was standing in the center of a crowd of perhaps a dozen people, hoping I could disperse them before Mrs. Dickson arrived, which would be at any minute.

I jumped up the steps to address the gathering. Paul Delvecchio was standing prominently among them. "Listen, all of you. I appreciate your coming here. However, we can't open the pool now. There's no water in it. It's not safe for people to be down there." It was a motley group, many of them old and weathered, some on crutches, others so odd-looking I could not identify their infirmities. My announcement brought forth a loud grumbling.

"Listen," I pleaded. "It's not up to you or me. We don't have the authority to do this."

Paul Delvecchio spoke up. "Who do we have to talk to then?" he pleaded. Isabella was moving through the collection of invalids, attempting to shoo them away.

"Please, let me handle this," I said, exasperated.

"It might be more convincing if I talked with them, don't you think?"

All I could do was stare at him, waiting for something logical to click in my brain. I stuttered out some words that fell away into silence.

The old gentleman ascended the steps. "I'm sorry; I've acted rashly," he said gently. "I used to hang out at the bar where Isabella works, and I went down there last night. It seems that her daughter and I have had similar experiences recently. You yourself told me I was healed for a reason. I wanted to do *something,* that's all—can you understand?"

"I . . . of course, yes, I do. But, you need to talk to your son, sir." I felt dizzy, breathless. "He can tell you about the kind of people we're dealing with here. We've got to be careful how we approach this situation."

Mr. Delvecchio emerged from the crowd. "I'm sorry about this, really. I should have been more adamant." He seemed on the verge of tears. "But to have him back again . . . you just can't imagine."

The crowd had heard the story before, and they appreciated the retelling with a chorus of affirmations. I turned back to Isabella, who shrugged.

It was still cool, but I could feel drops of sweat rolling down between my shoulder blades, puddling at the small of my back. I only faintly heard the sound of the car door slam and Mrs. Dickson's heels on the sidewalk. Heads turned in silence to watch her pass by us without a word, unlock the door, and enter the church.

I looked back at the silent crowd. They stood quietly shuffling, waiting for me to do something. "One minute. Give me one minute," I said, and pounded up the steps, leaving them all waiting outside like chicks in the nest.

Mrs. Dickson was settling in at her desk, deliberately avoiding me. I saw no point in the customary greetings. "As you can see, we have a situation here. I think we need to put our heads together and deal with it."

"Oh?" She looked up with that hateful look of which she was so proud. "Aren't they friends of yours?"

I held back my anger long enough to speak calmly. "I'll ignore that remark. In fact, these people are friends of Mr. Delvecchio's father. They came here for some help, and we need to get them some."

"Is that so? Well, what did you have in mind, Reverend?"

My mind searched for a response, and the only thing that came out was the wrong thing. "Well, I suggest you get to work on some benevolence kits."

This response unleashed what could only be described as a fury kept hidden for several months. The queen of passive aggression had finally lost it. "I will *not* spend my morning in that filthy closet stuffing cans and scraps for that horde of human refuse you've led to our door! Look at you! You're a disgrace! You can grovel in the dirt with them if you want, but don't drag me down with you. I'm going home. Get Mr. Hamber to help you feed the multitude!" She snatched up her purse and moved at me like a charging rhino.

"Wait . . . What?" She was bearing down on me, and I was overmatched.

"That's right. I've already called him." I stepped out of her way, and she flung open the door and descended the steps. The sudden action energized the crowd, and they surged forward. Mrs. Dickson picked her way through them haltingly, afraid of contamination. Seeing her enraged expression, they soon parted to let her pass.

"Mr. Delvecchio!" I shouted. "Hamber's coming! Help me get these people out of here!"

"Where?" He looked around helplessly, and I had no suggestions. "The basement?"

The careless remark inspired the people to cry out with joy, and they rushed up the steps. I held out my hands like a traffic cop. "No! *Not* the basement!"

Mr. Delvecchio, red with embarrassment, tried to pull the people back. I stood helplessly at the top of the steps, biting my lip with worry. I was surrendering emotionally to the reality of my predicament.

Hamber's huge Lincoln sedan pulled up slowly along the street. The sheer majesty of his arrival halted the crowd's advance, and as he approached, they watched silently, like island natives eyeing the first white man to set foot on their soil.

"You have an explanation for this, Miss Donovan?" The "Miss" was intended to extinguish any spark of authority I might have thought remained.

"Yes sir," I answered calmly. "I'm handling it."

He stood unmoving with both hands behind his back, his camel-hair jacket buttoned neatly. "Exactly how are you planning to do that?"

I drew in a deep breath. "I'm working on it."

"I see." He slowly ascended the steps. "Mrs. Dickson indicated this was something of a riot. I'm glad she appears to have been mistaken. So, are these people waiting for tickets to your Sunday worship service, or what?" His smile was mean-spirited.

"We are waiting for an explanation about the pool," stated Paul Delvecchio, who had crept up behind Hamber. I closed my eyes, deflated.

"Is that so, Miss Donovan?" I opened my eyes to see his face inches from mine.

"Yes. They believe the pool to have medicinal qualities. Somebody found her way down there when it still had water in it, and . . . look, Derrold, this has gotten way out of hand. A big misunderstanding. It's not any cause for concern." He bristled at my casual use of his first name in public.

"I thought we made it clear that you were not to go near that pool!" he yelled, barely under control. Isabella was saying something like, "It no her fault," but Hamber ignored her. "Consider this an official reprimand, Miss Donovan," he warned. "There will be a called meeting of the board tonight, and I'm quite sure this matter will be written up and presented to you formally. I strongly suggest you disperse this crowd at once and apologize to Mrs. Dickson."

"She's gone home," I said feebly.

"Then call her and apologize. I will see you tonight." He spun and walked back to his car, still ignoring Isabella's protests. She walked back to me and gave me a hug.

"I see now why you worry," she said. "We pray for you and that man." I sniffled into her shoulder, but could not answer. "We go now. It be okay." She whispered in my ear, "Since we all here, you have beets?" I laughed through tears and hugged her hard.

An hour later they were gone, their arms full of food and clothing, traipsing off like refugees to the relatively few cars that had carried them to the church. I was numb. The situation had become serious. I was in jeopardy of losing my job, and a rumor about the healing pool was spreading.

My relationship with Michael was strained; I was certain my reservations had made me that much less attractive to him. I wasn't even comfortable in my own house, and I thought I might be falling apart. I knew I couldn't work. I locked up the building and went home. I could hear Motorhead's desperate wail from inside, and I smiled. At least I mattered to someone.

◆　◆　◆

The advent of spring weather seemed to invigorate Sister Louise, who talked incessantly as we sat in the park with our salads. I think she was also happy to have some company, and to tell the truth, so was I.

"There has never been any place in this country approved by the Vatican as an official miracle site," she was saying. "But the standards are very stringent. The last thing the Church wants is to leap to false conclusions, which may later turn out to be scientifically explained. We have enough trouble with credibility these days."

"So, let's say the miracles are documented and determined to be inexplicable apart from supernatural intervention," I presumed. "Then what?"

She smiled. "Hold on now. There's more than one issue here. First, miracles are usually considered in an effort to elevate a person to sainthood. Catholics recognize saints as those who live on in heaven to intercede for those of us who remain on earth. Miracles are required for canonization; they must be attested, carefully scrutinized, and approved by the Congregation for the Causes of Saints, then passed higher up for official confirmation. The vast majority are never confirmed. So the first question is, are these miracles to be understood as related to the persons, or to the location?"

"Definitely the location," I answered quickly. "We're not talking about spiritual giants here."

"Are they Catholic at least?"

I thought for a moment. "You know, as a matter of fact, they are: Miranda is a small child whose mother is kind of inactive in the parish; Paul Delvecchio is an older man, but I think he's Catholic too; and Cornelia Shepherd started out Catholic but switched when St. Winnie's became St. Fred's."

"St. Winefrid's."

"Sorry."

"And what kinds of healing took place?"

"Well, the first one was arthritis, then deafness, and Alzheimer's. However, the arthritis was mild, and the woman is a little off the beam. The deafness belonged to the small child, and I was skeptical of that one too. With the Alzheimer's, it's hard for me to tell—I didn't really know the man before—but it sure looked real to me."

Sister Louise pondered this reply and crunched on some croutons. "What then would have been the purpose of these miracles?"

I knew this was coming. "I can't really say. But Michael's theory is that God is reactivating Father Calabrese's vision. He thinks God wants the church to reach out more. A 'house of mercy,' I think he called it."

She dabbed the corners of her mouth with a napkin and folded her hands in her lap. "Carla, I don't think you have anything solid here. The miracles are questionable, and there seems to be no good reason for them occurring. Perhaps your congregation should reach out more, but that is already commanded by our Lord. I think you should listen to your board and stop worrying about it. I also think a series of sermons on miracles might be in order."

Her wisdom was hard to refute. Why had I allowed this situation to trouble me so much? A rational person would have handled it entirely differently. I had let superstitious people influence me, and I vowed that wouldn't happen again. The only real question was the source of the water in the pool, and the board had an answer for that. In any case, the results of Phil Garrison's water testing would probably confirm it. The old nun was a mature woman who knew the difference between faith and fantasy. She would be an ideal mentor to me. Just sitting on this bench with her in the sunshine made me feel better. We prayed and parted ways, and with renewed confidence I went home to rest and prepare for my meeting with the board.

🜄   🜄   🜄

"I think the terms of our relationship need to be revisited. I am the pastor of this church and, as such, I am well within my authority to direct its ministries. I do not appreciate your efforts to control my every activity, and I consider your intrusion into my personal life unacceptable. I simply will not tolerate further invasions of my privacy. If you fail to recognize my professional competence and personal space, I shall be forced to seek another position at my earliest opportunity."

It sounded good standing in front of the mirror. The board would just have to deal with it. But then I reconsidered: where was my leverage to speak so strongly? I had nowhere to go, and I hadn't been at St. Fred's long enough to have overwhelming support from the members if I challenged the board's authority. They were overreaching, to be sure, but not enough that I had any real recourse to shift the balance of power. Any freedom they gave me would be graciously given. Perhaps I had not yet earned that consideration. The collar lacked only a leash. I suddenly felt foolish.

The one thing I had going for me was the fact that, in my heart, I had no problem complying with their demands. I would explain the situation fully, which should justify my actions to this point. I would assure them the pool would not be opened over their objections. Then, having pacified them, I would ask their permission to investigate the matter. I would assure them that there would be no digging up of anything to reveal whatever skeletons might be lurking, literally, in the basement. It would be okay.

Derrold Hamber was in a jovial mood as I greeted him in the conference room. It worried me. Was he rejoicing in having brought me to the brink of termination? The "Fab Four" were all in attendance—Hamber, Egan, Kerry, and Lutz—along with a few others. I knew beforehand which ones would do the talking.

"I guess we underestimated you," Kerry quipped, causing the others to snicker. "You've managed to do something we've been trying unsuccessfully to do for years."

I had no idea what he was talking about and could only wait for further illumination.

"You might even have earned yourself an early raise," added Egan. This remark provoked louder laughter.

"I'm kinda lost here."

Hamber sat back pompously with his arms folded. "It's Mrs. Dickson. She quit. Called me back this afternoon."

The news petrified me. Mrs. Dickson was a longtime member and very well connected. I couldn't quite rationalize the information with the levity in the room.

"We've been trying to get rid of that old battle-ax for years," said Kerry. "Never had the guts to do it. We all thank you profoundly, Reverend."

I hesitated to smile with them, thinking this some kind of trick. "Okay, well, that's fine . . . but I would like to—"

"Now, as for the public spectacle this morning, I think you'll agree that we'll have no more of that," Hamber intoned. "As for you, we have decided not to issue a formal reprimand, but some punishment is in order for your disregard of our directives concerning the pool. As you probably know, I've personally insured that the shell has been drained and the locks changed, so I'm not anticipating any further problems."

"I understand, but I want you all to know that I never did anything deliberately against your wishes. Even so, I—"

"Yes, you said things got out of hand," Hamber lectured. "We agree that you couldn't help the little girl finding her way down to the basement, but that is where the matter should have ended, and you should have informed us immediately. Now, this talk of a healing pool cannot possibly be good for our church's reputation. Had you handled this matter more professionally, we wouldn't have had to deal with it."

He obviously had some information from somewhere. "But I didn't really—"

He held up his hands to silence me. "Did you not speak to Mr. Delvecchio about the matter?"

"Well, yes, but—"

"But nothing," he said, stopping me again. "This matter is closed, and it will not be discussed again. The board will consider repairs to the pool at the appropriate time. As for you, we suggest you pay closer attention to your pastoral duties from now on. There is a sick list as long as my arm which, to my knowledge, you have not tended to, and I am told you have only made a handful of visits to the nursing homes."

Lutz whispered something in Hamber's ear.

"Oh yes," Hamber said. "As I mentioned, some punishment is in order." He was smiling wickedly, and I had no idea what to expect. "For the next several weeks, at least, you'll have to handle the load in the office without the benefit of a secretary."

CHAPTER TEN

GOD'S SENSE OF TIMING was never so evident as when the Parable of the Talents loomed large before me. In Jesus' story, a lazy funds manager steals the show, for his awful misjudgment overshadows the praiseworthy accomplishments of his peers. Like him, I had been fearful of my masters' wrath, so fearful in fact that I had incurred a greater chastisement at their hands. It was evidenced by the board meeting, in which Hamber didn't respect me enough even to let me have my say. Afraid to lead my congregation at the risk of unpopularity and criticism, I had buried my true calling, trying, as it were, *not* to get myself in trouble. It had led to a timidity exposed by this pool episode. If I had been closer to God, more active in the affairs of true ministry—as Hamber had pointed out—I might have been bolder, surer of what might actually be happening. Instead, racked by self-doubt, I felt I had let the Lord down when all he wanted me to do was trust him. Would I get another chance?

I committed myself to making this sermon introspective for the first time. I would be transparent before my congregation and renew their trust in me as their servant-leader. It was time to stop all the hand-wringing about what I couldn't do at St. Fred's and start doing what I could—love the people. Then, new horizons would open up for our church.

The situation with Michael troubled me. My newfound resolution dictated that I call him and make things right. *This is the way things are: I like you, I think you like me, let's admit it, and by the way I was right about what the board would do to me, and don't you feel guilty for throwing me to the lions?* No, that wouldn't do. He was not the type to accept defeat so candidly. I would have to ease into it, make him think he was right. To do that, I would have to own up to my insecurities, then rationalize them as a weak-minded feminine tendency. I would have to make him feel sorry for me, allow him to say that it was okay, that he shouldn't have pushed so hard, that the board had made its position clear, so we should simply pray about the matter and wait to see what God would show us. I liked this idea. It was definitely the way to go.

It was another fine spring morning, and I thought the afternoon might even be warm enough for the season's first milk shake. I envisioned a ride out to the Curry Freeze with Michael, all things made new. My blissful daydream was interrupted by the realization that my time was not my own and that I had a long sick list to be concerned with, not to mention piles of stuff to do at the office now that the witch was gone. Thus sobered, I dressed in khaki slacks and a blue blazer over a peach-colored cotton blouse with button-down collar. Thinking my attempt at professionalism made me look a bit too masculine, I ditched the blazer and decided to walk down to the church.

I had forgotten all about the newsletter, which had to be mailed that day to arrive in the members' homes by Saturday. The folding machine was on the blink, and Mrs. Dickson had been folding each letter by hand. Since she hadn't worked on Tuesday, I found that most of the layout remained unfinished. As I sat at her desk arranging the little strips of paper and cartoons she had cut out previously, I saw that nearly half the inside was still blank. So I gave up on making my intended list of visits and tried to dismiss the tantalizing taste of chocolate shake from my mind. I was going nowhere until I got that job done.

The telephone buzzed, and I stared at it menacingly. The little light flashed and didn't seem to want to stop. Four rings, five, eight, nine. I answered, regretfully, in my most pleasant secretarial voice.

"Good morning, this is—"

"Reverend? Is that you?"

"Yes, this is Carla. Can I help you?" I recognized the voice but not the name that went with it, a terrible malady that strikes all ministers in their first year on the field.

"Well, hi ya, Reverend. This is Phil Garrison. Didn't know if anyone was there yet."

I looked through the drawers for the glue stick as I made small talk. "Yeah, well, I was hoping you would go away. I'm alone in here today."

He laughed. "I was planning to let the phone keep ringing until I got you since the last time you didn't get my message. But actually, I'm just calling to let you know it's going to be a few more days before we have the water analysis."

"Oh, that's fine," I said, poking around in one of those multicompartmental plastic trays. "I don't suppose we'll be needing it anyway."

He inquired why, and I told him that the board had been aware of the problem, and that they were sure it was ground water, because it had happened before. I assured him he would be the first person I would call when they decided to renovate.

"I see, well, to be honest, I'm a bit relieved to hear that." Curious, I asked why. "I'm embarrassed to say I think we lost your water sample, and I doubt we will ever find it. I was calling just to buy us some time."

I found this answer extremely amusing. Everything seemed to be moving toward closure. "So what were you going to do when a week went by and you had no results, huh?"

"Oh, we've got results," he chortled. "They're just not the right ones. I have the lab report right in front of me. It's obvious the lab mixed up your sample with someone else's. It's a big place, and that happens sometimes."

"Wow, you guys are that good?" I said in a mocking tone. "How can you be so sure?"

"Well, it can't be yours. The sample came back showing high salinity. *Very* high. I haven't ever seen this kind of thing before, so I called on a technician this morning."

"What exactly is salinity?" I asked, only half listening, still rummaging around in the drawers.

"Salt concentration. The sample came back showing almost 200,000 parts per million. There's only one place on earth with salt levels that high."

"Oh?" I said absentmindedly. The glue stick suddenly appeared. It had been hiding among the highlighters. I snatched it out and slammed the drawer shut. "Where?"

"The area near the Dead Sea, in Israel." He laughed again. "Can you believe that? What a screwup."

I sat there suddenly frozen, gripping the receiver tightly, my back rigid, every muscle tense.

"Carla?"

"Yes, I'm here. You were saying something about the Dead Sea?" My nerves tingled with apprehension.

"Well, according to the lab, it's probably not the Dead Sea, actually. That would be 250,000 PPM or higher. They think it might be just north of there though; I think they said the Jordan River. It's quite interesting. Apparently, as the Jordan winds down to the Dead Sea, it actually flows below sea level in some places. The Dead Sea itself is four hundred feet below sea level, and there's no outlet, so as the water evaporates, the salts accumulate. We're talking seven times saltier than the ocean. Did you know that people go there like it's some kind of natural spa? They say it helps with arthritis and stuff. People are nuts, ya know?"

I could literally not believe what I was hearing. "And you say this isn't my water?"

He paused, probably surprised by the anxious tone of my question. "Uh . . . well, the code on the lab report matches the label, but . . . how can it be?"

"It can't, obviously," I said, twisting the cord around my fingers nervously. "But I appreciate your efforts. No point in following through though. Will there be a charge?"

"For what? Just keep us in mind when you get ready to do the work, okay?"

I gave him my assurances, and hung up the phone. As I struggled to free my hand from the phone cord, it only tightened around my wrist, a fitting metaphor of this whole affair. Was it really possible that the pool had been holding Dead Sea water? What would Michael say if he knew that?

There were voices and a commotion outside, then Joe the plumber suddenly burst in. He was carrying a small pump and had a garden hose coiled around his shoulder.

"Hey, Miz Donovan. Didn't expect to see you sitting there."

Still shell-shocked and left speechless from the phone call, I could only wave.

"I'm here to check to see if any water came back in through the drains since the storms. I'm supposed to pump it out if there is any." He reached down into the deep front pocket of his jumpsuit and pulled out a key. "No need to get up. I'll probably be right back up." He happily went to the door leading to the basement, unlocked it, and trudged down the stairs, whistling.

My heart was racing. I began to think of what to do next. Should I call Michael? Sister Louise? I jumped up, dragging the phone off the desk. It fell with a crash, and I muttered under my breath as I tried to extricate my hand from the tangled cord. I had to get downstairs before Joe pumped any water out.

I yanked my hand free and stumbled backward into Joe's big arms. I twisted around in his grip; he was grinning over the cozy arrangement. "What are you doing back up here so fast? Is it still empty?" I said, gasping.

He seemed disappointed that I squirmed free. "Nope. I must've got this all backwards. I thought he said Mr. D *drained* the thing on Monday. Now, I don't have time for the job. I've got appointments, and I might need this little pump with me, but maybe not. I s'pose I could leave it, but it's gonna take a long time, and I might not get back, and you'd need somebody to watch it." He rambled on, as if he were arguing with himself.

"Joe! What are you talking about!" I yelled. My nerves were just about shot.

He appeared to be confused. "Well, the job's too big. And the pump's too small. And like I said, I can't leave it—"

I rushed around him and flew to the stairwell.

"Mr. Hamber wanted me to make sure it was still empty, not full!" he shouted after me. He kept on talking, but his words became muffled noise as I descended to the basement.

The warm air engulfed me, and I slowed to a walk as I entered the large room. It was humid, almost like a sauna, and I opened my mouth to breathe deeper. I shielded my eyes from bright rays of sunlight, which streamed in through the windows and glimmered on the water. It took a few seconds to adjust to the glare. I could feel perspiration welling up at my throat and on my back beneath the blouse. My palms were sticky with sweat, and my jaw dropped as I stopped and stood squinting on the deck, staring in disbelief.

The pool was completely full of water—right up to the rim.

◊　◊　◊

The day seemed to be warming up rapidly, though I admit my body temperature had risen dramatically due to the events of the morning. I felt trapped in a constant state of panic, suffocated by stress. I veered the car onto the gravel drive of Shekinah Church and hopped out, scattering the loose rock as I ran to the door.

Michael wasn't in the office. The secretary indicated that he usually visited the hospital at this time of day, and I asked if I could have a copy of the members he might be seeing. I rushed out the door and roared out of the lot in a cloud of dust.

It amazed me how quickly I had succumbed to the board's wishes, explaining away what I had seen for myself. If God was forcing the issue of a so-called healing pool, I would have to accept it, regardless of the consequences. My gut feeling was to drag Hamber and the rest of the board down to the basement, demanding they see the supernatural at work; but I knew that they wouldn't believe me, no matter what evidence I presented, especially since the healings were subjective. These men had authority, but they were not spiritual leaders. They were so far from God that it was almost laughable if it wasn't so tragic, bullies who had attained their position through intimidation and tenure. The church was their place and, like the Pharisees of old, they would resist anyone who challenged their control. Salt water or not, I would have a fight on my hands. And yet, the fill line was still full of cobwebs—or was it? I hadn't bothered to look. Could someone else have filled the pool? Were Mr. Delvecchio and Isabella Ruiz somehow conspiring against me? No, they had already received their miracles—why would they undertake such a crusade now and risk the wrath of the board? It wouldn't be in character for either of them anyway. Still, it was definitely possible that the lab had indeed mixed up the results, and I grumbled at my own stupidity for rushing out of the pool room without a water sample.

I turned the car up the huge hill and into the parking garage of Ellis Hospital, hoping I could track Michael down. Emotions were ruling my mind—I was indecisive, nervous, and unable to focus on anything for very long. I could do nothing without advice. Maybe that's why my vision had been so clear earlier: I had hidden in the wise counsel of Sister Louise and then followed the banner of the board's unwavering decrees. Removing myself from responsibility gave me peace of mind. Perhaps I needed to face up to the sad fact that I wasn't fit for leadership at all.

As I rode up in the elevator, I reviewed the list of names the secretary had given me. Two of the four were on the same floor, so I started there. At the first room, the door was ajar, and the lights were dim inside. I poked my head in and saw that the patient, an older man, was sleeping. An IV was hooked up to his arm, and I could see the red blip on the machine repeating its cadence. On the bedside table was a white business card. I stepped closer and saw it was Michael's.

Down the hall, I came to a small group of people arguing in front of the room that was on my list. They looked to be Mediterranean—Italian, or Greek most likely. The discussion was animated, and I felt immediate discomfort as I approached. A young man was making his case rather loudly, something about "what did you expect?" The woman, probably his mother, was holding a clear plastic bag with pajamas inside, and she was crying. "He never wore pajamas, Ma, so what makes you think he would want any now?" the young man insisted. They noticed me standing there awkwardly and paused. There were two ladies also present, and they stepped aside. I asked if they had seen Reverend Montefiore, and the man said yes, he had just stopped by. Then he asked me a question:

"Do you like a man to wear pajamas?"

Four sets of dark eyes were staring at me, waiting for an answer.

"Well, I guess that depends. I mean, I'm not married, but I think, well, I don't usually wear nightclothes to bed myself. I mean, not nightclothes *specifically* . . . I *do* wear clothes, of course, not very much sometimes but usually something, nighties but not night*gowns* or that type of thing, but maybe if I were married . . ." They seemed to be losing interest in my ramblings, so I just summed it up. "It depends on the guy, I guess."

"There, see?" the man announced. "Dad's not the kind of guy to wear pajamas, not even in the hospital. Thank you very much." He seemed satisfied, and I tried to inch away.

"But this is a *public* place," the mother protested, and reached out and grabbed my sleeve. "He can't wear his boxers here." She looked at me. "Do you think a man should wear his boxers in a public place?"

"Well, I—"

"He's in bed, Ma, for Pete's sake," Mark said. "He's all covered up."

"No, no he isn't," she insisted, pulling me closer. "Ask this woman. Go ahead, ask her if a sixty-five-year-old man should be lying around naked in public, especially a man who is fat as a house and has hair poofing out all over his back and shoulders, hmm? What kind of a sight is that for people to see, hmm?" She began to yank me toward the door, I assumed, to see for myself and render a verdict.

"Look, I mean no disrespect, but I really have to be going," I said, stepping back. The mother looked at me as if I had just slapped her face. "I vote pajamas, okay?" She smiled and released me. I nodded at the two other ladies, who peered suspiciously at me, and I imagined them disgusted by the confession that I wore only skimpy bedtime attire.

I ran to the elevator and pushed the down button. There were only two names left, and if I chose the wrong one I might miss Michael entirely. The doors opened softly, and I walked in without looking, still preoccupied with making the right choice from my list. I stumbled headlong into a stretcher covered in sheets with what resembled a horrified shrunken head sticking out from under them, rolling on the pillow from the sudden jolt; bags of various colored liquids hanging about jangled wildly as I inadvertently rammed the stretcher backward, pinning the orderly to the elevator wall. Apologizing profusely, I hopped backward and watched the doors quickly close on both of them, trying to avoid their outraged faces.

I fretted, waiting for the next elevator. Finally I caught one and descended two floors. From the first moment I stepped out into the hall, I was affected by the inevitable dread that hung in the air, despite the brightly colored walls and carpet. *Oncology.*

Michael stood beside the bed, one hand holding the patient's hand, while the other held that of the patient's wife. It was a beautiful prayer, long but not tedious, thoughtful but not preachy. He possessed a masterful skill that I hadn't expected of him, a tender assurance in bearing burdens that wasn't his, really, but lent from on high. For a moment, I felt a twinge of jealousy, kicking myself again for my own wishy-washy ways. So unlike me, Michael had every-thing under control.

When the prayer was over, he noticed me, and I thought I saw a faint, brief smile. That was good. Time heals all wounds. I backed out of the room and waited as he shared a private moment with his people.

"Very sad," he said to me as he came out into the corridor and closed the heavy door gently behind him. "He's a good guy. Only fifty-three."

We walked together silently as this information sunk in. I was almost embarrassed to explain why I was there. "How many of yours are here?" he asked abruptly.

He had assumed that ours was a chance meeting, that I had been walking by and overheard his voice in prayer. "A few, I think."

"You think?"

"I forgot my list."

"You can call Mrs. Dickson and get it, can't you?"

"No, she quit."

"Really?" He seemed pleased with the news. "You know, you seem to have a very interesting life, Carla." He put his hand on my shoulder, and my heart rate elevated immediately in response. "Let's check downstairs and see

if they have a book for clergy. Sometimes the church memberships are listed."
Then he stopped.

"And what were you doing all the way up here . . . if you didn't know where you were going?"

Okay, here we go. "Well, I was looking for you actually."

His eyebrows arched in surprise.

"Something came up."

Determining that this would take some time, we agreed to discuss it over lunch. We left my car in the garage and took his Honda, cruising about until he spied a deli that looked promising. The day was bright, and Michael was obviously pleased that no permanent damage had been done to our budding relationship. Did I really have to dredge the whole thing up again?

"So, you were looking for me?"

"Yeah. I'm in trouble again."

"Oh, I see. A little problem with Mrs. Dickson, I'll bet. What, did you ream her out real good?"

I tried to shake off the images associated with such descriptive language. "No, that isn't it. You think maybe I could borrow that sweet lady you have working for you? She's a peach."

"Sorry. Maybe she can help you out in the afternoons though. I'll ask."

We took a number, and the line moved rapidly. Michael ordered something with mustard on rye; I opted for turkey and tomato, no mayo, on whole wheat. We found a table for two alongside a plateglass window facing the street. It was noisy and overcrowded and wonderful.

"And you told those people you didn't wear anything in bed?" He was laughing hard, a mustard dollop clinging perilously to his lip.

"No, no, just not the traditional stuff. Did you go in to see the guy?"

"Oh, yeah. These folks are relatives of one of my members, and she asked me to see them. Wants to get them in church, of course. I got there in the middle of the argument over the pajamas."

"Did you vote?"

"Definitely!" he hollered. "PJs all the way. Remember, I saw this beast up close."

"The husband or the wife?" I quipped. He nearly gagged at my joke. We both tittered happily until our mirth finally gave out.

"Michael, the pool is full to the top with Dead Sea water, and I'm clueless as to what to do now."

He forced down his mouthful and beheld me staring at him in all serious-
ness. I could tell he was working hard to process the full impact of the
message. I backed up to my meeting with the board and explained everything
that had happened since in detail.

He took a long drink of his black cherry soda. "Why are you telling me all
this?" he said at last, irritated. I could tell the effects of our quarrel still lingered. "You and I both know you have no intention of opening that pool to
the public."

The words wounded. "I'll get fired if I do, but—"

"But what? What does your spirit tell you? What is God telling you?"

"That I have to do something."

He chewed some ice obnoxiously. "You want my opinion?" I nodded yes.

"Okay, then. Here's what I would do. I'd test the theory. Let's select some
people and have them take a dip under our direct supervision. We'll have
someone reputable there as a witness. See what happens. If God is in this,
we'll know. If not, what's the harm? Drain the darn thing and forget about it."

The suggestion was so rational I knew it wasn't his true opinion. Michael
was all feelings; he went with his gut on everything. This was too sane to be
on the level. If Michael were in my place, he'd have the board kneeling
outside the church praying for the infirm as he led them forth for healing.

"I'm going to open that pool, Michael."

"No, you're not," he sang with a lilt in his voice, almost taunting me. "Not
yet, anyway."

I sighed. He crunched some more ice and watched me, smirking. He was
so cute with mustard on his chin.

CHAPTER ELEVEN

I Lugged The Big plastic tub full of folded newsletters down to the post office, regretting the particularly sloppy job I had done on the cut-and-paste part. But I was already a day late, and they had to go out or there would be talk of revolution in the air come Sunday morning. As it stood, some members still would probably not get theirs and would unload on me anyway, and since, from all the little scraps of paper Mrs. Dickson had lying around, I most likely lost at least one, I was already preparing myself for the fallout.

It had been a hectic morning, beginning with a tour of the newly filled pool with one euphoric Frankie Delvecchio. Inspecting it together, we found the fill spout still dry, the water line disconnected, and a decidedly salty taste in the water. He could barely contain himself from the excitement over what he had seen and insisted I demand the board to come down to the church and see for themselves what God had wrought. I dampened his flame by reminding him that, while I no longer had difficulty believing in our miraculous healing pool, the board could easily see it a different way. We would be accused of filling the pool ourselves and disconnecting the piping. Mr. Delvecchio had to admit that such a scenario was entirely plausible, since he had the know-how to have done exactly that. The salinity was a bit trickier, but we knew they would never taste the water, and even if they did, the deed would be ascribed to us. It was a lot of salt, but salt is relatively cheap, and we, in their opinion, would be written off as nuts enough to concoct such a scheme. Involving the board would only lead to two quick dismissals, and no one would ever be healed. I recalled the rebuttal of Cornelia Shepherd's ardent testimony, and the dark decades that followed.

Yet, we knew that there was a greater purpose in all of this, so we agreed that we should follow through. The plan was simple: Michael and I would bring candidates for healing to the pool one by one, documenting any divine intervention that occurred. Then, armed with incontrovertible facts, we would submit a report at the appropriate time. If nothing happened, we would know that someone was playing a cruel trick—someone who would go to great lengths to get me fired. Having incurred the wrath of people like Al Lintz who blasted me for "dishonoring the pulpit with vulgar slang and crass gestures," nothing would surprise me. Mr. Delvecchio consented to my proposal but solemnly declared that his father's healing was for real, to which I could only agree.

I could not risk any of the members blabbing about the pool, so I was forced to find people who had no contact with our congregation to conduct the experiment. Perhaps ill-advisedly, I phoned Isabella Ruiz at the bar on Wednesday night to explain what had happened and to ask her to recruit someone who really needed help. She exuberantly agreed to participate, and I arranged to meet her at her home early Thursday morning to meet the person she had selected. I warned her sternly, as was Jesus' custom early in his ministry, "not to tell anyone about this under any circumstances." In the background was the commotion of the crowded bar, and I knew Isabella could not possibly do what I had asked. Jesus, of course, had fared little better. Let them talk, I reasoned; many of them had already heard the tale and had been helped by our church. As long as they didn't interfere, what harm was there in keeping hope alive?

Forgotten in all of this was my appointment with the eye doctor, which I suddenly remembered while twiddling my thumbs in line at the post office, and which I determined to keep. First the collar, now the glasses—I was shedding aspects of my former self left and right. Hopefully, the external changes might have some positive effect on my mental and emotional state, which these days ranged from critical condition to Code Blue. I collected the church's mail from the clerk in exchange for the heap of newsletters and went on my way.

I am one of those people whose glasses dig deep ridges in the skin of their nose or ears, and having mine taken from my head by the soap-smelly hands of the young optometrist was traumatic indeed. I reached out into the blur to reclaim them but found only air. I had to be led to the spot from where I would be forced to read the famous chart, which I did, having no idea how well or poorly I was doing, though the fact that the doctor and his attendant started making small talk behind me as I stuttered out my guesses suggested he had stopped keeping score. In any event, I was told my eyes were severely afflicted and that common disposable contacts were not available. I needed new ground permanent lenses, which would take about a week to obtain. The disappointment lifted only as my glasses were returned, and I stroked the rims affectionately before mounting them firmly in place.

Isabella did not live far from the church, but my detours had taken me in the other direction. Despite the delay I was right on schedule until I circled several blocks looking for the last left turn indicated by the directions she gave me. It was humbling to realize that I didn't know my own neighborhood, but then, I had not been encouraged to go exploring. These were not the kinds of prospects the members wanted to see popping up in their pews. Sagging porches and streets littered with broken furniture reflected our church's neglect, to my dismay.

I found the duplex easily once I turned onto the correct street. Her place was the one with the large hole in the front steps and the storm door with the glass broken out. Isabella was waiting out in front with a waif of a girl who could not have been more than seventeen. Miranda was playing with a battered, naked Barbie on the porch.

"This Marita," Isabella said proudly as I stepped out on the curb. "She go with you to pool."

I extended my hand and felt the delicate bones of the girl's limp fingers. I immediately relaxed my grip. "Are you okay?" I asked.

"This Reverend Carla," Isabella said. It was evident already that Marita wouldn't be doing much talking. "She very quiet," Isabella whispered to me, as if Marita wasn't supposed to hear. The girl opened her mouth in an uneasy smile, revealing stained and crooked teeth.

She was Hispanic, though very light-skinned, with artificial blonde streaks in her long dark hair. There were two small studs in her nose and several rings hooked around the curve of one ear. She wore skin-tight purple Capri pants and a white T-shirt knotted tightly above her navel. The outfit was not flattering to her bony frame. With as much sensitivity as I could muster, I asked of her particular disability. Isabella pulled me aside.

"She into drugs bad, and walk streets outside bar where I work. After you call, I go to talk to her. She only fifteen."

This was not the kind of thing I had in mind. I was hoping for a withered hand, or a war wound, or a skin disease maybe—something that would be easy to discern before and after. But Isabella persisted, and I felt sorry for the girl. Even if Jesus should choose not to heal her of her affliction, a bath couldn't hurt.

"What if she goes into withdrawal?" I protested, still trying to weasel out of the situation.

"She already do that, last night."

I looked over at Marita and saw that she was trembling slightly and that one of her eyelids was twitching. She had sat down on the sidewalk, her skinny legs outstretched. I couldn't ask Isabella to take responsibility for this lost soul another night, not with the burdens she already had to bear.

"Where does she live?" I inquired.

"She no say."

Great. "Okay, Miss Marita. I have to make some hospital calls. When I get back this afternoon, I'll pick you up here, and we'll go for a swim." The child looked up at me with sunken eyes, as if she had not a care in the world.

♦　♦　♦

Marita floated in the pool like a stick of driftwood. I was new to this kind of water baptism, and tried everything: pouring, sprinkling, immersing—you name it. The immersing was actually quite fun, which I performed in the fashion of a black Baptist minister I had once seen, dunking Marita three times, once for each member of the Trinity. Marita came up gasping for breath the third time, and after that she tended to avoid me, so we swam in circles for a while. I had given her a swimsuit that had somehow shrunk, as all of my clothing seemed to do over time; it was black, with a bold red stripe, and we had to twist the straps and tie them behind her neck to make it fit. As for me, I wore one of those matronly styles, aquamarine with a little skirt attached. My skin was ghostly pale in contrast to Marita's, which was richly toned and stood out clearly as her most appealing feature.

Marita spoke only a few times, once in the car, again when trying on the suit; both expressions I interpreted as happy, though I couldn't understand a word of Spanish. She muttered to herself often while in the pool in a musical voice, having given up all hope of communicating with me, apparently content to splash around peacefully. I wondered if this might be one of the effects of a mystical healing taking place somewhere, and I watched her intently, glad if for no other reason than to have granted her this brief respite from what must have been a pained and troublesome life.

Pete was waiting on my steps when I drove up. He stood hesitantly when he spied Marita in the passenger seat. He leaned toward his home, and I saw the right hand flutter in a half-hearted wave, but then he righted himself and walked over to the car.

"Who's she?" he said curiously.

"Pete, this is Marita," I said loud enough that he stepped back. I always do that—as if the person who doesn't speak my language might somehow understand me if I shout. "She's coming over for dinner. She doesn't speak English."

Pete arched his unibrow at this news and followed us inside. Marita dropped the towel on the kitchen table and started fiddling with the knot in the back of her swimsuit as Pete's eyes widened in amazement. I told him to have a seat and hustled her into the bathroom where she had changed before, suddenly realizing that Marita's attire might not be suitable for dinner with a small child. I led her by the hand to my bedroom and gave her a pair of jeans which had to be cinched tightly with a belt around her tiny waist, along with a white sweatshirt with a picture of Mickey Mouse in the center which I had never worn. She was delighted, and I sent her back to the kitchen with wet hair and bare feet, while I changed.

Hot chocolate pleased them both, especially the whipped cream ritual of which Pete was so fond. Motorhead was under the table licking Marita's toes, making her giggle like the adolescent girl she was. Pete was inching closer, fascinated by the dark-eyed stranger, his eyes fixated on her nose jewelry. I ordered pizza and watched as Pete sprayed the whipped cream on his tongue to impress her. Then, he chased Motorhead repeatedly from the kitchen, only to roll with laughter along with Marita when the cat would try to sneak back in. I had difficulty imagining this young woman engaged in the lifestyle Isabella described, and it grieved me to know she might soon return to it. I decided right then, healed or not, I would see to it to find a way to help her.

We had arranged to return Marita to Isabella's that evening. I let her keep the clothes she was wearing, and she carried hers in a plastic grocery bag. Isabella's mother was there, and she received Marita warmly. The girl looked at me sadly and gave me a hug that nearly forced tears as she stepped inside. Tomorrow Isabella would call me to verify if, in her opinion, the power of addiction had been broken. Things were looking good so far.

As I walked back to my car I heard breaking glass in the distance, and the sound of angry voices. Cars roared up and down nearby streets unseen. The night was soon to be alive with all sorts of nefarious activities, and I was glad Marita was safe from them, at least until tomorrow.

I had accomplished several good things today, and I reflected on how much better I felt because of it as I slipped behind the wheel. I had gotten that newsletter out, had actually made my hospital visits, and had done something—weird as it may have seemed—about this healing-pool mystery. I laughed to myself at the secret nature of this new ministry. Carla Donovan, conductor of an underground railroad, snatching up the afflicted and setting them free, under cover of darkness! I wondered how long it might go on and considered picking up a new bathing suit.

The daydreaming got me lost in the neighborhood again, and I panicked momentarily, searching for something familiar. This was not a good place for a woman alone to ask directions. I circled around and saw a sign for Isabella's street and quickly made the turn, thinking I could start over and get my bearings again. As I approached her house, I saw the elder Mrs. Ruiz standing in the street. I slowed the car to a stop and rolled down the window.

"She gone," the agitated woman was saying. "I go to phone, she gone."

The woman's anxious fretting was strong enough for both of us, and I kept a cool head. "She couldn't have gone far. You just go back inside, and I'll look for her."

Mrs. Ruiz obeyed, and I was off. There were several side streets off this road, and Marita could have ducked down any of them. I drove slowly, worried that she might have had friends in one of these houses. I had no idea where she had been staying. Then, a thought occurred to me.

I headed back to Congress Street, this time having no difficulty with the route. I passed my house, and St. Fred's, then turned toward The Dutchman, the bar where Isabella worked, which was just a few blocks away. I was so intent on getting there I almost missed her—the flash of her white top in my headlights was all I needed to make the identification.

Marita was standing halfway up the block, in a shadowy area at the edge of the light afforded by the street lamp. With her was another woman, taller and darker skinned, wearing an outrageous body suit with some animal-skin pattern and a shiny gold jacket. They were huddled close together, enjoined in intimate conversation.

I drove past, intending to loop around the block. In my rearview mirror, I could see Marita leave the woman and start to walk up the street toward The Dutchman, only a block and a half away. I didn't hurry, assuming I knew her destination. She would probably go in to see Isabella, and I was relieved. I was already rehearsing the lecture I would give her, using Isabella to translate.

Upon returning to the street, I passed the wild-looking woman standing alone where she had been before. I continued to the stop sign and looked beyond to where the lights of The Dutchman could be seen down the street. There was no sign of Marita.

I parked in front of the bar and regretted not having my collar as I crossed the street to the front entrance. Several unsavory characters were milling around outside the front doors, eyeing me closely, and I slowed my pace. I swallowed, nervous at being so dramatically removed from my element. I stopped in front of the door as if faced by an invisible wall. What was I thinking? I couldn't go in there.

I smiled awkwardly, not knowing exactly what to do next, and greeted the men on the sidewalk, but they only seemed confused. The doors opened, and two burly men walked out, causing me to stop and wait. It was then I heard the rapid, familiar chatter in Spanish, and the telltale giggle that came from a dark alley just beside the building.

Marita was leaning back against the brick wall in the darkness, with a larger form hovering over her. The headlights from passing cars cast brief flashes of light on the scene, enough for me to know what was going on. Marita was making no effort to discourage the man's advances. In fact, she was, by means of certain well-planned movements, leading him on.

Something inside me boiled into fury, and I ran into the alley. I grabbed Marita's arm and led her away from a man in a cheap wrinkled suit that, even in the dim light, I could see was too small. He was stunned, then angered, and he flew at me in a rage, no doubt inspired by the alcohol I could smell on his foul breath. I pushed Marita out of the way as he stumbled into me, and I screamed, my shoulder blades scraping painfully across the rough brick. The shriek was right in his ear, and he fell forward. I jumped across his writhing body, but he managed to grab my ankle. I crashed to the ground, losing my glasses but breaking the fall with my hands. By now some of the men who were standing out in front of the bar were jogging into the alley toward us, blocking what little light there was available from the street. I kicked viciously and freed myself as the men closed in. Scrambling to my feet, I ran from the alley and saw the white blur of Marita's shirt making a hasty getaway. She was walking briskly, but I closed the gap quickly, and she turned to face me. Even through the blur I saw a look of regret mixed with fear that I will not soon forget. I put my arm across her shoulder and turned her around, taking her back to the bar, not looking back toward the alley where a crowd was now gathering.

A figure I assumed was Isabella came running toward us. A range of emotions passed through me, settling, at last, on pity for this poor creature trapped in a depressing cycle of self-destruction. It was all she knew, and it would take more than a swim in the healing pool to effect a lasting change.

Isabella embraced us both. The searing pain in my upper back caused me to wince at her touch, but I suddenly felt strangely exhilarated, almost euphoric, and I laughed out loud as I considered the headline that almost was: Lady Preacher Stomps Sinner in Bar Fight. Marita stared at me in wonder, not sure if it was okay to smile. I took her small hand in mine and squeezed it as the three of us stumbled, arm in arm, through the night.

CHAPTER TWELVE

I Awoke The Next morning with a throbbing headache and a sore back, mementos of my tussle in the alley. Distracted by these localized pains, I shuffled to the bathroom unprepared for the larger horror that awaited me there.

Mirrors do not lie, and mine was no exception. All of my careful cosmetic work had faded to distant memory. Thankfully, I had little time to gaze at my reflection wearing my only pair of spare glasses, which were constructed with black plastic frames and cast me firmly in the 1950s, though, in fact, they were just over ten years old and purchased while I was in seminary because they were the cheapest frames available. Had I not scheduled an important meeting with Michael, I probably would have considered going out in public without them, but I could visualize myself falling headlong down the basement stairwell, thus becoming another test case for the healing pool. If the failed experiment with Marita had taught me anything, it was that God never promised to repair the consequences of our own foolish choices. At least the clunky frames obscured the deep circles under my eyes.

The shower helped clear my head, though a bath would have been better if I had had more time. I tried to approximate the new hairstyle of which I had grown so fond, tilting my head in several odd directions to ascertain the effect from different vantage points, and was semi-pleased at the result. I pulled on a pair of jeans and a fuzzy pink cardigan, a loaner from Margaret, which almost redeemed the glasses by giving me a kind of stylish retro look. I noticed the clerical collar on my nightstand and smiled. "You've come a long way, baby," I said to Motorhead, who looked away, eyes at half-staff.

As soon as I hit the street, I saw the white truck parked in front of the church. Corning Lutz was the patriarch of the board, and the primary benefactor for St. Fred's. His windy speeches of how he personally saved the church from bankruptcy on several occasions were the stuff of legend. I liked him even less than I did Hamber, but if I ticked off Lutz, everyone stood to lose, not just me. Whatever Lutz was doing in there couldn't be good, but I would have to play it cool.

A silver Honda whizzed by before I could flag it down, but then it braked up ahead in the middle of the street, and Michael leaned his head out the window.

"Need a lift?"

"Hold up," I answered.

I walked up beside the car, which lurched ahead just as I reached the window, catching a glimpse of Michael's passenger—a stocky man wearing a sling—but I couldn't see his face.

"I said wait!"

The Honda stopped again, and I jogged up to it. Michael was grinning. I bent over at the waist and saw the other man. He was youngish, probably around twenty-five, with thick limbs and a puffy, stubbled chin. "Meet Jess. He's one of our new members." Michael leaned out farther and whispered, "He's got a stress fracture in his ulna."

The car rolled along slowly, and I picked up my pace, power-walking alongside. "Ulna?" It didn't sound like something a man would have, and Jess laughed at my confused expression. He leaned down and looked up at me through soft green eyes.

"It's that skinny bone in the forearm," he said. "Broke it at work. Guy smashed his thumb with a hammer, got mad, and threw the hammer. I tried to shield my face with my arm. *Crack.*"

The sound effect was inauthentic but nothing further needed be said. We were almost at the church, so I quickly ran through the game plan. "Nice to meet you, Jess. Maybe we'll shake hands in a few minutes." Jess said something like "cool" but I was rushing to the rules of procedure. "Now you guys drive around back and wait until I tell you it's safe to come in, okay?"

"Oh, man." Jess was looking at the white truck with Lutz Constructors emblazoned on the side in blue script. Before I could react, the front door of the church opened, and Corning Lutz came bounding down the steps at a brisk octogenarian clip. Out of the corner of my eye, I could see Jess slinking down in the seat.

"You don't come to work very early, do you, Reverend?" he said.

I walked around the car and stood in front of the passenger window. "I'm sorry, stayed up late last night working. Is there something I can do for you?"

He laughed and coughed simultaneously. "For one thing, you can visit the list of shut-ins I just put on your desk—and soon. They may not be important to you, but in days past they contributed to the life of our church and deserve to be looked after now that they can't attend. Like we said at the meeting, you haven't been putting forth what we consider a minimum effort at . . ." He stopped in mid-sentence, crinkling his brow. "Who are these people?"

"Hmm? Oh, this is Michael Montefiore—"

"The minister?"

"Hmm? Yes, that's him."

Michael was springing out from the driver's side, skipping around the car to meet Lutz, but the patriarch ignored him, trying once again to peer into the car. "And the other gentleman . . . he looks somewhat familiar—"

"Jess Petruski," Michael said.

"*Petruski?*" Lutz bellowed. He reached for the door handle, but the door opened from within, bumping me out of the way.

"Are you *hiding* from me, Petruski?" Lutz demanded. "What are you doing here?"

Jess stood to face the old gentleman and was a good eight inches taller than he was. He was a huge man, but it was clear that Lutz intimidated him, as he did almost everyone.

"I want to work, Mr. Lutz, that's all. I can't get disability, and I'm having trouble getting by."

"You should have thought about that before you started that fight with Jones, Petruski."

"Sir, like I said before, it didn't happen like that."

"Three eyewitnesses said it did. I don't like troublemakers on my sites, and if you think you can cry to my pastor to get her to persuade me to give you your job back, you are greatly mistaken."

"But that's not why I came, sir. This whole thing is a big misunderstanding. Jones and those guys don't want me around because I read my Bible on breaks and don't swear all the time—that's why they lied to you. Jones is the one who threw the hammer."

"*After* you threw it at *him,* because he uttered a profanity, isn't that so?"

"No. Look, I don't even want my job back—I just need to work, sir. I don't have any money coming in, and our baby is due next week, along with the mortgage. That's why I came here, Mr. Lutz. I thought if I could just—"

"Stock up on diapers and canned goods, you know, the typical stuff," I interjected, reaching into my pocket for the keys and tossing them to Michael. "Here, why don't you guys go on in—I'll be there in a second. Mr. Lutz is a very busy man and doesn't need us wasting his valuable time."

Michael took the hint and pulled the confused Jess Petruski up the walk while I remained to calm the fuming Lutz. "He's kind of a sad case, that guy," I said after they were inside. "Goes to Michael's church. Lots of problems. I didn't think you wanted to stand around and listen to his tale of woe."

"Well, if you want my opinion, he doesn't deserve—"

"I figured we should do what we can, you know, so he wouldn't . . . *sue* you or anything."

"What? Sue *me?*" Lutz was outraged.

"Something about unsafe working conditions, harassment . . ."

"He wouldn't dare!"

". . . violation of building code requirements, a few other things. I thought a little charity might ease his troubled mind."

My risky tactic proved effective. It wasn't much of a stretch to assume that Lutz ran a shady business. I listened to a long speech about how the code could be interpreted any number of ways, about how difficult it was to settle conflicts between employees, and about how OSHA had made it nearly impossible to build anything these days, much less make any money doing it. I assured him I would tend to his list, and sent him on his way. After he was well out of sight, I dashed up the steps.

I found Michael and Jess in the benevolence closet, where Michael was stacking cans in a large box. My entrance surprised them, and they stopped their talking, allowing me to capture the scene in freeze-frame. Jess was in the process of reaching up with both hands to get a pack of disposable diapers from a high shelf. The sling was gone. A ball of wet bandages lay at his feet.

Several well-placed karate chops against Jess Petruski's ulna left my hand smarting, but did not so much as make him flinch. We concluded that yet another miracle had occurred, though it was altogether possible that this guy was not what he seemed. The healing didn't surprise him in the least, and he spouted a few Bible verses in support of God's goodness with a bit too much flippancy for my tastes. I surmised that he had only recently come to

Michael's church and had plunged into the congregational life with zest, while his shy, pregnant wife remained in his shadow, unknown by most of the members. Perhaps he was a con artist who went from job to job, getting himself fired to receive unemployment benefits, and maybe he did start the ruckus with Jones, as Lutz said, and now he was taking advantage of us as well. Or, he could have been the real deal—a simple man who trusted God and who had abundant faith, at least more than I had.

Michael returned from dropping Jess off at home to find me in the basement sitting on the pool deck, struggling not to be distracted from prayer.

"Where'd you get the cool goggles?"

"It's a long story," I sighed, but he listened intently as I told it. I felt incredibly stupid for thinking that a dip in Dead Sea water would turn a teenage prostitute into a paragon of virtue, but I tried to justify my actions. "I was told she was an addict," I said. "I thought it was worth a try."

"That's all you can do, Carla. If the truth be known, I have doubts about Jess myself." This confession was encouraging, and I expressed my similar concerns. Suddenly we were immersed in doubt, questioning even Paul Delvecchio's recovery. It was unusual for Michael to waver like this, and I probed deeper.

"Well, I can't help wondering why all this is happening—*if* it's happening," he said. "Why are these people being healed? Is it because they are Christians, or that God wants them to become Christians, or what? I don't doubt that something weird is happening down here, but what's the purpose? If the pool hadn't suddenly filled up with salt water, I'm not sure I would believe it myself."

I didn't like the tone. "But Michael, what's changed? Yesterday you were the one so sure of the miracles."

"I don't know—it's just that . . . are you *sure* the lines are disconnected?"

I blinked. "Michael, are you saying Mr. Delvecchio may have staged this whole thing?"

He looked away, ashamed. "The thought did cross my mind."

"But why would he do such a thing?"

"How about to try to get you into trouble? Maybe he wants to run you off. Shoot, maybe somebody put him up to it, paid him off or something."

"This is just ridiculous," I said, standing up. "Go and see for yourself then." I pointed to the hatch door in the floor. Michael shrugged and walked over, lifted the hatch, and descended. There was silence for a moment, then

Michael said, "He could have connected the pipe, filled the pool, and disconnected it again." I huffed and shook my head for no one to see. "No way, and you know it," I yelled bitterly down into the hole.

Michael's head popped up like a woodchuck's. "Okay, look, we've got to get to the bottom of this somehow. You've got arthritis, deafness, Alzheimer's, and a suspicious broken arm—nothing we can really prove, because we don't know these people all that well. And, your Marita didn't get her miracle at all. We've got to have something we can verify before the news gets out. If it turns out to be a sham, you'll be considered a crackpot. But if it's true, we better be able to prove it."

I helped him climb out of the pit. "What would Jesus do?" I muttered.

Michael hesitated, as if struck by a thought. "That's it!" he exclaimed. "Remember the healing of the leper? First chapter of Mark?"

"Uh, yeah . . ." I said, vaguely becoming aware of what he was getting at.

"Jesus heals him and warns him not to tell anybody because it's too early to start a conflict with the Pharisees and scribes. But he *does* tell him to go to the priest—to certify that God healed him. That's exactly what we need—a certified miracle."

"Fine," I said. "Should I call a televangelist? How much cash have you got?"

"Don't be facetious. I know how we can do this. Remember when you came looking for me in the hospital? The man I was visiting, the one with cancer? Well, his doctor is an outspoken Christian who prays with his patients, goes on mission trips to Africa, you know the type. But he's also one of the most respected physicians in town."

"So you want your friend to come to the pool and have his healing verified by this doctor," I summarized.

"Can't come to the pool. We take the pool to him. The doctor won't even know what's going on."

"And if it doesn't work?"

"Well, there's always your lousy eyesight. But let's not go there quite yet—I kind of like the nerdy look." I blushed and fiddled with the glasses, which only reinforced his point.

♦ ♦ ♦

I spent the better part of the day making calls on the shut-ins, most of whom were delighted to see me. Surprisingly, I enjoyed it quite a lot, especially talking with Mrs. Klovak's parrot and looking through photo albums of the Perrimans' trip to Niagara Falls. Mrs. Harold was originally from Brookline, so we swapped stories of home. When the clock showed it was time to head over to the hospital, I wondered why I had neglected this blessed duty for so long.

I had emptied a bottle of natural spring water, or so the label read, and submerged it under the surface of the pool before leaving the church. Lifting it out, I had examined my wetted hand to see any effect, but found none. What was I expecting—a firmer grip? Smoother skin? Manicured nails? Before leaving, I retrieved the bottle from my oversized handbag. The water had a dull sheen to it as I watched it swirl inside the clear plastic container. The apostle Paul once used his sweat rags as healing cloths, so why wouldn't an anointing from the Lord's pool be just as good?

As I drove to the hospital, I pondered Michael's flip-flop earlier that morning—a chink in his righteous armor. Apparently I wasn't the only one with doubts. I wondered which Michael would be awaiting me—the crusader, or the skeptic? Our faith is rock steady when we're preaching, or teaching, or defending our way of life. But when we come face-to-face with something holy, something truly sacred, it scares us, all of us, out of our wits. It is almost as if we want to keep God at arm's length, for if we draw too close to Him, all our sins will be exposed. We are like the escaped Hebrew slaves at the foot of Mount Sinai when it quaked and thundered and rained fire, who said, "Go on, Moses, you go up and face God—we'll stay here and do whatever *He* tells you." Even a part of the ordinarily courageous Michael Montefiore wished it really weren't true, or he would have to deal with it, just like me. He was troubled to know God's purpose in all of this. Were we to become like those faith healers we laughed at—and have everyone laugh at us? Did God want to bring about a power struggle between the board and me? Would Michael eventually have to take a public stand on the issue, and if so, how would it affect his ministry? His reputation? I kept coming back to the necessity of proving—if only to ourselves—that God was at work. On the other hand, perhaps in the searching we would learn something else he wanted us to know.

I walked the well-lit corridor like a spy in a foreign land, clutching my bag with both hands. When I arrived at the room, I felt the heavy burden of terminal illness that hung in the dimness like a stagnant cloud. Michael was already there, along with a woman I assumed was the patient's wife. She smiled weakly at me, and I nodded, treading lightly toward them.

The man was sleeping, though not restfully. He was emaciated, ravaged by chemotherapy, on the last leg of the journey. I listened as his wife, a thin, dark woman named Patricia, told of how robust he had been just a year ago, how they had hiked in the Adirondacks and taken camping trips with their children. He was a good man, this Carmine Russo, a man who loved God and his family and fishing and the Mets and Rocky his spaniel mutt and his buddies down at the lodge. His love of God had not wavered, she said, and, in fact, it had increased. He had witnessed of his belief in Christ to everyone who had come to see him, and several had professed faith. She had found many quiet moments with her husband in the past months—special times she would always treasure—to talk and remember and get ready for what was coming. God had been so good to them. They were blessed, she said. They were so blessed.

The petite Italian woman was a spiritual giant, and I felt a rush of shame to presume that my little splash of pool water could reverse the effects of the disease which they had struggled against for so long and with such dignity. With trembling hands, I removed the bottle from my purse, and with my finger rubbed the water gently into Carmine's forehead. Then, we joined hands and Michael prayed, his voice clear and true, his strength overcoming my weakness. This was followed by tears and hugs and the peace of our Lord, whose presence was strong and lifted our crying faces into smiles.

◊   ◊   ◊

When I returned to St. Fred's, I found Isabella waiting for me on the steps along with a haggard gentleman who was coughing so hard I could barely understand his name when he gave it. It was clear why they had come, and I quickly ushered them inside.

Ralph was a retired carpenter who had emphysema, and his labored breathing between coughs was so unsettling that I was tempted to pull out my water bottle and have him chug the elixir that remained so he might instantly relieve his burden. He was hunched over, bowlegged, and bony, with pronounced worry lines carved deep in the ruddy skin of his face. It broke my heart to see him suffer so.

It was unclear to me exactly how to proceed, and my mind was scrambled as we helped him to the basement. I naturally gravitated toward the rite of baptism in my mind and settled on affusion as the preferred method: I would not submerge the man entirely, but pour the sacred water over him. From somewhere deep in my mental closet of clerical formulas I tried to summon the words appropriate to performing such a ritual, but of course there were none, so I decided to approach it as responsibly as I knew how. For Jesus, it was faith that made so many of his petitioners whole, and it would be required of Ralph as well.

Isabella and I carefully removed his shirt, revealing a stained T-shirt underneath. I retrieved a bucket and towel from the janitor's closet at the end of the hall and dipped it in the pool. Then I asked the questions.

"Ralph, who is your Lord and Savior?"

He responded with such horrendous hacking that his body convulsed violently, and we had to grab onto his shoulders to keep him from falling into the pool. I panicked, worrying that the poor man might drop dead on the spot.

"Ralph, is Jesus Christ your Lord and Savior?" I was leaning down, looking up into his eyes. They widened, and he seemed to nod his head in the affirmative, though it could have been the effect of the muscle spasms from all the coughing. But the man was turning blue, and his confession of faith, flimsy as it was, would have to do.

I plunged my hands into the bucket and cupped them to hold as much of the water as I could, then opened them over Ralph's head. I wasn't particularly good at this, and most of the water was lost on the way up. I handed the bucket to Isabella and tried again. Since he was still doubled over, the water level was just right for me to splash a goodly portion onto him, and I was so pleased with this procedure that I did it twice more. The coughing immediately abated, and Isabella and I stood back in wonderment. A crooked smile could be seen forming on Ralph's wet face, and though exhausted and wheezing, he slowly stood straight on his bandy legs.

Isabella put her hand to her mouth and muttered something in astonished Spanish while I hustled to help Ralph dry himself with the towel and put his shirt on. He was trembling from weakness and cold—bless his heart—but the coughing had definitely subsided. Slowly we made our way back upstairs when, just before I opened the door that led to the office, I heard the front door open.

"Stop," I whispered. "Someone just came in. You two stay here, and don't even breathe." Regretting my poor choice of words, I turned back and said, "I mean, keep quiet."

I opened the door to find Derrold Hamber standing at the end of the short hall.

"Hi," I said cheerfully and totally out of character.

He frowned. "What were you doing down there?"

"Oh, just checking," I said, not knowing what else to say. "I just got back. I've been visiting shut-ins all day."

He arched his eyebrows in surprise as I walked around him to take a seat behind the secretary's desk, hoping to draw his attention away from the basement door. "Now, is there something you wanted?"

The usual grim visage clouded his face. "Yes, in fact. I received a disturbing call from Corning Lutz a few hours ago."

I crossed my arms defensively. "If it's about the shut-ins, I know I've been remiss about making the rounds, but after today it won't be a problem getting—"

"He didn't mention that," Hamber interrupted. "He spoke to me about a person named Jess Peruski or Petruski, something like that. Do you know this man?"

"Uh, well, yes, I do. He came looking for help this morning. I think he used to work for Mr. Lutz, a weird coincidence—"

"And Corning fired him, some kind of religious zealot. And apparently you have something to do with it."

I swiveled back and forth on the squeaky chair. "All I did was give the guy some diapers."

"You don't know anything about the broken arm scam?"

"Scam?" Now I was visibly nervous.

"That's right. This man Peruski went to see Corning today at his office, demanding his job back. Said his arm had been miraculously healed and that it was evidence that he had been treated unfairly, and Corning should hire him back or face the wrath of God."

I was stunned. "That's . . . I can't . . ." Words half formed got caught in my throat. "He actually said that?"

"Those very words. And he said *you* would back him up. Corning is furious."

I stood up, suppressing the urge to run into the street. "I would never say such a thing." I was emotional but apologetic. "Please tell me you know that."

"I do. Just tell me you did not encourage this man to go back to Corning and plead for his job. *That* I can see you doing."

"Well, you're right, I might have, but I didn't."

He nodded. "I see. And you didn't know this man before?"

"No, sir. He goes to Michael's church. They've helped him quite a lot, I gathered, and he just thought—"

"He could pawn him off on us, eh?" Hamber was lightening up. "Taking advantage of your kind heart, like all these indigents do around here. Well, I suppose that's okay, but just be careful you don't get—"

A violent eruption of coughing from behind the basement door caught us both off guard. I held my breath, terrified, as Hamber stared down the hall.

"Did you hear . . . ?" He paused his question, probably because he realized it was just as easy to see for himself as ask me. I held my breath as he marched toward the door.

Isabella and Ralph were cowering on the stairs in semi-darkness. Another long barrage of coughing was launched at Hamber, and the board chairman stepped back.

"What . . . ? Who . . . ?" He was the speechless one for a change and, if not for the anxiety of the moment, I would have delighted in it. I rushed up behind him, putting my finger to my lips, frowning at Isabella and Ralph to say nothing.

"This is Isabella Ruiz, Mr. Hamber." She smiled and tilted her head like a little girl. "And this gentleman is Ralph . . . uh, Mr. Hamber, can I speak to you privately for a minute?" I ushered him away to my study, afraid to look at his face. As soon as I shut the door behind us, he exploded.

"Carla! What in blazes are you—"

"Shhh," I cautioned. "Don't let Ralph hear you. I don't want to upset him."

He stared at me, his jaw hanging.

"He was waiting on the steps when I got here. I think he's homeless. And probably sick. Did you see the way he was shaking? And that awful cough—he's in bad shape."

"That's all well and good, but—"

"I was trying to talk to him when Isabella came by. She comes over sometimes in the late afternoon to get canned goods for herself and her young daughter."

"It seems I've heard something about that from Mrs. Dickson. But that doesn't explain—"

"I'm sorry to interrupt you, sir, but please listen. I don't want Ralph to wander off again before getting help. When I went into the benevolence room with Isabella, he slipped away, and we found him in the basement."

"The basement is off limits, Miss Donovan." The formal address wasn't a good sign.

"Yes, I know it is. But the plumber apparently forgot to lock up when he left the other day. Do you know Joe? He left his pipe wrench here last week, the big goof."

My story seemed to have enough plausibility to convince Hamber. "Yes, I know," he said through gritted teeth. "And that numskull helper of his."

"Right. Well, I was checking all the locks while I was down there and came up to get Ralph some clean clothes. Isabella was having some success communicating with him, so I left them in one of the side rooms. I didn't see the point of explaining all this to you. Homeless people come in here all the time."

"I understand perfectly," he said. "It was a bit of a shock seeing them there though."

"Yeah, I suppose it was." I laughed uncomfortably.

We went back out into the office to find them gone, as I expected we would. When Hamber left, I dropped into the chair and, reaching into my purse for the water bottle, I placed the cool plastic against my throbbing forehead and closed my eyes.

CHAPTER THIRTEEN

For Several Hours I tortured myself with the alarming fact that I was getting pretty smooth at stretching the truth. Although, in the end, I justified it by the easy rationalization that I was lying for the greater good, that is, to keep the healing pool a secret. Telling Lutz and Hamber what was actually happening in the basement would result in my swift dismissal, and God's mighty work would grind to a halt. But maybe I was assuming too much here—maybe God *wanted* me to be bold about this. Isn't that what faith is all about anyway? We didn't really have any solid evidence yet, so making the pool story public would definitely be a faith statement. And, if unbelief prevailed, what was to stop God from turning another swimming pool into Lourdes?

Lourdes. The little grotto in France where the Virgin Mary supposedly appeared to the teenager Bernadette Soubirous more than 150 years ago, where thousands visit every year seeking a glimpse of the mother of Jesus and healing of their infirmities. I knew about Lourdes because my parents' church in Boston incorporated the name and was adorned with beautiful statuary of Mary herself. More than fifty healings have been declared official miracles by the church over the years, my mother often said. She was a firm believer. The thought provoked a chuckle. If it turned out that her daughter presided over a certified healing site, would it change Mother's opinion of me? It was hard to imagine.

Harder still was getting my hands on incontrovertible proof of our collection of miracles. I had asked Mr. Delvecchio to have his father examined by his attending physician, and though he promised to do it, he was having trouble convincing Paul to go. Then there was Isabella, who to my knowledge had not yet taken Miranda to the doctor either. My sense of urgency was selfish, of course, for these people needed no confirmation of what they already knew. I didn't want to push them too hard and reveal my skepticism—or worse, undermine our relationships. But I had to know. I hoped Carmine Russo would show signs of recovery soon.

Guilt rolled over me like a wave. Did I care at all that these people were made well, or was I more concerned with my job security? But then, I reasoned, why punish myself needlessly? After all, Marita had evidently not been helped, nor Ralph. And I had no idea what to make of Jess Petruski. In the end, of course, it didn't matter what I thought about the pool, and it wasn't important to know why or even how God chooses to heal someone. Nobody is running tests to see if there is something funny about the water at Lourdes. I was the problem. I had been from the beginning. I was afraid. But Michael's words kept rolling around inside my head: *Faith trumps fear.* The proof I was desperately seeking was nothing more than an excuse for my own cowardly faithlessness.

I didn't like my growing tendency to fib, and I worried that keeping the secret from the board might actually turn out to be the worst thing to do, since when they did find out, they would know that I had been deceiving them, no matter what evidence I produced. I picked up the phone to discuss the issue with Michael when it rang under my hand.

"I've got another swimmer," he said, using our pet term for the healing candidates.

I slumped at the news. "Really?"

"Yeah. Ted McCorkle. Came in to see me this afternoon. Guy's a diabetic—a list of medical problems as long as your arm."

"Really?"

He laughed. "Yeah. But the thing is, that's not what he wanted to talk about. He's raising money for juvenile diabetes, wants a place to bring the kids for a special event. I said I knew the perfect place. Can you guess?"

"Michael . . . please tell me you didn't volunteer the pool."

"What's wrong with that? Think of the data it would generate for our research. And the publicity . . ."

Now I knew he was kidding. "But seriously," I said.

"Okay, seriously, I'm letting him use our church, but we started getting theological about disease and stuff, and he made the statement that even with all the money and medicine in the world, it's always God who does the curing. Real health, he said, is in Christ—even if you stay sick. That's what he tells the kids. Ted's a pretty devout Christian. So I told him."

"What? About the pool? Did he laugh at you?"

"No way. He was very interested. Not for the kids, though. He said it wasn't right to play with their emotions like that. If it didn't work, you know. But he'd go for a swim himself if we wanted."

"If *we* wanted? Hang on, here, Michael—I'm missing something. Doesn't he want to get well?"

"Sure he does. But he said that's not the most important thing to him. Serving God is."

"Then why do it?"

"To increase his faith. Why else?"

"But if he does get well, don't you think he'll want to bring all those kids down to the pool?"

"I don't know, maybe. But if he does, what's wrong with that?"

Yes, Carla, tell us please exactly what's wrong with that? "Well, nothing, I suppose."

"Great. He'll meet us after lunch on Saturday. By the way, are you free that night?"

"Huh? I think so." I was still woozy from the thought of a hundred kids showing up at the church with inner tubes and snorkels.

"'Cause Mama wants you to come over for dinner. You like pasta?"

◆ ◆ ◆

Saturday morning found me refreshed and eager to meet the day, I think because, for the first time in several weeks, I felt ready to deliver Sunday's sermon. I even found time to play catch in the front yard with Pete. The day was so beautiful even Motorhead came out on the stoop to watch us. Pete babbled excitedly about the acquisitions the Yankees had made in the off-season and, once again, he announced that he had an uncle who might take him to Florida for a few days during spring training. Knowing his family, I doubted his high hopes would be rewarded. But hope is always a good thing, and as Pete imagined himself in pinstripes performing various feats of skill—deep fly ball caught over the fence to end the World Series, perfect throw from right field to nail the runner at the plate, unassisted triple play, etc.—I kept Ted McCorkle in the back of my mind. From Michael's description, he seemed to be the kind of man so imbued with hope that he considered his illness almost a trivial matter. He was energized by the knowledge that God *could* heal him, not necessarily that he *would,* and so, how could he be disappointed? The great hope of his life would materialize after, not during, his time on earth. This was comforting to me, and reflecting on it altered my perspective about the pool. God would reveal his will in his time—for me as well as for the pool—and I would accept it.

I fixed myself an amazingly healthy lunch—turkey sandwich, no mayo, and a fruit cup—a further indication that my emotions had stabilized. It was stress, I reasoned, that made me doubt, made me worry, made me eat all the wrong foods at the wrong times and in the wrong portions. The sermon was done, and it was good, so what did I have to worry about? All those eyes staring me down tomorrow morning would see their minister in perfect form, and in total control—for a change.

I was still a little hungry after the sandwich, but resisted the urge to eat anything else, knowing that later on I would be joining the Montefiores for dinner. Ordinarily I would be at my wit's end about something like this, but the invitation had come from Michael's mother, not from him. She liked me! I tried to visualize myself as part of such a loving, accepting family, and I fantasized about it off and on as I prepared to go to St. Fred's, though not letting myself get carried away, of course. Michael's older and younger brothers were both married, and I wondered if his mother simply wanted to push things along. Still, it buoyed my spirit to think I interested her, and not merely what I represented.

The sun was nearly blinding as I walked down to the church. The snow had entirely melted now. Spring was here, and Easter was coming right behind it. I felt as if I were walking into a new dimension, and meeting Ted only added to the surrealism of this day; he was balding, overweight, and yet extremely appealing. A warmth I can't adequately describe seemed to ooze out of him. He was wearing faded blue swim trunks, one blue sock and one green, and a brown T-shirt; apparently, in addition to his many ailments, he was also color-blind. He and Michael made a good match.

Michael commented once again on my glasses, which I had decided to keep for a while based on his earlier compliment, and I wondered if he had just said it to be nice and was expecting me to get another pair after all. But I said my next change would be contacts, and he just nodded, thinking. Ted suspected there was a history behind our exchange.

"Yeah, I broke my good pair trying to rescue a prostitute from a guy in an alley behind a bar a few blocks from here," I said.

He looked at me as if he couldn't believe I was serious, then broke into a smile. "God bless you, sister. No wonder God is moving in your church."

I glanced sideways at Michael, who was smirking. "I guess we ought to get moving ourselves then," I chirped and led them up the steps.

Ted swam playfully in the pool while we watched from the deck. It was strangely like closing time at the YMCA, and we were the parents of the kid who kept saying he'd get out "in one more minute." This person was so infinitely happy already despite his imperfect body that I didn't see how God could improve on him, or why he would even want to. But, if anyone ever deserved a miracle, Ted was probably the one.

He spoke to us at length about his program to help the kids, and I was impressed at the bigness of his heart. In fact, though he did describe what he had been through fighting his illnesses over the years, he never once mentioned the possibility of healing. He was doing this, it seemed, for our benefit, saying he "would never want to get in the way of what the Lord was doing." After he left, Michael and I reflected on those words.

"Do you think we're going about this all wrong?" Michael asked. "Maybe you and I should have just gone to your board and said, 'Look, guys, there's Dead Sea water in the pool, and here's the lab report, and Frankie Delvecchio says his dad's been healed, and we don't know what to make of it, so what do you guys think we ought to do?'"

"It's a bit late for that," I answered.

"Maybe so. But maybe we aren't struggling so much with faith in God as we are with faith in the board."

It was a fair assessment, but he didn't know them like I did. It was obvious, though, that we were ready for the suspense to end. Either this was a healing pool—at least sometimes—or it was not. Speculation was getting us nowhere. What did we really believe? We had to go one way or the other: drain the pool and forget it, or step out on faith.

💧　💧　💧

A loud clamor from deep within the house flowed out into the street as soon as Michael opened the front door. From the kitchen window his mother had seen the Honda drive up and was making haste to meet us. She was sweating heavily from the heat of the kitchen, where I could see large steaming kettles on the stove, and the small home, which before had seemed plenty big for Michael's parents, strained to contain the mob that had now invaded it.

I was ushered in by Michael's mother, who I was sure must have had a name but insisted on being called Mama. Mr. Montefiore, Angelo Sr., was shouting at a man I took to be Angelo Jr., as the television blared, forcing their voices even further up the scale.

"They switched it? Did you see they changed to another game? It just started." He was ranting at the TV.

"It's over, Pops; they're already behind by twenty-five. Who wants to watch that?"

"*I* want to watch it, that's who."

Michael took me aside and whispered, "March Madness."

"Yeah, well you always pick losers anyways, Pops. Nobody in his right mind picks Siena to go to the Final Four."

"Yeah, but *Duke?* Why all the time we gotta play Duke? What's so great about Duke? Where in blazes *is* Duke, huh?" He was waving his arms like a windmill.

Two longhaired little girls were hiding behind Mama, taking quick looks at me, and giggling. "My grandchildren," Mama proclaimed, like a miner discovering gold, "Mary and Daniela." She spun around trying to catch them, finally laying a hand on the taller Mary, who might have been around eight, and she hauled her in for a sweaty kiss.

"Those two are Junior's," Michael said. He was clutching my elbow as if afraid I might get crushed by the herd if he let go. "And this is my little brother, Anthony, and his wife, Patti." I turned to see an extraordinarily handsome young man, who had apparently been standing there all along. His cute, blonde wife—with whom I immediately formed an unspoken kinship based on our mutual recognition that we were the only non-Italians in the house—rushed up and took my hand. "He's the quiet one," she said, referring to her husband.

Mama then began shouting at the two Angelos to turn off the basketball and come to meet me. They stopped arguing and obeyed, but left the TV on.

"Hey, Pops."

"Michael!" shouted the older man and threw his arms around his son. Then, backing off, he turned his attention to me.

"Hi," I said.

He nodded and looked nervously at the other Angelo. Michael tugged at my elbow.

"Uh, Duke's in Durham, North Carolina," I said. "They have a fine divinity school there."

The two men looked at each other once more, puzzling over my statement.

"You're the lady minister?" guessed Junior.

"She's the pastor at St. Fred's," Michael said. "So, Siena's getting killed, huh?" His deft shift of the subject to more familiar territory seemed to relax the men, and they resumed the earlier debate, this time drawing Michael in with them. I felt someone pulling me away. It was Mama.

"Come meet Theresa," she said, hauling me into the kitchen with Patti and the girls trailing behind.

Theresa was a stout woman with dark strands of hair pasted to the side of her face. We found her slinging a lasagna noodle at the wall.

"If it sticks, it's done," Mama told me. "You know this?"

"Hey!" Theresa yelled over the rumble and hiss of the boiling pots, perhaps saving me from a lecture on the proper preparation of pasta. "So this is Carla." She had a pretty face and a nice smile, but like her husband, she was *loud*. Patti was at my side, showing moral support, while Mary and Daniela begged their mother to let them throw a noodle at something.

We girls talked of cooking, husbands (bitter complaints, except for Patti, who had only good things to say about Anthony), the break-in at my place, and the decline of western civilization in general and the city in particular. I contributed a travel promo about Boston and anecdotes concerning Motorhead, in which the kids were vitally interested. During this time, we constructed two impossibly heavy tubs of lasagna, which was more than enough to feed the ten of us—but there was also homemade chicken soup, fresh-baked crusty bread, and a huge bowl of salad. We drank cappuccino as we worked—I was instructed that real Italians always drank it before the meal, *never* after—and the actual sitting down to dinner seemed anticlimactic to me.

Angelo Sr. was still grumbling about basketball and was told by his wife that "our guest" wasn't interested in such things. I smiled and remained silent, remembering Michael's warning that these were Knicks fans and, under no circumstances, should I mention that I liked the Celtics. But the silence created an awkward pause in conversation, which the other men sensed as they came into the room. Since all eyes were on me, I felt led to say *something*.

"Would you like me to say grace?"

If the silence was awkward before, it had now become embarrassing, and I blushed. It was a knee-jerk reaction to fill the void, a natural enough response, in that I was often asked to perform this function everywhere I went. But these folks were not accustomed to women taking spiritual leadership, and I feared I had offended them. Somewhere inside my disconnected thoughts, I could hear Michael laughing, which triggered a similar, if delayed, response from them all. As it turned out, Mama practically had to beat the Angelos to offer the blessing at these family meals, and the duty ultimately fell to Michael, who would complain about not wanting to work when he was at home. Then, all eyes would turn to Anthony, who was forced against his will to eke out some ill-conceived sentence fragment studded with "Thee" and "Thou," only to face the ridicule of the others. Friendly abuse seemed to be the communicative glue that held the clan together: harsh words, which became expressions of love when understood in context.

The prayer, culled from childhood memory, was a traditional Catholic recitation of gratitude to God for his gifts from his bounty of good things, and I nearly blushed again at their praise. A flurry of sound and motion commenced from there—dishes passed, bread torn, cutlery clinking on china, salad scooped out in leafy mounds, Theresa grating Parmesan cheese over every plate, the TV bleating play-by-play from the den, Mama crying out above the din to see that the grandchildren were not overlooked. It was disconcerting and overwhelming at the same time, unsettling and intoxicating, not like my family's formal affairs in Boston; I loved being in the midst of all this *life*.

For some reason, Mama attempted to serve me the last slab of lasagna from the first tub, but I waved her off. The magnificent dripping heap of baked pasta hovered on the end of her spatula, unwilling to return to its place. Then, ignoring my apologies, Mama dropped it onto my plate.

"She's not that hungry, Mama," Patti said, likely recalling flashbacks of her own lost wars trying to refuse food in this house.

"Hey, you don't have to be hungry to eat," said Junior with a shrug.

"I'll just have to throw it out," Mama complained.

Michael reached over and severed the huge square of layered pasta, removing half to his own plate.

"You're a glutton all of a sudden?" barked Theresa. Michael did not respond. It was my first indication that he didn't much care for his sister-in-law.

"Hey, remember that girl, what was her name, Michael? Ally? Sally? The one with the garlic thing?"

"Ceil."

"Yeah, *Ceil*. Real pale girl, remember, Angelo?" The husband nodded, though he was leaning back to hear the TV from the other room.

"She was allergic to garlic, that one," said Theresa. "She only got pale after dinner. And sick too. Remember, Michael?"

I could almost hear his teeth grinding. "No," he said.

"C'mon, you remember, *Ceil*—like the honking animal. You gotta remember *that*, huh, Michael? We can laugh about it now, though it wasn't too funny then when she started honking and turned white just before she—"

"I said I don't remember!"

"Hey, that reminds me," interrupted Junior, a rude habit which seemed to come naturally to him, "guess who I saw the other day, Pops."

Theresa, thus stifled, went back to eating. Angelo Sr. looked irritated. "Sixty thousand people in this city, and I have to *guess* which one you saw the other day?"

The oldest son brushed off the sarcasm like dandruff from his oily head. "Your old shop steward, Paul Delvecchio."

Michael and I froze, and our eyes locked momentarily.

"Yeah?" Pops said, suddenly sanguine.

"Yeah, down at the plant when he come by. I told him you were on third shift. He said he'd put in a good word with the bosses to get you back on days. Guy looks great."

"Yeah? What about the . . . old-timers' thing?"

"*Alzheimer's*, Pops," said Anthony, shaking his head. Everyone paused to stare at him. Then, the discussion resumed.

"He's the smart one," Patti whispered in my ear.

"Ah, whatever," Angelo Sr. answered. "Last time I saw him, he couldn't remember my name."

"He's better now," Junior said. "Said God healed him."

"Yeah? How?"

I was twisting in my seat, beginning to perspire, as if just now realizing the house was hot as a sauna.

"I didn't hear that part, break was over. But I heard it from a bunch of guys. Hard to argue with though. Guy looks great."

Everyone slowly swiveled to look toward Michael and me.

"What do you guys think about that, huh?" Michael's father inquired.

Michael cleared his throat. "Well, all healing is from God."

"Yeah?" I could tell Angelo Sr. was skeptical. "So why Paul Delvecchio and not your Uncle Aldo?"

Michael took a deep breath and replied patiently, "Uncle Aldo had a stroke, Pops." I guessed the subject had come up before.

"Sure, but he hung on for two days after that. Why not your Uncle Aldo, when he went to mass every Sunday, and confession all the time, huh?"

Angelo Jr. interpreted this as a good time to sneak off to the basketball game.

"It's not for us to ask those things!" Mama Montefiore shouted. "Your brother lived a good life, and he didn't suffer. Now he's in heaven with God."

Angelo Sr. stood up. "Yeah, well where did it get him, huh? He only got fifty-eight years to show for his good life. That's why I don't go to church." Mama genuflected and nervously muttered something under her breath. The little girls fled the room.

"It's not about church, Pops," Michael said, sighing.

Patti pulled Anthony from the table.

"You said it, son, it's not about church, or God, or nothin'. Work like a dog all your life, and where does it get you, huh?"

"Pops, I don't know why God does what he does. But I believe Paul Delvecchio was healed." I looked at Michael, astonished. When provoked, his true faith glowed brilliantly. "And out of gratitude he should repent and find what Uncle Aldo always had."

"You don't know," Theresa said to no one in particular. "You just don't know."

"As a matter of fact, Theresa, I *do* know," Michael snapped.

"Is that so?"

"Hey, Pops," Junior called out from the den, "Siena's making a run."

"Yes!" Michael said. His temple throbbed with tension. "If he says God healed him, that's what God did."

"Okay. But you don't got proof, do you?" Theresa continued.

I gripped Michael's knee under the table to abort his answer and, inspired by his witness, gave my own. "If God offered us proof, what would be the value of faith? He wants us to *trust* him. Like your beautiful girls, Theresa. Don't you want them to trust you when you tell them something?"

"Sure. Because they don't know what I know."

"Fine. And do you do good things for them to show you love them?" She nodded. "Well, that's what miracles are."

"They're coming back, Pops!" Junior shouted.

"Hang on a minute!" Pops yelled. Turning back to me, he said, "I like what you say, Carla. But you go to church, so what? You say a few prayers, hear the priest talk, eat the bread, so what?"

"For me, worship is an act of faith, not an obligation," I answered. "God delights in our worship because it is an expression of our love for him. Or at least it should be. He wants us to *want* to follow him. Hasn't he done enough for us? He gave us life, salvation . . . He shouldn't have to prove himself over and over again. But every now and then"—I looked at Michael and smiled—"he makes a miracle, just to let us know he's there. And that should move us to follow him more."

"Nah," said the frustrated patriarch, "I just don't see it."

"There are miracles every day, if you look for them," Mama said, blessing me with a warm look of approval.

"Not today," said Junior, who appeared suddenly at his father's side.

"Siena lost then?" Michael asked, ready for the controversy to end.

"Yeah. We made a game of it, but these big-time programs always win in the end. What can you do?"

"How bad was it?" Pops said.

"Devils ninety-nine, Saints eighty-one."

I glanced at Michael, whose eyes reflected the sad irony in the score.

"Maybe next year," Angelo Sr. said, "we'll have our miracle, huh?"

"Yeah, Pops," said Michael. "Maybe next year."

CHAPTER FOURTEEN

I Awakened Sunday Morning grateful for the peculiar phenomenon that shows us our deepest convictions most clearly when we are threatened. (As in the case of a teenage girl who abuses her little brother mercilessly, only to rush to his defense when the neighborhood bully tries to do the same.) Michael and I both realized we really did believe God was performing miracles in the basement pool of St. Fred's, but only when we were forced to bear witness to our faith about such things in the presence of his skeptical family members. We understood now that there would be no proof coming, at least not in the way we would have liked it—no bolt of lightning, no writing in the sky, no pillar of fire to show us the way. It was our job, we reasoned, to interpret what we had been blessed to see, and to show others the way.

But, to where? That was *The Question*.

The urgent compulsion to do something did not erase the nagging question from our minds, but only made it bigger. It loomed large over the text of the morning sermon I had so carefully prepared, based on the powerful parable of the kingdom recorded in a single verse. There was a treasure hidden in a field, Jesus said, and a man found it, hid it once again, joyfully sold everything he had, and with the proceeds bought the field to gain the jackpot. What he had found in the field was of such value that all he owned paled in comparison to it. The kingdom of heaven, Jesus said, was like that. And to think it had been lying there, undiscovered, all along.

Ordinarily the sermon would have had a distinctly evangelistic flavor, you know, the-cross-leads-to-the-crown sort of thing. The manuscript I had prepared and thoroughly rehearsed was a safe bet, well researched, solid, not the least bit controversial. And yet that seemed to be the biggest problem with it; the neatly typed pages I had been so pleased with just yesterday now sat lifeless in my hands. Why was I preaching this, an evangelistic sermon to a church full of Christians? Some of them, I knew, weren't Christians, but the result would be the same. Because they *thought* the message didn't apply to them, they wouldn't really hear it. In fact, they had heard it many times before, and it had not borne fruit in their lives yet. I was forced to deal with the reality that the sermon had pleased me so much because I thought, in hearing it, my congregation would also be pleased with *me*. And now *The Question* returned, bigger than ever, relentless in its insistence to be answered.

I tossed my robe in the back seat and drove to the church early. It was a stunning, sunlit day, a pledge that the expected rebirth of springtime was actually underway. Michael and I had agreed the night before that I should not hide the pool from the board any longer. They had told me to leave it alone, I did, and the thing filled up again! What was I to do? What were *we* to do? I was sure that the only way we would ever answer *The Question* was if we all came humbly before God in light of these bizarre developments and sought the truth in prayer together. If I lost my job, so be it—I had to take the step of faith required of all spiritual leaders. If not by this, by what other measure can one be called a spiritual leader at all?

This did not mean, however, that I should stand behind the pulpit and boldly proclaim to the whole gathered church that we were the proud owners of a miracle pool. Instead, I planned to ask Hamber, Lutz, Egan, and Kerry to see the pool for themselves, after everyone had gone, and discuss the matter as spiritually sensitive people should. But as I arrived at the church—realizing only then that I subconsciously chose to drive instead of walk because I might need to make a quick getaway later—I was gripped by a strange foreboding, a premonition that if I followed the original plan, things would turn out all wrong. It simply didn't feel right, like the sermon I knew I somehow needed to modify within the hour. I paused to pray, my distracted thoughts successfully sabotaging my focus, so that I received no real assurance—just the sense that today would bring with it some unpleasant surprises.

It was in this attitude of fragmented prayer—snips of holy phrases marked by words and phrases like "please" and "if it be your will"—that I rushed to my study unseen. An envelope had been slipped under the door by Mr. Delvecchio, who had already unlocked the building, adjusted the thermostat, and performed the usual preparatory rituals. "I was asked to deliver this to you," it read—signed "Mr D." I closed the door behind me and opened the envelope to find a handwritten note from Michael: "You can do it, Carla. I'm praying for you."

I could hear people entering the office. Sunday school would begin soon. In minutes, the lonely halls of the church would be filled with the familiar hubbub of chitchat, unfolding metal chairs, badly sung hymns, and the rumble of the organ. Normally this energized me, but today I shrank from it in fear. Once I opened the door, I would be the professional servant, and for the next two hours there would be no place to hide. I inhaled deeply, glanced down at the envelope for comfort . . . and knew immediately how I would open the morning sermon. I smiled; perhaps God would get me through this, I thought. *He will show me what to do.*

Ten minutes later I was walking the corridors, enduring endless ribbing about my glasses. Most everyone seemed to be in a good mood, remarking on the pleasant weather—all but Al Lintz, who went out of his way to point out typographical errors in the newsletter and who interrogated me about the departure of Mrs. Dickson, pinning me against the wall until Jameson Kerry rescued me.

"Excuse me, Reverend, but there are some . . . guests of yours waiting in the sanctuary." Kerry didn't seem particularly pleased to report this information, searching for the right word to describe the visitors before calling them my guests, though rather distastefully. It was only ten-thirty, a full half-hour before worship, and the sanctuary would be empty until the organist cranked up the preservice music in twenty minutes.

"Thanks so much—I'll just go see to them." The smile I flashed at Al Lintz disappeared as soon as I turned away from him and hustled down the hall.

Amber light was pouring in through the colored glass, creating a kaleidoscope effect. I burst in through the choir loft door to find three young women standing at the far end of the center aisle. "I'm Carla," I called out. "Can I help you?" It was the wrong thing to say—normally I would have come out with "Welcome to St. Fred's" or something equally chirpy—but these girls (and that's what they were, I saw as I approached) appeared to be troubled souls indeed.

"We're friends of Marita," said the tallest girl. She was likely the oldest, maybe nineteen. The outlandish clothes, which had probably shocked Kerry, identified them plainly. The tall girl stood in the center, her long arms curled around the shoulders of the others. The girl on the left was perhaps fourteen, dirty, and extremely frightened. The other was very dark, Puerto Rican perhaps, or Cuban: her eyes were deep wells of neglect. She bore all the marks of hard time on the street.

"I'm disappointed you didn't bring her with you today," I said, probing. "Is Marita all right?"

"Missing since Friday night," said the tall girl.

This was awful news, and I flushed with anger and worry. "I haven't seen her, if that's what you—"

"We have no money," the dark one cried in a thick accent. "We are flat broken."

"Are you in trouble?" It was an obvious question, but it needed to be asked. The words brought forth a torrent of tears from the young one. I sensed that they feared whatever happened to Marita might soon happen to them.

"We have nowhere to go," the tall girl said. "Sabila is sick."

"Do you want me to take you to the hospital?"

"No!" shouted Sabila, who I began to suspect might be illegal, not to mention suffering from withdrawal.

A door creaked behind me. Astrid Huggins, the church organist, peered over her bifocals in wonder.

"Marita told Sabila about the pool," the tall girl said, "and we were hoping—"

"Shhh," I said, pushing them back to the vestibule. "Not now . . . do you understand worship is starting? I have to preach in a few minutes."

"Can't you take us to the pool while church is going on?" asked the tall girl, who, despite her seniority over the group, suddenly seemed just as fragile.

"It didn't do much for Marita, so I doubt—"

"Please!" she squealed, and tears welled up in her eyes. She seemed desperate. "You did help Marita. She said she was going home. Then . . ." Sobs erupted, and the three huddled close. I drew near, and we all four held hands within a small circle.

"Tell me why you are afraid," I said calmly.

"Marita keep her money to go home with," Sabila said.

"He found her," said the tall girl, "and he's got her somewhere. He'll get us too."

"Who? Why?"

"Richie. Because last night, he took everything we had. Gave us nothing back, not even a penny of our share. He's watching us."

So that was it. They were seeking sanctuary from the bad guy. Astrid Huggins's stout fingers descended on the keyboard, and we jumped.

"Look," I said, "you have to go to the police."

"We be molested," Sabila cried.

"No, no. You won't be arrested. I promise."

They sensed that my promise was hollow; I didn't know the first thing about these poor souls—who they were or what they had done.

"If you could just take us to the pool," the tall girl begged, "we would be safe down there. And if we get better, it will be easier for us to get away."

Easier for them? Drop in at the church and grab your miracle to go? The loud reverberations of the organ overwhelmed the commotion I knew must have begun. I looked over my shoulder to see people filing in from the classroom wing.

"Okay. But then you'll go to the police?"

All three of them nodded.

I opened the big front door to see four dark suits coming up the steps. *Ushers.* One of them would surely volunteer to take care of my problem for me, since the service was about to begin, and there's no telling what these girls would say to them. I whirled and led the girls back down the center aisle, darted down an empty pew, and yanked them quickly along the wall behind Astrid, who looked up, but continued playing as we skirted by. I pushed open the swinging door and nearly ran into Al Lintz, who was sneezing as he came out of the rest room. Behind him were Hamber and Lutz; there was no way I could get past them without giving some explanation.

Al Lintz was still wiping up something with his hanky as we sped by him. "Mr. Hamber, could you give the announcements for me? They're printed in the bulletin. I need to take these girls to my office and call their parents. I'll be right back." It was a weak story, and after looking the girls up and down, he was most suspicious. But I gave him no time to object, which I knew he wouldn't. I would probably get a reprimand later, but he loved the spotlight and would prefer to do the announcements anyway.

I slowed down, smiling and greeting each of the surprised members by name as they came up the opposite side of the corridor. By the time I reached the office area, everyone had gone into the sanctuary. The booming notes of the organ ceased; Hamber would be striding to the pulpit to welcome the worshippers and make the announcements. I had a clear path to the hall that led to the basement door. "It's down there," I said as I hauled my stumbling human cargo forth. Then, a voice called out to me and stopped us cold.

"Mr. Kerry? Oh . . . I didn't see you there."

He was smiling, almost blushing, standing just inside the benevolence room. "I got to thinking, and I thought your, uh, guests might need some assistance." I saw that he was packing three boxes with food and clothing. I was so amazed to see it that, for a moment, I couldn't speak. Was this the greatest miracle yet?

"You girls are staying for the service, aren't you?" he said.

We looked at each other. The young one was nearly hyperventilating at the sudden change of plan.

"Um, well, actually, I was going to—"

"Naw, I can do this, Reverend. You show them a good seat, and I'll fix these up for them. Don't worry—I'll be done in time to hear the sermon." He was obviously proud of himself.

I sighed. Pointing my head back in the direction we came, I took one step before the tall girl squeezed my hand and pulled me toward her. "We need to go to the pool," she whispered, intelligent enough to have learned by now that the pool was something of a secret.

"*We?* What's all this about 'we'?" I snapped. "I thought Sabila was the sick one."

"I have a . . . condition." She whispered in my ear, and I closed my eyes in frustration. For some reason, I just couldn't see this as the kind of thing that would get her to the front of the healing line at the next crusade.

"*After* the service," I said through gritted teeth. "Just come with me now." I pulled them along, stopping only to snatch my robe from the chair where I had tossed it.

We entered to a room full of eyes. I pointed to the empty pew down front—there were always several rows of them—and the girls filed in. Hamber was elaborating about the upcoming Easter schedule, describing every event in such detail that if it weren't still late March we would have thought he was reliving the experience for those who weren't here. Or, more likely, he was dragging out the announcements, waiting for me.

I quietly ascended the platform and slipped into the throne-like chair that was reserved for me. Across the platform was the choirmaster, a layman named Custis Doyle who had inherited his position from his father, a band-leader from the Swing era and retired music teacher. Custis knew next to nothing about choral music, but he waved his arms fairly well and could carry a decent tune, and since no one else wanted the job, he was quickly installed. The choir, which pretty much ran on autopilot, wasn't in the loft that day because Custis did not want to preview any of the Easter music they had been preparing, as he explained after taking the pulpit from Hamber. I interpreted this message to mean either he didn't have enough members to pull off the anthem, or they sounded so dreadful he didn't want to scare off the potential audience, deducing this conclusion from the fact that an anthem was listed in the bulletin.

We stood for the opening hymn. I could hardly hear my own singing, much less that of the people, because of the proximity of the organ to my chair. My eyes ran ahead of the words in the hymnal so I could cast quick glances at the three girls down front. The third time I looked, I noticed that I wasn't the only one looking; the fourth time I saw that they had noticed the same thing, and had closed their hymnbooks. They looked so uncomfortable that I thought they might simply fly down the side aisle for the exit, but they sat down with the rest of the crowd. It was then I noticed something I hadn't seen before, hanging on the tall girl's neck.

Corning Lutz came up to give the Old and New Testament readings from a lectionary off to the side of the platform. He read from the big King James Bible that was placed there (did he even have a Bible of his own?) and tripped over many of the words. I only half-heard the readings, staring at the girl with the gold pendant in the second row. She saw that I was staring and clutched it self-consciously. She looked down at it then, and back at me. In that moment she must have seen the outrage in my eyes. I gripped the arms of the throne in hot anger, radiating resentment at this brazen prostitute who had the nerve to come into God's house asking for help while wearing my stolen jewelry—the pendant that had been given to me by my grandmother and taken from my house just a week before. Where had she gotten it? I doubted that she could have been the thief, but she was obviously connected to him somehow. Did she know it was mine? Now, she does—I could read the guilt in her eyes.

My rage cooled as Egan gave the invocation, and Custis led us in another song. We stood again, but the girls remained seated, huddled together for some reason. At first I thought that they might be praying, so lost in their desperate petitions that they carried over into the hymn, but then I saw that Sabila was trembling severely, and the others were trying to comfort her. The ushers came down to receive the offering; one of them gave a brief, ritualized prayer, and the congregation fell into their seats with a loud thump and rustle. The tall girl removed the pendant and dropped it in the offering plate as it passed by, and as soon as the usher had moved past the row, she led the other two girls out into the aisle and out of the sanctuary, exiting behind the organ as we had entered, in full view of everyone.

My mind raced. What to do now? I couldn't chase after them—I was scheduled to preach in less than a minute. Were they going to the pool? I scanned the room for Jameson Kerry—had he come in yet? Yes, there he was, standing in the back. He must have gone around to the front so as not to disturb the service in progress. Then, I saw him dart out into the vestibule; my worst thought was that he had seen the girls go out and wanted to catch them to give them the boxes he had packed. I hoped—ashamed to say I didn't pray—that they would escape him somehow. The anger of a moment ago had melted into regret; the poor girl had been given the pendant as a gift or possibly as payment, probably knowing at the time it had been stolen, but not from where or from whom. She had figured it out because my reaction gave me away, and now she was gone. Embarrassed? Ashamed? Certainly no more than I. The ushers carried the plates full of envelopes, checks, and loose change back to the table below the platform in front of me. The gold of my pendant shimmered among the coins.

I walked to the pulpit without my Bible or manuscript, heavy-hearted, wanting to just blurt out a confession to the world. *Those three hookers you are all despising are God's children. As much as we might wish they didn't exist, they do. And God brought them here for help. So let's stop this charade of a worship service right now and go after them.* But I didn't do that, of course. Instead I preached one of the shortest sermons on record at St. Fred's. I gave the congregation all that God had given me.

"I found a note slipped under my door today." I paused. "A note of encouragement." This seemed to relieve the people, though I don't know why. "It was from a person who cares for me very much, who doesn't judge me, who tries to understand. Do you know what it feels like to be judged? I do." On an ordinary day they would have related these words to my personal plight as a woman in ministry. But not this morning. They were thinking about the girls.

I read the text from memory.

"When I was about seven, my father arranged a surprise for my birthday. He said he wanted me to meet someone he knew from business. This was exciting, because my dad worked all the time and never seemed to have much of an interest in my life. But every now and then, he would do something completely unexpected to remind me that he loved me. So, we got in the car on Saturday afternoon, and we went to a place called the Boston Garden, to see a basketball game.

"They had these little windows there, I'm sure you know what they look like, and my dad told me to go up to the one that had a sign that said Will Call and tell the lady my name. She gave me an envelope with my name written on the outside; inside were two tickets: one for me, and one for Dad.

"We went into this huge arena and kept going down, down, passing all the seated people, right down to the court level, where there was this cool parquet floor. Our tickets were special, Dad said, because they were given to him by one of the players. When they came out for warm-ups in their green-and-white suits, one of them came over to where we were sitting and spoke to me by name. He asked me how I liked the seats. I was just in awe at the size of this man. People started crashing in around us, holding out stuff for him to sign. He signed a few things, and then took me out on the court, let me dribble a little, and my dad took our picture together. This player had to pick me up, because if we stood next to each other his head would be way out of the frame. That's when he told me his name was Larry Bird. I laughed and thought it was a joke at first, because I thought he kind of looked like one."

The crowd stirred, enjoying the story. Jameson Kerry had reentered and was quickly walking down the side aisle. He whispered something to Derrold Hamber, and the two of them went back out. I took this as a bad sign.

"I still have the picture, of course. And the envelope, and the ticket stub, and the autographed ball, safely put away in my parents' house back in Boston. Larry Bird scored forty-two points in that game, and the Celtics beat the Lakers in overtime. But the funny thing is, it was *years* before I realized how big a deal this was, how big a star Larry Bird was, and how big a treasure I had. And I thought about it this morning, when I got that little note with my name on it. You know what the treasure is, right? It's not what you're think-ing—the personalized memorabilia—though it's probably worth a small fortune by now."

I waited, watching them think. But I couldn't wait too long; I had to get back to the office and deal with the mess that was waiting for me before things really got out of hand.

"The *real* treasure, friends, was the day I spent with my dad. He gave me his undivided attention that day. Popcorn, ice cream, anything I wanted. He's a broker, and he's met a lot of famous people, but I didn't know it back then.

All I knew was that he had set aside that one day to share with me the riches of his kingdom. And now, looking back, I can't think of anything more valuable than that—to know the love of a father, who knows all my faults, and still makes me feel like I'm the only person in the world that matters. What would that be worth to you?" Their eyes showed that I had connected. The truth was hitting home.

I read the text again, slowly, with emphasis.

"Would you trade all that you have to gain this treasure? That's what Jesus is asking. You can answer that question for yourself. But to it I will add another: How tragic would it be to find that God had placed such a treasure right under our noses—and we paid it no mind? To think that he would bless us with his presence, here at St. Fred's, and we were too preoccupied with our own affairs to notice? That God, having already given us all we could ever want or need, would suddenly and inexplicably give us even *more*—the opportunity to be used by him to bless others who are less fortunate—only for us to ignore what he wants to do right here in our church?"

The question confused them. To be honest, it confused me. I wanted to talk about the pool without talking about the pool. How could anyone understand that? The sermon, which was nothing more than an effective illustration—had peaked and was fizzling out.

"So Mr. Lutz, if you don't mind, please close the service with prayer after the final hymn. I need to excuse myself to tend to some young women the Lord sent to our church this morning." And with that, I fled through the vacant choir loft, not looking back.

I found Hamber and Kerry conversing in the center of the office area. There was no sign of the girls.

"Miss Donovan, this simply must stop." Hamber was stern, intentionally intimidating.

"I'm sorry? I . . . I don't understand."

Kerry's face was ashen, his mouth tight.

"These young lady friends of yours tried to rob us. Mr. Kerry here found them attempting to force their way into the basement when they heard him coming. It's locked, of course, so he had them cornered."

"They gave the excuse that you said it would be all right," Kerry added.

"But . . . where are they now?"

"I went to get Mr. Hamber, and when I came back, they were gone," said Kerry.

"But these girls just needed help. I can't imagine they were trying to steal anything."

"Really?" said Hamber in a mocking tone. He walked over to a side table and picked up an engraved pewter chalice that had been used by the priests during communion many years ago. "Mr. Kerry took this from them when he caught them."

I stared at the object, which we kept on display in the office on a high shelf. Were they really stealing? Or did they just want something to use to dip into the pool? "I—I—" Before I could find an answer, the phone rang.

"The church will be secured during services from now on," Hamber said. "And a member of the board will be on duty to watch the building during worship services. We plan to install an alarm as well. All this is your fault, Carla, for turning this place into a hospital."

I could say nothing in response. Wasn't the church supposed to be a hospital of sorts—for sinners—or a hotel for saints? The phone had stopped ringing.

"These kinds of people just can't walk in here like they own the place," he continued.

But wasn't it God's place? Couldn't he invite anyone he wanted?

"If we're not careful, we'll lose this church, Carla. People will stop coming if the riffraff are free to roam about the halls. It's bad enough that they defile the sanctuary during worship. I'm sure you'll agree that we need to raise the bar here. Ungodly people are not welcome, do you understand? Just look at what this neighborhood has become—is *that* what you want to become of our church?"

I glanced into the benevolence room to see the boxes that Kerry had so lovingly prepared, and my heart sank.

"See to it that my directives are followed." With that pronouncement, Hamber led Kerry, still tight-lipped, from the room.

Stunned and ashamed, I began to weep. What was happening? No way could I tell the board about the pool now. What was I going to do?

I walked to the blinking light on the message machine and pressed the button, hoping it might be one of the girls we had so poorly treated that morning. Could anything be done for them now, or had we wasted the chance they had given us, driving them far from the courts of God forever?

The message was not good news. It was from Michael, just finishing up his service. He wanted me to know that Carmine Russo was dead.

PART 3:

DO YOU WANT TO BE MADE WELL?

CHAPTER FIFTEEN

I GREETED THE SHEEP with reserve, a more human response to the situation, this weekly ritual which I usually masked with a chipper ministerial tilt-of-the-head congeniality, like politicians do at fund-raisers, caring nothing for the splashes of flattery cascading from the lips of those who write the checks. Such inauthenticity is permitted at the front door of the church, where anything less would be considered rude, but this morning I could not muster so much as a smile. Grieving inside at the harsh rebuke handed down in the back room, the tragic (though not unexpected) death of Mr. Russo, and distracted by fears of what might have happened to the girls, I simply shook the hands and hoped it would all end soon. There were many compliments, more than usual, though they were the vague kind: good sermon, I really enjoyed that, you gave us something to think about with that one. *Don't tell me when I've preached a good sermon,* I thought, *because I know what's good and what's not.* Such thoughts were indicative of my attitude. The compliments probably stemmed from the fact that we were getting out of worship early because of my brief remarks, and the day was brimming with crisp light. Only Al Lintz had to ostentatiously check his watch and frown. Not a single soul said anything about the girls.

Retreating to my study, I phoned Shekinah and was captured by the answering machine. It was no surprise. At Shekinah, the welcome center opened at eight, the early service was at eight-thirty, Sunday school was at nine-thirty, and the second service began at eleven. Michael had probably scooted out during the offering to call me; it was almost noon, and he would still be preaching. I didn't bother to leave a message.

I sat there, biting my nails, listening to the ticks of the cheap wall clock in the empty church. I felt the urgent need to do something, as if decisive action could erase the tragic events of the morning, but I had no clue what to do, which only made me more anxious. I didn't know when Mr. Russo had passed away—last night? This morning? Probably the latter, since Michael would have had a message when he got home from his parents' house if it had been last night. Or maybe it was in the middle of the night—too late to call him. No point in going to the hospital. Should I go to the home? No, it wasn't my place to do that. Should I swing by Shekinah and go with Michael? No, weird as it sounds, that would be presumptuous: he had his flock, and I had mine. The Russos didn't even know me. And since Michael's message didn't provide clear instructions, I decided to leave things to him.

I walked around the office like a mouse in a maze. There were the boxes Jameson Kerry had packed. My thoughts turned to the girls. They were running from some person named Richie, most likely their pimp, who they suspected had done something to Marita. Where would they go? There was only one place I could think of. If I could find them, I might be able to take them to Sister Louise, who could surely provide safety and possibly treatment. In retrospect I realized that this was a reckless course of action, but acting on the impulse seemed to ease my distressed mind.

I drove home, changed into jeans and a white, long-sleeved T-shirt, fed Motorhead, and heated up the square of lasagna Mrs. Montefiore had insisted I take home. The passing of time often can reveal the stupidity of our ill-conceived intentions, but as I nibbled at the edges of the steaming square, still too nervous to eat, I became only more resolved. My own church was not the least bit concerned for the harvest. Yet, who was worse? I was concerned, but had done nothing about it. My good intentions in ministry, long ago forsaken, rose up to condemn me now. I hung up the robe in its usual place on the back of the bathroom door, wondering if I could ever wear it again. Robes were for the sterile confines of the church, which discussed and rehearsed the practice of religion during convenient, scheduled intervals. With all that practice, I should be more than ready for the real thing.

🜄　🜄　🜄

Jesus thought so little of his reputation with the religious leaders that he touched lepers, joined Samaritan women in conversation, and even presided at a party at the home of a well-known tax collector, so what was I worried about? Still, I parked well down the street, fearing that lightning might strike ere I crossed the threshold into this den of iniquity.

The Dutchman was decorated almost tastefully in rich red tones, much like a fashionable Italian restaurant. A decent crowd had already gathered to watch the ball game on a TV that was suspended in the corner behind the bar, one of those burnished wood counters with a brass footrest running along the bottom. Isabella saw me and waved with delighted surprise. I did not smile and tried to avoid eye contact with the other patrons. I was all business.

"Have you seen three call girls this morning? One's name is Sabila."

"You know them?" Isabella asked. It was obvious that she did.

I explained the circumstances of the morning encounter at St. Fred's, leaving out the unpleasant details of their flight. "And you haven't seen Marita either?"

She shook her head slowly. A few of the men had crowded around us, listening.

"You the lady with the pool?" one of them asked from behind me. "I got this back problem . . ."

I sighed, trying to contain my impatience. It was perfectly logical that I would be asked such questions, since I myself had drafted Isabella to find candidates for our research, and since Paul Delvecchio, whom I knew frequented this bar, had been telling the whole world. I clicked off possible responses in my mind, deciding to calmly explain that my first concern was for these girls, and then we could talk about the pool. But when I turned to face the man, my professional airs quickly evaporated.

"*You!*" I yelled, flabbergasted.

The man stepped back, shocked.

"This is the guy that was feeling up Marita in the alley!" I shouted to Isabella, and sensed an immediate reduction in volume to the conversations around me as a bar full of ears inclined to listen. The man was already so inebriated that he couldn't recognize me, and he showed no inclination to defend himself.

"His back hurts because I stomped on it outside when he came after me!" I shouted in disgust to anyone who was listening.

"You must be wrong; he hurt his back and lose his job, that's why he drinking."

Her innocent complicity infuriated me. "Isabella, just stop and listen. I listened to you, so now you listen to me." I tried to calm down, but my nerves were frayed, and my skin tingled with heat and anger. "He's drinking because he's a drunk, and that's probably why he lost his job, and why he doesn't want to work, and why he's preying on good-hearted souls like you."

At this outcry, the man stepped forward, thrusting out his chest the way male toads inflate their throats to impress the ladies, so close that I noticed the stains on the lapels of his cheap jacket. "You better shut up," he slurred.

"Oh, this is just ridiculous!" I threw up my arms and rolled my eyes dramatically. I stared him down. "So, you like to pick on girls, you loser?"

His face showed a tremendous capacity to redden, even beyond the effects of the alcohol. This fact seemed to energize me further, and I resumed the verbal assault. "Didn't you learn your lesson before?" I was nearly out of control, done in by my own exhaustion and pent-up frustration. "I doubt you could do much damage in your pathetic condition." My voice oozed with contempt.

The mockery was not being received well by the rest of the crowd, which shrunk back from me uncomfortably, whispering as I continued the tirade. This only infuriated me more, and I turned to face them. "What is it you people want from me, huh?" I screamed. "And what—is God supposed to hand out miracles like Easter candy, no matter how badly you screw up your lives? Sure, just go on getting sloshed and shooting up and turning tricks in some dirty alley and then wait for Carla to come to the rescue, is that it? Just go for a swim, and it'll be all better, just so you can go back to your selfish, sinful ways? Well, I've had it! Is anybody here really sick? I mean *really* sick—cancer, diabetes, anything?"

No one moved. I was making an incredible display, carried along by a continuous rush of adrenaline. It was as if I were outside my body, watching the whole scene, wanting to end it, but not until I had finished having my say. Incredibly, they kept listening, perhaps amazed that a lady preacher would barge onto their turf and just unload on them like this, or maybe my message was sinking in. I would have stopped if I could have, but I really didn't want to. It was as close to a sermon as any of these folks were ever likely to hear.

"I thought not," I said arrogantly. "Your problems are mainly of your own making, aren't they? And you know what? I'm no different from you—I'm probably going to get fired just for walking into this place, just for caring, just for trying to do something for you people. What do I get for my trouble, huh, can you tell me that? A pair of broken eyeglasses, cuts and bruises thanks to this oaf here. And the end of an honorable career, that's what. And I'll never get it back, you know that? I'll never get it back."

I felt a hand grip my arm just above the elbow. Too overwrought to realize it was Isabella's, I jerked my arm away and marched toward the exit. I stopped at the door and whirled around. "Now I'm going out to find those girls before something bad happens to them. Anyone want to join me?" They just stared at me, amazed, and I bolted out of the saloon like Marshal Dillon from *Gunsmoke* chasing down a band of cattle rustlers.

♦ ♦ ♦

Misdirected anger is the worst kind, because once it is spent, then comes a flood of regret. Halfway to my Cavalier I stopped in the middle of the street, contemplating going back with an apology: *Please forgive me for my tirade. I'm under a lot of stress and concerned about these four scared teenagers. I never meant to insult any of you,* I would say. But that would have made me appear even sillier in their eyes. The truth was, I was a tight little ball of pent-up frustration, angry with myself for neglecting the very thing I had a moment ago so self-righteously proclaimed. Did I *really* care? Or, did I care only when caring presented no risk to Carla? How astonishing and revealing that I hadn't even asked the girls their names. I was mad at myself, too, for not standing up to Hamber. So it would have done no good to go back to the bar and apologize to those people. Let them think me the world's biggest hypocrite. It was probably true. The whole scene, as I replayed it in my mind, was laughable. But I wasn't laughing.

It is a peculiar phenomenon indeed that drives a person to watch opportunities blow past her like the wind, then overreacts when the chance is gone and nothing good can be done. Not unlike the preschooler in his first soccer game—who lags just behind the kid with the ball, then runs to the goal once it is kicked as if he were truly part of the game—I had been on the fence, waiting for someone to push me over to one side or the other. And now that I had finally decided to jump off, there was no one left on the playground, and I was throwing a fit, to make sure no one came back to play with me. I would have made a landmark study for an ambitious psychoanalyst, had one been remotely interested in whatever drove me to such folly. "Donovanism," the report would read, "a debilitating affectation of the human thought process that cultivates self-doubt in gargantuan proportions, triggering irrational, compulsive, self-destructive behavior and isolation in thirty-something-year-old ordained females." At least I would become famous.

But this was no time for the paralysis of analysis. Marita was missing, and her three friends might be in danger. Worse, the guy who frightened them so much might well have been the one who broke into my house. Suddenly, my pool problem seemed far away. Carmine Russo was dead, and it seemed foolish to pursue such fantasies any longer in the face of real danger. I strapped myself in the car and began to scour the streets I should have known by now from hours of ministry in them. If I was lucky, I might come across the girls or someone who had seen them. I wouldn't play the hero for long though; if nothing turned up quickly, I planned to call the police. At least I could give them a lead and a name—Richie—in connection with the robbery. And I would have satisfied myself that I had tried to help in some small way.

I drove slowly, overwhelmed by the deplorable condition of the neighborhood, as if seeing it for the first time. I tried to imagine it a generation ago, when the dilapidated homes were new, and children played in the streets without fear for their safety. It was still a quaint place, but time had taken its toll: sidewalks were cracked and split by weeds; trash was scattered on curbsides, blown into the road by the wind; porches sagged; weather-beaten houses suffered from neglect. Many good people lived here, I knew, people who worked hard at difficult jobs and who made just enough money to get by. But there were also others: the ones who had fallen into drugs and crime, juvenile delinquents, drop-outs, operators from parts unknown who preyed upon the locals' misfortune. As I looked into the windows, searching for any sign of Marita or her friends, I prayed quietly for those inside, whoever they were.

I made my way through parallel streets, then doubled back and criss-crossed the same blocks on the intersecting roads. There was no sign of the girls. A few cars passed me, and I stared the drivers down but recognized not one of them. I was only ten blocks from my house, but I was the stranger here.

A somber grief captured my spirit. I was past the anger now, possessed by an uncomplicated sadness. The neighborhood had changed, but our church had stubbornly refused to minister to the needs of this new generation. Hamber's attitude of suspicion and resentment was born in isolation and nurtured by years of separation. I had fallen into the same trap—me, Carla—the kid who never lived up to expectations, the adult who chose the untrod path, the beggar who dedicated her life to helping other beggars find bread. I realized that I had traded a life of sacrificial ministry for the antiseptic life of the Pharisee, and it had made me miserable. I shepherded a group of nice people who had no idea what they were missing. And what had I done about it? Not a thing—because I wanted their approval. I wanted to be accepted, assured, admired. I wanted to be just like them.

I pulled over to the side and began to pray hard, harder than usual, asking God to do something to show me that all was not yet lost, that there was hope for me, and for St. Fred's—that this community could be redeemed. I was struck by a thought, a Spirit-planted thought—a revelation that is supposed to come upon all of us in prayer but which had happened only rarely to me—a conviction that what I was seeing around me was happening *because of our church, not in spite of it.* In the absence of light, the darkness had enshrouded this place, and only the shining of a true light could dispel it. An incarnation. A rebirth. An epiphany. In that moment I didn't care what it would cost me— *Please God, please let me find those girls!*

When I looked up, I saw a broken-down grocery and liquor store across the street.

I hopped out of the car and ran to the door. There were two small boys hanging around in the little yard, throwing sticks and rocks around. I pulled on the aluminum screen door and pushed my way inside.

It was dark and cool. The linoleum beneath my feet had worn away. The scuffed path led to a counter where a balding African-American man sat on a stool reading the Sunday paper. He smiled at me and asked if he could help, and I leaned over the counter.

"I'm looking for some young women," I said, my voice wavering. "One of them is taller than me; two of them are Hispanic, the other—"

"I know them," he said, rather disgusted. The corners of his mouth turned down.

"And . . . you've seen them?"

"No. Not usually during the daytime."

I hesitated. "Thank you for your help, sir. By the way, I'm Carla Donovan, pastor of St. Fred's church. Here's my card. If I can do anything for you, please let me know. And I'd appreciate a call if you happen to see the girls."

He beheld me suspiciously, then nodded. I got the impression he didn't know quite what to say.

I headed for the door, noticing other men, black and Hispanic, all young, perhaps a half-dozen of them, milling around in the aisles. They didn't seem to be paying much attention to me.

I walked briskly to the Cavvy and started the engine. Might as well give up, call the police. What else was there to do?

There was a strange, sharp prick at the back of my neck, and my eyes flashed to the rearview mirror. What I saw there nearly stopped my heart.

The man made no attempt to hide his face. Against his dark skin I could see the glint of the long blade. His voice was high but menacing.

"I'm very sorry, but there has been a change of plans this afternoon. Let's get going now, exactly as I say. Don't be foolish and try to run. You'll not get far if you do. Just do as I say, and I won't hurt you. Go ahead, put the car in reverse. That's good. Nice and easy."

CHAPTER SIXTEEN

I DROVE SLOWLY AND obediently as directed by the intruder who retracted the knife and relaxed in the back seat. He was instantly pontificating, and I feared provoking him by missing a turn, but I dared not interrupt. From the rambling discourse, I discerned that this must be none other than Richie, and as far as he was concerned, these streets were his realm—and they and all who entered them belonged to him.

At length he indicated that I should pull in to a narrow driveway beside a wreck of a wooden structure in the heart of a particularly seedy area not far removed from my own neighborhood. Two thugs milled about in front of this drooping house, which might have been painted white at one time, but now sported colorful graffiti and what could only be described as obscene street art all along its front and sides. My hands trembled badly, and I felt a tightness in my chest as I made the turn. I had the distinct impression that it was not Richie's intention to harm me, but if creating sheer terror was his objective, he was definitely succeeding.

We got out, and Richie asked for the keys. As soon as I handed them over, he tossed them to one of the thugs, who jumped into the car and drove off. The other stood at attention like some kind of ghetto soldier as Richie led me inside. I stopped at the door and confronted my abductor, scared to death.

"Look, I don't know what you want, but I can help, if it's money—"

"Hush, lady. I know you can help. That's a problem with me; you help too much. Get inside. I said I won't hurt you."

I walked stiffly into the broken-down house. It was filthy, with sleeping bags lying on the floor along with junk food bags, wrappers, and cups. There was no power, or at least no lights, and no furniture; a foul smell permeated the place.

He waved me over to a wall and told me to sit, which I did. For the first time, I was able to get a good look at him: narrow face, bony, with long dark fingers, cropped black hair, several earrings, a suit jacket (double-breasted with no shirt underneath it), dark slacks, and black boots. I shivered at the thought of what he might be planning to do.

"I heard around town that you have plans to clean up the neighborhood. I advise you to forget about that. Consider this a warning: stay away from my girls. My business is well established in the community, much more desired than yours. I understand you're relatively new around here, and so I'm going easy on you. Future indiscretions will not be tolerated."

"What have you done with the girls who came to my church?"

"It's not any of your concern. I will tell you that they are safe—transferred to another location where they can work under more controlled conditions. They bring me too much business to cut them loose. Besides, I provide certain incentives to keep them on the job."

Indignation replaced fear, and I stood up to him. "You're a drug dealer, then."

"Wait now, I didn't say that." He held up his hands defensively, grinning.

"You didn't have to say it," I snarled. "That's how you keep girls like Marita working for you—you get them hooked and supply them with drugs."

"Yeah." He smiled wickedly. "I'm an equal-opportunity employer . . . if you're interested."

"You make me sick," I said defiantly.

Richie didn't seem to appreciate my attitude. His smile faded. "Consider this fair warning. I'm not a violent person. But you stay out of my hair. Or I'll put you out of business, hear?" He turned his back on me, walked out, and locked me in.

Hours passed. Night came softly and swallowed the house. I wondered if Michael was worried about me. I worried about my car. I imagined the thugs ransacking my house, terrorizing my poor cat. I paced back and forth, checking every door and window. There was no escape, nothing to do but wait in the darkness.

I heard the growl of custom engines in the street and voices on the porch outside. One of Richie's comrades unlocked the door and called me outside.

"Come with me. We'll be needing the house soon," he said. I nearly choked at the smell of beer on his breath.

He escorted me to a car, not mine; it was gold with dark-tinted windows, mag wheels, and some kind of chrome thing protruding from the hood. I had an inclination to run, but what was to stop this brute from gunning me down? I would fight for my life if it came to that, but there was no need to provoke him.

He tied my hands with an elastic cord and sat me down hard in the passenger seat. I decided not to speak, though I wanted to tell the goon how much he disgusted me. At this point I had lost any shred of Godly love that might have been lurking in my tired spirit.

He reached over and took my glasses, tossing them out into the driveway. *Great.* Then he tied a bandana across my eyes, as if it were necessary. I felt a little sick as the car rolled out into the street. It was incredibly loud, and I almost laughed at the thought of this goofy Joe Cool cruising the mean streets in this absurd vehicle.

When the car finally stopped, I waited for him to walk around the car and let me out. He pulled off the blindfold, cut the cord around my wrists, and pushed me down in the dirt. The ground was hard and cold. I honestly thought he was going to shoot me in the back of the head, and my muscles were paralyzed. I prayed; then I heard his heavy footsteps and the opening of the car door. I managed to look behind me in time to see him drive away.

Relieved but immediately aware of how tired and sore I was, and hungry, I scanned the horizon to get my bearings. I couldn't make out anything. There were stars, and lights in the distance, and large, blurry objects nearby. I was standing in a parking lot—no, a junkyard. I was close enough to one of the cars to tell it was mangled and rusted. I headed for the distant lights, weaving my way around the cars, bumping into them and tripping over parts and rocks beneath my feet. I came at last to a tall chain-link fence, and from there I was at a loss. There was no sound of traffic. I sat down, leaning against the fence. I figured it must be after midnight, how much I couldn't tell. I decided it was best not to wander any farther, aware that a practically blind woman in a place like this might be easy pickings for marauders such as inhabited these parts. For the moment I was safe. I would try to sleep now and find my way home in the morning.

◆　◆　◆

When dawn came, I groped my way along the fence that led to a small shack and a drive-through gate that was closed but not locked. I pushed it open and embarked along the dirt road leading to the highway. I could hear a car pass by now and then, and eventually I could see them zooming along. Hopefully, I would find a kind soul to offer me a ride back to town. My back hurt badly again, and the pain was aggravated by my uneven steps caused by one broken heel. I removed the other shoe and smashed it on a large rock embedded in the road until its heel dropped off too.

Once on the highway, I caught a glimpse of a white blur coming toward me. It hardly made a sound, and it floated like a cloud, slowing as it approached. I side-stepped out of the way as the driver pulled over, his tires scrunching the gravel along the shoulder. I peered in. The driver was a young man wearing a T-shirt that read His Pain, Your Gain in huge block letters large enough even for me to read. This was a godsend, for sure.

"You look like you could use a lift," he said. His voice was sweet, and my heart leaped with emotion at his invitation. My eyes brimmed with tears as I jumped into the car.

The engine purred as we sat on the side of the highway. I could not see his features clearly, but he struck me as kind of grungy, with scraggly dark locks and heavy stubble. A torrent of words poured forth as I described my plight. "Wow. There's a bunch of people looking for you, Rev. It's all over the radio," he said.

He told me that he could get me home in about a half-hour. We decided first to stop and call the police to tell them I was okay. A mile or so down the road a small filling station with old-style pumps beside the new ones was open, and the man gave me a quarter to make the call. As it turned out, I was told to wait there and an officer would pick me up in a few minutes. I went back to the car to inform my Good Samaritan.

He rolled down the window as I walked up. "I can't thank you enough for your help," I said. "If there's anything I can ever do for you . . ."

He seemed to blush, though I couldn't quite tell for sure. "No, no, I'm only happy to have saved you," he said, chuckling to himself. "I may stop by the church one of these days though. I bet you'll have an interesting sermon."

I hesitated, not wanting to pry. "Are you a . . . uh, do you go to church around here?" I stammered.

"Well, churches fascinate me, but I'm not really into the membership thing. I'd like to visit them all, but to be honest, I don't sense that I'd be welcome in a lot of places." It was then I noticed him fiddling with what I thought might be a gold cross glinting in the lobe of his left ear.

I smiled. "Frankly, you'll probably get some strange looks at St. Fred's if you show up dressed like that, but that's okay. I'll introduce you as my special guest."

We shook hands as the police cruiser drove up, and he sped away, apparently not wanting to speak to the officer. Suddenly I realized to my deep regret that, once again, I had been so self-absorbed with my troubles that I had neglected to ask his name.

The patrol car offered a powerful sense of security, so much so that I wondered if I could muster the energy to pull myself out of the seat once the officer delivered me home. I gazed out the window at the beauty of the spring morning, ignoring the squawking of the radio, until I thought I heard "St. Fred's" blurt from the little box amid a stream of words unintelligible to the untrained ear.

"What was that?"

The officer seemed surprised that I spoke. "Oh, just some kind of disturbance at a church somewhere; I think they had a fire or something earlier. Probably a minor crowd-control problem. No need for me to respond; I'm not close to there."

"St. Fred's?"

"Uh, yeah, that was it."

"That's my church! We need to get over there!" I cried, recalling Richie's threat.

"You've been through a lot, Miss. And we still need to file a report—"

"Go! Go! Go!" I shrieked.

The officer wriggled uncomfortably in his seat, then casually reached for the radio and pressed the button. He relayed his intentions to the dispatcher.

In what seemed like only a few minutes we were whizzing past my house and coming to a sudden stop right in front of the church. It was like pausing a videotape—there was a fire truck parked along the side of the building, and a crowd, which consisted of two groups on either side of the street totaling about twenty people, who stopped and gawked as we came barreling in. I immediately popped out of the car, and the scene started moving again, a fluid explosion of sound and color. A white van with a satellite dish on top, from one of the TV stations, was parked curbside.

Shouts permeated the clear air, and several figures ran toward me, shouting my name. At the head of the line was Isabella Ruiz, and I felt the claws of Miranda's tiny fingers pawing my legs. Surrounding us and closing in fast were faces I recognized from the bar. It was overwhelming and confusing at the same time.

From somewhere beyond this joyous throng came the equally threatening thunder of Derrold Hamber's voice, calling my name. The welcoming committee backed away, and I saw Our Leader approach, accompanied by a thin person wearing a white polo shirt with some writing on it I couldn't discern.

"Miss Donovan, I know you must have a good explanation for all of this," he snarled, "but before we attempt to unravel the mystery, this gentleman has a question about the pool."

This was very bad. "I'm sure I'm not the best person to answer that—"

"Oh, I'm sure you are!" Hamber barked. "As a matter of fact, this acquaintance of yours, this Ms. Ruiz, has already explained matters quite well to the greater metropolitan area." He was speaking through gritted teeth, snarling in Isabella's direction. "According to her, you—"

His lecture was interrupted by Corning Lutz, who called out from the top of the stairs in his ragged voice, "Derrold, it's true! The pool is full of water!"

A television reporter in a particularly snazzy blouse and short skirt appeared behind Hamber with a cameraman, but before I could say anything or Hamber could resume his discourse, the thin guy in the white shirt entered the fray, poking a pencil at Hamber and declaring, "Operating a pool without a permit is a violation of the New York State Sanitary Code, Sub-Part Six-Dash-One, Point Four. I am empowered by the state of New York to close this facility immediately. Should you fail to comply with the items cited on my inspection report within thirty days, you will be subject to—"

"Shut up, you idiot!" Hamber yelled. "We have no intention of opening this pool!"

The little man held his ground. "It is clear, sir, that you *have* opened this pool. It's my job to see that the safety of the public is ensured, and that, sir, is what I am endeavoring to do."

Hamber seethed and pointed his finger into the man's chest. "This is private property, and you have no right to be here just because you saw the news this morning and decided to put on your cape and play Super-Bureaucrat! You will not enter this church, and you will not do an inspection, and we will not need a permit— because we are not opening this pool!" He was steamed, and it was almost comical. Then he turned to me, and I swallowed the tiny giggle that was bubbling up in my throat. I was light-headed and weirdly giddy.

"Carla, you and I need to go inside and have a talk with the rest of the board right now."

I was so famished that I responded without fear. "Okay, but not now. I'm kinda tired, and . . ."

He grabbed my arm. The officer, who all this time had been trying to disperse the crowd, slipped between us. Isabella took hold of my other arm in a vice grip.

"Are you okay?" she squealed in my ear. "I tried to find you last night but you no came home. We all felt so worried for you out in the streets. And then we heard on the news about the church on fire, and we came running."

Conscious that the camera was capturing this lunacy on tape, I tried to calm Isabella down. "Listen, it's okay. I'll just talk to them for a few minutes, and we'll settle this." I turned to Hamber. "What caused the fire?"

"Arson," he sneered. "But apparently there was very little serious damage done. It seems the *swimming pool* in the basement somehow overflowed and saturated the carpet down the hall, which stopped the fire from spreading. Now, you wouldn't know anything about that, would you, Miss Donovan?" His face was a blur, but his voice buzzed with sarcastic hostility.

I could only stand there blinking, trying to focus, processing the words. "You say the pool . . . *overflowed?*"

The officer had now turned his attention to Isabella, since Hamber had taken the hint and released his grip on my arm. She was fussing at him excitedly in Spanish. "He say we start the fire!" she shouted in mangled English.

"Mr. Hamber, you can't be serious," I said. I was still reeling, relieved to be free despite the bizarre situation, visualizing a picture of God in heaven waving his hand, saying, "No, no, Richie, we'll have none of that at my church," and summoning the Dead Sea water to surge against the flames. I spurted out an inappropriate laugh. "I must be going crazy," I said to myself, then doubled over, laughing uncontrollably.

In a moment I recovered and became aware that everyone was staring at me.

"Well, for a while I *thought* I was going crazy," I added, speaking in the general direction of the camera, "after this pimp had his bouncer dump me in a junkyard last night." This statement generated shrieks of amazement from the throng. The reporter was now trying to wedge her way in closer.

I was offended that Hamber completely ignored my remark and chose instead to verbally assault Isabella. "Then what are these people doing here, if they have nothing to do with this? Why are they so interested? Only yesterday we foiled a robbery attempt, and now this happens? What a coincidence. Any fool can see what's going on here. This woman, who apparently holds some sway with these people, has been taking charity from us for weeks, and when I confront her about this malicious act of treachery upon God's property, she announces to the whole world on television that we can all go to the devil. It's madness, and slander. I won't tolerate this kind of treatment from such a person."

The put-down didn't evoke a retort from Isabella, but the slur wasn't lost on me. I was strung out, exhausted, and emotionally wrecked, so I had no power to think of a politically correct response. "This *woman,* as you call her, Mrs. Isabella Ruiz, is a fine person who has more compassion in her little toe than our entire church board combined." I said. "All you care about is your precious reputation, which, as far as I can tell, ought to be pretty well shot after today."

"You can make all the snide remarks you want, Miss Donovan," he snorted, "but this is *our* church, and we'll conduct its affairs with dignity, if you please! All you've brought is disgrace to our congregation, you and these . . . these *people!*"

The reporter nosed her way forward. "Tell us again about the pimp, Reverend. It was a *pimp* who abducted you, is that right, Reverend Donovan?"

"How do you suppose God feels about *these people,* huh, Mr. Hamber?" I demanded. The reporter shoved her fuzzy microphone in front of my face, and I pushed it away. "Has it ever occurred to you that he might actually *care* about them?"

"And what about those who pay your salary?" he bellowed. "Are they somehow less entitled to your pastoral services? You seem to be more interested in wallowing in the streets with the dregs of society than in doing your job!"

I stepped even closer to him menacingly, prompting the officer to grab me by the shoulders. He had big muscles, and the embrace wasn't altogether unpleasant, but I twisted free. The reporter was still looking for a crevice in which to insert herself, and all I could see was the top of her mussed head from behind the policeman's bulging bicep, as she whined in muffled tones, "The pimp, Reverend, what did he do to you? Our viewers need to know—"

"My *job?*" I screamed at him. "Do you have any appreciation for what I've been through in the past twenty-four hours?"

"Certainly!" he shot back. "We all know about your little sojourn down to the local watering hole as soon as church was over. Is that any way for a minister to behave? Is that any way for a *lady* to behave?"

"That's it," exclaimed the officer at last. "You'll have to take this inside now. The party's over. All you people can go to your homes," he called out, but there was now such an uproar in the small crowd that his order had no effect. Some of them, it seemed, were pushing even closer in, enraged at Hamber. "I think you had better come with me, sir," the officer advised the chairman.

"Okay, but she's coming along!" The *she* was me, but I was too fed up to continue the fiasco.

"Forget it! I'm going home to my cat!" I yelled defiantly.

"You'll come right now and stand before the board!" Hamber shouted as the officer tried to pull him away.

"Don't talk to me like that! I'm not your slave!" The people whooped with pleasure, and I heard at least one "Amen!"

"That's insubordination, insubordination," he sniveled. "There's no debating this now—you're fired!"

"Fine. *I quit!*" A mighty shout arose from the decidedly pro-Carla crowd.

"Have your things cleared out before tomorrow!" he called out as the policeman whisked him up the front steps. Sirens blared, and two more patrol cars appeared on the scene. The people were flaring out now in the street, and I saw the other cluster of people across the way: probably church members, who, I assumed, had come down out of curiosity or concern.

"Are we live? Are we live now?" The reporter anxiously positioned herself in front of the building, desperate to get her update in before the drama played out.

Isabella, who had retreated with Miranda into the background, came forward to give me a hug. Her body shook with sobs as she searched for words to explain her actions. She was distraught, feeling responsible for the whole fiasco. I held her at arm's length and tried to offer consolation and an overdue apology for my own outburst at the bar. Human beings are such fragile creatures. She quieted herself and nodded, acknowledging but not accepting my judgment that it was all for the best.

"Let's get out of here," a voice whispered. An arm reached around my shoulder. It was Michael.

I said a final goodbye to Isabella and promised we would talk later. We walked to his car, me leaning on Michael, my legs heavy and sore. I became dizzy with hunger; my head throbbed from eye strain. The events of the past twenty-four hours seemed surreal, as if the traumatic experience of the night might never have happened, and yet its devastating effects remained, landing on me all at once, crushing me under its weight. I was suddenly drifting, floating, finding it impossible to focus on anything, concentrating hard on simply putting one foot in front of the other.

"Did all that really just happen?" I asked.

"Yup," he said.

CHAPTER SEVENTEEN

MOTORHEAD'S TINY THROAT WAS hoarse from crying. He was half-crazed, scampering about the place, directionless, almost dog-like, euphoric at my return but also letting me know he didn't appreciate my extended absence. He finally leaped to the top of the kitchen table, then to the counter, and finally onto the curtains, which tore rather badly as a result, prompting Michael to make some cute remark, trying his best to lighten the mood. I ran to disengage Motorhead from the fabric, then stopped, realizing the curtains weren't mine anymore; they belonged to the church and were there when I moved in. *What a lousy attitude,* I thought, then excused myself from further self-flagellation, considering the circumstances.

I fed the cat and poked around in the refrigerator to meet my own need for nourishment, but I soon lost interest and let the door rattle shut. My headache was gone, and I no longer felt hungry. In fact, I didn't feel much like anything. Michael was asking questions; the words came into my head very softly, nearly inaudible. I sat at the table watching Motorhead wolf down his food. Perhaps he was more like a dog than I had thought.

What was I going to do now? There weren't many people in my life that I felt I could really count on. I had always had a good relationship with my father, but not a particularly close one, and we had grown apart in recent years, due to the challenges of my profession to which he could not really relate. I had certainly never been my mother's ideal daughter, and so I had cut the emotional cord early, which had only widened the breach. My parents seemed more like an aunt and uncle now, and our contacts were irregular and superficial. I knew it was partly my own fault, having become more distant with the years. It may have been the persecution complex I had developed, never revealing my true self for fear of criticism. I didn't miss my parents' natural scrutiny of my life, but in giving that away I lost some intimacy too. But now, I didn't know where else to turn. When the world crumbles around you, the first place you think of to take refuge is home.

"I need to go to Boston," I said out loud.

"I'll take you. When do you want to go?"

I stared at the blur of Michael's dark features. "I don't think that's a good idea."

"You don't have a car."

Oh. I sighed. Here was a true friend. There was a limit, I knew, to what I could ask of Michael, especially now, since I would probably be leaving the area. Was there anyone else? As far as church members were concerned, I had chosen to avoid close personal relationships in order to maintain some level of impartiality, which I felt was important to leadership, so there was no one to call. Ironically, the strategy had often backfired, because few people knew me well enough to support my positions, so I had rarely gone out on a limb. Instead, I had settled for hiding in the majority view, afraid to advance my own agenda. Look where playing it safe had gotten me!

My thoughts turned darkly to the revelation of the previous day. Would God answer my prayer, or not? Tears suddenly streamed down my face. What had become of my life? Michael said I should try to sleep, but forcing myself to rest never worked; the physical inactivity seemed to spark some chemical in my brain that produced anxiety. All I could think of was what I had lost—my job, my family, my friends, my self-respect. I felt violated and abused; I had been robbed, abducted, threatened, bullied. Even Isabella, despite her good intentions, was hurting now—because of me. And the regulars from The Dutchman—they had taken my side, it seemed, though their support this morning could have been attributed to loyalty to their bartender, resentment toward the establishment, a selfish curiosity about the so-called miracle pool, or simply the excitement of the controversy against the routine of their often regretful lives, and not necessarily because of my personal merit. Perhaps I belonged among them, part of the masses of those more sinned against than sinning who were forced to accept their lot because they did not have the resources or the fortitude to do otherwise. *Yeah, that was me.*

I looked down at Michael's hand, holding mine. He had proven faithful, and the time had come for both of us to lay our cards on the table. The thought of him frantically searching for me all night warmed my spirit, and I clung to the emotion. I attempted to banish the thought of leaving, taking no pleasure in the prospects of finding another pastoral position, especially after the debacle at St. Fred's. The search committee would talk to Hamber, and that would be that. Why even try? Maybe I should talk to Sister Louise about entering the convent . . . that way I would stay close to Michael. No, it was dishonest even to think of such a thing. I wasn't even Catholic anymore, for heaven's sake! I realized now that I was deeply depraved, too ashamed even to pray.

We talked. I would allow him to take me home to Boston—where, at minimum, I could have my optician fit me for some new glasses, since I had canceled the order on my contacts. The plan right now was for me to get some sleep, and Michael would take me to dinner later. Concerned for my safety, he invited me to stay the night at his parents' house, and I was seriously considering it, though I felt reasonably secure, since Mr. Delvecchio had fortified the place. Plus, I didn't think Richie would be making a repeat performance, since he had already gotten his message across, and I would be no threat to him now, though, no doubt, the hawkish newswoman had blabbed the word *pimp* to the watching world. I had declined to identify him even to the police, fearing he might retaliate in some way, not necessarily against me. But a guy who would set fire to a church was capable of anything. And I was worried about the girls. So I decided to call the cops and turn him in after all; at the very least, the cops could watch him—and my place—tonight.

After the phone call, I escorted a relieved Michael to the door and shuffled off to bed.

The next thing I heard was the doorbell. I strained to make out the glowing numbers on the bedside clock—had I really been lying here for nearly two hours? My body was stiff and sore. Moving my limbs was excruciatingly painful. I knew I should eat, whether I felt like it or not.

There was no one at the door, but when I opened it, an envelope fell inside. It was an official letter from the board accepting my resignation. It was printed in extraordinarily large boldface type. Were they sensitive to my poor eyesight, or did they just want to emphasize their point? In any case, I was to have all my belongings out of the office by Saturday night, since an interim pastor had already been secured and would be moving in on Sunday, right after the morning service. I was to leave my keys on the front desk. I could stay in the house for thirty days and would receive my normal compensation and insurance coverage during that time. It was signed by each member of the board. There was a postscript: arrangements had been made to drain the pool, and the health department had agreed to waive the penalties for operating without a permit; therefore the board would not be passing any fines on to me.

I crushed the note into a ball and threw it out on the lawn. They finally got me, after all.

◆ ◆ ◆

Michael took me to an elegant restaurant and spent way too much money for the companionship I provided. I was dreading the trip home to Boston, especially after calling my mother. Word of my dismissal provoked a restrained "how unfortunate, dear," which flowed seamlessly into the news that my sister had received a promotion, *while on maternity leave,* and was moving up to associate editor for another magazine owned by the publishing group, something called *Movers & Shakers,* having to do with the personal lives of high-profile, job-hopping "Baby Boomer" executives. Maybe I could land a job as a copy editor, Mother wondered aloud, or with all the travel Margaret will be doing, maybe I could be Ryan III's nanny—interviews were currently being scheduled. I decided not even to tell her about my all-expenses-paid night on the town, courtesy of the local crime lord.

"You've hardly touched your eggplant."

"I guess I'm just not hungry."

"You don't have to be hungry to eat, remember," he said with a wry smile.

I smiled back. "I'm sorry. I'm trying to get all the despair out of my system before tomorrow."

"So, why are you even going?"

It was a legitimate question. "To see my sister," I said, thinking this to be true. I hadn't really thought about *not* going home, assuming this was simply what one did when one's life fell apart. "She's one of those happy people who can make you believe there's good to be found in everything."

"Romans 8:28."

"Yeah. It comes naturally though. She probably doesn't even know the verse."

"Do you believe that?"

"What?"

He slowed down. "That all things work together for good to those who love God and are called according to his purpose?"

"Sure. It's in the Bible, isn't it?"

He didn't answer, but I thought he nodded. It was difficult to see.

"Isn't it?" I repeated.

"Yes, but . . ."

"But what?" Suddenly I became alert, anxious to know what was troubling him. Was this a chink in his spiritual armor? Was my misfortune so disastrous that he could see no hope, no promise to claim for me, that he could find no words of wisdom?

"I was just thinking of Carmine, that's all."

Of course. Lost in the sea of my misadventures was the hard reality of the funeral scheduled for Wednesday, which must have continually bobbed up in Michael's mind, as such things do with ministers until they're over. "Are you ready?" I asked.

"Kind of. The guy's life was a far better sermon than any I could give. I've got the drive back from Boston tomorrow to mull over it."

"It'll be okay, Michael. You know where he is. Death is a blessing for a Christian." It was good to play counselor to him for a change.

"Then why did we believe that anointing him with miracle water was what God wanted?"

I could tell from the strain in his voice that this question was really bothering him. "Gosh, Michael, we just assumed—"

"Well, we were wrong, weren't we?" he snapped.

This reaction was normal. I waited for a moment for him to calm down. "People are so attentive to grieving families, but no one thinks about the pastor in these situations, who feels he must be strong, even though it hurts to have lost a friend," I said.

"Who has to stand up there and say everything's fine when it's not."

"Romans 8:28," I said.

"Yeah."

We left the restaurant and arrived at my house rather early. There was an unfamiliar car parked two houses down, across the street. Over my objections, Michael walked right up and spoke with someone briefly who was sitting inside. "Everything's cool," he said, coming back to escort me to the front door. "I'll sleep better knowing you're being guarded," he said.

"So will I."

"Hey, Carla," he called out just before I went in, "you're not thinking of going home, like, *for good,* are you?" He sounded like a little boy.

I was touched by the intent of the question. "I can't say. But you know, all things work together for good . . ."

"Yeah, yeah, yeah," he said, laughing, as he walked back to the car.

◆　◆　◆

The next morning, Michael greeted me with his familiar intensity. "I've got this figured out," he said, accepting my suitcase. No "hello," no "how are you feeling today?"—just that.

"I guess I'm supposed to ask you to elaborate?"

He chuckled. "It's a long drive," he said.

"Save time for instructions on what not to say or do when you meet my mother."

We drove past St. Fred's slowly, and I asked him to go around the side so I could see the damage done by the fire. The brick wall was charred black almost halfway up, a basement window was knocked out, and debris was everywhere. "Hang on," I said. "I need to go in."

Michael and I went in the office entrance and down the basement stairwell. The pungent smell of smoke was heavy as we descended. The carpet in the lower hall was still damp, and I opened the door to the storage room where I assumed the fire had started. The window near the top of the wall was shattered, and most of the carpet was burned up, along with the draperies. Even without my glasses I could see that the aged posters had melted off the walls, along with the paint. The box of old ledgers was little more than ashes.

"Man, this must have been an oven," Michael said. "All they did was throw a bottle with gasoline and a torched rag through the window. With the door closed, it's a wonder the heat didn't cave this side of the building in. Metal door, concrete walls—"

"But the carpet didn't all go up," I said. "It's almost as if—"

"The water came to meet it, right here, before the fire went under the door."

"This is so weird," I said. "They probably doused the place with fire hoses to put it out."

"But you heard what the guy said—it was already out when they got here."

"They said the pool overflowed. What they meant was, it stopped the advance of the firewall. They probably still turned the hoses on the burning room."

We wandered in silence back out into the hall, our feet squishing on the soaked carpet. "Carla, there must have been a huge wave coming through here. How did that much water get out of the pool so fast?"

I pushed the open door to the pool room all the way open. "It's still full," I said.

Michael laughed in disbelief. "So, this thing spontaneously overflowed in response to the fire, then just receded?"

"Not spontaneously," said a rugged voice from behind.

"Mr. Delvecchio," I cried, recognizing the voice, but not the face in the dim light with my bad eyes.

He came out on the deck to greet us. "Remember that pipe I showed you, down in the filter room?"

I looked in the direction of the hatch in the floor. "Uh, huh."

"Well, somebody connected it. That's why there's no mystery here, as far as the fire department's concerned. The pool is full, so Hamber figured you had the thing fixed behind the board's back. They already questioned me and Joe. I couldn't say you hadn't done it, but we sure didn't do it for you. The fire department guy thinks somebody was in here when the fire started and went down and turned the valve."

"Wouldn't a fire extinguisher have made more sense?" I asked.

"Checked those. Only have one on each floor. Neither one works. We'll be getting a fine—your fault, Hamber said. He'll probably send you a bill."

"But how would someone get in here?" Michael asked.

Mr. Delvecchio shrugged. "I changed all the locks," he said. "Again, 'Carla had no alibi, she had been drinking.'"

"*Whoa!* Stop right there!" I shouted. "I was *not*—"

"I'm just telling you guys what they said, okay? I know what happened here, and so do you."

Michael and I looked at each other, afraid to say what we were thinking. We sloshed back down the hall in silence, and when we got upstairs I retold the story of my abduction to the kindly custodian.

"The good Lord was looking out for you, Reverend. There's a reason for all this. You'll see."

"Okay, I hear you. Just remember you're saying this to a person who's practically blind," I said. He laughed like someone who knew what he was talking about.

♦ ♦ ♦

We had driven for nearly ten minutes without speaking, until finally I broke the silence. "So, what do you have all figured out?"

"Oh, *that,*" he answered. "I was talking about Carmine. You were right, his death is a blessing. I was thinking of how many people believed in God because of how he lived with the cancer. It's an unbelievably long list. And more will be added to it tomorrow."

"So you have a peace about it," I said.

"Well, *no,* not yet. But I at least have something to help me deal with it. Sickness is related to the human condition—theologically, it's connected to sin, not necessarily to the person who is sick. There's no rhyme or reason to it—everyone and everything in creation is affected by it. God rescues us from the eternal consequences of sin, so death isn't final for the believer. The tragedy is not that a good person dies of cancer; the tragedy is when a person doesn't know that sin is the real sickness."

"That's what the head says. But will the heart ever accept it?"

He smiled. "Nope. That's why we believe in healing pools. We all die because we're all sinners. God decides when and how. We like to think he occasionally intervenes and spares us pain. But he is known best when his people respond to those who are suffering. It is a reflection of his goodness, his power at work in the redeemed."

"I guess you do have a pretty good jump on the sermon," I said.

"I'm not trying to preach to you. Just think with me for a minute. We did what we could for Carmine and the rest of them. But he wasn't healed. Nor were others. Why do you think that is?"

"Well, Marita kind of created her own problems. So did Ralph."

"Okay, so, does that mean God's not merciful?"

"No, no, it's just that. . ."

"What about Jess Petruski?"

I laughed. "You think he was really healed?"

"Yes. Because his healing was a witness to your friend Lutz."

I thought a minute. "Oh, so your theory is about *witness bearing.* Carmine in his sickness, Jess in his health. What about Ted?"

Michael shook his head. "No change . . . yet. But he's another one who does more good being sick than a hundred who are well."

"But Paul Delvecchio—"

"Paul Delvecchio went out and told everyone who would listen, according to my brother."

"And Miranda—"

"So, do you think Isabella hasn't given God the praise? The healing has only strengthened her faith at a time in her life when things aren't going so well."

"Cornelia—"

"Who boldly told what had happened to her before the whole church— and to *you*." I didn't quite catch the significance of the emphasis on my hearing her story.

"Me? What have *I* got to do with anything?"

"Well, c'mon, Carla; you needed a shot in the arm yourself, didn't you?"

I stiffened. "Maybe a little," I murmured.

"Don't you see the pattern here? It's not that God *will* heal anybody; it's that he *can*. That's what he wants us to know," he insisted. "That's what he wants *you* to know."

"So, what are you saying, that this whole thing is a sign from heaven . . . for *me?*"

"No, not just for you, for all of us."

It sounded good, but I wasn't interested in pursuing the matter; listening to Michael, I kept hearing the sound of my mother's voice.

CHAPTER EIGHTEEN

THE MANICURED LOTS OF Upper Falls made quite an impression on Michael, and I sensed seeing the place of my origins may have altered his opinion of me. He was tentative, apologetic, fearful of another insensitive trampling upon my fragile ego, and by the time we arrived at my parents' house, he was ready to turn back. It was refreshing to see how different he was when removed from the security of his natural habitat, but I had neither the energy nor the desire to explore this facet of his personality. I had my own demons to face.

"Oh, boy, won't this be a glad reunion," I muttered, seeing both parents' cars, along with my sister's, in the drive. "Looks like you get to meet Dad." I wondered if the family had convened not to gather around the wounded chick like mother hens, but to get a glimpse of Michael. He was already clearing his throat in preparation for the grand entrance.

"Is that him?"

I looked to the front porch. Dad had seen us drive up and had already come out to greet us. He stood with his hands on his hips, his feet spread wide, looking like a giant, though he was only about 5 feet, 7 inches. He was wearing a red flannel shirt and twill trousers, his typical stay-at-home-on-a-workday attire.

"That's him. Nervous?"

"Nah. Italians and Irishmen have a lot in common." Neither of us laughed at the weak joke.

"Stay close to Dad; he won't bite. Avoid Mother. No drooling over Margaret."

"Gotcha."

Dad walked to the car and greeted Michael with a vigorous handshake. "Brian Donovan," he said. "Thank you for all you've done for Carla."

"You're welcome, sir, I mean, it's nothing, I—"

"Sweetheart!" Dad had turned away from Michael to offer me a warm embrace. He patted my back and said, "You look tired, honey. It'll be okay now."

This was Dad's predictable approach. Say a few words, do nothing about the problem, forget the whole thing, go back to life. But it was good to hug him and to borrow a little of his strength.

"So, Michael, I understand you're a preacher," Dad said as we walked up the brick path to the front door.

"Yes, sir. In fact, I can't stay long. I've got a funeral back in Schenectady."

"The city that lights and hauls the world," Dad said.

"Sir?"

"That's what it used to be called, you know, when I was a boy. A major industrial center during the war, the big one."

"Oh, I didn't know that. Things have kind of slowed down since then, I guess."

"The General Electric plant is still there, right?"

"A lot of my family works there. It's about half what it used to be though."

"Ah, foreign labor's awfully cheap. Tells you something about a country when it costs less to buy foreign goods than to make them here at home. Unions rule this country today. You know, Ronald Reagan worked at the GE plant way back."

I feared the gap was widening between my father and Michael, who was about to get a lecture on what's wrong with the world. Michael was right; they didn't have much in common: Catholic vs. Protestant, Rich Family vs. Poor Family, White Collar vs. Blue Collar, Republican vs. Democrat . . . I prayed the Red Sox and Yankees wouldn't come up.

"Carla!" It was Margaret (Margo, Mags, Maggie to the family) bursting out of the door, saving Michael unwittingly from further interrogation. "Are you okay? Gracious, where are your glasses?" She reached out to haul me inside like a fisherman pulling a prize marlin into the boat.

"Broke both pairs," I said into her shoulder as we embraced.

"Oh. As if losing your job weren't enough." Her voice turned to a whisper in my ear. "He's cute!"

We separated. "Margaret, this is Michael." Dad had his hand resting paternally on Michael's shoulder.

"So nice to meet you. Call me Maggie." Her voice oozed sweetness. I rolled my eyes.

"Where's Mother?"

"Putting Ryan down for a nap." Almost instantly, Mother emerged from the back room.

"Hello, dear," she said. "Your glasses will be ready by four. I've already called the optician."

I was put off by her neat way of using practical matters to avoid dealing with sensitive emotional issues. I should have let it go, but couldn't. "Thank you for making the arrangements, but I was planning to get contacts." This was not true; why had I said it? Michael had liked the intellectual look afforded by my clunky frames, and I had decided to stay with glasses.

All movement in the room stopped; it looked like an exhibit in a wax museum.

"Contacts? Whatever for?" She glanced at Michael, irritated, apparently, that I had not yet introduced him to Her Highness.

"Tell you what, Mother. I'll have my prescription transferred to a local optician at home. I can get the contacts when I get back."

"Home? But you *are* home, dear. I thought we were to discuss your future plans, now that things have—"

"*You* wanted to discuss that. All I want is to get some rest. I've had a tough few weeks."

"Well. Margaret can take you then. I'm sure you'll trust her judgment on the frames better than mine. I wouldn't do these things for you, Carla, if I thought you could do them for yourself. But, I suppose, we all grow up some-time. If you'll excuse me . . . I think I hear the baby crying." She backed away and darted down the hall, out of sight.

Margaret was immediately at my side. "I can't handle this now; I really can't," I was saying.

"Listen, honey," Dad said, closing in. "Your mother's been worried sick about you. She's just trying to help."

"Oh, please. Getting fired just gives her another reason to put me down. I can't believe I came here," I sobbed.

"Look, I'll leave Ryan here for a few days," Margaret consoled. "You come stay with me."

I looked up, wondering what had become of Michael during all this family turmoil. I found him back at the door, having quietly edged his way along the wall.

"I really should be going," he said. "The funeral and all." He looked as if all the blood had been drained out of his face.

"Well, young man, it was certainly good to meet you. And thanks again for your concern." Dad spoke in summary fashion, like he always did, the perfect picture of denial, acting as if everything was normal. For us, I guess, it was.

"I'll walk you out," I said. I took his arm and yanked him along.

"You don't have to leave now," I said, outside. But we both knew it was for the best. How could I expect him to hang around in the middle of this circus?

"I'll call you," he said.

"I'll call *you*," I corrected. "I'll give you Margaret's number then. Be good to Motorhead, okay?"

"Sure." He paused. "Carla," he said gently, "I never meant to imply back in the car that there was anything wrong with you. Do you know that?"

I slouched, deflating slowly. "No apology needed. I should have seen this coming. I've got baggage to sort through. Maybe here is where I need to start."

He looked to the right and left, then straight at me. "Frankly, after seeing where you come from, I'm amazed you haven't been institutionalized before. Good luck," he said, "but don't think twice about shaking the dust from your feet if things don't go well."

I smiled as he climbed in behind the wheel. I missed him already.

"Got to go," he said, his smile masking the pain of separation.

"I'll pray for you tomorrow."

He nodded and backed out quickly. I turned back to the house, when I heard him call out. He had stopped at the end of the driveway and was hanging out the window.

"See you at home!" he shouted, waving. The words sounded more like a welcome than a farewell.

◆　◆　◆

Ryan Castleton Cavanaugh Jr., Esquire, was conveniently out of town, taking depositions in Philadelphia for some important case Margaret couldn't quite describe and in which she apparently had little interest. His return was scheduled for Friday, so we girls had three nights to spend together. Margaret, who was armed with a full arsenal of credit cards and was well trained in their use, planned on a shopping spree each day, though this wasn't entirely for my benefit: she was toning up nicely and needed a new wardrobe for her job, she said. Also on the agenda was an introduction to my first-ever aerobics class, a regular afternoon date with a cooking show to which she had become addicted while on maternity leave, and video rentals.

Did I want to meet with a career counselor? She could set me up with someone at *Boomers* magazine who was an expert in mid-life transitions.

I declined the offer.

Did I want to have dinner at Le Soir? The rabbit potpie is nationally acclaimed.

No thanks.

So, how about a pedicure?

Sure.

Have my hair done?

Sure.

How about a body wrap down at the spa?

Sure, my pores were pretty much clogged.

Margaret was enjoying this probably more than I was. In a mere three days, she said, I would return home a changed woman. But first I would need to pass the acid test of my renewal: dinner at my parents' house on Thursday night.

I marveled at how well my sister, who was vain, self-absorbed, and care-free most of the time, had morphed into what I might describe as a model mother. She knew just what to say, and when to say it; she knew when comfort was needed, and applied it in just the right quantities. I told her about the board, and she likened Hamber to Torquemada of the Inquisition, and I felt better about the situation. I told her about the demands of ministry. When she said that she couldn't possibly have met them herself, I felt a twinge of pride wriggle around inside me. At length, I even told her about Richie and my night of terror; she listened, took me for an ice cream, and we sat in the car at a park and talked it through. For the first time, I felt close to her, like a sister rather than an aunt. But the one thing she didn't do was bring up *The Subject,* and this was perhaps what I needed most of all. Things went so well between us, though, that I came right out and asked what she thought.

"Margaret, what's the deal with Mother?"

"Ooh, boy, that's a weird thing, there. I can't answer that one. Why she picks on you, I don't know. She basically stays out of my way, except when she's had one drink too many."

"You're her idea of the perfect daughter, that's why. Me, I'm an embarrassment, and always have been, as far as she's concerned. She can't accept who I am."

"Well, from what I can tell, if she doesn't do something about it soon, she'll lose you. Maybe she already has."

I frowned. "I don't know. It's not that serious." I was regretting bringing up *The Subject*.

"Yeah, I think it is, Carla. You keep coming back, calling, whatever. And all you get is criticism. I mean, it's always been bad, but lately I don't know how you stand it. We all recognize how you visit less and less. She knows it's her fault; she just won't admit it. That makes it worse. I talked to her about it last time."

A lump stuck in my throat. "You did?"

"Sure did. She was absolutely awful that day. Anyway, she wouldn't talk about it, said it wasn't my business, and said she didn't talk to either of her daughters about the other."

"Ha! Really?" I was incredulous. "She talks about you to me all the time."

"I know. Funny thing is, we're not that close, me and Mom."

The balance of the conversation had shifted, and neither of us had any more to say. Margaret started the car, and we headed out. "Whatever. Let's go get your glasses. Tonight we chill, tomorrow the mall." She fiddled with my hair and sighed. "Enough heavy stuff for one day. We've got important work to do."

◆ ◆ ◆

At Margaret's suggestion, I went for black metal frames that blended the look of my wire-rimmed glasses and the clunky ones into one style. From there we hit the fitness club, where I joined two dozen rock-hard women shadowboxing to the thump of a sound track that seemed more appropriate to a full-scale military invasion. The spandex outfit Margaret loaned me started cutting off my circulation about two minutes into the routine, so I walked off and slouched against the mirrored wall, gasping for air. My sister spoke to the instructor at the break, and I was soon being led into the brightly illumined recesses of the gym by a tall, disinterested brunette where I was introduced to the masseuse. From the looks of her, I would have guessed her to be named Helga or Hilda or Gert, but it turned out that her name was Jane. The punishment that she inflicted relaxed me.

By this time it was almost seven, and I was fading fast, but Margaret was still juiced over the girls' getaway package she had put together. It was as if she was trying to make up for a decade of estrangement in these short three days—every second counted. We feasted on a presumably low-fat, paper-thin, albino pizza, served in an art-deco café that had about six tables and a forty-minute wait to snag one; not exactly Le Soir, but fancy enough. A skinny vanilla latte (coffee: decaf; size: grande) followed the meal, served at a busy coffee bar/bookstore in a shopping center near Margaret's house. There was no need for videos tonight, Margaret said, because she had three tapes of the cooking show she hadn't seen yet, and I would just *love* those, so we lingered in our booth. I watched a crowd gather as Margaret punched out Mother's number on her wireless phone and rattled instructions, as if Mother had no idea what to do with a baby. The crowd collected into a clot of people crammed in front of the door, then fell silent before one lilting voice floating above the heads from somewhere out of sight. I couldn't hear what was being said, but when Margaret clicked off she leaned back and caught a glimpse of what was going on. "Carla—I had no *idea!* Do you know who that *is?* It's Alisharia Smith—she's getting ready to speak!"

Margaret snatched up her latte and pulled me into the horde of needy fans, nearly all of them women, with a few annoyed husbands in tow. After some polite pushing and shoving we popped into a clearing near the front, where I could see a narrow-faced, platinum-haired ice queen sitting behind a table stacked with books. A placard proclaimed the title of the book she had written and would sign tonight, after a few brief remarks: *Forgotten Suffragettes: Exploding the Myth of the Modern Woman.*

"Margaret, I'm kinda tired, do you think we could just—"

"Shhh! Here she is!"

Alisharia Smith unfolded herself from behind the table and hovered over the small podium like a prehistoric bird. "Thank you all for coming. Before we begin, I would like to say how encouraging it is to see such an outpouring of support for my work in city after city . . . but I cannot accept praise for something that really isn't mine."

The crowd held its collective breath. *What?*

"It's *your* story, ladies—you write it every day with your tireless efforts to break the shackles of expectations placed upon you by society, and I am truly humbled to give voice to your courageous, unknown struggles."

A relieved cheer of joy went up from the women. "Let's go," I said in an older sister's tone I had not used for twenty years. Margaret ignored me, just as she had back then.

Alisharia Smith was suddenly flapping her wings with passion, ignited by the love of her fans. "I speak of your right to be what God made you to be—not what your husband wants, or your boss wants, or your mother wants, or some militant feminist wants."

"Did you hear that?" Margaret chirped, her eyes fixed on the speaker. "We've got to get you that book. Maybe if we hang around later, you can actually speak to her."

"I would rather have my fingernails pulled out with pliers," I snapped. But she had surged forth to the front of the pack.

Alisharia Smith's eyes narrowed. "Don't any of you settle for someone else's dream," she scolded affectionately. "Together, we can forge a new vision of independence for the twenty-first-century woman."

I retreated back through the wall of people, using my hands in a prayer gesture to pry open spaces like a machete against the untamed jungle, finally poking through the masses and landing just in front of the coffee counter, where I ordered a café au lait and waited for Margaret to return. She appeared some twenty minutes later bearing her booty.

"This book jacket is nothing but the woman's face," I said. "You can see the pores in her skin right through the makeup." I turned the book over to see another picture of the author on the back.

"She is *so* down to earth!" Margaret squealed. "Open it up."

Inside was an inscription. *I believe in you, Carla!* The swirling print was in bold red marker and covered the whole page. It was signed: *Ali.*

"How very nice," I mumbled. "What does yours say?"

"Just *To Margo, with Admiration, Love, Alisharia Smith.* And look, she gave me a press card too."

"This is booking information," I said.

"Well, I mentioned *M&S*, you know."

"*Movers & Shakers.* The magazine."

"She would make a great story, don't you think?"

"Margaret, the woman has nothing to say. It's a message with universal appeal. I mean, here she is with her diamonds dripping, tooling around the country with her publicist, promoting herself to women who dream of having what she has. Well, it just isn't realistic."

"What's wrong with telling people to follow their dreams?"

"Nothing. But look at this—she's got her photograph on this dust jacket in three places. This is all about *her own* dream, which she gets to live by exploiting these poor unfulfilled women."

"Well," Margaret huffed, "at least she *has* a dream."

◆ ◆ ◆

Many hours later, when I sat beneath the warm glare of the bedside lamp in Margaret's guest room at 3:00 A.M., I actually reached for my personalized copy of *Forgotten Suffragettes*. The first three pages accomplished something I desperately needed. They put me to sleep.

I awakened a few hours later with a soreness attributed to Jane's muscular hands and stumbled out into the kitchen, where Margaret was whipping up something she had seen last night on one of the taped TV shows, after I had gone to bed. It was obvious from her demeanor that the slight friction from the previous evening would not derail her plans for a pleasant day. We ate the sumptuous breakfast, and I answered questions about Michael, though whenever a thorough answer required dragging in a theological explanation for this or that ("You mean he doesn't drink at all, either? What do you guys do for fun?"), she deflected them gracefully and veered the conversation in another direction. In time I surrendered to subtle insistence that today would be full of fun and games, with no controversy between us.

The mall was not crowded, and Margaret led me from store to store, where we tried on matching clothes, usually in the same sizes. For some reason everything seemed to look just a bit better on her, which gave rise to her suggestion that I meet with her personal trainer that afternoon to put together a fitness regimen I could take back with me. Whenever I went shopping for myself, price and time were the key factors, but after a while I stopped looking at the price tags and leisurely tried on everything I liked. Amazingly, when freed to think this way, it turned out that my sense of style was similar to Margaret's, if only a tad more conservative. In the end, she purchased six spring dresses—three identical ones for each of us—four business suits (three for me), three swimsuits (two tankinis for her, a modest one-piece for me), and several pairs of shoes. She also bought herself a drawer full of new jewelry, saying I could have my pick of some of her old items, and an elaborate makeup kit for me. By the time we were cleaning up from our lite-vegetarian lunch, I felt a pang of guilt, thinking about Michael, who by now would be concluding his remarks at the graveside of Carmine Russo. The urgent desire to flee the mall and rush back to Schenectady finally subsided when the clock passed one-thirty, and I knew the ceremony would have been all over.

Greta (I'm serious, but she looked more like a Jane) was a short, muscular cheerleader-type who carried all of her forty-five years in her face, but she was pleasant enough. She walked me through a series of exercises on weight machines, marking down the proper settings so I could repeat the routines on similar equipment back home. From there, Margaret took me downtown to a spa she sometimes visited in the afternoons, an amenity offered by the magazine for top-level performers. I treated myself to the full package, including the seaweed body wrap and subsequent steam bath, which left me feeling like I had been simmering in a pot, the warmth seeping deep into my bones. The room became like the moor of a gothic novel, and as my mind floated in the mist I thought of the pool, of the moment Cornelia must have known her arthritis was gone, and I opened my eyes wide, strangely invigorated.

I could not remember a more wonderful day—a day of indulgence, sheer self-love. Encouraged by Margaret, flattered by sales clerks, pampered by masters of the healing arts, I was soaring beyond all reason, pondering my future. Did people really live like this? What had I been trying to prove all these years? *It was time I started tuning in to my own needs,* I told myself, beginning to imagine the possibilities. After pillaging Margaret's jewelry box and watching two old movies that left us both in tears, I retired to the guest room and read two whole chapters of Ali's book before drifting off to peaceful sleep.

◆ ◆ ◆

When Thursday morning came, the euphoria had ebbed away into a comfortable resolve. Practical matters had crept into my head during the night, and I awakened to a clear agenda: have dinner tonight with Mother and Dad, move out of the church office over the weekend, begin the search for a new life on Monday morning.

We could not leave the house that morning because Margaret needed to spend several hours on the phone with the office. The days were drawing nigh for her return, and there was much to do to get the first edition of *M&S* off and running. That afternoon she whisked me downtown and showed me her new office. The view of the Boston skyline and the endless flattery of her subordinates cast her in an almost ethereal glow, like a queen returning to court after a long absence. I was nearly starstruck myself.

"You know," she said, as we descended in the elevator, "I'm sure I could get you a job here. If not here, there are plenty of people I know, and of course Ryan does too. Maybe you should consider staying."

Staying? Here was a member of my family inviting me to stay. As if I were really a part of the scheme of things. As if I really mattered to them. Hearing these words had the effect of a powerful drug.

"I'll think about it . . . *Margo*," I said. We laughed like little girls the whole way down.

The sight of his mother threw Ryan Castleton Cavanaugh III into hyperventilation, just now realizing, perhaps, that she had been gone. Margaret scooped him up and rocked him until his distress subsided. Dad was in his favorite chair, watching the news, oddly without his customary glass of evening wine; Mother, who was orbiting around Margaret and Ryan, greeted me with a warm half-smile that had me staring at her in wonder for some minutes.

"Your hair looks lovely," she said.

I didn't know how to respond to this compliment. "It took two stylists and Margaret to get it this way," I answered.

"Mmm-hmm. They did a good job. It's a nice complement to your new glasses. I see you changed your mind."

I just looked at her, waiting to hear, "I told you so," but she just smiled. "Mother, are you okay?"

"Would it be possible for you to call me Mom?"

"So . . . you're not okay, are you?" She sighed, just as Dad appeared.

"Well, how are we doing? Feeling better?"

"Much," I said. The three of us watched Margaret cooing at the baby.

"We've had quite a couple of days, your mother and I," said Dad. "Felt like old times, just the two of us and the baby. Remember that old house on the other side of Newton, where you spent your preschool years?"

"Vaguely."

"Rode by there the other day. It's for sale. Your mother suggested we buy it."

"What, to rent out?"

"No . . . for *you,* honey."

I whipped my head back to look at Mother. She was puffy around the eyes, trying not to show it, tickling Ryan's chin.

"Mother?" This was strange. What was happening? It felt like the villain had tied me to the railroad tracks, and the train whistle was blowing in the distance.

She pulled herself away from the baby and awkwardly hugged me, not looking into my eyes. I froze. "I . . . I can't just move back here," I said. "I've got loose ends at home."

"I know, dear. It was just a thought."

We held each other for a moment. Margaret was grinning; Dad was looking down at us with pride. For a moment, all was confusion. Then, I figured it out: she was remembering the past, wanting to go back and right the wrongs, start over somehow.

I only knew one way to respond to her, so I spoke what was natural. "Mother, I know I haven't been the perfect daughter . . . I'm sorry, I—"

"No, no, no, Carla," she said, pulling back to meet my gaze. "I won't hear of it. We both know I'm the one with the problem." Problem? Was I missing something? Sensing the weight of the silence, Dad practically pushed Margaret out of the room, leaving us alone. I didn't know what to do.

Mother's confession shocked me. I couldn't handle it. My lack of a response seemed to open the floodgates, and she poured out her pain. The words struck me with the force of a tidal wave—how Dad had always spent time with me instead of with her when he wasn't working, which made her jealous; how I had rejected her efforts to mother me during adolescence; how she had felt lost when Margaret left the nest, which made her turn to alcohol, on which she was now hopelessly dependent; how her regrets over never having her own career spilled over into resentment toward me; and on and on. It had the effect of an anesthetic rushing through my veins, slowing my mental and physical functions. It was a revelation indeed, but I had always known it, just wouldn't admit to it, because that was too hard. To know that it wasn't just in my imagination; it was real. I couldn't face it, and I nearly shut down.

"Transference," I said, emotionless. "You take out your frustrations on me. Like coming home from a bad day at work and kicking the cat for no good reason. It's very common."

"You were always such a *good* person, Carla. You didn't need what I needed to be happy. You were a reflection of what I should have been. I know that now; I've known it for a long time. But I had no idea how much I've hurt you until I realized that my own daughter didn't want to come home, that my home would never be your home again . . . because of me."

"Dad put you up to this, didn't he?" She didn't answer, just wiped her eyes and nose.

"You're getting help then?" I was struggling to feel something other than pity.

"I've been to confession. Your father and I have agreed to counseling. Maybe a treatment center."

I nodded. *Well. There it is. What else should I say?* I was numb.

"Carla, will you forgive me for being such a terrible mother?"

I looked into her eyes. I wanted to forgive her, but something in my spirit blocked the words from coming out. I was slowly filling with rage—I wanted to scream at her, as if laying all the guilt out in the open had given me justification for doing so. This pitiful woman's self-loathing was the reason I had struggled with insecurity for so long, the reason I lacked confidence, the reason I had stopped believing in myself. In my mind I replayed the steady stream of put-downs and criticisms she had unleashed over the years. I broke from eye contact and crossed my arms tightly across my chest, trying to keep from exploding like a mad Irishwoman.

Her face fell before I could answer. "I understand," she said weakly.

"I need time," was all I could say. And I left her there.

Dinner went perfectly well on the surface, with Dad and Margaret carrying the brunt of conversation, which volleyed between the baby and business. The food, which had been catered, was served on silver trays with little blue flames underneath; Mother had been so busy with Ryan that she had ordered everything brought in. I guess she envisioned all could be made well by staging one pleasant dinner: "Just forget about all that stuff, and let's start over; Carla, buy that old house, and we'll be mother and daughter again."

Dad abruptly raised himself from the table and left the room. No one spoke until he returned. "Here's the name of someone I know in Albany," he said. "He's a broker, always looking for good people. If he likes you, I'll pay for the courses you'll need."

I accepted the slip of paper. "Thank you, Dad." There was an icy silence. "It's not that I don't want to come home; it's just that, well, if things work out with Michael . . ."

"It's fine, dear," Mother said, patting my hand. "It's just fine." Her weak smile almost seemed sincere.

CHAPTER NINETEEN

I WASN'T VERY TALKATIVE on the way back to New York, and Margaret didn't provoke me to discuss the events of the dinner Thursday night, perhaps because what she heard of Mother's sob story bothered her as well. She was not one to get bogged down with such things, preferring to live her life above the fray. If she gave the impression that she was superficial, she didn't seem to mind; I knew my sister was sensitive deep down, and watching her forced mannerisms as she sought to make light conversation while we traveled made me wonder if she was masking some inner hurts as well.

Forgiveness is easier said than done, but as a Christian it wasn't optional for me. This may have been what allowed my anger against my mother to persist throughout the night and into the next day—not that it was merely difficult to forgive her, but that I was required to do so. I had been given the opportunity, but I had spurned it, dishing out a little of my mother's own medicine in my petulant refusal to accept her confession. Now that she had accepted the blame, was I to simply patch up my wounds and act as if we could have a meaningful relationship? My faith demanded that I do so, and I resented it, clinging to my anger, not wanting to be freed from its grasp. All the compassion had been bled right out of me.

I was angry at a lot of people, I admitted to myself, recalling the shame of my earlier bitterness toward Margaret, who never intended to diminish me by the inevitable comparisons to her. The church board was the main object of my seething rage, and the more I thought of their piddling micromanagement to the disregard of the great challenge before us, the more I felt entitled to hang on to my anger. Michael had not exactly endeared himself when he implied that I might be somewhat flawed emotionally, though he had every reason to imply it. Even God was not faring too well with me these days; why had he chosen me, of all people, to play host to his miracles, only to abandon me in the end? What was the point of it all? Someone once said that we can know God's will only when we look at it through hindsight. Well, I was looking, and I could see nothing good bubbling up from the healing pool, unless the healings were real—in that case, I supposed there were blessings for Cornelia, Miranda, and Paul. Funny though, how all that seemed far away now, and I—husbandless, childless, jobless, and apparently motherless— seemed unwilling to trust in anything. *Miracles?* I felt like the wandering Israelites who forgot all about the parting of the waters and the pillars of fire and cloud, wanting only, in the face of their present desperate need, to go home. And yet, as I gazed out at the birches along the highway through the glass that held the ghost of my reflection, I worried I might never know where home really was.

Why was it that Mother, in the midst of her confession—at that moment when the years of disrespect were washed away in a flood of truth, when the way was made to heal the wounds, finally—seemed more like a stranger than ever before? Why was it that, now that it was all out in the open, I felt dead inside toward her? As long as I had endured her criticisms, I had hoped someday to come up to the standard she had set for me. But now, I realized that it wouldn't have mattered anyway. I felt robbed somehow, having wasted my life trying to attain what was unattainable. The eldest child, the father's favorite, the mother's scapegoat for an unfulfilled life—what could I have done to change it? The cards were all on the table, at last, and I had been dealt a bad hand. So I had sought, and found, a relationship with God and security in the church. There, I would be accepted. People would love me. Respect me. Need me. When they failed to do so, I worked harder. But the appreciation required to fill the hollow in my heart never came. All I earned for myself were more unrealistic expectations.

My mother's alcohol-induced harping had destroyed my life. That was all I could think or feel. My mother had ruined me. Sharing her guilt may have eased her burden; it gave shape and weight to mine. There was no reason to bluff with my bad cards in hand anymore. I folded.

Margaret rolled the car slowly up to the curb in front of my house, the way people do when they still have something to say but can't find the words.

"That's a relief," I said. "At least my furniture hasn't been tossed out onto the front lawn."

We hugged and made the usual commitments of calls and letters and visits. She really was a wonderful girl; so much so, in fact, that I actually smiled when she began to review what I had learned about clothing, makeup, proper diet, and exercise. I was making a new start, I assured her. Without her these past two days, I would have been lost, I said.

And I would have been. I watched her from the porch as she drove away. I walked inside the house and looked around. It was quiet, especially since Motorhead was at Michael's, which reminded me that I needed to call him right away. But instead I just sat down at the kitchen table, staring incoherently at a stack of pepper cookies that by now were hard as rocks. I missed Margaret, her beautiful home, the vicarious experience of her life I had enjoyed. Dishes were stacked in the sink. Junk mail and magazines were piled on the counter, where I usually tossed them upon coming home from work. There were bits of cat food spilled on the floor around Motorhead's dish. It was silent, and I was alone. Lonelier than I had ever been. I didn't want to move. Or stay. I felt forsaken. Empty.

Lost.

◆　◆　◆

When Michael arrived later that afternoon, he knew right away that something was wrong. At first he kept filling the void with words. He was good with words, and I was content to let him talk. Every now and then he tried to pull me into the conversation. "So, what did you and your sister do all week?" *Girl stuff.* "Was it fun?" *We had a great time.* When he finally tired of the game, the empty space between us triggered a sudden, alarming thought.

"Where's my cat?"

"Under the bed," he said, clearly disgusted. "Won't come out. The thing has terrorized me the whole time. Claws at me from under there when I try to get in. And there's this low growl when I turn off the lights and try to sleep. You may have to come get him. He's just waiting for the right moment to do away with me."

"I'll speak at your funeral if you want."

"Your compassion is truly touching. Speaking of funerals, I wish you had been here for Carmine Russo's. It was incredible, Carla. Powerful. Place was packed. Four people came right up to me at the graveside and said they wanted to learn about being a Christian. It wasn't the preaching, of course, it was Carmine. They all said there was something different about him. It proves my theory."

"What theory?" I was staring off somewhere, not really listening. I still had to fill the dishwasher.

"The pool theory. God was made visible in Carmine's suffering. He became an awesome, undeniable witness."

"So why doesn't he just zap us all with some disease then?" I snapped.

He moved closer to me, warily, not affectionately, as if he feared I might take a swing at him. "Carla, you don't look well."

"I'm still recovering."

"Look at me."

I didn't want to, fearing the whole mess would come gushing out. But I did anyway, holding my mouth tight in defiance.

"I think you're depressed," he said. "Are you sleeping a lot?"

"No, Michael." I spoke like a bored teenager barely tolerating her father's good advice.

"How's your appetite?"

"Margaret's got me on a health kick. Listen, I'm fine. Just . . . preoccupied."

"Sure. I know you've got to be uptight about your job. Actually, I wanted to—"

"I've got some options," I said.

The statement seemed to startle him. Where did that come from? I said it without thinking, I suppose to try and scare him off. He fixed his dark stare on me, waiting for me to explain. "My dad," I said.

"Your dad what?"

"He knows a broker in Albany. I'm going to call him on Monday."

"A *broker?* You're quitting the ministry?" He was aghast, and my dormant anger flared at his reaction.

"What do you suggest, huh? If you hadn't noticed, it's kind of hard for a woman to get work in the church these days—especially one who got fired. I obviously have to get a place to live, and I have to pay the rent somehow. What do you want me to do, beg for alms? Or maybe you want me to just go back to Boston and leech off my rich parents."

"I don't think you're in the right frame of mind to be making these decisions right now," he said sternly. "We ought to stop right now and pray about this. You're obviously—"

"Oh, like we can crank out a little prayer, and I'll be back the way you want me?" It was all coming out now, the whole ugly pile of junk that had polluted my spirit.

"Carla, listen . . ." He reached out, and I pushed his hand away. He reached out again and caught my hand. "I have a way you can continue to do your ministry. I don't think you should make any big career moves yet. Get a part-time job and do this ministry. It's a small stipend, but it will help. God will make his will clear for you if you'll just—"

"Clear? *Clear?* How much clearer could he have made it? Try this: F-I-R-E-D—you're fired, Reverend Donovan! Sorry about all those years of thankless work; we got the wrong girl; you're totally inept, you say the wrong things, do the wrong things; you obviously don't fit the mold."

"But Carla, the pool—"

I stood up, throwing his hand down. "Don't even go there, Michael. The stupid pool is the reason I'm out of a job. The pool is the reason I nearly got killed the other night. And guess what—they're draining it, if they haven't already, and I'll just bet we find out why it filled up with water."

"Okay, you're not yourself, that's what this is. You need to see someone. I'll make some calls."

"Why?" I demanded. "Because I don't want to spend the rest of my life wearing that slave collar, serving other people with no appreciation for practically no money, and zero respect? Because I don't want to be publicly humiliated on live television, and kidnapped, and hated by my own mother? Is that so crazy?"

He stood up to face me. "No, it's not. You've been hurt; there's no way around it." He looked like he could cry, and it only made me angrier. "But I know God can heal your hurts. He's not through with you yet."

"Yeah? Well, I wish he were—because I'm through with him."

The words stunned even me. Surely he knew I didn't mean them. Michael just looked into my puffy eyes, his face melting into sympathy. I crashed into his arms, let him hold me while I cried. Ashamed as I was to have said such an awful thing, it was good to let it all out. Eventually, he spoke.

"I'll make some calls, okay?"

"Okay," I sniffled.

There was a long pause. "You know, I really think you need a steak sandwich, Carla."

I couldn't help feeling my mouth try to turn up at the corners as I nuzzled his shoulder. "I'm on a healthy diet."

"Fine. Then order the meatball sub."

The little smile turned into an abbreviated laugh, which pleased Michael immensely. Now that the venting was passed, we both felt a welcome relief. I had a long way to go, I knew—emotionally, professionally, spiritually. But having Michael there was enough to make me want to try.

"So, what's this great ministry idea?" I said, courageously trying to hide my disinterest.

"No way. We'll talk about that tomorrow, when I help you pack up the office. Tonight, let's just have fun. I mean, hey, it's a Friday night in Schenectady. You want to go bowling?"

I just shook my weary head at him. He was a keeper.

♦ ♦ ♦

The third and fourth chapters of *Forgotten Suffragettes* were little more than a regurgitation of the first two, and I quickly lost interest. By 8:30 A.M. I had already done the dishes, thrown out the pepper cookies (and half the contents of the refrigerator), and sorted through the pile of papers on the kitchen counter, before settling down to read. My head was swimming with possibilities. Could I make it in the world as a real person, with a real nine-to-five job? Finding no help from Ali, I took out a blank sheet of paper and listed my options. The evening with Michael had been so reassuring, with him listening patiently to the whole saga of life with Mother. While he would not let me off the hook, he knew I needed time before I could begin the process of reconciliation. Thus consoled, I completely dismissed any thought of returning to Boston right away. I would definitely call the broker; the job should pay well, and I fantasized about living Margaret's life—a nice place, money to burn, maybe even a husband and baby. But I wouldn't go back to Boston even if things didn't work out with Michael, not for a while, at least until I was ready to deal with my mother. A six-month lease on an apartment here in the area would be a smart move. I wrote that down. I also listed some miscellaneous tasks that I deemed high priority for Monday; to pick up my car from the impound lot across town was first on the list. I was relieved when I was informed it had been found, none the worse for wear, in a motel parking lot, keys in the ignition. Well, at least part of my life would be back to normal. I had really missed the old gal.

Figuring out what to do with myself on Sunday would be a problem. It would be weird, not preaching, but I realized that I probably wasn't capable of pulling it off anyway. I could feel my heart rate rise, just thinking about St. Fred's. I decided what I needed was a few weeks off from church, maybe even a month, to work out my emotional conflicts, but I didn't see how I could avoid attending Shekinah. Whatever ministry Michael had in mind for me was probably associated with his church anyway—delivering children's sermons, working with youth, doing short-term evangelism, something like that. Like Jonah fleeing from Nineveh, I knew I could not escape dealing with my spiritual issues for long, not with Michael around. But I didn't want to face God quite yet, either, not with all the resentment I was harboring inside. I wrote down Shekinah, with the notation "volunteer only." If I could get away with it, I preferred just sitting in the pew for a while. I was sick and tired of serving God out of obligation, which had been my pattern for so long. If and when he wanted me, he could let me know.

It was still only mid-morning, and I was bored. Michael was due to show up around lunch, and we were to spend the afternoon packing up my stuff from the office. I wondered how I would feel when I dropped my keys on the desk for the final time. I went to the back porch and selected some boxes Isabella had brought, deciding to get a head start clearing the shelves in the study. They were liquor boxes, of course, and I laughed out loud—how ironic, my mother was the alcoholic, and I took the rap for that too. Just my luck, someone would see me traipsing down the church steps with these cartons, which would only add to my infamy. Let them talk. What did it matter now? I snatched up two large boxes and headed out.

A white car was parked in the street in front of the church, and as I came closer, I knew whose it was. He was sitting on the front steps by himself, reading. It was the same grungy guy who had picked me up on the highway, though he had a different T-shirt and was wearing cut-off jean shorts now that the temperature was rising. Through my glasses I could see that he was still unshaven and had a mop of dark, mussed hair, but his clothes were clean, and his eyes were sharp and clear. This was no bum, as I had previously thought.

"Nice day," he said.

"Yeah. You do know it's Saturday, right?"

"Sure. Figured I'd get here early and get a good seat."

"Didn't you see the TV?"

"Don't watch it much."

I left the boxes on the sidewalk, climbed up, and sat next to him, one step below. "Nice shirt. What's it say?"

He looked down at his chest. "It says Killed in the Line of Duty. Kinda cool for Lent, I thought." I squinted at the navy-blue shirt and saw what looked like a white chalk outline, the kind police officers draw around murder victims, roughly in the shape of a cross, above the red script.

"You give up anything?" I asked. "For Lent, I mean."

He was silent for a moment, then said, "Quite a lot, actually. You?"

"Same," I said.

We sat without talking for a while, thinking.

"What's that you're reading?"

He closed the book and held it up. It was a thick paperback Bible with a white cover. He had written something on the front; it looked like the number 108. "The *NMT*. Ever heard of it? *New Millennium Translation*. Targets young adults, ages eighteen to twenty-five. Supposed to be more applicable to the problems of today."

"Such as?"

"Oh, things like addiction, low self-esteem, depression, you know, stuff we've never heard of before. It's 'filled with notes for precise application to your unique challenges from today's leading Christian thinkers.'" He read the phrase right off the back cover.

"You don't seem impressed."

He smirked. "Not really. We live in an affluent society, and affluence breeds sin. The rich want more, and the poor want what the rich have. To me, sin isn't a modern problem. How are we supposed to be pure with all the corruption in the world, right? So, last year's Bible is out of date, I guess. Same stuff, just coming from a different angle. It'll probably sell a million copies."

"The miracle of modern marketing," I quipped.

"Speaking of miracles, what's the deal with the pool? These guys were here earlier with pumps and hoses and stuff. They had a key. One guy named Joe said he was draining the pool. Told me about some little girl who went playing in there and got healed of deafness or something?"

Ah, so it was done then. A wave of sadness passed over me. "Supposedly," I said. "Nothing's been proven yet." I had trouble looking him in the eye; he had an intense stare. At first I thought he was going to interrogate me about

Miranda, but he just crinkled his brow and waited for the rest of the story. I intended to tell him everything, but my story gravitated toward my personal frustrations in ministry. The more I talked, the more I felt he might be someone who would understand. He was a thoughtful young man, sensitive, with a hint of ambivalence toward organized religion. So I told him about Miranda, my talk with Cornelia, the pool filling with water, and the repeated reprimands, climaxing with my secretive and foolish attempt to heal Marita, and its disastrous consequences—leaving out, of course, any suggestion that I was anything but a hapless victim.

"That's quite a tale," he said. "You sound defeated."

I shrugged. "Well, let's think about it. God wants to do something, and his own people stop it cold, again and again. They always seem to get away with it. That's just the way things are."

"And the way things have always been. If they understood the heart of God, they would recognize his works. Since they don't, they won't. But, so what? Does God need these people to do what he wants?"

"I suppose not. But God doesn't seem to be trying hard enough," I said bitterly.

He raised an eyebrow. "Really? Looked in the mirror lately?"

I was stunned at his accusation. I didn't think we knew each other well enough for him to be so blunt. "And what about you—just drifting around, not even committed to any church," I snapped. "You're one to talk."

"You're avoiding the question, and you're angry because you don't want to face the answer."

That was true. I backed off. Maybe I should just let it out and be done with it. Maybe it would be better to get it out of my system here and now, before Michael showed up with talk of some menial ministry opportunity and I blasted him. "I *have* tried," I whined. "These people won't let me do anything. It's the same everywhere I've been. I have to do everything myself. I get no help, and it's never good enough. The ministry is a joke. You can't win."

"That's why you're quitting?"

"I'm quitting because I'm sick of doing all the work for people who don't even care."

"You're sick all right."

I felt a rush of hot anger well up inside me. Part of me wanted to run away, and part wanted to cry. "You don't know me, so you have no right to judge. You have no idea of the sacrifices I've made." I stood up and headed toward the door of the church.

"Carla," he said softly.

I stopped and looked back. He had turned his scruffy dark head in my direction, the gold cross earring twinkling in the sunlight.

"Do you want to be made well?"

I just stood like a stone. I recognized the question. "Did you just read that or something?" I didn't need any more preaching.

He got up and slowly descended the steps. When he reached the bottom he turned to me again. "Your friend was right, you know, when he said God uses miracles to get people's attention. You know now that he can heal the body; you've seen it yourself, if you will accept it. If he can heal the body, why not the soul? Which do you think is more important?"

I opened my mouth but couldn't speak. There was something . . . Did he say, *my friend?* I hadn't even mentioned—

"Yes, your friend, Michael. He has a good head on his shoulders, but he makes for a lousy priest. By the way, tell him he did an excellent job at the funeral. Mr. Russo was very pleased."

I began to tremble. My knees buckled; I had to sit down.

He spoke reassuringly. "I know it seems bad now, but things will change. Unless a grain of wheat falls to the earth and dies, it remains alone. But if it dies, it bears much fruit. So shall it be with you. Trust me."

I tucked my head down between my knees and wept. My heart burned with a strange, not unwelcome emotion.

I heard his steps as he returned to me. I felt his hand rest gently on my bowed head. "Enough excuses now. It's time for you to rise up and walk," he said softly.

My tears flowed freely. I heard him laugh, and I looked up, peering into the sun through wet lashes. He smiled and said, "You know, Michael's right; you really don't need contacts to be beautiful. Besides, those glasses are sharp. Margaret has good taste."

He walked back down the steps to his car and started the engine. I watched as he rolled down the window, raised a finger to his lips, smiled again, and drove away.

PART 4:

HOVSE OF MERCY

C H A P T E R   T W E N T Y

THERE IS A PLACE where, when you find yourself there, you know you've hit bottom. In that place you begin to make excuses: "It's not my fault; it isn't fair." Or promises: "If I ever get out of this mess, I'll do this or that." But nothing happens to move you forward, and you sink even deeper. You never expected it to get this bad, but it did, and now you've got no clue as to what to do. So you claw at other people and rationalize things and feel sorry for yourself. You go home, if they'll have you, and if you won't have them, you run away again. But you don't do the one thing that will start you on the way up and out of the abyss—you don't ask for help.

I suppose you do if you're desperate. Or if you have no sense of shame. But I was far too proud to admit that my condition was as serious as it was, that my problems all found their source in one root cause, my own fanatical obsession with myself, with what people might say or think or do to me, with what they had already done to me. You can never win the game when all you do is defend the goal; in time, the opponent wears you down, and you are overrun by a horde of those who are more aggressive than you, though not necessarily more intelligent or skilled. Like the man lying on his pallet by the pool in Jerusalem, I had watched, envious of others, waiting for something to happen without trying for it, preferring passive self-pity instead, allowing myself to be stepped over and shoved around until I wasn't a person there at all, just an object in the way. Until *he* came, and showed me I was worth more than that.

Looking back on it now, I cringe at the thought of what might have become of me if he had not encountered me that day, when, after packing my life as a minister into cardboard boxes, I walked, still grieving, into the shadowy basement of St. Fred's church, where I climbed down to the lowest place I could find—into the damp, empty bottom of the healing pool—to kneel in the dark on the hard cracked plaster, alone.

I repented of thinking less of myself than God thought of me.

I repented of the doubt that leads to fear and petitioned God for the doubt that leads to faith.

I repented of my bitterness toward my family, and toward those to whom I was accountable in the work, asking God to show me how to love and forgive them.

I repented of the superficiality that had stifled the vision God had given me.

I repented of the insecurity that had led me to question my calling.

I repented of seeing and not believing, of hoping against the truth, for the sake of my safety. I celebrated the imperishable inheritance that was mine in Christ. I praised God for his deliverance. I dedicated my life once more to a life of unwavering service, felt once again the power of humility surging in my spirit.

I'll never forget that day, when I climbed up from the depths of the pit, fearless.

🔹 🔹 🔹

Later on, I was flipping through a worn paperback copy of Dietrich Bonhoeffer's *The Cost of Discipleship* when I heard the door open. I tossed the book I had pored over during my seminary days into the open box, chiding myself for not having mined its wisdom in the succeeding years. It had been sitting on the shelf my whole career, a neglected relic from a former time, when God-things once captured my mind and heart, before the slow death had set in.

"Anybody home?"

I appeared in the doorway of my former study and leaned on the frame. Michael was holding Motorhead in his arms; as soon as my beloved pet saw me, he scampered down. But instead of rushing to rub his head against my shin, he darted for the corners of the office, creeping along the woodwork, prepared for any unexpected danger in this foreign place.

"It's worse than I thought," I said. "What have you done to my poor cat?"

He smirked. "He finally emerged from under the bed, howling to be fed. That beast of yours made me buy four different brands of cat food before I finally broke down and gave him tuna fish. Then, he tore my curtains and shed all over my recliner. And he sat in my bathtub and wouldn't come out for hours."

"Did you speak to him nicely?"

"Yeah, and he hissed at me. I finally just yanked him out of there and threw him in the car. I warn you: I haven't had a chance to shower today."

I laughed, and Motorhead finally discovered me, his nose nudging my shoes and his motor humming. I knelt to pet him.

"Bunky Willembeck?" Michael had advanced slowly toward us, possibly afraid to touch me while the cat was within clawing distance, but stopped at the secretary's desk. He was holding a peach-colored paper plucked from a stack of worship bulletins I hadn't noticed before.

"You see this?"

"No. Who's Bunky Willembeck?"

Michael chuckled. "The new interim pastor, according to this. This guy's about eighty, I would guess. Had two fingers blown off in World War II. He's been filling pulpits for years around here, always tells war stories."

He handed me the bulletin. I looked at it, seeing nothing.

"So. You okay?"

"Yeah." My smile was genuine.

We embraced. The feline motor at our feet filled the open space of the office.

We moved to the study, where one box was already sealed with tape, and the other was half full. Motorhead immediately jumped inside it. I dropped into my chair and looked wistfully at the half-empty shelves. Should I tell Michael what had happened? He was perusing the volumes, probably searching for the right words to say.

"Great book," he said, picking up a dusty hardback by Jürgen Moltmann.

"I didn't know you were into the deep stuff," I quipped.

"What, are you kidding? I love the German theologians—Barth, Bultmann, Moltmann . . . I've read all those guys."

"In seminary, right? Required reading."

"Well, yes, but that's beside the point." He was grinning.

"So, did they affect your thinking at all?"

He cocked his head to one side. "If they did, I suppose I'd remember some of what they wrote."

"You know, I'm thinking of revisiting some of these writers, now that I've got some time," I said. "I need to work out some stuff, put things in perspective."

"It's amazing how we're exposed to all these ideas in school, and when we're out there in the trenches we just drift to the newest ministry fad. Like me—I'm always buying these leadership books, but you can read through them in an hour, and there's nothing we haven't heard before."

"The fact that there's a new one every five minutes ought to tell you something," I added. "We're looking for that magic elixir—take one dose and the church will grow like Jack's beanstalk."

"But what we should be doing is building on a theological foundation and not a practical one. If we understand the mission, we can adapt the methods to carry it out. At Shekinah, for instance, we've gone the contemporary route in worship because that's what the leadership gurus say will reach people. It's working, but only with one segment of the population responding. But look around here. I'm not sure drums and video projection would work in this neighborhood."

"You couldn't get it past the board anyway."

He sat down across from me, his dark eyes sparkling. "Jesus dealt with the same thing though. And it didn't stop him, did it?"

"No, but—"

"So why should it stop us? You're in an ideal position to implement a truly New Testament ministry—not bound by the restraints of institutionalized religion."

"*Now* I see where you're going. This must have something to do with this big career opportunity you were talking about."

"Okay." Michael settled in to make his pitch. "Jesus was outside the system, just like you are now. He went out and met the people where they were. Our church would like to set you up as a mission pastor—at the bar."

"*The Dutchman?* You're kidding, right? Tell me you're kidding."

"Nope. Already talked to Isabella, she checked with the owner, and he's cool with it. There's a fee to rent the place on Sundays before one o'clock, and my deacons have already approved it. We've got a band lined up and everything."

"Did Isabella put you up to this?"

"Shoot, no. My idea. But she did say now she understands why God hasn't let her find another job."

"All part of the plan, huh?"

"Yep. The *big* picture. Now, before you start objecting, just think for a minute about—"

"I'll do it."

Michael stopped abruptly, leaning forward, still wanting to plead his case, his brow wrinkled in confusion. "You will?"

"Of course I will. I'd *love* to do it. It's perfect. And you are so sweet to do this for me." I leaned over and kissed his cheek.

My response embarrassed him. "The pay's not much, but—"

"It will be enough. I just want to serve. Tell your deacons I accept."

"Fine. It's a deal then. Tomorrow you can come to our service, and we'll make it official."

"Deal," I said, extending my hand to seal it with a shake.

He grasped my hand and eyed me suspiciously. "Carla, are you sure you're okay? Last night you weren't too crazy about even the suggestion of doing ministry. What happened to change your mind?"

I shrugged. "I had a little talk with Jesus, that's all."

"Ah." He made like this was perfectly understandable, and of course it should have been. We all know that prayer changes things. Still, I could tell he was not quite convinced. Motorhead suddenly jumped into Michael's lap, purring robustly.

"Oh, so you like me now?" he said to the cat. "What's gotten into you people?"

"People?" I said, amused. Motorhead lifted his chin and let Michael rub his vibrating throat. "See, anyone can change. All it takes is a little love and affection." He looked first at me and then around at my piles of books, smiling to himself at the simplicity of it all.

◆ ◆ ◆

It was nearing eight o'clock by the time we had transferred the last box to my back porch. We went back to St. Fred's for one final look around, lingering for a while on the pool deck, where we stared silently into the empty shell. Michael was lost in thought, still trying to make sense of what had happened there. I took his arm and watched him closely. For Michael, everything had to fit perfectly; there was always a quick solution to every problem. Faith for him was a simple, practical matter, and to tell him that I had been visited by God would have troubled him even more. How strange it was that I, who had always struggled to find peace, had finally found it while he searched for answers that would probably never come. He had been right, of course, about the miracles pointing to something greater—the overwhelming, incomprehensible love of God, which I had so personally come to understand—and, for all I knew, about the witness-bearing theory too. As for me, I couldn't worry about the pool anymore, for I had been charged with the greater responsibility to bring not just healing, but wholeness, to others. The pool had been emptied out, like this chapter of my life. I would leave the keys on the desk and close the door on it all and start over with the dawning day.

We returned upstairs to the remains of the now-cold pizza we had ordered and took the trash out to the dumpster. I left a note that if the church planned to cease the benevolence work, I would have a use for the canned items and clothing. Michael kept his eyes on me, waiting for a tear or at least a glum countenance. But I was the picture of contentment all the while, and in time his look of concern melted away.

Saturday nights were there to polish up the next day's sermon, and I knew it would be a short evening for Michael, but I made one request of him.

"Will you go with me to see Cornelia?"

He cocked his head to one side. "Now?"

"If you don't mind. I've been worrying about her lately." The truth was that I wanted to tell her about my experience, to encourage her somehow, to let her know that there was at least one other person in the world who didn't think she was crazy.

"Sure. Be nice to meet her anyway."

In the space of half an hour, we were checking with the irritable desk clerk, who raised an eyebrow at the mention of Cornelia's name. "You're the second visitor today," she said with an air of contempt. With no family nearby, Mrs. Shepherd didn't get many visitors, which she probably interpreted as a lack of concern on our part. "When they get like this is when people start to come," she said.

"Like what?"

The woman just sighed, handed us our visitors' passes, and returned to her filing.

Michael stopped along the way several times to speak to the wheelchair-bound, and once to help a man who was walking like a snail down the hall adjust the cardigan sweater that hung askew on his crooked frame. We finally arrived at the dimly lit room 108 and found Cornelia asleep. We stood at the foot of the bed, not knowing if we should stay.

"She's had a rough time lately," said a dark-skinned nurse who was probably nearing retirement herself. "Cranky old thing. But she can be so nice when her mind is working." The nurse had slipped in behind us, unnoticed.

"She seems fine now," Michael said.

"Since about four o'clock, after her visitor came," the nurse said. "Nice young man. Then she just drifted off to sleep, happy as can be."

"Was this person from St. Fred's?" I asked, hopeful and suspicious at the same time.

The nurse shook her head. "Maybe he was, but I've never seen him before. He prayed with her, though, and he read to her for a while." She pointed to the bedside table.

Michael picked up the book. *"The New Millennium Translation*. Huh— I've never heard of this one. You?"

"I might have," I said, hugging myself, turning the angle of my head to read the room number written on the white cover. I felt a warmth within, there in the quiet room, so glad that I had come.

🌢 🌢 🌢

For the first time in many years, I awoke on Sunday morning without having to don the vestments and take up the role of the vocational pastoral servant. There had been intermittent vacations throughout my career, but each time I worshipped in other places, I could not focus on God, but instead viewed the service as a kind of seminar, making notes on what I liked and disliked, doodling on the bulletin those ideas that appealed to me for future use. This day was different; I had no such future work for which to prepare.

Michael arrived right on time and talked excitedly about how he had planned the service, as if he felt he had to explain it to me to minimize any potential criticism. The early "worship celebration" at Shekinah turned out to be very high tempo, almost shattering the limits of my comfort zone, which embraced a more traditional, serene way of doing church. Michael, of course, was supercharged despite the early hour, nailing his points with powerful, descriptive language and deepening their meaning with finely constructed illustrations, articulately told. He was clearly the star of the show, if such terms are even appropriate to describe the experience. It looked like entertainment, but felt like worship; it energized and comforted at the same time. Especially when Michael introduced me as the proposed pastor of the new "Matthew's House" mission, and the congregation responded with a collective "Amen" followed by applause.

After church, I returned home to scour the Help Wanted section in the Sunday paper. I circled a few promising opportunities and pulled out a blank white sheet to draft a cover letter for my resumé, which I presumed was saved in my computer and could be updated quickly. As I sat at the kitchen table, hovering tentatively over the stark white page, I noticed a slow line of traffic stream past: worshippers leaving the service at St. Fred's. I paused, waiting to see if any would stop. None did. What had they been told? I could only guess about the one-sided presentation that Derrold Hamber would have made to explain my sudden dismissal, if the board had not issued a church-wide letter already. But most of the people had probably seen the TV spot, so Hamber would have to do a little apologizing for himself too. I chuckled to myself, imagining the spectacle.

I was sure I could find a part-time job to supplement my ministry stipend. That was reason enough for me to stay in Schenectady, rather than run home to Mom and Dad and, God forbid, their whispering neighbors. I had thirty days left in the parsonage, and if I found a job soon I could get an apartment. If for some reason things didn't work out, I could fly to parts unknown if I wanted and start again. I had some funds stashed away to pay the inevitable pet deposit for Motorhead, and I figured that waiting tables or working as a receptionist would do fine—something not particularly mentally taxing to pay the bills while working on the ministry. And, if Matthew's House really took off, what then? I was so grateful to God for the freedom he had given me; it was like emerging from a dense wood where all was confusion and finding I had not been far from home all along.

◆　◆　◆

In the days that passed, I interviewed with three potential employers and two temporary agencies. The screeners at both agencies knew nothing about the demands of professional ministry and blitzed me with silly questions.

"Do you know Windows?"

"Yes."

"Can you format a spreadsheet?"

"No."

"Do you have any special skills?"

"I know how to use a Greek lexicon, and I can fix a folding machine. I'm also fairly competent with a glue stick."

"Are you good at filing?"

"I'm a piler, actually. I put things in piles and set them around on the floor."

"Do you have good people skills?"

"It depends on which people you're asking about."

"Do you have any disabilities?

"You might call me romantically challenged. And I'm practically blind."

"I see."

"So do I, except when my glasses get busted in tussles with thugs."

The prospects of finding an office job thus diminished, I tried less challenging positions. The first, a job as a clerk during the night shift at a local hotel, paid the most, and the woman who met with me was very interested. There was a fountain out front in which intoxicated guests liked to cavort after hours, and whoever worked the desk needed to be assertive enough to handle that event. This was apparently the main focus of the job, and she thought my previous line of work somehow prepared me well for dealing with irrational and stubborn people. I declined that one. The second job was as a waitress in a deli, but there would only be two of us, and the other—a thin, chain-smoking, middle-aged, fake blonde—looked mean. The third opportunity turned out to be a charm: I found a rare-and-used book dealer who appreciated my education and needed someone to take orders off the Web site and occasionally handle the front desk. Perfect.

These were liberating days indeed. The part-time job at Fenimore's proved to be quite fulfilling: I was able to locate several resources for a professor at Union College for his summer course in nondramatic literature of the English Renaissance, and he e-mailed me daily with new requests. There was an estate sale in which Fenimore's acquired several boxes of old books, and cataloging them proved to be quite enjoyable. The small bookstore, crowded with obscure volumes and papers, dispensed a distinctly nineteenth-century air, aside from the presence of the computer. Dust motes played in the streams of sunlight that gave the place its ambient glow. Sometimes Michael brought sandwiches at lunch and helped me search for obscure titles long forgotten by everyone except the customer, to whom they represented something treasured and lost, or clues to some vital, arcane fact.

The days were warming, and I set upon the task of apartment hunting in the afternoons, which proved to be much more enjoyable than expected. There were amenities galore: pools, tennis courts, exercise rooms, and clubhouse activities. I daydreamed of the crowd from The Dutchman hanging out around the pool for a summer afternoon social with Bible study afterwards in the clubhouse, and I giggled obnoxiously to myself, causing one young apartment manager some self-circumspection while showing me around. After an enthusiastic orientation to the cardio-machines at one yuppie community, I decided to follow Margaret's advice and begin a work-out program, so I checked out a health club on my way home. The young chicks strutting around were somewhat intimidating, but I noticed a few forty-something soccer moms striving mightily against the ravages of time, and, since I thought I compared favorably with them, I signed up.

I devoted much of my free time to preparing a complete manuscript of my sermon, something I hadn't done in a long time. Some of the folks at Shekinah painted a bright red Matthew's House banner to hang each week, and three of the youth who had a band were already rehearsing for the music part of the worship. Elated with how quickly everything came together, I prayed fervently for the work, pondering whether this was what God wanted me to do after all. Our first meeting would be on Palm Sunday; I eagerly awaited the coming of the Lord.

🔸 🔸 🔸

"Not long ago I was standing right over there." Heads turned, following my accusing finger. "Had I been thinking clearly, or if I had just stopped to consider the consequences of what I was about to do, things might have turned out differently." I paused, giving them time to return their gazes to me. I was standing behind the bar on a wine crate. "But I acted out of frustration, got carried away with my emotions, and said some things I regret now. Many of you were here. You saw what happened, and you know where it led.

"Have any of you had a similar experience?" Nods and murmurs filled the room. "You know, then, how easy it is to choose the wrong way out of a bad mess, which only makes things worse. There is a right way, but you're blind to it; all you see is anger and fear, and you revolt against it—you keep drinking, you quit that job, you throw that punch. Big mistakes, every one of them. And then you wake up and say, 'What did I do to get myself into such a fix?' But you know there's no going back."

A somber silence greeted my words, but not like the disinterested tranquility of my former congregation when I preached. They were attentive, thoughtful, introspective. "Now imagine being there on that day when Jesus rode into Jerusalem. You and I would probably have been among the crowd, shouting praise to him. We would have heard about his powers and would have seen him as a potential deliverer for us. He might have been the answer: no more Romans, no more poverty, no more sickness, no more empty living. But then, a week later, when it appeared that Jesus would accomplish none of these things, you and I would have joined the crowd that turned on him, not thinking, just shouting in anger and frustration that he should die. 'Release the murderer Barabbas instead,' we would have cried with them, because at least we would have known that he was on our side, that he wanted what we wanted, that he was one of us."

I had long since abandoned my prepared manuscript, trying to connect with this unusual collection of two dozen hearers. They looked odd sitting at their tables without drinks, quietly listening. It was impossible to know if I might be getting through; curiosity seemed to be the most identifiable expression on their faces. The whole scene was surreal, but I forged on, hopeful.

"The crowd wanted the blessing Jesus promised. He had told them how to get it, but they weren't paying any attention to the words. They wanted no part of him if he demanded anything from them. They wanted no part of the cross. And yet, the cross is the key to the blessing. Any one of us in here can carry it with us; all it takes is faith. And obedience. And a willingness to put the resentment away, and start serving one another in love."

The subtle movement toward my invitation was met with a visible response. Some of the men who were standing in the back ducked out. There were guarded looks about the room.

"No one is asking you to change your habits today. What I'm asking you to do is ask yourself three questions, that's all. First, are you happy with your life as it is? Second, do you believe that God can help make your life more meaningful? Third, are you willing to give him a chance to do that? If you are, I would like you to raise your hand as the band plays, with all our eyes closed. Hands in the air means we'll be back next Sunday, and we'll start slowly walking through what the Christian life means. With God's help and guidance, we'll deal with your issues and find some new direction for your life."

The band, which had opened the service with an unplugged, modified version of "I Can't Get No Satisfaction," now launched into a rather weak cover of "Let It Be." At least ten hands were raised. I prayed a corny benediction that seemed so appropriate I would later try to recall it for regular use: "May God bless all who come to this house, which by his presence is made holy, and as we also are made holy, let us go forth to bless others in Jesus' name, amen."

Fifteen minutes later, I was lying on my back on the bar after the small crowd had gone, looking up at the glasses hanging upside down above me, listening to Isabella chattering away excitedly about my preaching prowess.

"It has nothing to do with that," I said casually. "I have credibility with these people. I've been roughed up by a bad guy, and I lost my job. So they listen. They're testing me, but it's way too early to know for sure what might happen."

"We have very many next week," she said.

"Naturally. It's Easter."

"Yes, but you make promise to help them."

I closed my eyes, praying for patience. "It takes time, Isabella. Don't expect . . ." I caught myself, but it was too late.

"Miracles?" She grabbed my arm. "I give testimony next Sunday then!"

I rolled over on my side, propped on one elbow. "Sure. That would be great," I said.

She said something in Spanish and kissed my forehead. I fell back and laughed, and she joined in with me. I stared up at the rows of glasses, then looked around as if for the first time. "No communion, though," I said, and this increased her laughter all the more.

CHAPTER TWENTY·ONE

I HAVE HAD THE feeling on several occasions that the person I am talking to is completely disinterested in what I am saying, and I should just save my breath, but I continue for the sake of one who is eavesdropping on the conversation. It is often like this in preaching, because people rarely want to show that the sermon is having any effect upon them, or that it speaks to a matter of critical importance in their lives. Rather, the preacher is assumed to be talking to somebody else, while the true target of the message displays a merely speculative interest in what is going on. The Word always finds its mark, and I can usually tell where the arrows lodge, though it is something of an acquired skill to do so. But when I took my advertisement to the newspaper offices for publication, the man with the shaggy mustache and ink blot on his breast pocket made no attempt to hide his curiosity.

"Excuse me, but don't I know you from somewhere?" I looked up, somewhat bemused at the line, but answered the man with the same honesty with which he seemed to be asking the question.

"I don't think so . . . unless you've visited my former church."

"That's it!" he said, punching the air. My impression was that this odd fellow was passionate about everything. "But I didn't go to your church. I saw you on television. Incredible story."

The woman behind the desk had not yet responded to my inquiry about the ad department, and went back to her personal call, assuming the man was taking over the responsibility for my presence in the office.

"Oh. Well, that was rather unfortunate," I said, not embarrassed anymore at the repeated acknowledgment of my fifteen minutes of fame, but not particularly enthusiastic about retelling it either. He wanted to know what had happened since, and I'm sure I told him way more than he cared to know, though his sincere interest never waned. This was a professional listener. He took the ad from my hand and praised it.

"Matthew's House," he read. "Can I come?"

I hesitated for a moment. "Of course, but . . . you might feel—"

"This is great," he commented, absorbed in the ad, his expert listening function suddenly switched off. "'No shirt, no shoes, no service,'" he read. "That's classic."

I blushed a little but didn't let on. "That's what it says on the door. We're kind of opposite from what you usually get on Easter. Listen, I'm not sure you'd care for—"

"I'll be there," he said abruptly. "Will you have a few minutes afterward for the interview?"

"The . . . what?"

He laughed. "The interview. I'll do a story on your new church, how's that?"

I was speechless, but extremely gratified. He escorted me to the advertising department where I found another disinterested person, but that was okay. All this guy had to do was stick the ad in Saturday's paper. And all I had to do was be ready for Mr. Mustache the next day.

◆ ◆ ◆

My boss at Fenimore's allowed me to use his copy machine to make flyers promoting the Easter service, and I put the first one up in his window. During the week, Michael and some of his faithful members helped me pass them out and staple them to telephone poles around the neighborhood. The results were overwhelming: about seventy people crowded around the tables down at The Dutchman to worship. Isabella offered her story of Miranda's healing, and I preached vigorously on the subject of hope, focusing on the women who first went to the empty tomb. I noticed that Mr. Mustache hardly wrote a word on his notepad until after the service, which concluded with an invitation to write a prayer on a three-by-five index card and a request to talk with me privately during the week. The band sent us forth with a rousing rendition of "Spirit in the Sky," and I gave what I thought was a rather bland interview, until I saw the headline on Tuesday morning: Holy Spirits! Radical Reverend's Tavern Talks Stir Seekers. The story began like an old-time radio commercial: "Thirsty for something new and refreshing?

When it comes to religion, Carla Donovan, formerly of St. Fred's church, is certainly the straw that stirs the drink."

This was not exactly the kind of press that would earn for me the glowing admiration of my peers, but it did make points that would resonate with the great unwashed. I was quoted accurately, repeatedly cataloguing the flaws of the modern church, with its fortress mentality and resistance to change. My comments about how ministers are trapped in the machinery of the church, unable to effectively reach out for fear they might neglect to oil the gears and have the whole thing grind to a halt, made even me smile as I read them. On the subjects of pretense and formalism, I was unmerciful in my criticism; on hypocrisy, I simply echoed the sentiments expressed by most people who don't attend church. My indictment was complete, but the interviewer was careful not to portray me as vindictive—the vision for Matthew's House was vividly clarified: to bring the gospel to where the people are already, to where they are comfortable enough to (pardon the metaphor) "drink it in." I wanted to emphasize that God touches the heart first, then a person responds as God leads, and only then does his or her life begin to show it. So many people think they have to be perfect before they can come to God, and they've got it backward, thanks to the self-righteousness they encounter every day from contemporary Pharisees. "If the church isn't willing to change for the sake of those outside its walls," I contended, "how can we legitimately ask those outside the walls to change for the sake of the church?"

"Great line," Michael said as we talked once again about the article when he called me at Fenimore's on Wednesday morning. "You sure I didn't say it first?"

"Probably, but God gets all the glory anyway."

"Hmm. Sounds like preacher talk to me. Better watch that, or you'll lose your following."

An e-mail from my book-loving professor had appeared, and I read excerpts from his favorable review of the article to Michael, who seemed suddenly interested in changing the subject. I suppose my burgeoning celebrity status was a bit awkward for him, and though he didn't speak of it, I sensed he didn't find the change in me altogether appealing at times.

"Let's forget church for a while. Want to go to the gym with me this afternoon?" The words sounded almost foreign coming out of my mouth.

"You're pretty serious about this workout stuff. That's—what? Three times now?"

"Four. You have to be tough if you want to be buff," I boasted.

He didn't laugh, and this worried me. Not even a fake laugh, which I would have accepted as a good sign. Still, I felt so good about myself and life in general that confidence oozed out of me, and I couldn't step back to let Michael do the macho-man thing without effort.

"You know, I think you liked me better before, when I was weak and weary," I said, peering up to a sagging shelf above the door where a carved figure of a raven perched. Michael answered in some roundabout way, but my ability to concentrate was shattered by a deep foreboding, and I sat, Poe-like, hovering over the keyboard, wondering where it came from.

The bells jangled harshly above the door as I made a totally unsatisfactory stab at ending the conversation.

"Mr. Kerry?"

He wore a wool jacket despite the gorgeous weather, with a narrow tie and a brimmed hat. His lined face was drawn and tired, but pleasant, which struck me as odd. I whispered a quick goodbye to Michael and turned my attention to the source of my dread. Just seeing him conjured up unpleasantries; my chest tightened, and I felt my throat go dry. "What a coincidence," I croaked, "to run into you down here. Do you have an interest in rare books?"

My attempt at common civility was strained, and he removed his hat and held it, almost apologetically, with both hands fingering the brim in front of him. "Carla," he said without looking at me, "since you were, um . . . since you left, we've been having a few . . . um . . . problems."

I might have at least tried to show surprise, but instead asked for details.

"Well, it's only been two weeks, but for one thing, attendance is way down. In fact, we had fewer than a hundred people on Easter. The fire, I think, scared some people, and of course the media attention . . ."

"You'll bounce back," I said, secretly pleased by the news. "People will forget."

"But if we can't find someone to preach, things can only get worse."

"I thought you guys had Bunky Willembeck filling in."

"Yes, Reverend, but you see, Mr. Willembeck had a heart attack two minutes into his Easter sermon and collapsed on the platform. He's in the intensive care unit at Ellis."

"That's terrible," I said, at last sincere.

"It is, it is," Kerry went on. I couldn't tell if he had been sent against his will like Jonah to Nineveh, or if he was truly sorry for the events leading up to my dramatic departure. "I need to inform you that not everyone feels this way, naturally, but there was a special meeting of the board last night to discuss the newspaper piece, and some of us would like to invite you to return to your position. The members have been calling us ever since you left, upset about what happened. They feel ashamed, you see, and now that you're apparently reaching people, albeit in an unconventional way, there is a deep regret over your . . . resignation. The people feel you were never given a chance to do what you had in your heart to do. There is the opinion that you should be given that chance now, if you'll accept it. I'm here to see if you are even the slightest bit interested."

"And Hamber? Lutz?"

He fiddled with the hat nervously. "As I said, not all are in agreement. But most are. Frankly, I'm not all that enamored of your new methods myself. But I'm willing to try and be more open-minded."

I watched him closely. This conversation was making him extremely uncomfortable. "I'll certainly pray about the matter" was all I could say.

He smiled weakly and put on his hat. "I'll pass the word," he said, and walked out in front of the clang of the bells on the glass door, below the frozen stare of the painted black bird.

◆　◆　◆

It couldn't have been an hour after Jameson Kerry left that the calls began; my former members had found me, thanks to the mention in the newspaper article of my part-time employment at Fenimore's. I had no real desire to return, of course, but I couldn't dismiss the idea entirely, and I said so to at least four of the callers who dared to ask the question. I had made a commitment to another ministry, I said, and I owed it to the people who frequented The Dutchman to give it my best shot. But Kerry had soft-pedaled the situation; I learned that there were not only fewer than a hundred present on Easter, but actually no more than fifty. I also discovered that there was a rumor afloat of the church's impending sale, because apparently the health department had done a thorough inspection following the fire and had issued a severe warning. This information came from none other than Al Lintz, who had a son who worked down in the city government offices: The church would need to address these problems soon—lead-based paint, asbestos, faulty plumbing, etc.—or face a heavy fine and possibly closure. According to Al, an unnamed entity had already approached the board with an offer to buy the property. It had been hard enough to find me, some said, and there were great concerns about anyone wanting to become pastor of a church in such a situation. Just getting someone to fill in once a week was a major challenge. Furthermore, hoodlums had begun to loiter around the church in the evenings, scaring off many of the elderly who made up the lion's share of the membership. If ever a miracle was needed, St. Fred's needed it.

Later that same day, I phoned Michael to make a proposition.

"You *what?*" He wasn't offended, just astonished.

"I want to move Matthew's House to St. Fred's."

"Carla, the whole point of the mission is to *not* be in a church. Those people won't even consider going there."

"They will if I open the pool."

There was silence on the other end of the line. His skepticism, however, was shouting back in soundless waves.

"Listen, the church building can become a ministry center for this whole area," I continued. "We can still have services in the bar—I'll do them at both places. We'll use St. Fred's to meet their physical needs, to help the whole person. I know I can gain support from the businesses in these neighborhoods. When some of the people profess faith, they can be discipled at Shekinah or St. Fred's. It can work, Michael, I know it can."

"But what if no one else gets healed? The whole thing will backfire."

"Michael, you heard Kerry. And I've found out that he didn't tell us the half of how bad things really are. God is judging that church, Michael. He's going to shut it down, if we don't act now. It's a bad witness; it's actually doing harm to the gospel as it is, but God wants to change that. He did miracles in the basement just a few weeks ago, remember?"

"I don't know . . . do you think the church will buy it?"

"The real question is, who will buy the church if they don't. It's up for sale, you know. They've got the health department on their backs."

"Serious?"

"Yeah. So what do you say?"

He hesitated to answer. "You seem awfully sure about this. Frankly, you've been so weird lately, I'm not sure you know what you're doing."

"And you gave me a job?"

He laughed. "Okay, you got me there. But I had other motives too."

His comment almost made me blush. I wanted to tell him everything. "Michael, you know that passage in Genesis where the strangers come to Abraham's tent, and they ask for Sarah?"

"Sure. She was hiding in the back."

"And one of them made the promise that she would have a son a year later, and she laughed?"

"Yeah, so what's that got to do with—?"

"She needed reassurance, Michael. She thought it was all over for her. And God made a personal visit, just for her. She named the baby Isaac—for her laughter."

"I know the story. So what does—"

"And the other passage, in Luke, where the stranger appeared on the road to Emmaus with Cleopas and that other guy?"

"Carla," he said in that chauvinistic tone of his, "I know all about that one too. Do you mind explaining—"

"In a second. But you know how they were so emotionally wrecked because of the trial, and the cross, and the missing body, and how they were crying on each other's shoulders about it, right? So why didn't Jesus just identify himself? *'Cheer up, fellas! Look at me–I'm alive!'*"

He sighed. "Well, because they would have missed the point. He wanted to show them that the cross was necessary, that the Messiah had to suffer to bring about redemption. He wanted them to see that, so he walked through the Scriptures with them until they did—then he revealed himself."

"Just like Sarah, they were hopeless," I summed up. "And Jesus came quietly and personally to them and gave them hope. Michael, I had an experience like that."

I could tell that he was having difficulty processing the statement. "An experience . . . *like that?* In what way . . . 'like that'?"

"A personal visit."

More hesitation. "Carla, listen, honey. I put together a list of names. I could give some of them a call . . ."

"I know, I know. And I'll go to your counselor if you want. But I'm telling you, I know this is going to work out. If Jesus appeared to Sarah, why not me? Why not Cornelia Shepherd? Can you answer that?"

"I'm not going to argue with you," he said. I knew I had him trapped.

"Good. Then you'll support me?"

"Well . . . I suppose. *If* the people at the mission say yes, and if St. Fred's says yes. What else can I do?"

"You can fire me."

"Aw, that's been done. You just keep coming back, like a bad habit."

It had been easier to say over the phone. I hung up, shut down the computer, and headed home for a quick change, supercharged for my evening workout at the gym, as if a tremendous weight had already been lifted from my shoulders.

◆ ◆ ◆

It was easy enough to spread the word to the crowd at The Dutchman since, by seven-thirty, most of the regulars had already gathered around the bar. I spoke to them in clusters of two or three or five and was greeted with a stunning display of indifference. It occurred to me that the Sunday services were simply a curiosity to many of them, and since these would continue, they saw no objection to anything we might do at St. Fred's. Maybe we had made a tactical error in planning the mission in the first place; by bringing church to the people, we may have simply made it more convenient for them to excuse themselves from religious commitment. Now, they could always ease their minds by saying, sure, they go to church, sometimes every week. But the fundamental issue—that of the need to change their lives—wasn't getting through. Of particular interest was the pool, however, which still held a certain fascination for many of the ones like Isabella whose faith operated on the simplest of levels. I would have been better off if I had left the matter with her, for she was a powerful inspiration. In truth, I believed that the healing pool was somehow a means to an end, and not an end in itself, but I would never again try to relegate God to that which was controllable or predictable. Not knowing any better, we would plunge ahead. It was a church with a pool. Why shouldn't it be open?

Deciding at last to allow Isabella the chance to tell her story fully, I went home to call Jameson Kerry. He answered on the second ring and seemed pleased that I had even considered his proposal. Since St. Fred's had no preacher for the following Sunday, he asked me if I would fill the pulpit. I agreed, under one condition: I would use the time to share my vision for the church, and it would need to be voted on, not only by the board, but by the congregation present in the service, immediately afterward. If they said yes, we would get started right away. If the answer was no, we would part ways forever. The fact that Kerry agreed to my terms on the spot suggested one of two things, or possibly both: They were desperate, and Derrold Hamber was no longer in charge, perhaps due to his public, televised outburst at my expense.

Emotionally drained, I drew a warm bath in the claw-footed tub and began to undress. I felt no nervousness about what I would say on Sunday, probably because it was already swirling around in my head. These were things I had known all along, but had buried under the rubble of my own bitterness for years. My vision, or more accurately the vision God had given me, was bubbling forth even as the waters of the healing pool had lapped against little Miranda's feet. I settled into the bath thinking on these things, excited at the second chance that was mine, happy to know that, despite the enormous challenges ahead and the improbability of success, I had a God who cared deeply about such things, and who would not let me fail, so long as my own faithlessness did not get in his way.

The telephone rang, and I jumped, scaring Motorhead from his perch atop the commode lid. I laughed, thinking of an earlier time just a few weeks before, when my happiest thoughts were mere daydreams, and reality was nothing but drudgery and doubt. How things had changed!

I threw on the robe, which clung uncomfortably to my wet skin, as I ventured out onto the kitchen linoleum in bare feet, like a diver in flippers fresh from the sea.

"Miz Donovan? This is Eldon Doby."

"Yes, Mr. Doby?" I puzzled, trying to place the name.

"At the grocery. You said call if—"

"Yes. Yes, of course." I hadn't known his name, but the deep voice was familiar, ringing clearly now as the water ran from my ears. "Have you seen the girls?"

"Got 'em right here. All four. What you want me to do?"

"Just don't let them leave. I'll be there in ten minutes."

I dressed in haste, panicking for a moment in search of my glasses, which I found on the bathroom sink. In minutes I was running out the door, ignoring Motorhead's distressed face in the window, fumbling with the keys to the Cavalier, and speeding off into the night.

Once behind the wheel, I realized I could not remember exactly where the grocery was, so I drove to The Dutchman and began to retrace my steps of that fateful Sunday afternoon to find it. I did recall that I had envisioned the neighborhood as a grid, traveling along two sets of parallel streets, and I knew that the grocery lay along the second route. But that first expedition had been in daylight; now it was night, and so I drove slower, worried that every minute I delayed might result in a lost opportunity. Crawling through the dimly lit streets, I felt a pang of fear mixed with frustration, as if I were venturing back into danger unnecessarily, glancing into the windows of the shabby roadside homes for anything or anyone that might be a threat. Finally, some twenty-five minutes after the urgent phone call, I spied the little grocery bathed in a circle of light afforded by a street lamp. Standing outside the door was Mr. Doby, anxiously looking out, I assumed, for me.

He pointed toward the back of the small building, and I followed his direction, the car bumping along uneven and broken pavement. I parked between a rusted car on blocks and a battered snowplow, and he appeared at my window as soon as I turned off the ignition. Without a word he waved me to follow him through the back door and into the store.

"In there," he said, pointing to a wooden door, then marched back to the counter, which he had left unattended.

I opened the door onto a tiny windowless room with a cheap metal desk pushed against the wall, piled high with papers and junk. Sitting atop the desk were Marita and Sabila; the tall girl was standing in the corner, talking down to the youngest of the group, who sat below her. The five of us could hardly fit in the little space.

Marita rushed to embrace me, muttering something in Spanish that made Sabila smile. I turned to the tall girl, who seemed impatient.

"Where are we going?" she wanted to know. It was clear that she was willing to go to just about any safe place, and soon.

"How did you make your way back here?" I asked.

"We ran into Marita a few blocks away. We were on our way back to Isabella's house when this guy told us to wait here for you."

I took a hard look at Sabila, who seemed relaxed, despite the dark circles under her eyes. All of them were dirty, but I decided not to ask too many questions.

"Well, there's no use going back to the church. The pool is drained, and Richie's henchmen are watching it, I'm told. I can take you to the police."

This brought forth loud, untranslatable objections. "Okay, just calm down. I know a safe place, better than Isabella's. But you have to allow us to help you." At that, Sabila started to cry, and while Marita tried to comfort her, the tall one nodded to me that they were ready to go.

I cracked open the door to find Eldon Doby selling beer to a youth with low-slung jeans and a floppy hat. He didn't check for identification, but I figured he had, a long time ago, decided not to make trouble for his customers, or they might make trouble for him. I waited until the creaky door slammed shut and the deep rumble of the overbuilt engine rattled the walls as it pulled away, then I poked my head out of the room and saw the store was empty. Mr. Doby was content to sit on his stool and smile pleasantly at us as we sneaked out the back door to the car.

My passengers began to chatter as soon as we pulled away, reminding me of the car pool after school. I drove fast, worried that en route we might encounter those who might not appreciate my rescue attempt. I told the girls to slump down in their seats, which was difficult to do in the compact car, but they did their best. The tall girl, who I finally learned was named Patrice, laughed through the space between the bucket seats at the three in the back, intertwined as if engaged in a game of Twister. In a relatively short time we had emerged onto the highway and were scooting across town. Relieved, I let them relax.

The small building behind the diocesan center was brightly lit, indicating that Sister Louise was at home. I left the girls in the car and rang the bell.

"Carla?" She looked surprised to see me, but not displeased. From my expression she must have known this was not merely a social visit, and she instinctively looked past me to the car.

"They're prostitutes. Young ones—at least three of them are teens, I'm pretty sure," I said. "Probably runaways. At least two of them have drug problems. They're running from their pimp—"

Sister Louise had brushed by me and was approaching the car to see for herself, looking like a wise hermit with her crocheted shawl, despite the comfortable evening. She opened the back door, and the girls came tumbling out, not saying a word, intimidated, I presumed, by the sheer power of this woman's presence. The nun put her arm out to Sabila and covered her shoulders with the shawl, as the rest followed obediently back toward the house. "They can come in tonight," she said to me, "and tomorrow I'll make arrangements to have them cared for." Her gentle smile was reassuring, and for the first time in well over an hour I felt calm.

I stayed with them for quite a while, listening to things I wish I had never heard from the lips of these girls who were half my age but who had had a lifetime's worth of experience already, while Sister Louise talked with them, encouraging their confessions. In time I found myself sharing my own burdens, which lay sleeping just beneath the surface of my newfound confidence, and I realized that we are all broken people, each with our own story of rebellion and, hopefully, return. All was not lost for these girls, after all. I entrusted them to Sister Louise's care, and retreated to my car for the ride home, carrying in my heart the urgent, inexplicable urge to call my mother.

CHAPTER TWENTY-TWO

"Mom?"

The greeting came in the form of a question, not because I didn't recognize the voice that answered the phone, but because of the strangeness of the intimate term, and I strained to utter it, fighting against years of emotional distance. Despite the greater span between heaven and earth, Jesus called his Father "Abba"—*Daddy*—and yet I struggled to call my mother "Mom." But then, they were much closer than we are, and God's not an alcoholic.

There was a sniffle on the other end, followed by a pause. "Is this . . ."

"Carla," I answered for her. Of course she knew it was me. She was wrestling with the discomfort as well. "I was calling to see how you're doing."

Such a simple statement, but enough implicit tenderness to shake her. *She cares,* she was thinking. "Oh? I'm . . . okay." Silence. What to say now?

"You know, I was thinking, uh, you and Dad have never been here and . . . Hey, I might get my job back."

"You might?" I couldn't read surprise, disappointment, or pleasure in her tone.

"Yeah . . . Probably. It's complicated. But if I go back to St. Fred's, I was thinking maybe you might want to drive over one Sunday? For the service?" My voice was spiraling into an elevated, thin pitch.

"Oh. Yes, yes, that would be wonderful, but . . . *can* we do that?"

Ordinarily the question would have been funny, but for some reason I found it irritating. "Sure. We don't shoot Catholics or anything."

"I'll have to ask your father, you know—"

"Well, you can come any time, if this week's not convenient. And . . . maybe you could bring Ryan and Margaret?"

"Yes! Oh, that will be good if they can come!" We both shared the feeling that Margaret's presence would definitely ease the tension. "And little Cass too."

"Cass?"

"Oh, we've taken to calling the baby by his middle name, Castleton. It's so confusing having two Ryans, and his great-grandfather was called Cass—he's the one who started the law firm."

"Oh."

Mother hesitated, perhaps sensing a familiar despair in my soft, monosyllabic response to the inevitable chorus of adoration that was about to resound as she ran on about the Cavanaughs and their stupendous feats, which would seamlessly merge into praise for Margaret, and culminate with criticism of me. This, at least, had always been the pattern. Instead, she changed course. "Yes, but you know, every generation has to blaze its own trail. That's what I was telling Doris Mayflower the other day, about your work as a minister. I'm so glad you didn't decide to go do something else, like that stockbroker thing your father thought up."

I was completely dumbfounded by her intentional flattery that words literally caught in my throat. Did she mean it?

"And it's such a lovely old church you have. You know that photo you sent me a few months ago? I framed it and hung it just inside the front door. Everyone who sees it always asks . . ."

The monologue faded from my hearing, though I hungered for every word, a physical reaction to the surreal quality of the conversation. I soon found myself speaking freely, recalling the tale of the pool, the bar, the fears and the doubts, and (amazing even myself) the faith. She listened carefully, sharing my frustrations and cheering my victories, like someone who was really not all that interested in the facts of the story, but in the person telling it. Like a mother.

An hour had passed when I hung up the phone. Putting it down was a happy relief, like setting down your heavy baggage after climbing a long flight of stairs to arrive at last in your room with a view of an exotic, alluring land.

◆　◆　◆

I walked to the pulpit without notes and stood before a pitifully small congregation, the majority of the pews empty or peppered with one or two persons at the most, probably about forty all told. These were the true saints, predominantly older folks, who had marched into the sanctuary in clear view of the handful of delinquents sitting on the front steps—the same who now filed in and parked themselves in the back row. In addition to these were Isabella and Miranda, along with a half-dozen people she had brought along. There were plenty of smiles all around, as if I might be one of their children accepting an award for an elementary school essay. Clearly, the majority was in my favor, but those few who resented my reappearance by popular demand made their presence felt with frowns, crossed arms, and fitful squirming as I spoke. This was the way Pharisees operated; with no real grounds to oppose the people's choice, they would express their disapproval in less obvious ways. I should be wary. Egan was one of them; Hamber and Lutz, however, were nowhere to be found.

My remarks were brief. About halfway through I realized I was practically regurgitating the opinions I shared with the reporter that had been printed in the paper, but it didn't seem to bore anyone. They were delighted with my forthright honesty, and I wondered if this is what they had been expecting from me all along. At length I came to the matter of what it would take for me to return to St. Fred's. My sufferings at the whims of an insensitive and abusive board had been publicly displayed, and I now had the upper hand. I relished the moment, but was careful not to take advantage of the situation in stating my conditions.

"I believe the old adage that a church should not be a hotel for saints, but a hospital for sinners. I want you to support my efforts to reach out to this community with no expectation of return. That means we will divert a significant portion of our budget to benevolence, counseling, training, and other ministries to the whole person. In doing so, we will not shrink from our greater cause to share the gospel with these people and invite them into our fellowship. We must acknowledge that, in God's sight, we are no better than they. They belong here as much as we do. This church should be called a house of mercy."

No one moved, knowing perhaps that such generalities were toothless without details. No one could argue with a commitment to a nonnegotiable aspect of Christian ministry like caring for the needy. I would not return as senior pastor only to find them not supportive when the time came to apply these eternal truths. Now was the time to lay all the cards on the table.

"In order for this to happen, we will need to change the way we do things. Dress for our worship will be casual, the music will be contemporary, and the tone of our services more relaxed and informal. Believe me, I'm not that comfortable with this kind of thing myself. But what I want isn't important. We have to do whatever we can to make people feel at home who are uncomfortable with church because they don't come from religious backgrounds. Our place must become their place. That shouldn't alarm us, because, after all, it's God's place."

There were stirrings now. But still, I felt a warmth there from most. It was time to be direct.

"As you are probably aware, there's a swimming pool in the basement that is in desperate need of repair. It fills with water sometimes, and I'm sure you've heard a lot of things about that. Some people believe that miraculous healings have occurred down there, and I'm one of them. But I don't believe that God dispenses miracles arbitrarily. I do think he has been trying to tell us that he can do miracles in people's lives through our church if we will just be obedient to him. So, I say we commit to a long-range plan to establish what has come to be known in recent weeks as the Matthew's House ministry, here, on our property. That means sleeping quarters for the homeless, a kitchen and food pantry, and rooms for vocational counseling, medical care, and other services. I won't come back to serve as pastor without your commitment to do this. And you will have to vote yes or no today."

I looked out over the faces and watched expressions change from elation to confusion to concern. This would be a major challenge, financially and culturally. Was this the only way the vision could be fulfilled? I saw people who wanted to see such a thing happen, but couldn't imagine it within the crumbling walls of St. Fred's, not with things looking so grave at present. They needed help to take the plunge.

"Look, I know this sounds like a lot, especially for us. We're used to talking about things for months, appointing committees, deliberating some more, compromising on the proposal, raising funds, then finally giving up from exhaustion and doing nothing. Where has all that hand-wringing gotten us? Look around. The building is falling down around us, the congregation is shrinking fast, and nobody wants to be pastor. If we don't act now to define our ministry, we'll be gone in a few years. Worse, we could be a restaurant or a gift shop a lot sooner than that. Or, we could be torn down. That will be our legacy. And look at our neighborhood. How many of you have ventured just three blocks from here at night? There are prostitutes, drug dealers, and all kinds of criminals roaming about. Kids are dropping out of school and ruining their lives. This is fast becoming a slum, and if you think St. Fred's will ever be a nice, all-white, upper-middle class congregation again, you are sadly mistaken. We have three options: move, close, or carry out the Great Commission right where we are. To me, it's not something we debate. We just decide—and if you accept the third choice, I'll be with you all the way."

The vote was too close for a showing of hands. I fidgeted in the throne-like chair, wondering if this would be the last time I would ever preside so royally, while index cards were found, torn into small ballots and distributed, and ultimately collected in the offering plates by a quartet of sullen ushers. When the final tally was read, twenty-nine people had accepted my proposal, twelve had not. I had a choice to make; I knew it would be tough going. But it wasn't about easy or hard—it was about what the Lord wanted. I had questioned him enough in my life. It was, in my opinion, simply a matter of trust.

The silent congregation sat nervously awaiting my answer as I walked to the pulpit, emotionless but resolute.

"How we will be able to do this, I have no clue," I said. "But if you're willing to try, so am I." A short riff of applause drifted toward me, catching me unprepared. Very few of these aged saints would live to see much more than the beginning of renewal; their lot would be great sacrifices for small rewards. I nodded and offered a brief benediction. They began to inch their way to the edge of the pews, more aware than I was of how difficult our task would be. I paused before departing the platform to watch one older gentleman greet Isabella, who in turn introduced him to her guests, and I marveled at how the kingdom advances, slowly but with certainty, on the strength of such small things.

♦ ♦ ♦

Sweat soaked through the back of my T-shirt as I lugged the last box of books from my car toward the church. My muscles were already sore from working out, and I felt my weakened fingers slipping under the heavy load. A car drove up behind mine as the box crashed to the sidewalk.

"Need a hand?"

"Naw," I said between short breaths. The pool man always seemed to catch me at my worst.

He bent down with me and helped me repack the books. "I was in the area and thought I would drop by," he said. "Don't suppose you've had any discussions about the pool?"

I smiled at his persistence. "Sorry, Phil. Health department shut us down. No money right now to fix it, but we're hopeful."

He didn't appear too disturbed to hear the news. "That's fine. It would have been big bucks." He started to leaf through a Greek parsing guide, and I wondered if he had any idea what he was looking at. "So," he said while perusing the pages, "would you like to grab a bite for lunch maybe?"

The nonchalant manner of his question carried an unmistakable intent. "Are you . . . asking me out?" I yelped as if bitten, unnecessarily stating the obvious. It seemed to embarrass him, and he froze momentarily, the book open somewhere in Romans. We knelt there awkwardly, looking everywhere but at each other.

"Well, I . . ."

As he searched for an answer, straining to determine if my incredulity centered on the absurdity of my going out with him or of simply being asked, I felt a strange numbness in my thigh and longed to stretch it.

". . . I was hoping you . . . well, yes, actually, I am."

The words tumbled out freely and seemed to relieve the tension. I opened my mouth to politely decline when a sharp shooting pain erupted in my leg, and I screamed. He stumbled to his feet and stepped out of the way as the cramp took total control, and my body contorted into a violent seizure, my leg jackknifing toward him wildly. It was like a scene from a bad martial arts movie, complete with sound effects.

"I take that as a no," he said as I jumped up and tried to shake out the pain, hopping around the box of books as if dancing for rain. I clung to the side of the car for balance and started to apologize for my sudden convulsions.

"That's okay," he said cheerfully, perhaps grateful now that I had not said yes. "I understand. By the way, I've got something for you." He reached inside his car and flipped open the latches of his briefcase. When he emerged, he was holding a small plastic vial, which he tossed to me. I dropped it, naturally.

"Your water sample," he said. "No sense keeping it around the office just so we can get it mixed up with someone else's again. I'll fax you the lab report when I get back to the office, just for kicks. But please, keep this a secret, okay? I wouldn't want the word to get out that I'm a complete moron."

"Oh no, Phil, I would never tell anyone that," I assured him, immediately regretting my choice of words.

After he was gone, I spent the rest of the day putting my office back together. Michael had informed me that he would try to come by to help, which irked me somewhat, especially since he didn't volunteer any details. I wondered again if my new take-charge attitude had changed his view of me. Perhaps he preferred me as the "weaker vessel." I apparently had much to learn about the mating habits of the male minister.

The desk vacated by my erstwhile secretary was now covered with unopened mail. There were several letters hand-addressed to me, and I hauled them into my office to consider them in peace. I expected both praise and anger and got both. Several people threatened to leave the church, and others planned to withhold their contributions, but this didn't worry me much, since very few of these folks had even been at church on Sunday. They were getting their information through the gossip line and no doubt had heard things I hadn't even said. And yet, there were other letters from those who pledged their unwavering support of my courageous stand. These I read many times over, drinking deeply from the well of encouragement.

A letter from Al Lintz was especially charming. He was a tough old bird, steeped in silly traditions, but duty bound to serve the Lord. He cared about the church and its future. As long as I didn't use *darn* in my sermons, he would be in my corner all the way.

I reached for the phone to call Michael, wanting to share the blessing.

After about ten rings he finally answered. "Michael. You'll never believe what I found in the mail."

He hesitated, then replied in a shaky voice. "I know. I got one too."

The tone of his response was mournful, almost a whisper. "You . . . got what? Are we talking about the same thing?" I asked.

"I'm talking about the postcard," he said. "Didn't you get one?"

Confused, I rustled through the letters. "No, no . . . maybe it's still in the outer office. What postcard?"

"Go look," he said gravely. "I've been getting calls all day. My guess is that they're all over the city."

My assumption that no one could possibly take the accusation seriously was premature, as I began to hear from worried members that they had received the postcards. No one asked if the story were true—that Michael and I had been meeting each other at a sleazy hotel—but wanted only to let me know what was happening. They listened as I offered my opinion that this was typical of how certain kinds of people act when they are angry with a religious leader, and that we should not be troubled by it. More often than not, this proved to be unsatisfying; they wanted a public denial, as if any shred of doubt would be enough to convict me of immorality in the eyes of their peers, which would only hurt the church further. After all, there *had* been some legitimate questions raised about my conduct before, and I really ought to set the record straight, not that I *needed* to, of course.

In order to appease the masses, I sat down at my computer and banged out a sniping retort for the weekly newsletter:

Dear Church:

In recent days our congregation has agreed to embark upon an ambitious plan to reach our community, and I am grateful to God for the opportunity to lead you through this important work. Your support of me, in spite of all that has happened, is truly appreciated. It is nice to open the mail on my first day back to find your letters of encouragement. I'm excited about what lies ahead.

Please know that I will keep an open door throughout this process to address your individual concerns. Feel free to call on me at home if you consider it necessary. And, if you can't seem to find me, check your mailbox: you may be one of the lucky members who are receiving breaking news on my whereabouts from an anonymous reporting service. Just meet me at the location on the postcard—the more, the merrier! I'll be glad to interrupt what I'm doing to give you my undivided attention, because I'm committed to being more "hands-on" in my relationships.

Of course, if you go to the appointed place, and I'm not there, chances are I've already moved down the road to meet someone else's personal needs. Or it could be that the reporting service simply got the facts wrong. I'll leave it to you to decide. The bottom line is, I will do everything I can to be the best servant-leader I can be. All I ask is that you judge me by the Word of God—not by the words of others.

See you Sunday,
Carla

When the typing, cutting, pasting, and folding were done, I cheerily stacked the newsletters in the bin and hauled it to my car. My muscles were still sore, but it felt rather pleasant, each twinge of pain a reminder that I was growing in health and strength. I shoved the plastic bin into the back seat and headed to the post office.

I missed the job at Fenimore's. It came suddenly in a jolt of remorse over losing the freedom I had felt doing my simple tasks, helping others, seeking and finding. Why had I given it up so quickly to embark upon this risky mission? The answer eluded me. The odds were against me, and I had enemies from within (the poison pens among our membership) and without (Richie and his band of brigands). I was forever locked, it seemed, in the heroic struggle to be a leader, hungry for the odds against me to make my exploits that much more glorious, but up to now I had accomplished little. Would I fail yet again? I prayed that God would renew my spirit for the simple tasks of ministry, to find peace somehow in praying with the sick, listening to the troubled, feeding the sheep. I could not make the ministry into a monument to myself, a self-glorifying endeavor in which people became a means to an end. Matthew's House was the vehicle for the vision, not the vision itself, which was leading people, one by one, to find wholeness. I realized that I had to somehow learn, then, to discover peace in that calling.

Out of the corner of my eye I caught a flyer tacked to a telephone pole, and I chastised myself for forgetting to take them down. It occurred to me that it might be wise to run a shuttle from The Dutchman to St. Fred's, to take people to worship who might not have heard about the change. Or, if I held services in both places, I would need to establish and publicize a new schedule. This was all happening too quickly, I fretted, *and I'm not prepared*. Suddenly, for the first time in days, the old doubts burrowed their way deep into my soul, and I gripped the wheel with anxiety. What was I doing? Did I really think I could herd these people into the church just like that? Who was I that they should follow me? And who was I to make such demands of the members, many of whom had supported that church longer than I had been alive?

Still preoccupied with these questions, my mind went vacant as I stood in line to mail the newsletters, nudging the bin along with my foot. I was vaguely aware of a woman staring rather rudely at me from her place ahead of me in line. As we shuffled forward, she came around the rail, and we were face-to-face.

"You're disgusting," she spat. The words were made all the more vicious by the contemptuous glare. I recoiled against the rail, stunned.

"Excuse me?" I sputtered, embarrassed not so much by the epithet as by the fact that so many people must have heard it; I felt several sets of eyes honing in on me. "Do I know you?"

"No, but everyone knows you, what with your reputation for carrying on like you do," the woman barked. The line was moving again, and the distance between us lengthened.

"What are you talking about?" I asked innocently, louder than necessary. "Do you go to St. Fred's?"

"No!" she yelled. "I wouldn't dream of it. Those people are nothing but hypocrites. Why they would want you back, I'll never know. You belong down at that watering hole with the scum, not behind a pulpit."

A lump lodged in my throat. "I'm afraid I've missed something somewhere," I called out. "Are you talking about the newspaper article? Doesn't sound like you read the same thing I did."

She fumed. "Don't get cute with me; you're a lush, and the whole town knows it. As soon as you arrived, you filled up a whole shopping cart with wine, and your only friend is a bartender, for heaven's sake. My neighbor drove past the church the other day and saw you carrying boxes of booze inside."

I held back the insult. "Those were boxes filled with *books*." We were about fifteen feet apart now, but the line had stopped moving. Everyone in the post office was absorbed in the exchange.

"No wonder you don't wear the collar anymore—you're a disgrace, that's what you are!" she hollered. I could only stand there helplessly as the onslaught continued. "You and that boyfriend you've been shacking up with!"

I could take this no longer. Flushed with anger, I marched along the rail toward her as the people moved to let me pass. My fingers tingled, and the back of my neck was scorched. Praying I would have the strength not to haul off and whack this woman, I walked right up to her and said sternly, "You have no right to accuse me of these things. None of them are true. Tell me, where are you getting your information?"

She would not look at me. Instead, she moved straight to the front of the line and presented her parcel to the clerk, who posted it without a word. Then we all watched as she marched defiantly out. Her exit breathed life into the crowd; the people started to move and talk excitedly, waving their arms for emphasis. I slipped back to my place where I had left the bin of newsletters, red-faced and hurt. Stamps and envelopes of various kinds were hung on the wall, and I imagined the mail in everyone's hands containing more gossip about me, the words on their lips repeating the lies, which grew with every retelling. But then, some began to turn toward me and whisper their support. Even so, I felt shamed by the spectacle. Now that it was over, I felt like crying.

In a few moments, the line of customers seemed to have forgotten the incident and returned to their affairs. An overweight twenty-something guy draped in black clothes with several small metal items piercing his nose and eyebrows noticed that I was still upset and walked over to me.

"Personally, I would have slapped her," he said.

◆　◆　◆

The Wednesday night crowd at Shekinah Church was almost boisterous, greeting each other with all the hushed reverence of a stampede as they swarmed around the folding tables in the small activities building constructed with volunteer labor. Several folks stopped to chat while I picked at my baked chicken, rice, and carrots, but as soon as the last one moved on, I quickly devoured a moist square of carrot cake. Michael had been gone for several minutes, weaving his way around the tables, speaking to each person. He had apparently abandoned his plate, since it was almost time to start the prayer service, so I snatched his cake also.

Historically, nerves marked the beginning of my downfall, so I knew I'd better watch it; I put down my plastic fork, having only scraped off the cream cheese topping. Even in this casual setting I was uptight, stressed from the pressure of criticism and the discussion that would mark this evening's program. I looked at the good Christian people, trying to lock into their relaxed manner, musing to myself that this was about as informal as church could be (reminding me a bit of dinner at Michael's parents'). Just then the voices quieted down almost automatically in anticipation of Michael's approach to the small handmade podium. He was less than fifteen feet away now; paper plates were being carried to the trash bins, Bibles were opening, and children were skittering off to their various activities. I folded my hands in my lap and tried to look self-assured.

Michael began easily with a short devotion on the apostle Paul's commitment to taking up offerings wherever he went for the poor believers in

Jerusalem. It was part of Michael's continuing series of teachings in support of the mission work at Matthew's House, though he never specifically mentioned it. He urged the people to develop a heart for the needy, recognizing that such compassion was "Spirit-led and Spirit-bred." I knew that evangelism and counseling training were part of the total program, along with kids' Bible clubs for the summer, literacy work, and other ministries. But Michael started slow, and in the right place. It is in the heart where every good work begins, he noted.

There was an extended prayer time, using a long list that was printed and distributed to all. We prayed in small clusters—something I could never imagine happening at St. Fred's. My three partners—an older man and his wife, and her friend Janice—took the whole time. That was good, since they prayed for everything on the list and more, including everything under the sun, and I could think of little else to add. At length, Michael reconvened the meeting and brought up the issue of Matthew's House directly.

"Our deacons have already met to discuss the changes affecting our mission work, and I bring this to you for information tonight. Our mission pastor, Carla Donovan, has been asked to return to St. Fred's church, with the understanding that the work of Matthew's House will continue there. This is really great, because it gives us a facility from which to establish ministries to the surrounding neighborhood. So, our stipend will no longer be given to Reverend Donovan directly, but to a special fund for the work. Services will continue at The Dutchman, though the schedule isn't firm yet. Most of the people we reach will, hopefully, eventually seek membership at St. Fred's, but we will have a hand in discipling them. Through the relationships we establish some will likely come here. We took a step in faith, and the Lord has blessed it—now, there are *two* churches committed to helping these people."

He made it sound so positive, even I became excited hearing the amens filling the little room. This wasn't so bad after all.

"And there is one other matter we need to be in prayer about."

What?

"As many of you know, there have been accusations made about my relationship with Reverend Donovan."

Heads snapped back to stare. This was awful. I felt I was shrinking in my metal chair, but I was frozen with fright. Then I noticed the stares weren't suspicious or contemptuous—they were *sympathetic*. Michael continued speaking, but I couldn't follow the words, preoccupied with the people who were slowly approaching, gathering around me to pray. Out of the corner of my eye I saw another group converging around Michael. I felt hands on my shoulders and fell deeply under the power of love in action. I don't remember anything that was said in those few minutes, but when it was over I felt a tremendous weight lifted, both physically and emotionally, like coming up for air after being swallowed by a raging current.

CHAPTER TWENTY-THREE

THERE WAS NO TELLING how many of the postcards had been mailed, but I had heard from at least a dozen people by Thursday, and Michael from almost as many. The indications seemed to be that people outside the church had also been mailed cards, and everywhere I went I felt oppressed by stares that weren't there. It is an incredible phenomenon, really, that someone could be so threatened by the prospect of change that they would lash out like this, hoping to scare me away, or at least distract me from carrying out the vision I had proclaimed. Hamber, of course, had the capacity for such a despicable act, but harboring suspicions would only spoil my spirit further. And yet, I couldn't shake the shock that a person associated with the church—a profess-ing Christian—would deliberately try to destroy my ministry without dis-cussing his or her complaints with me in a rational manner. Michael's theory was that, since the church welcomed everyone, it tended to attract people who got beat up every day in the big, bad world, and once they were inside the church, they wanted to take control of everything and everyone almost out of resentment. They might be a bit twisted, but the church was the one place where they could have their way and be in charge. Pondering this thought, I considered those who had risen to positions of leadership, and while many of them were influential people, quite a few were not. Big men (and women) on the church campus were they, but inconsequential outside its walls.

We determined not to allow the poison pen to intimidate us. Michael met with his deacons, and they all pledged their support; one even recommended a pulpit exchange between us one Sunday—me preaching there, and Michael at St. Fred's—to show that the two churches were not influenced by the rumors. Of course, no one at Shekinah believed that the nefarious campaign had been originated by one of its own members, so Michael had it relatively easy. Unfortunately, this was not to be the case for me.

On a whim, I punched the speed dial connecting me with Derrold Hamber's direct office line. He answered inside of two rings with a pleasant, lilting voice. When he heard that it was me, the tone grew dark. "I can't imagine why you're calling me," he said, "unless it's to apologize."

This made me smile, and I was glad he couldn't see it. "Honestly, sir, I was calling to see if you had left the church."

"Do you care?"

"Of course I do," I said, careful not to elaborate that his departure would be more cause for celebration than concern. "Our last discussion was a little heated, and since I'm starting over, it would be nice to know who I'll be working with."

"I've heard about your new endeavor. It will never get off the ground, with or without me," he growled.

"With God all things are possible."

He grunted. "Even those with their heads in the clouds should plant their feet solidly on the earth. You have no idea what you are getting into. It might be possible with God, but not with you. You're not capable, Miss Donovan."

I tightened my grip on the phone, wanting to yell any number of insults at this man who had been instrumental in hiring me—an ostensibly courageous decision, which I knew now to have been motivated solely to allow him to retain power in the church. "I guess that means you're leaving then," I said instead.

"Not exactly. Better to say I'm sitting on the sideline for a while to watch the carnival. I wasn't in favor of your return, as I'm sure the few board members who remain have told you, and I can't in good conscience offer my support, so I'll wait for your plan to fall apart, and then I'll come back to pick up the pieces."

"Seems to me you would want to stay close to the situation, either to claim responsibility if the ministry prospers, or to minimize the damage if it doesn't."

He took a deep breath, the way self-important men often do before issuing pronouncements. "That would be hypocrisy," he said.

My smile returned, a bloom amid the desert heat of my anger. "You don't like me, do you?" I said, laughing.

"Not particularly." He wasn't laughing with me.

The slight release of tension triggered the question that had prompted the call. "Mr. Hamber, did you send the postcards?"

"I don't know what you're talking about."

That was all he would say. Why didn't he just hang up on me? What could he gain by having this conversation? And then it struck me—he *enjoyed* this little game, and he would play it as long as I would let him. I got the impression that he had been waiting for this, wondering when I would call to beg the great man to come back, probably at the urging of the other board members. Then he would lead his cavalry of malcontents back to fill the pews with fannies and the plates with cash. He craved attention and control, and by holding out so conspicuously, he was enjoying both.

"Someone is sending anonymous notes around town questioning my morality. You don't know anything about that?"

"I said I didn't. But I'm not surprised."

I needed to end this war of words quickly. He was better at it than I was, and soon I would make a fool of myself, lashing out irresponsibly in anger. "Okay, then. I've enjoyed talking with you, Mr. Hamber." I hoped he could hear the sarcasm.

"Is that all?"

"Yes. Have a good day now." I hung up and stared at the phone, thinking it might ring right away. I couldn't know if he had sent the postcards, and it really didn't matter. I wished I could be rid of him, but I doubted if that was possible. Power was intoxicating to people like Hamber—once it was gained, they were loath to give it up. He would be a nobody at some other church, and we both knew it. Besides, Hamber was out to get me, and if my plan did work, he could never realistically regain the influence he once had at St. Fred's. I knew he couldn't stay away too long.

I emerged from the study to find the light on the answering machine blinking; someone must have called while I was speaking with Hamber. I hate answering machines because, when you're the minister, they tend to obligate you to respond. Sometimes the messages they convey concern trivial matters, other times not—and I was mindful of this fact as I depressed the button: the last such message I had received was from Michael informing me that Carmine Russo had died.

I didn't recognize the voice until she identified herself. It was the woman from the nursing home informing me that Cornelia Shepherd had been moved to Ellis Hospital, and that the family had been notified. She was not expected to live through the night.

I locked up and made for the door, then backtracked to disconnect the answering machine from the phone before heading to the hospital.

The brief conversation with Derrold Hamber, self-deposed chairman of the church board, rattled around in my brain as I traveled through town, merging like a fast car in heavy freeway traffic, with my worries about Cornelia. The two things had nothing to do with each other on the surface, but somehow they seemed connected. It could have been sheer anxiety: wondering when Hamber was coming back and when Cornelia was going away—the stressful waiting for unpleasant things. Or maybe it was the sense that events were taking a downward turn all of a sudden, despite my recent foray into forgiving my mother—calling her daily, even—and the vote of confidence given to me by St. Fred's. I kept replaying a certain conversation in my head, trying to dispel the doubts—this was no time to sit and fret; I was commissioned and empowered to rise up and walk.

I parked in the clergy space at Ellis and tracked along the familiar route into the belly of the hospital. Michael said he sometimes prayed as he walked through the corridors for the unknown patients behind the doors, each one of whom had a story, he said, and hurts to be healed. I wanted to do that, but I was far too nervous, thinking only of what I might see when I pushed open the door to Cornelia Shepherd's room.

She seemed smaller as she lay in the bed, the sheets folded neatly around her still form. It was apparent she had not moved since some nurse had tended to her last, and even as I came close I could not tell if she was breathing. I stood there awkwardly, then went back to the nurses' station.

"Excuse me, I'm Carla Donovan from St. Fred's. I was wondering about Mrs. Shepherd."

"Yes, of course, Reverend." She was dyed blonde and plump but bustling with happiness, apparently undaunted by the sadness all around her, like a bouquet of fresh-cut spring flowers hung on the face of a mausoleum. "I was asked to give you this."

I took the envelope. "Is she—"

"She's resting now, heavily sedated. I don't think she has much longer." She pointed to the letter. "You just missed the attorney."

I looked down at the envelope, thanked her, and backed away to the wall. I scanned the neatly typed note and was pleased to know that the lawyer's office would be in touch with the next of kin, and that the funeral home would be contacting them directly with the funeral arrangements. I was urged not to make immediate travel plans if possible because the reading of the will would take place while the family was still in town; apparently Mrs. Shepherd was leaving a portion of her estate to "St. Winefrid's Church." Enclosed was a paper written in Mrs. Shepherd's own hand outlining the specifics of her funeral service; I smiled to see she had listed the congregational hymn "Pass It On"—a mantra from the sixties. A former pastor whose name I recognized had been originally scheduled to speak, but his name was crossed off, and mine was written in the margin. I was so moved by this gesture that I wanted to rush into the room and give the old woman a hug. But the biggest surprise of all was the name of the person she wanted to bring the eulogy: Fr. Bruno Calabrese.

I tucked the letter in my purse, and, as I did so, noticed the small plastic vial Phil Garrison had delivered. I went back to the room with it hidden in my hand, and I stood there awhile, wondering what to do. This woman's life was over, I thought, and I knew her in relation to one defining moment, when God had wondrously intervened in her life. But what else had she done over these years? How many lives had she touched? It shamed me to think that I had never asked, that I had used her as a conduit for information to help me deal with my own troubles. Could I sprinkle her with miracle water and bring her back, if only for a day, or an hour, or a minute? To apologize, to tell her that her life did matter to me? No, that too would be selfish. It was time for her to go home. Whatever I would discover about Cornelia Shepherd I would hear from Father Bruno—if he was still living, and I could even find him.

I thought I noticed a smile on Cornelia's face, but it was probably only in my head. I pulled up the chair and sat with her quietly. Time went by, and my mind began to slow to time's pace, perhaps an hour, perhaps two. Clouds obscured and revealed the sun outside. A nurse came and went to check the equipment. Plastic numbers flipped on a digital clock. And then, Mrs. Shepherd turned her head to me ever so slightly, and I knew she was gone. I kissed her on the forehead and turned to go. Pausing, I poured the water from the little vial into the bathroom sink, and dropped it in the trash basket. I closed the door to the room and spoke briefly to the nurse.

I prayed as I walked—for the unknown patients—and sped away from the hospital, anxious to talk with Sister Louise.

◆ ◆ ◆

A long talk over coffee with a nun who was rapidly becoming my best friend, a long talk with a woman who shared my name and who was finally becoming a parent, and a long bath with a good book under my chin and my faithful cat perched nearby helped ease the pain of my loss. I grieved not so much for my personal loss, for Cornelia and I were hardly friends, but for what she represented, to me and to everyone else. She had been a true witness. Now she was at peace, Sister Louise said, and it was up to me to carry on her work. I didn't know exactly what that meant, and I didn't ask. But I slept that night more peacefully than I had done in a long time.

Friday was Michael's day off, and I should have known before I called that he would be looking for something to do. A natural workaholic with a thousand irons in the fire, he had been chided by his deacons for working seven days a week some time back, and they insisted he stay away from the church on Fridays for his own well-being. This act of love was interpreted by Michael to be punitive, in effect if not in spirit, and his restlessness had led to a number of ill-fated hobbies, excursions, and activities, none of which seemed to satisfy. So when I called to say that Cornelia Shepherd had died and had apparently left money to the church in her will, he insisted on seeing the attorney's letter, and hopped right in the car before I could object. The fact that Sister Louise was busy tracking down Father Calabrese only height-ened his interest, and it was all I could do to dissuade him from assisting with the search.

It's not that I wanted to keep secrets from Michael, but rather that he moved so fast, that made me hesitant to give him any information. Invariably, he would thrust himself into whatever unresolved problem I might divulge and carry me off in some unwanted direction, before I could even get used to the idea. He didn't quite grasp that sometimes people just want someone to *listen,* and not necessarily to prescribe the cure for what ails them. When we first met, his boldness was a good match for my insecurities, but now things had changed. I wasn't the wimp he thought I was anymore, and while I was sure he had sensed the change in me, I also worried that he might prefer the old Carla. He undoubtedly held on to the assumption that I was, at best, still depressed; at worst, a little unbalanced. I decided I would try to balance the scales between us by staying calm, rational, and steadfast. The old Carla, after all, was still lurking there, itching to get out.

The doorbell interrupted my makeup routine, which wasn't going particularly well anyway, so I just scrubbed off what I had so amateurishly applied; Margaret would see me tomorrow and would discover that I hadn't learned a thing about the cosmetic arts. I would have to tell Michael about the visit, too, that Mother (okay, Mom) and I were poised to patch things up and that the whole family was coming to hear me preach on Sunday. He didn't much like my family (who could blame him?), and it would be important for this situation to change if we were to have any future together. A post-church Sunday dinner might be a good starting point.

Michael was all smiles and ushered in the morning sunshine as I opened the door. Motorhead curled around my legs, and Michael greeted him first, but an electrostatic shock from his fingers sent the poor animal galloping away.

"That cat's a lint bag," he said.

"No need to vacuum when he's in a floppy mood," I said. "C'mon in."

The letter was on the kitchen table waiting for him. "I've heard of this firm, Van Antwerp and Weiss. Wow, this is from the head 'Twerp himself. Let's go see this guy."

"No way, Michael. This isn't any of our business, really."

"Well, let me tell you something. You need to find out what's going on here. I'll bet there's a pile of money at stake. Last year this guy left his house to the church because we were the only family he had—*we thought*. Turns out he had a grandson in Ohio who never visited, never cared a bit for the old guy, but who contested the will, saying we had done all these nice things just to get the man's assets. It almost went to court, and we settled to avoid the negative publicity. All I'm saying is, be prepared."

"Look, I don't want to come off as a money-grubber. I mean, if what you say is true, wouldn't pestering the lawyer just prove the relatives' point?"

"I don't think so. The church hasn't exactly been good to this lady over the years, and I bet the family knows it. They will fight this, I'm sure. See all the names on this letterhead? Van Antwerp is the senior partner, and he's handling this himself. What does that tell you? Carla, this could be God's way of saving St. Fred's. Did you ever think of that?"

I hadn't, and my face said so.

"And there's another thing I'm curious about. Why would she want Bruno Calabrese to speak at her funeral?"

"Well, that's easy. She was a Catholic who converted when the church changed hands. She would have known him. A lot of people like to be remembered as they were when they were young."

"I guessed that part, but she updated this paper recently. See, this other guy was crossed out, and your name was written in, but she left Father Bruno on the program. What do you have in common with him?"

"Nothing, unless—"

"Unless he knew about the miracle and believed her."

I sat down at the table with him and reread the letter. "So what this means is, she is leaving money to the church because of the pool. That's no surprise . . . she doesn't even believe in women ministers. It's obvious that she wants the story told." I put the paper down. "Oh, boy."

"What?"

"Well, we have to do this at the funeral, both of us, assuming Bruno is still living and Sister Louise can find him. It's what she wanted; we can't just leave it out. Now this family sitting there will *really* think she was nuts. How can such a person be 'of sound mind'? They'll say we encouraged her delusions. Michael, in order to justify our claim on the estate, would we have to actually *prove* this miracle occurred?"

He drummed his fingers on the table. "Let's go see the lawyer," he said.

We stopped at the diner for breakfast on the way. As we were eating, I casually mentioned that my brother-in-law might have some advice for us, since he was a big-shot attorney in Boston. He might even take the case if it went that far. I said I would discuss it with him the next day when he arrived in town.

"He has business here?"

"Uh, no, the whole family's coming—to see me."

Michael paused in mid-chew, his fork dripping maple syrup.

"I meant to tell you, but these other things seemed more important."

"No, no, it's fine," he said. "You need the time with them. No problem. I think it's great. So, should I expect you to be emotionally wrecked when it's all over?"

I laughed. "Well, you still have those counselors' phone numbers, right?"

The offices of Van Antwerp and Weiss leaned slightly to the left, and the narrow steps inside the door were worn and uneven. The building was located in the historic district known as the Stockade, the site of the first settlement in the area back in the late seventeenth century. Many of the existing structures dated to the 1700s, including this one; I kept falling into the wall as we climbed the creaky stairs.

An attractive receptionist indicated that Mr. Van Antwerp was meeting with a client, and though she was polite, it seemed to me that her immense surprise that we just kind of crashed in without an appointment was meant to communicate that such things simply weren't done. She would be happy, she said, to give him a message, and whipped out a notepad. Translation: If you expect to see the man today, you're flat out of luck.

"We're here about the Shepherd estate."

Her eyes filled with white space. *"Oh,* of course. Just a moment." She hopped up like a bunny and disappeared around the corner. I only had time to flash a look of bewilderment at Michael before she returned.

"Mr. Van Antwerp will see you now," she chirped.

We followed her down a short corridor and were ushered into an office that could have served as an exhibit in a museum of colonial life if not for the huge man in the gray suit who was stabbing his PDA with a stylus. The door shut behind us, and he looked up.

"So very nice to meet you folks," he said, putting down the gadget. He cocked his head to one side, oozing sympathy. "She was such a fine, fine lady. Please have a seat."

We placed ourselves gently in the rickety chairs. I looked at Michael, wondering if he expected me to speak up first.

"Now, let's see," the lawyer said, opening a file. "I think you should know that Mrs. Shepherd had very strong feelings about her church, um . . . oh yes, St. Winefrid's. She had the finest medical care throughout her later years, I'm sure you know, but she could have lived in a much nicer facility, but she wanted to preserve as much of her estate as possible for the church. I hope that won't be a problem."

"And why would it be?" I asked.

Van Antwerp raised his big head from the file. "Well, some folks aren't really religious, I guess, and they don't understand these things." He smiled. "I take it we can expect smooth sailing then. I must say I personally think you're being extremely gracious. Three hundred thousand dollars is a lot of money."

I gripped the arms of the chair. "Three hundred thousand dollars?"

He frowned. "Why, almost, yes. Didn't you get my phone message?"

I moved up to the edge of my seat. "I got your letter, the one you left for me at the hospital."

"Hospital?" He stared at me, confused, then at Michael, then at me again. "You're not the Stewarts? From St. Louis?"

I realized immediately he had mistaken us for the nephew and his wife. "No, sir. I'm Carla Donovan from St. Fre . . . Winefrid's, and this is Michael Montefiore. Three hundred thousand dollars?"

He flopped back in his well-oiled executive chair. "For heavens sake, forgive me. I just assumed . . . well, when you just showed up, I figured . . . I'm sorry, it's just that most people would be mad as blazes . . . uh, excuse me . . . and I expect the Stewarts will be too. But frankly, there's probably not much they can do about it."

"Why not?" Michael asked. "I've heard there are challenges to provisions like this all the time."

"That's correct," Van Antwerp answered," but in this case, there's nowhere for them to go. You see, there's a clause in the will that says if one party makes a legal challenge, the other party gets it all."

"But, did you know Mrs. Shepherd that well?" I asked.

The big man gave up a loud chuckle. "I know what you're thinking, Reverend. That's why I had a psychologist meet with her the day we drew up the documents. She was of sound mind, at least that day." He patted the file. "It's all in here. Of course, nothing is ever ironclad."

I stood up to go, and Michael followed suit. I wanted to get out of there, fearing the news was too good to be true, and the longer we talked, the more likely a loophole would be discovered.

"Besides," the attorney added, still sitting down, "it all makes sense."

"What's that?"

"Oh? That Mrs. Shepherd would leave so much to the church. Her husband was a very successful contractor in the years following the war. I'm pretty sure it was his company that built the old swimming pool down in the basement. You didn't know?"

"Actually, no," I said. Now I was standing rock still.

"Well, I believe he did. They say he did fine work. Tell me, is the pool still operational?"

Michael looked down at his shoes, embarrassed to reveal his wicked grin. "Better than ever," I said.

After a mid-afternoon fried chicken and ice cream splurge at an outdoor restaurant beside the Mohawk River just over Scotia Bridge, Michael took me to a movie and back home for an early evening. His behavior was erratic—one moment euphoric over the potential windfall for St. Fred's, the next pouting over being left out of my family gathering, though I invited him repeatedly. I think he reasoned that, since I didn't tell him about the visit right away, I didn't really want him there, which may have been true, but I doubted it. In any case, I went home to clean the house, and he went home to see his mama and watch the NBA playoffs with Angelo Sr.

I rolled out of bed around nine on Saturday, dressed rather haphazardly in jeans and pocket-tee, and went directly to my desk, where I scribbled out notes for the coming days' messages. The thoughts flowed, and time passed quickly until hunger called. So around noon, satisfied with my morning's labors, I heated up a frozen low-fat dinner of enchiladas and bean glop in the microwave, relishing the prospect of a quiet day. I would need the time to prepare myself mentally for the arrival of my family anyway; now that I had released my brain from the serious business of study, I fixated on this one event so much that I could not concentrate on anything else, not even the big Sunday worship service or Cornelia's funeral. But it wasn't fear that gripped me, more like butterflies in the stomach, the bizarre effect of worrying over something gladly anticipated. Motorhead repeatedly crashed his humming head into my hand as I tried to steer a forkful of smashed beans into my mouth. I finally gave him a taste, which he found revolting and skittered away, whiskers twitching at the offense. I was halfway through the first enchilada when a familiar rapping came from the front door.

"Hey, Pete. C'mon in." I was in an agreeable mood and was glad to see the little guy, who could clear my mind of tension with one cornball remark. He didn't move, other than to slap a rubber ball into a leather baseball glove several times, in hopes that I would take the hint. "Okay," I said. "But hang on for a minute while I finish lunch." This pleased him, and he happily followed me inside.

The Yankees were on TV but were already getting thrashed, and Pete was too hyper to wait patiently for them to mount a comeback in the later innings. He had a theory that he could somehow vicariously assist their efforts by playing the game himself, and upon his return to the TV later on they would have things well in hand. I was still struggling to grasp this mystical union so many males around here seemed to have with the pinstripers—even Michael, who ranked Don Mattingly among his heroes right up there with Martin Luther and the apostle Paul.

It was a gorgeous day, and we assigned ourselves positions parallel to the street, with me, of course, looking directly into the sun. I was further handicapped by not having a glove but, after watching Pete bobble my accurate throws, I considered us evenly matched. I could see why Sheila, although a part-time mother at best, had not allowed him to use a real hardball, since he demanded I throw him grounders and pop-ups, which he invariably missed, causing the rubber ball to conk him somewhere more often than not.

"It's one to nothin' in the ninth, and the Rocket has a perfect game with one out to go." He had a habit of obnoxiously narrating imagined game situations as we tossed the ball around. "Hey, sports fans! That ball's hit deep to center field . . . it's way back . . . Williams is racing to the wall . . ." With this, he faded back, urging me to throw him a high one.

I looked up into the sunshine and tried to judge the arc on which to hurl the ball. The sun was blinding; I let the ball go, then shielded my eyes to see if Pete would save the perfect game. I tried to blink him back into focus, zoning in on his voice. "That ball is going . . . going . . ." There was something flashing suddenly in the picture. I froze as Pete jumped for the ball. It bounced off his glove and bounded away as the object approached. *Fast.* Pete stumbled after the ball, losing his balance.

"Pete!" I screamed, and bolted toward him. The obscenely customized gold hot rod roared up onto the sidewalk, nearly striking the child. My eyes fixed on the driver's. He was looking at me. There was no mistaking his face.

I tumbled onto the yard—falling across Pete, who had buried his face in the grass—whispering words of comfort that lost all power in my frantic tone. I looked back to see the car peeling around the corner, a bizarre sight on Congress Street on a sunny Saturday afternoon. This had been a warning. Richie had told me once before not to mess with his business, and he knew, or assumed, that I had disregarded his instructions. Sister Louise had quietly shuttled the girls to a treatment center downstate and had already been in touch with their parents. Richie could not have known this, of course, but he did know they were missing—and I was the logical culprit.

Pete finally responded to me with a weird sound, spoken down into the soil.

"You okay?"

He turned his head back to me slowly. "Yeah. Did he run over my ball?" I smiled at the resilience of children and patted him on the back. "Let's go look for it," I said.

The rubber ball had struck the grille of the car and ricocheted into the street, where it had come to rest in the slot of an iron sewer grate recessed into the curb some twenty yards away. We fetched it, and Pete tucked it inside his glove, then marched hurriedly home. As I followed, I saw where teardrops had swept away the dirt on his cheeks.

Sheila came outside, hanging onto the door as if she was afraid she could not return if she let go. "Pete's a little shook up," I said. "A car went out of control and almost rode up on the lawn where we were playing catch. But nobody's hurt."

The woman ushered her son inside, and from within I heard the whimper of a scared child, who finally felt safe enough to let loose his emotions. Sheila stared me down with a look of confusion that melted into anger and retreated to the interior of her home to tend to her crying son. The look said she would keep him away from this irresponsible neighbor in the future, and if she meant it, that was good: it wouldn't hurt her to be more involved in Pete's life. But I knew it wouldn't last.

I hustled back to my place, leaping up the front steps, and rushed to the phone to call Michael.

"Carla? I was just about to call you. Slow down . . . are you out of breath?"

I told him what happened, and, typically, he went logical on me. "Did you get the license plate number?"

"No."

"The make of the car?"

"No. It was gold."

"Are you sure it was the same guy? Maybe it was some drunk, or a guy talking on a cell phone."

"Accept reality, Michael. It was Richie's guy. But I'm not worried. Richie's a coward. If he had wanted to kill me, he could have."

I could hear Michael huffing with frustration on the other end. "Have you called the police yet?"

"He's gone. What do I tell them? I already reported him once."

"Call them anyway. They can send a car to watch the house."

"Fine, fine." My mind was reeling. There was an awkward silence, but I didn't want to hang up the phone just yet. "My parents are coming over," I said absently.

Michael paused. "Right. About that, uh, that's why I was going to call, actually. I was thinking, um . . . what are you guys doing for dinner?"

I exhaled deeply to continue living, since I had been subconsciously holding my breath. "Well, I'm meeting them at the Desmond, up by the Albany airport. Dad knows the place, and he and Mother are staying there. I'm keeping Margaret's family."

"So, have you made plans? For dinner, that is?"

"We were going to either eat at the hotel or go out. Michael, what's wrong? You sound funny."

"Well, I thought it might be nice if we all kind of ate dinner over at my parents' house." He spoke this so fast I hardly had time to react. "Mama's insisting, Carla. In fact, she's already cooking."

"Oh, *Michael*. Are you insane? They have nothing in common—what will they talk about? This is crazy. You come from crazy people."

"Look, I just mentioned it in passing. I always get the twenty questions about you: when am I taking you out, where are we going, when am I bringing you over again, you know. She just insisted. What was I supposed to do?"

I chewed my lip, having already torn off two fingernails with my teeth. "You could have just told her *no*."

"Carla. Think about what you just said."

Stray thoughts zipped here and there and finally came together. It probably wasn't all that bad of an idea—at least it would deter the possibility of a conflict among the Donovans. Things had been going well over the phone, but face-to-face was another matter. I decided to back off a bit. "I see your point," I said.

"If I say no, I'm disrespectful. That's a big problem with Italians. If I say *you* said no, that's a worse problem."

"But, Michael, it's not like we're married or anything."

"Tell that to my mother. She's probably already planning the menu for the rehearsal dinner. Does your dad like baked ziti?"

I laughed. "My dad will probably leave early and take Mother out for dinner anyway. They did that when I graduated from seminary. The dean had this big dinner party on the grounds, and they just turned up their noses at it. No alcohol, I suppose. Now, Margaret's rehearsal dinner was another story.

The Cavanaughs had everything imaginable to eat there, and an open bar. Dad had to practically drag Mother out—"

"I mean tonight. We're having baked ziti tonight."

"Wha—?" The random thoughts split apart and whizzed away again.

"Can you have them there around seven?"

"Oh, sure. Fine. We'll be there."

"Great. Now call the police. I'll call you back in ten minutes to make sure you did."

◆ ◆ ◆

The dispatcher wasn't particularly enthusiastic about locating an officer to take my complaint, but he finally sent a car—an official city patrol car, naturally—to my house. I wanted to leave a note on the door that the resident had been robbed, beaten, and hauled off in the forty minutes it took to respond, and maybe he should look for her in the dumpster down the street. But I decided that a bad attitude wouldn't be particularly helpful, especially since the young cop was just doing his best to help. He wrote everything down carefully and muffled something into his radio when we finished; less than a half-hour after he had gone, a graphite-colored Dodge van appeared at the curbside three houses down the street. I considered knocking on the window on my way out to let the occupants know they could break for donuts, but maybe their presence was a deterrent to whatever sinister activity Richie might have planned to perpetrate in my absence.

I drove up to Albany pondering how to explain the dinner arrangements to my parents. Had it just been Margaret and me, we probably would have had a great time, since she was so fond of cultural experiences. Knowing her, she might have even profiled the Montefiores in the magazine, representing a refreshing slice of real life. Mother (okay, okay, *Mom*) was unpredictable given her medicated state, and Dad would surely object to inconveniencing himself; he preferred long, late dinners with several rounds of martinis prior and a piano tinkling in dim light afterward. As for Ryan, I really didn't know him all that well, but I sensed he would show his breeding in subtle, though deliberately noticeable, ways, unless Margaret chided him for it. Little Cass, of course, would probably cry the whole time, frightened by the constant surge of loud noises. In Michael's family, asking someone to pass the Parmesan cheese sounded like yelling to the beer man at a Yankees game.

The Desmond is a fashionable, extraordinarily comfortable hotel, with its cavernous, open interior reflecting a pleasant blend of tropical and colonial styles. I called from the lobby on the house phone, and Dad summoned me up.

Ryan was pacing outside the room, talking on a cell phone. He glanced at me and went back to his conversation, then did a double take and flipped the phone off. The suave smile eroded in proportion to his gradual recognition that this chick in the short black dress was his wife's older sister.

"Any chance you can put that thing away and enjoy a relaxing dinner?" I said, knowing full well the phone might prove a convenient means of escape from the madness to come.

"Hi, Carla. I'm afraid I need to head back to Boston anyway," he said, animating with the exaggerated affectations of simulated stress. "The deposition's been moved to Sunday."

"What? Are you skipping church again?" I scolded playfully, but meaning it.

"I know. But the guy flew in to get the Saturday overnight fare, called Dad at home and said he couldn't wait until Monday now, he had to fly back Sunday night—something came up for him Monday morning at home." He sagged against the wall.

"Aw, c'mon, you love it," I joked.

"No, no," he said, amused, looking away. I was clearly correct.

The door opened, and Margaret peeked out. She was wearing a dazzling white cotton dress with lavender dots, making me look something like the evil twin. "Hey there." She gave me her little girlfriend hug. "I was just wondering what was taking so long." She shot a laser glare at her husband.

"I got a depo, Mags. Got to get back to Beantown tonight."

"Not for the Celtics play-off game tomorrow?"

"I said I had to take a depo, Mags." He writhed against the textured wallpaper.

"Not for the Red Sox doubleheader?"

I noticed Ryan wasn't making eye contact with Margaret either. "Well, it's like this," he huffed. "The client wants to go, and Dad said—"

"One lousy time in your life I ask you to do something. We've never even been to my sister's church, Ryan."

I tried to pry my way in. "You mean there's no deposition?"

"Oh, there's a depo, all right!" Margaret shouted, way too loudly for the corridor. "Let me guess; Tina will be going along with you to the game?"

"Mags, somebody has to take down his statement."

"Oh, so Miss Priss is going to sit in the stands with her little machine propped up on her knees, poking at the keys while drunks spill beer on her tube top?"

"Mags, you're sounding ridiculous. This is a perfectly legit—"

"You wouldn't *believe* this tube top, Carla," she said, ignoring him. "I drop in the office on a Saturday morning—another so-called working weekend—and there she is, wearing this . . . this. . . . "

"Now just hold on here!" Ryan demanded. "I came all the way out here, didn't I? I said I'd even go to her church, didn't I?"

"And you didn't bother to tell your father, did you?"

"No, but . . ."

"You *knew* he would call you to come back as soon as he found out. The man thinks he owns you, Ryan. And the incredible thing is, you said okay—for a crummy baseball game."

"*Two* games, Mags—two baseball games, back-to-back. And this is an important client. Do you realize how much money . . ."

If Margaret realized it, she didn't seem to care. While he was ranting, she grabbed my wrist and yanked me inside the room, slamming the door on her protesting husband. Mother and Dad were sitting quietly in opposite wing-backed chairs, apparently having heard the whole thing, while Cass slept in his Moses basket.

"Trouble in paradise?" Dad said, obviously displeased.

"He's a jerk," Margaret said.

"I told you that when he asked you to sign that prenup."

We remained silent for a moment, as if expecting Ryan to beg admittance, but no knock came.

"You were right, Dad, I should have known." She was visibly distressed, but showed a steely strength nevertheless. I flashed a look at my mother, wondering how she could have been so blind to the cracks in the façade projected by the perfect couple's marriage.

"It's all right," Mother said, getting up, completely missing the point that it certainly was not all right. She approached Margaret and me with open arms, and we huddled awkwardly. "We'll not worry about him. Tonight it will just be our family."

"Uh . . . actually," I began, "we've been invited somewhere."

"Oh?" It was Dad, left bushy eyebrow raised. "By whom?"

I released myself from the huddle. "Michael's parents. They insisted. I couldn't say no. I hope you're not—"

"That's wonderful, darling!" Mother gushed.

"Wait a minute here," Dad interrupted, physically breaking through the bond which held Mother and Margaret, to face me. "Did they pick the restaurant already?"

I knew what he was angling at. "Yes . . . I mean, no . . . they invited us to their home." I waited for the onslaught, but he just stood dumbfounded, as if he couldn't believe this was really happening.

My father continued to devolve steadily as we made our way down to the cars, asking the kinds of questions an insecure child might ask on the way to his first day of school. Are these people normal? Do they have to serve pasta? Are there a lot of them? Yes, yes, and yes, I said. My answers only seemed to trouble him more, so much so that he asked Margaret to drive.

It was fascinating to see my family members in such disarray, far from the comfort zone of Boston's social circle. Margaret, who made a living talking with strangers, should not have been this nervous; I attributed it to the embarrassing episode with Ryan, during which her usually well-hidden frailties became evident to all. I would play the unlikely role of big sister tonight, calming her frayed nerves and navigating her through the turbid waters of conversation with obnoxious, blue-collar Yankees fans, the type of people she had avoided all her life. As for Mother, she was peculiarly subdued, and there were long moments of silence in the car during which she would have ordinarily injected a barb or two. The depression medication had practically lobotomized her in my opinion, and I feared a dependence on prescription drugs would simply take over where the booze left off. Dad would be the one to watch. He would be outside his element, and the only one of the three in any shape to carry the ball for the family, so to speak. Other than me.

Dad's questions trailed off as we entered the Montefiore's neighborhood. It was still light, and children who were playing in the street as if it were an open field stopped to gawk at my father's silver S-Class. Mother and Dad looked deflated as I turned back to check on them; Mother was smiling blankly out the window like a mental patient recently sprung from the clinic, and Dad had the resigned look of someone about to be checked in. Margaret had flipped down the visor and was teasing her hair with a ballpoint pen as she tried to keep the car on the road, muttering something about an eyebrow pencil being the wrong shade. Up ahead, just past a line of used American cars (and one silver Honda) parked at the curb, Theresa was sitting on the stoop in front of the house, while Mary and Daniela were coloring something on the driveway with sidewalk chalk. As I turned in, I could make out a crudely drawn message: Welcom to Our House Donavens Red Sox Stink.

Hmm, I worried, *this ought to be interesting.*

"Just remember," I said to them over the seat back, "if by some miracle Michael and I get married, you'll be seeing these people again, okay?"

I hopped out and was immediately hugged by the girls. My father emerged from the car like a visiting foreign dignitary, buttoning his suit coat and tugging at his cuffs to expose his cuff links. Mother came forth slowly and was greeted by Theresa, who shocked her with a hug. The look on Mother's face suggested she was delighted by the greeting, and I was relieved. "You have a lovely home," she said.

"Huh? You kiddin'? Junior could never afford something like this!" Dad stared at the house, amazed at the statement, while I made the proper introductions. Daniela had released my leg and was pounding on the window on the driver's side, behind which Margaret continued to preen furiously. When she finally appeared, the girls backed up in awe. "She *is* beautiful," Mary whispered.

"And where did you hear that?" I asked, chasing them playfully. "Did Uncle Michael tell you that?" They giggled and ran into the house, easily avoiding my grasp. I extricated Cass from his car seat, and Dad got the Moses basket from the trunk, moving very slowly, I guess still hoping for a reprieve. Theresa led us to the front door like a tour guide, talking nonstop about her children, pausing several times to make points, nearly causing her guests to collide each time.

I was actually enjoying this.

Michael came out onto the stoop, wondering what was taking so long. "Nice dress," he whispered to me, and I hoped he didn't mean Margaret's. He then reintroduced himself to my family, and we crammed ourselves into the house like Alice falling through the looking glass. The TV was blaring from the den, and Michael wisely invited Dad to follow the sound with him, just as Mama Montefiore came bustling out of the kitchen. I was stunned to see she was wearing a lovely formal dress, and it looked like she had done her hair a new way.

"I'm Celeste," she said, clasping her hands in front of her. It struck me that this was the first time I had heard her name. "Come meet my other daughter." I knew this meant Patti, who was actually a daughter-in-law. Once you were in this family, though, you were *in*.

After ten minutes of listening to Patti praise Anthony's intelligence as if to say to these strangers *really, he's not one of them,* Junior came rushing into the kitchen with a six-pack of beer under one arm and clutching a fresh bag of chips, invoking a hard look from his mother, which might have been a backhand if we had not been there. "We're almost ready to eat," she said.

"Halftime," he said, in a hurry to get back.

"We have guests!" she shouted after him to no response.

"I'll see what I can do," I said, and went to the den.

Dad was sitting on the sofa next to Michael and Anthony, awkwardly but not totally uncomfortable. I noticed his jacket was still buttoned, but his tie was loosed. Junior and Angelo Sr. were sitting in matching blue recliners. "Who's playing?"

"Hornets and Heat," mumbled Junior through a mouthful of chips.

"Who do you like?" I said innocently.

Junior stopped munching and turned his head toward me slowly. "This is not about who we like, Carla. This is about who we *hate.*"

"We hate the Heat," clarified Michael, "because Pat Riley is a traitor, and all Knicks fans hate the Heat."

I looked at Dad, who was returning the can to his lips repeatedly. "We hate the Heat, too, because Pat Riley used to coach the Knicks, and all Celtics fans hate the Knicks," he said between sips. These seemed like contradictory arguments, but they allowed a shaky kinship, which was important at the moment.

"And Dave Cowens used to coach the Hornets," said Anthony, helping out.

"That's right," answered Dad, waving his beer in support of Anthony's observation. "Big Red. One of the greatest Celtics ever. And Paul Silas, another Celtic, coaches them now."

"Go Hornets!" shouted Junior, spitting chip fragments on the armrest.

I wandered back to the kitchen. "I couldn't persuade them," I said. "I guess we'd better wait for halftime."

"Fine," said Celeste Montefiore, walking toward me with a head of lettuce rolling around in a huge purple plastic bowl. "You can toss the salad."

♦ ♦ ♦

Halftime came and went, and the salad I had so expertly tossed was still sitting in the center of the table, covered with plastic wrap. Loud laughter could be heard from the den, and we interrupted our girl talk to listen in once in a while. Whatever was going on in there, the men were obviously having a grand time, the natural affability of the natives overcoming the stiff uneasiness of their guest. The baked ziti sat wrapped in foil on the stove, while Margaret was braiding Daniela's long black locks, and Patti looked on with admiration. Theresa lectured me on the bad habits of Montefiore men, and Mother and Celeste sat at the table, sipping coffee. The kitchen was unbearably hot, and I felt an urgent need to escape to an open space, so I suggested we check on the guys.

I followed Theresa. "Who's winning?" she bellowed above the blare of the TV. She showed no shock at the spectacle before her, and they paid her no mind, but I stopped cold, trying to make sense of the scene. The game was over, and some kind of sports talk show had taken over the screen. Junior lay sprawled out on the floor amid empty beer cans and bags, while Michael and Dad were laughing and elbowing each other in the ribs. Dad's eyes were half winking in that mischievous Irish way of his, and he seemed only partially aware of the voice from across the room—Angelo Sr.—who was trying desperately to get his attention. Anthony was dozing happily, slumped over the arm of the sofa.

"Gosh, Michael, have you guys been drinking?" I asked, stating the obvious.

"*They've* been drinking, Carla. I'm just trying to follow the conversation." He had a big, contagious smile on his face, and I felt a jolt of mirth myself. Theresa started kicking Junior to get him up, and he tried to shoo her away.

"There you are, Carla," Dad said proudly. "Maybe *you* can get this one. What do you call it when an Italian has one arm shorter than the other?"

"I . . . uh, what are you talking about?" I didn't like what I was seeing one bit.

"A speech impediment. You get it? A speech impediment." Michael elbowed Dad again playfully, acting like he appreciated the joke. He winked in my direction.

"That's nothing," Angelo Sr. interjected. "Everybody quiet. Hey, Brian— you heard about the Irishman who stole a pint of whiskey and hid it in his coat?" he asked, finally getting my father to look in his direction.

Dad shook his head.

"He fell down the stairs outside the pub, see, and the bottle smashed into bits. So, he gets up, and feels a trickle running down his leg. And you know what he said?"

Dad shook his head again.

Angelo paused for effect. "Please, God, let it be blood."

Dad squeezed his eyes shut and bent over, then began to shake with a low chortle, and when he raised his head, tears were filling his eyes. He gasped for breath, then laughed uncontrollably, along with Angelo, who was doubled over, nearly falling out of the chair, delighted his joke had hit home. Theresa was sitting on Junior now, yelling something in his ear.

Dad recovered and stood up. "Hey, hey, Angelo, how about this one—do you know how an Italian gets into an honest business?"

Michael's father harnessed his laughter long enough to reply, "No—you tell me. How?"

Dad puffed out his chest and said, "Usually, by picking the lock."

Angelo rolled in the chair, delighted.

The other women had appeared behind me, and Celeste marched forward and hoisted her husband out of the chair. As she stood him up, he pushed her away, and with arms waving declared: "An Englishman, a Scot, and an Irishman went into a bar . . ."

"Oh, brother," quipped Patti, who went to resuscitate Anthony.

"You boys c'mon and have some dinner now," said Mama, smiling. Michael and I shared a look of profound wonder at the conduct of our fathers in the center of the room. Junior was still fighting his wife off, trying to join the frivolity in the space above him. The whole scene was so comedic, we couldn't help but be amused.

"And each one of these guys has a fly in his beer," continued Angelo.

"Wait. I heard this one," said Dad, nearly stepping on Junior. "The Englishman says, 'This is disgusting. I could *never* drink this bloody ale now.'"

Junior struggled to his feet, with Theresa hanging on. "Right. And the Scot says, 'It's perfectly fine, lads. This wee beastie won't spoil the taste.' And he scoops out the fly and drinks the rest down in one gulp."

"Yeah," Angelo cried, nearly choking with excitement over the punch line, "but the Irishman—he *grabs* the poor fly by his teensy-weensy wings and screams in his face, *'Spit it out, you little monster! Spit it out!'*" He was pinching his fingers together to dramatically illustrate the point.

Michael was red-faced, hanging his head either in shame or to hide the laughter at these awful jokes. All of us were laughing now except Mother, who appeared petrified, whereas I was merely embarrassed. The effects of the alcohol scared her—that was a good sign. I couldn't exactly say that anyone here was drunk—*oiled* might have been a better adjective—though Dad had, for some reason, let his guard down enough to enjoy the trading of light-hearted insults, and I could only assume the beer had something to do with it. Seeing him like this suggested he might have been part of Mother's problem all along. It saddened me that this highly successful man depended on alcohol to help him navigate in uncomfortable social situations. It had certainly helped him find the lowest common denominator here.

Twenty minutes later, we were sitting around two tables: one in the kitchen, for our parents, the other in the small dining room, where the seven of us enjoyed listening to Angelo Jr. tell stories about Michael and Anthony when they were little kids. Mary and Daniela ate in front of the TV, with Cass wiggling next to them in his basket. Only Margaret was distant, and I felt sorrowful for her. I hadn't known her marriage had been a sham, but now it made sense—Ryan's frequent trips out of town, Mother's continuing praise to mask the reality of the situation, Margaret's exchange of emotional intimacy for status and money and self-indulgence. For the first time, I felt a real kinship with my sister. I had something, finally, to give her.

I looked around the table. Who were these people, really? On what had they anchored their lives? For Junior, I think, it was his parents; for Theresa, her children; for Patti, her husband. And what if they were cut loose from these anchors? I watched Margaret—the girl who had everything—fighting just to keep from crying in the presence of three couples. And I thought about the neighborhood around St. Fred's: just people who had lost their way, that's all. Some had never been on the right road to start with. But all needed to come home.

I paused to hear the laughter from the kitchen. Unbelievably, my parents were having a good time. When all the pomp and formality and best impressions were laid aside, they were just insecure people like everyone else, trying to connect to something. Here, far from the trappings of their shallow lifestyle in Boston, they were forced to engage in the business of being human, forced to reach out, and be accepted.

I suddenly felt a strong desire to walk around the room and hug all these people, but of course I didn't do that. I did pray quietly for them. Michael noticed that I had withdrawn momentarily from the banter, but he didn't try to lure me from my contemplation. For all I knew, he had been thinking the same thing. Of all the persons present, Michael was the only one who I was sure had a truly personal relationship with God, the only one who had connected securely to an anchor that would never be shaken. St. Fred's, I hoped, would be a place where anyone who was willing to follow God could find a home. It would be a home like this one—where rich men and men of modest means could find commonality, where differing cultures could come together as one, where the insecure could connect to an anchor—God, his place, his people.

"Hey guys," I interrupted. "Can I ask a question?"

Junior cocked his head to one side and grinned. "I suppose," he said. All heads turned to me.

"Well, I was thinking how nice it would be if all of you came to St. Fred's tomorrow as my guests."

"What, and miss the mass?" Junior said.

Theresa thumped him in the shoulder. "We don't even go to mass, you dummy. Of course we will, Carla. Won't we, dear?" Junior's expression was a cross between nausea and extreme worry.

"We would love to," said Anthony. Patti, somewhat surprised at first, took his arm and smiled back at me as if to say it was all right with her if it was all right with him.

"How come you never came to my church?" Michael asked his brother, half-serious.

"Well, we get to hear you all the time, big bro," answered Anthony. "But this"—he nodded in my direction—"will be interesting."

I didn't know what to make of this comment, but decided to interpret it as complimentary. "So it's a deal then," I said. They looked at each other and shrugged.

"Looks like the family approves of you," Michael quipped, "even if you *are* Irish." I couldn't tell if he was pleased or put out.

Junior stood and raised his wine glass. *"Salute,"* he said.

I clinked my water glass with his, then the others, and offered an Irish blessing—a joke of my own: "May you live forever, and may the last words you hear be mine."

"Ha!" shrieked Theresa. "When Angelo here darkens the door of that church, you might wish you hadn't said that. Don't be surprised if lightning strikes."

This brought forth a bemused objection from Junior, who apparently didn't think me an unwitting prophet. As it turned out, I should have listened to Theresa.

CHAPTER TWENTY-FOUR

Sunday Promised To Be a big day, and from the time I got out of bed I worried about the reception I might get upon entering the sanctuary. While ironing my vestments late on Saturday night, I struck upon an idea to diffuse any tension. I had to show that the rumors hadn't shaken me, that I believed in what I was doing despite the opposition. If they saw that, they would be willing to follow. If I showed fear or second thoughts, all would be lost.

I silently entered the sanctuary against the booming of Astrid Huggins's organ, just as the choirmaster was concluding the call to worship. The notes trailed off as the six robed singers saw me, and their leader turned his head in response. Custis squinted to read what I had written on the front of my collar, then smiled broadly as I walked past him to my seat, and I knew the risk would pay off. Choir members craned their necks and began to laugh as they sat and looked up the Bible reference I had written there in large characters—JOHN 8:7 (*Let him who is without sin cast the first stone*)—an obvious reference to the accusations in the postcards.

The mystified congregation shook their heads in confusion at what was happening at the podium. When Jameson Kerry stepped up to read the morning's announcements, he read the verse and offered his impressions of my stunt to widespread laughter. "By the way, Carla," he said, turning to me, "that load of gravel the board ordered should be delivered just about the time you get ready to preach." There was more laughter, briefly uproarious and heaven-sent.

The applause that greeted me upon my ascent to the pulpit was warm and completely unexpected. Though I recognized that it was prompted by Isabella, who sat with eight or nine people she had recruited from The Dutchman, along with Paul and Frankie Delvecchio, I was so moved that it was difficult to speak for a moment, so I stepped back and waited for calm. It was a relatively small congregation, but larger than the one I had last addressed. The majority of them were smiling. It was a sign from God: we were on our way. It was then that I noticed Angelo Jr., Theresa, Anthony, and Patti sitting together about halfway back, one pew behind my parents and Margaret, who kept the baby next to her in a little carrier lined with fluffy fabric. I could see his little hands waving above the fringe. All of them were dressed in suits and dresses, though Junior's tie was askew. Margaret's bare shoulders received a good bit of attention from the rows behind, and several of the men in front continued to glance behind them at her after I had introduced my "special guests." Another controlled wave of applause filled the sanctuary, and Junior fiddled with his tie, which Theresa noticed and adjusted for him, embarrassing him more.

Not all was perfect, however. In the far corner of the sanctuary, the street toughs who had been patrolling outside all week were sitting to themselves. They must have crept in early, since I didn't notice them across the street. I was acutely aware that Richie would continue to harass me, but I could not let the presence of his thugs intimidate me. I tried to ignore them, until Derrold Hamber strolled in and conspicuously marched down the center aisle and took a seat down front, surprising everyone. I saw the bullies mutter to themselves as he walked past, and as soon as he sat down, they slid out of the pew and went out, making a small commotion.

I led the congregation in the litany printed in the bulletin, and then offered an extended invocation. When I opened my eyes, I saw Jameson Kerry standing in the aisle, whispering something to Hamber. As the rest of the congregation stood for the hymn, the two of them went out, I assumed to keep an eye on the gang of punks.

The Matthew's House band, which had come dressed in their usual ratty jeans and oversized T-shirts, had huddled in the second row, intimidated by the formality of the service until it came time for them to play. Their version of "O Happy Day" was actually quite soulful, and the congregation seemed to enjoy it. While at least a few snarls were visible, I sensed such a unity among this otherwise disconnected group that it was difficult to believe this was actually St. Fred's. It was as if Winefrid herself had sprinkled each member with droplets from her healing well. But then, just as the band was finishing up, Kerry appeared at the door and waved for Frankie Delvecchio to come quickly, distracting almost everyone. Enough people had been coming and going by now to raise a few eyebrows—including mine—as to what might be going on.

I tried to focus on the Word from God and recapture their attention. The sermon was taken from the passage in John's eighth chapter about the woman who was caught in adultery. I made obvious allusions to the postcards but didn't specifically mention them. Here was a woman, I said, who had been watched for a long time. She had problems, to be sure, but rather than lift a finger to help her, her critics waited for the right moment and then executed a swift judgment against her. Why? Was she any threat to them? Why did they hate her so? Jesus knew the answer and addressed their hypocrisy. They punished sinners like this woman to maintain their self-righteous façade; they looked holy but, in fact, they were as corrupted as she was. As for me, I wasn't perfect either—who among us is? But God helped me, while others watched and waited for my fall. He would not condemn me, because he himself was condemned *for* me, for us, and for all people—even those we call bad, who are everything we say they are and worse: wicked, angry, misguided, lost. Who will sacrifice to lead them to sin no more? It was a good sermon. I wished Hamber had remained in the sanctuary to hear it.

I felt a bizarre thrill as I preached. It was effortless, almost *easy.* A few moments into the sermon and the people were intent, once more relaxed. I was carried along. May I say it? *Inspired.* And then, the door was thrown open, and Kerry appeared again—this time, he was frantic. "Someone call the police!" he shouted.

The congregation erupted into noisy, confused panic. In a split second, I took in fragments of the chaotic scene: Patti pulling out her cell phone, Margaret lifting Cass out of the carrier, Junior and the men from The Dutchman running up the aisle. I rushed down from the platform and picked my way through the people like a tailback, yelling to my frightened family to stay put as I went by, finally reaching the vestibule. From the top of the steps I gasped at the drama unfolding across the street. The gang had broken into a car that was double-parked on the curb, and now a fight had broken out. Junior was right in the middle of it, with the rest of the guys from the bar pounding away. The form of a man lay prone in the street. It was Hamber.

A siren could be heard in the distance, aiding the men's efforts to chase the gang away. I went to Hamber and could see that he had deep cuts on his head and hands. Isabella appeared at my side and took over for me, talking to him in Spanish.

"He be okay," she said to me.

"They would have killed him." The voice was Jameson Kerry's. He was standing over me, disheveled and sweating. The patrol car flew up the street and swerved to a halt diagonally, blocking the way. I listened as Kerry told the officers what had happened through labored breathing: The thugs had broken into the church through the back way. He and Hamber had gone to chase them away. When they found them, they had already done significant damage, and their first thought was to call the police right then. However, when the gang saw the two men, they fled, and Hamber gave pursuit. When Kerry came around the building, he saw them confronting Hamber, who had apparently tried to stop them from stealing his car. That's when Kerry went running back into the church, and the men came to Hamber's rescue, effectively saving his life.

I could do little to help, so I approached Junior, who was flushed and had torn his coat. The tie was gone, and his shirt was unbuttoned nearly halfway. He seemed euphoric, exchanging high fives with the guys. None of them appeared to be badly hurt. I let them retell the details of the battle as an ambulance rolled up to tend to Hamber. He was sitting up now, looking at me. Was he angry? Scared? The look held powerful emotion, and a touch of weakness. I went to him and took his hand as the paramedics surrounded us. "You'll be okay," I said. "God is watching over you." He nodded and collapsed into tears, gripping my hand tightly. Now I understood his feelings perfectly; he was grateful to be alive.

I went back into the church and informed my parents what had happened. They were sitting alone in the sanctuary in strict obedience to my command, as the others had spilled out all the doors. Most were still outside, watching from a distance, or had already gone home. Cass was looking around happily, not sensing anything but his mother's presence.

"Interesting enough for you?" I asked Anthony, trying to communicate that things were under control. The stunned look vanished from their faces, and they began to chatter incessantly, recalling every detail of their brush with danger—all except Mother, who slumped in the pew, no doubt desperate for a drink.

I asked them to wait just a few more minutes while I checked on things in the back of the church. I went through the office and down the stairs, where Mr. Delvecchio spoke with one of the police officers, who was carefully inspecting the damage. The punks had broken through the same window as before, but this time they had dropped down into the room, where they had spray painted slogans and epithets on the walls. A trail of red paint lined the hall, all the way to the pool. What I saw there nearly stopped my heart. The empty shell was gouged and defiled with painted graffiti, mostly profane, and several chunks of the concrete had been broken loose. The rusty fill spout had been smashed, and the tile deck was cracked in several places. "Did these guys have sledgehammers or something?" I asked to no one in particular. Mr. Delvecchio answered, "Come with me."

The cover in the deck was open, and he led me down into the darkened room. The pipe segment that connected the water line was missing. "You know, I removed that thing after the room flooded so it wouldn't happen again . . . by accident."

"That was no accident," I answered. "We both know that."

"So did the board. I mean, they couldn't prove it, but their first thought was that I hooked up the line to fill the pool in the first place, and you were down here turning the valve to flood the basement when the fire started. All except Kerry. But I can't say I blame them."

"What do you mean by that?"

"Well, a week or so after the pool was drained, Hamber came down here with me. That's when he made me disconnect the pipe, and I should have taken it out of here then. Instead, I forgot and left it up on the deck. That's what the thugs used to wreck the place; I found it in the pool, and the cop has it to check for prints."

I squinted to see the damage the intruders had wrought. The filter bypass piping had been dented and had separated in some places. The wheel on the water valve had been knocked off, and the threaded end of the pipe was crushed. "It's almost as if they knew what they were doing," I said.

"Naturally they did. No way are we going to fill this pool again without some major repairs being done."

We scrambled back up the ladder to the pool deck. I dusted off my shirt and sighed. "Mr. Delvecchio, you know it wasn't me who flooded the place, don't you?"

"Hey, I believe what you told us, especially now—that these criminals grabbed you that night. But you have to admit, the circumstantial evidence seemed to say otherwise."

I stopped him, intent on getting a straight answer this time. "What are you talking about? Why did the board think it was me?"

He looked down, ashamed, perhaps, to have known, as if a slight bit of suspicion remained. "When Hamber and I came down here, we had a flashlight, and it picked up something shiny on the floor."

"What?" I insisted. "What was it?"

"An *earring,* Carla. A little gold cross."

It was thirty minutes into lunch at the Desmond before the subject of my sermon came up. Michael arrived just as we were beginning, and we were forced to confirm the story he had already heard from his brothers about the disturbance at St. Fred's. He inadvertently asked if the Dodge van was still watching the house, which led to further inquiries from my father. He now expressed his grave concern not only for me, but also for Margaret and Cass, who planned to stay a few days. I assured him that arrests might soon be made and that the police had promised to step up their patrols in the neighborhood. I also mentioned that I thought our own version of a neighborhood watch program—courtesy of the regulars from The Dutchman—might keep things under control. In the end, however, it was agreed that Cass would go back to Boston with his grandparents, but Margaret would stay. She wouldn't listen to their attempts to get her to change her mind, and frankly, I was glad for the company.

We parted ways with my parents after lunch. Standing at the car, Mother took me aside and told me she was proud of me, hugged me, and asked me to pray for her. She had been struggling all weekend to get by without alcohol, and Dad's carefree imbibing on Saturday night hadn't made it any easier. They clearly had issues to work out as a couple, and I wondered if his problems would not be more difficult to overcome than hers. At least she was facing her demons, saying that she planned to begin an outpatient treatment program during the week.

"I'm proud of you too . . . Mom," I said as we embraced. "Thanks for coming." Dad patted me on the head, glad, I think, that the trauma of the weekend was over.

After the Mercedes was out of sight, Michael, of course, wanted to see us both home and check to make sure the van was there. He drove ahead and was already waiting for us, sitting on the hood of his car.

"I talked to the guy," he said, hopping down. "Twenty-four/seven until things stabilize."

Margaret stared after the parked van for a long moment and seemed relieved. We moved her luggage inside, and Michael and I took her for a drive around town and a nice walk around Central Park before he had to go back for his evening service. Margaret was quiet, but I knew she would want to talk later that night, when it was the two of us alone.

"So, are we on for tomorrow at two?" Michael asked when we pulled up again at my place.

I went blank at first, having completely forgotten about the funeral.

"From that look on your face I take it we're still on, and you're not ready."

"Oh," I said, remembering. "Actually, I'm fine with my part, almost. I can polish it up in the morning. But I haven't heard back from Sister Louise yet. Do you think the priest is coming?"

"I doubt it. Call her and see. I've got to go. You guys let me know if there's any trouble; Mama's always looking for people to feed."

Motorhead aggressively inspected Margaret and her baggage while I dialed Sister Louise's number.

"Yes?" came her pleasant answer.

"Hi. This is Carla. I was just wondering—"

"Oh, I'm so glad you called, I've been trying to reach you all afternoon. You really should get an answering machine, or at least a cell phone."

I had no interest in explaining, as I usually do, that answering machines obligate one to respond, as do cell phones, which cost money to use, and one doesn't need to have one if one has no one to call and doesn't want calls coming in. "I really should," I said, and I did mean it, especially now that my attitude toward the work had changed. "But I'm lazy. Do you have any news?"

She laughed. "In fact, I do: Bruno will be on a plane tomorrow morning from Santa Fe. We should make it just in time for the service at two o'clock."

I pressed the phone deeper into my ear as if I hadn't heard her clearly. "I don't believe you!"

"I'm a nun, Carla."

"Oh yeah. How is he?"

"He's not well. He called me back a few hours ago to say his doctor had advised him not to make the trip, but he had already purchased the ticket. He said he's been waiting for this for almost forty years. Nothing could keep him away."

"Waiting for Cornelia to die? That's kind of creepy."

"Oh, no, that's not what he meant. Waiting to *come home*. He was very sad to hear about Mrs. Shepherd. But he was quite excited about coming back."

I wanted to hear more but for some reason didn't ask. Motorhead looked up from his rubbing of Margaret's suitcase and silenced his loud purr. I know that cats have excellent hearing, but I doubt they can understand language. I must have shown that Sister Louise's news had not brought comfort but exactly the opposite, and I didn't know why. Motorhead evidently sensed my apprehension, for he raised his bushy tail, twitched his whiskers, and stood at alert, expecting a soothing word to set him at ease. When I hung up the phone I held out my arms, and he jumped into them, still keen to the fact that something wasn't quite right. I scratched the fur on the back of his neck, and he stared at me the way cats do, eyes blinking slowly in boredom or impatience or disdain, waiting for an assurance that I simply couldn't give.

♦ ♦ ♦

The fateful day arrived like any other day, full of promise or foreboding, depending on one's point of view. I knew I could not approximate Margaret's skills in preparing breakfast, but I was so nervous about the funeral that my bumbling attempts at culinary magic led my sister, after a grease fire and two eggs splattered on the floor, to suggest we go out for a bite.

"You seem edgy," she said.

"It's a big responsibility," I replied. This was certainly true. I had never been able to do anything productive the morning before a funeral. I would review my remarks over and over again, pacing around my office mumbling each phrase, terrified that I would misspeak and send the grieving family into deeper despair, an abyss from which they would never again emerge. It didn't help matters that, due to my haphazard habits in visitation, I didn't really know many of the deceased that well, relying on the hints and asides of their surviving relatives to form the foundation of my eulogies. Here was a real person who had loved and been loved, a unique individual who had done many things now unremembered. Here was a whole life—precious in the sight of God—now gone from our midst, and it was my job to make sense of it in twenty minutes or less. How could I possibly do it justice?

"But funerals are for the living," Margaret counseled as I hovered over an omelet at the diner. I knew this truth, naturally, but I had never chosen to think on it all that much before. I could let the people remember their loved ones in their own special ways; I should simply give them hope and not worry about what I didn't know or couldn't say. No need to preach them into heaven, or condemn them to hell. Just offer hope to the ones who remain. I could do that.

This funeral, however, was different. For one thing, I suspected the family would not be grieving at all. In fact, when we arrived at the church office to prepare the bulletin (Margaret was a wiz at such things), there was a message on the answering machine from Mr. Van Antwerp to confirm the reading of the will at his office on Tuesday morning, nine o'clock sharp. He mentioned that, after speaking with the Stewarts, he felt certain they would vigorously oppose the bequest to the church. He cautioned me against referring to Cornelia's eccentricities during the service, since he had learned just this morning that the psychologist who certified her sanity had recently lost his license. Unfortunately, turning the funeral message into a sales pitch was unethical at best, immoral at least. And, considering it was Cornelia Shepherd's funeral at St. Fred's church, I would be worried that as soon as I began to skew things in our favor, you-know-who might show up and relieve me of my job on the spot.

But I would not be solely responsible for the proceedings on this day anyway. An aged priest who once roamed the halls of this formerly grand building was coming to speak, and that is what made me woozy with worry. What if he started talking about visions of Winefrid? That would definitely not help our cause, especially if he recalled Cornelia's experience, which I was almost sure he would do. The healing pool was not only empty, it had been vandalized, and while I had every intention of reopening it someday, I didn't want to use a belief in miracles to spark the cause. What I wanted to do was simple: collect the money from Cornelia's estate, renovate the pool, invest in the community, and watch God do his thing. This way, I wouldn't have to confront anybody, cause a big commotion, or risk losing my job. Been there, done that.

Still, I have always believed that God rarely leads us down the easiest road. If it's easy, it probably isn't God's way. "Was it not necessary for the Christ to suffer and then enter into his glory?" Jesus said to the travelers on the journey to Emmaus. The road I was looking down was precipitous indeed. The small congregation could hardly pay my salary, much less support my vision. Even if they could, Richie and his pals would probably declare open war on the church. After yesterday, I worried that the wolf may have succeeded in scaring away some of my already diminished flock, though, thanks to Junior and the guys from the bar, the flock might have scared him too. Beyond that fact, there were rumors afloat questioning my morality, which hurt my credibility as a pastor and community leader. A legal battle loomed large over the Shepherd will, which might be publicized, thus bringing the story of the pool out into the open. But I had no way to verify the claims of healing, only the statements of a few people. And even if I filled up the pool, hoping for a dramatic vindication, I would be breaking the law. The headlines would proclaim the irony: Man Healed of Leprosy Later Dies from Disease Contracted from Pool Operated in Defiance of Health Code.

"Carla?"

I looked up from my daymare and blinked at my sister.

"There's a van full of flowers out front."

"Oh, of course. I'll be right back." I left her in the office to finish folding the bulletins while I headed for the sanctuary.

An older lady in jeans and a pink smock was already arranging the three flower stands beside the pulpit: orchids from the nursing home, roses from Father Calabrese, and a small basket of spring flowers from the Stewarts that might have run them around fifty bucks. The lady had left the front doors open, and a gentle breeze lifted a pleasant scent off the flowers. There had been no visitation since there was no local family, but the death notice had been printed in the newspaper, and Kerry had announced the funeral during Sunday worship, so I assumed more people would have responded. I supposed that some of our older members had known Mrs. Shepherd, but then, most of them had bailed out in recent weeks. I couldn't estimate how popular she might have been, but I thought she deserved better.

"Is there any way I can have more flowers sent here?" I asked.

"It's almost one, ma'am. The funeral's in an hour."

"Can you try?"

"Do you have a credit card?"

Forty minutes and two hundred dollars later, the white van returned, riding up just in front of the hearse. The funeral director, a hunched man who stank of cigarette smoke, had been hanging around in the vestibule. Already in my robe, I handed him the peach-colored bulletins Margaret had so lovingly prepared, helped the lady with the floral decorations, and scooted back to my office where my sister waited.

"Not here yet?"

She was speaking, of course, about Father Calabrese. "Sister Louise said it would be close. He's coming all the way across the country with a connecting flight in Dallas. Any unexpected delay, and he might not make it."

"You look like you might not make it yourself," she said.

"Will you quit telling me stuff like that?" I barked with an uneasy laugh. My palms were sweaty. I ushered her out of the study and told her to take a seat in the sanctuary; Michael would be there shortly, and she should look out for him. I needed time to get my thoughts together, just in case.

I closed the door and performed an act I almost never did; I knelt to pray, resting my hands and head on the seat of my chair. Why was I so nervous? Perhaps it was because of what I knew: that God is real, and there is a heaven; that Cornelia Shepherd was probably looking down from there, picking out just the right pair of hip-huggers and tie-dyed shirt for the occasion; that the future of my church, and probably my ministry, rested on the words I would say in a few moments. Perhaps it was because I also knew what I had to do and feared the consequences. So I prayed the old "not my will but thine be done," and opened my eyes. I pulled back my sleeve to check my watch. *Let's go, Carla. Time to rise up and walk.*

It would make for a splendid story to say that peace flooded my soul as I marched down the corridor. I jumped at the sudden blast of the organ, which shook the old walls on both sides. I took a deep breath, swung open the side door, and entered a room filled with about twenty people—almost all of them old. I quickly found Michael and Margaret; with his dark features and her brilliant fairness, they made a stunning couple, and this fact troubled me. I stepped up to the platform and took my place in the throne-like chair. The vestibule was crowded with dark suits: the director, and only four pallbearers. Jameson Kerry was one of them. I scanned the pews for Sister Louise in vain. But I did notice Isabella sitting in the back with Mr. Delvecchio, and a bouncy Miranda between them.

The casket had been set in place below the pulpit. I nodded to the director, stood, and motioned for the congregation to rise in honor of the family. Mr. Stewart was a distinguished man who looked trim in his navy-blue suit with chalk stripes; his wife was elaborately dressed in a long black gown, and their teenage children, both boys, seemed disinterested and unhappy. They all seemed self-conscious and walked circumspectly, either uncomfortable in these surroundings or contemptuous of them. None of them bothered to look in my direction. When they had filed into the reserved row, I signaled the organist to stop. She held the final note of the prelude too long, and when it ended abruptly, it felt as if all the air had been sucked out of the room. At my gesture, the congregation sat and adjusted and smoothed and coughed and waited to get this thing over with. I recalled Margaret's observation that a funeral is for the living, and felt sad.

A creak from the outer door slipped past the funeral director, and a slice of sunlight pierced the carpet at his feet. I came to the pulpit, almost tripping at the sight of Sister Louise assisting the old priest through the vestibule. He was shorter than she was, fragile, sun-spotted, trembling. From the lapels of his wool suit, I judged it to be at least forty years old; it was big for him now, but he walked proudly in it. I hesitated, watching the two of them take their seats. A few heads began to turn. I plunged immediately into my remarks.

"We have gathered here today to honor the life and memory of Cornelia Shepherd, a faithful Christian and member of this church, loved by many and missed by all. She passed away quietly, but she was not a quiet person. In the brief time I knew her, she never hesitated to speak her mind, which was as sharp as her tongue." A few of the older ladies in the pew smiled. "Cornelia spoke freely about the way her life had been touched by God, and it made people uncomfortable. Today I will not try to speak for her, but for the God who spoke through her. And his message is this: 'No eye has yet seen, and no ear has yet heard, nor has it entered into the heart of man all that God has prepared for those who love him.'"

My paraphrase of Paul's words from the first Corinthian letter made Father Calabrese shudder, I thought, but it could have been a sudden tremor. Sister Louise gripped his shoulders and spoke something to him, and he settled down. I continued my brief exegesis of the passage and concluded my message in the strongest possible words.

"This lady went swimming one day in the basement pool. She met a stranger there, and she claimed he healed her of arthritis. Why did he choose her? I believe it was because of her openness to spiritual things, her ability to see through the manmade muck of religion to find the truth. And because he knew she would bear witness to that truth: that God is a loving God who desires wholeness for all people. It was not particularly important to Cornelia Shepherd whether the church was Catholic or Protestant. She demanded, however, what *was* important, that the church reach out to this city, and she was rebuffed. Perhaps she went about it the wrong way. After all, the stranger told her not to tell. Of course, those were troubled times, and fulfilling her vision would have certainly invited controversy, possibly even serious conflict. But one thing is sure: St. Fred's would not accept her testimony, and we have been in steady decline for thirty years. You can challenge what she said she saw and experienced in that pool, but you can't argue with the prophetic power of her message."

Mr. Stewart was casually inspecting the stained-glass windows. His wife was examining her nails. One of the teenagers was playing a handheld video game. I looked beyond them to find Isabella, who was trying to hold Miranda in her lap. *Wow, she is hyper today!* I smiled at her, and she stopped her squirming to smile back, but only for a minute. I felt good about what I was saying. It was a long time in coming.

"You want to know the honest truth?" I continued, leaning over the pulpit. "I don't think the miracles are all used up around here. To see this church thrive in this community would be such a miracle. To see the lives of those living around us thrive—that would be an even greater miracle. Cornelia Shepherd believed in such things. If her life is to have made any difference, the rest of us must follow her in faith. We take comfort in knowing where she is today. A more profound question may be, where will we be tomorrow?"

Michael made a move to get up, as if to offer a one-man standing ovation, but then settled back down. It made Margaret laugh.

I led the congregation in a prayer, then suffered through an agonizingly slow stanza of "Pass It On," with Michael and me carrying the melody. As if to erase the memory of the poorly sung music, I quickly introduced our guest speaker.

"Mrs. Shepherd lived a very long time, and we are tempted to think of her as old," I said, "because old is how we last saw her. But it is good and right to remember her as a younger woman, in the prime of her life. And so we are fortunate to have with us Fr. Bruno Calabrese, who served here in the late sixties as parish priest, when this place was still called St. Winefrid's. He has come a long way to give the eulogy for this good woman." I nodded toward the old man. He was confused for a moment, and Sister Louise had to nudge him to get him to come along. His halting walk to the pulpit was of such duration that I returned to the microphone and said, "Father Calabrese is accompanied by Sister Louise, our mutual friend, and fellow laborer with Christ."

I sat down, relieved that the majority of my part was over. I had said my piece, and I felt good about it. While Father Calabrese slowly advanced, people took the opportunity to whisper and unwrap mints. One of the Stewart boys appeared to be doodling in a hymnal. His father repeatedly checked his watch.

The old priest ascended the platform and gently took my hand. I whispered an awkward "thank you for coming," and at length he let go with a soft smile. He took the pulpit with both hands and steadied himself.

"Jesus Christ appeared to me the first time on October 20, 1961, in this city, at Ellis Hospital," he said.

The words were spoken through the winded gullet of an old man, but they nearly knocked me over like a gale. I looked out at the people—they were equally stunned, even the Stewarts. I gripped the arms of my high-backed chair as if preparing for takeoff.

"I was visiting Angus Shepherd there," he continued. "He was dying of heart failure. I gave him what we Catholics called at that time extreme unction—the last rites. He was a good man, and I hated to see him go. He had a heart for the poor, you see. I prayed there as he clung to life, asking God to give him five more years. When I opened my eyes, the Lord was there, in the room with us. I was afraid! But he said that my prayer had been answered, and that there was something Angus had to do. Then, he was gone."

Father Calabrese struggled to clear his throat before he could go on. "Do you know when Angus Shepherd died?" We waited, already knowing the answer.

"It was October 20 . . . 1966."

The room was bathed in eerie silence. The funeral director, who earlier had sneaked out on the porch to smoke, now actually came back in and took a seat in the back.

"I never told him, or anyone, about what I had seen, just that God had answered my prayer. Then one day he came to me in confession and told me an awful secret. Angus Shepherd's father built this church, you know. And Angus, as a young man, helped lay the foundation. He was deeply troubled for not saying anything all those years, about how the church had been built directly over paupers' unmarked graves."

I stared at Michael, who was already staring at me.

"Angus wanted to ease his guilt. With a few of his men, we began to dig down under the basement level, which was still unfinished. When we exhumed the first body, I went to my bishop. He was less than pleased and told me to stop. Of course I did not do so. But I did not tell many people either. Angus bought the plots and the markers in various cemeteries around the city, where we buried the people properly. There were seventeen in all. The bishop was enraged. And then there was a rumor around town, that I had seen St. Winefrid weeping, that I had lost my mind. Angus died, and I fell into despair. There was talk of sending me away to a mental hospital. Why had the Lord done this to me? I asked. I wanted to take my life. And then Jesus Christ appeared to me a second time, as I petitioned him for mercy right here at this altar. I shall never forget his words."

Miranda was sitting still on her mother's lap, her arms wrapped around Isabella's neck, *listening*. Seeing her listening made me shudder with holy fear.

"*If it is Winefrid they say you saw, it is Winefrid's healing well that they shall have. As for you, Bruno my servant, I will prosper your work if you will not deny me. I will not leave you or forsake you.*'"

The trembling returned, and the old priest staggered. Sister Louise, who was seated across the platform, came aside to steady him.

"But you know of course that I failed him. I didn't have the strength to stand firm. The church officials threatened to rescind my ordination. I had nothing to my name . . . what would I do if I could not serve as a priest? That was when Cornelia came to me and encouraged me to oppose them. Trust God, she said. Many would understand. I could start a new church, she said, I could have a ministry among the poor. She had the means to see to it that I would succeed. But I was afraid of them, of what they could do. It was 1968; how could I oppose the Church? It was better, I thought, not to fight them. So, I agreed to be sent away."

He wept quietly, and we all waited respectfully for him to recover. Sister Louise rubbed his feeble arm. It was an amazing scene. Graves of the unknown dead right under the church. How ironic. And, how tragic. I felt myself beginning to weep with the old cleric. Margaret was already dabbing her eyes.

"She wrote me letters, Cornelia did," the priest said. "She was studying the Bible, growing in her faith. I thought that the Lord was carrying out his work through these new people, in spite of me. And then, the Lord came to Cornelia . . . and as Reverend Donovan said, the people could not accept her testimony. In time they broke her spirit. But they cannot change what God has ordained. He will not leave us or forsake us. He waits for those he has called to love the world boldly in his name, to bear his cross, and to receive his reward."

Father Calabrese looked at me for a long moment, his deep-set eyes freezing me in my place. "Do not follow my example, Pastor Donovan. Do not use the unbelief of others as an excuse for your own. Has he not said it plainly? A healing well you have known in this place, and a healing well you shall have."

I watched as Sister Louise, her face bathed in tears, helped her old friend from the platform. It was time to dismiss the assembly. I raised myself with great effort and strode to the pulpit. My sister Margaret had buried her head in her hands. *There is hope for you, Margaret,* I proclaimed inaudibly. *And there is hope for our mother, our parents, and me.* The funeral director had already opened the outer doors, and light flooded in. *There is hope for those outside these walls too,* I thought, *for this is a house of mercy.*

"May the grace and peace of our Lord Jesus Christ be with you all." I nodded to the pallbearers, who came forward on cue. I stepped down from the platform, beckoned the congregation to rise with the lifting of my hand, and walked forth ahead of the casket toward the square of sunshine streaming in.

Outside, I stood at the back of the hearse until the casket was stowed away, then walked quickly to the family limousine to speak to the Stewarts. They were already in the car, so I had to knock on the window.

"I'm Carla Donovan. It's unfortunate we haven't had a chance to speak until now," I said, bending down to talk through the opening as the glass scrolled down.

"We'll talk tomorrow morning," the nephew said behind dark glasses.

"Of course. Cornelia was very special to me. I'm sorry for your loss."

He removed the shades slowly. "And I'm sorry for yours."

I flinched, sensing there was a deeper meaning hidden in the words.

"If you think for one minute that I will allow any of my family's money to flow into this broken-down relic of a church, you are sadly mistaken," he said. "I intend to do everything in my power to see that you get nothing—especially after that sideshow you put on in there. I'm not sure who's crazier, my great-aunt, or you and that old fool you dragged in from the nursing home with that ridiculous story. How long did it take you to script that performance? Well, all you did was make me angry. As a matter of fact, I plan to sue you for defamation of character after the estate is settled, for portraying my family as a bunch of religious kooks."

"Hold on there, sir," I pleaded. "We were just trying to honor Cornelia's wishes."

"Aunt Cornelia wasn't of sound mind—we all know that, for heaven's sake. You manipulated her to get her money, and I'll prove it. By the time I'm through with you, there'll be a For Sale sign nailed to the door of this place. If I were you, I'd start looking for a job. You might try acting, since you seem so good at it . . . *Reverend*."

I stepped back as he rolled the window up and turned away. There was a tug at my elbow.

"Michael . . . hi." I was still reeling from the verbal assault and couldn't quite think clearly.

"That was great in there. Listen, they're lining up the cars right now. I assume you'll ride in the hearse, right?"

I nodded, still stunned by the exchange with Mr. Stewart.

"I'll take Mags with me to the cemetery, okay?"

Margaret appeared from nowhere and hugged me. "You're a really good preacher, you know?" she said into my ear. I saw that there were only a few people still on the porch, and one of them was Isabella—waving wildly. She shouted when she caught my eye.

"Carla! Have you seen Miranda? She no in church!"

"No, I—"

"Oh, *I* saw her," said Margaret. "That cute little girl in the blue dress who was with that lady? She was talking to Father Calabrese after the service."

"She what?"

"Uh, she was talking to the priest and the nun just a few—"

But I was already rushing back toward the hearse. "Can you wait a few minutes longer?" I asked. He shrugged, and I bounded up the steps. "You check around back, I'll check the office," I told Isabella. I raced through the empty sanctuary, my open robe flowing like a cape, banging off the corridor walls to get to the office.

The door to the basement stood wide open. I felt sure it had been locked. Other than me, only one person had a key.

"Mr. Delvecchio!" I yelled. I knew now what they were up to, and I didn't like it. With the pool in its current condition, that old priest could trip on some loose plaster and crack his skull—assuming he could even make it down the stairs. Frantic, I hung onto the railing and took the steps two at a time, nearly tripping over the hem of my stole, which finally fell away behind me.

There was no one in the basement hall. I ran past the vandalized room, embarrassed at the thought that Father Calabrese had read some of the awful words painted along the walls. How would we ever clean this up? Just seeing this profanation of God's house would have been enough to give this old priest a heart attack. He probably had some distant relative who would sue me too. Fear quickened my pace. I almost ran smack into Frankie Delvecchio, who popped unexpectedly out into the hall.

"Slow down," he said, smirking. "C'mere."

We stepped out onto the deck together. There were Father Calabrese and Sister Louise, sitting like lovebirds in a dusty pocket of broken tile. His trousers and her skirt were rolled up to their knees. They dangled their bare feet over the edge of the pool, giggling like little children, while Miranda echoed their laughter from below, splashing with joy in the swirling, rising waters.

Paul A. Nigro graduated from Clemson with an English degree in hand and a writing career in mind. Instead, he nearly became a professional grad student and served ten years as a pastor before retiring at age thirty-five to explore life on the other side of the pulpit.

He is currently president of Paddock Pool Equipment Company in Rock Hill, South Carolina, and continues to speak and minister in local churches. When he is not playing with imaginary people, he spends time with the real people who matter most: his wife, Cindy, and their two children, Julia and Vinny. This is his second novel.

For further information, see *www.paulnigro.com.*

Additional copies of this book
and other titles by Paul Nigro
are available from your local bookstore.

If you have enjoyed this book, or if it has
impacted your life, we would like to hear from you.
Please contact us at:

RiverOak Publishing
An Imprint of Cook Communications Ministries
4050 Lee Vance View
Colorado Springs, CO 80918

Visit our website at:
www.riveroakpublishing.com